PRAISE FOR *CLYTEMNESTRA*

"Casati masterfully brings us into the [ ]
might see what burns inside her, and [ ]
ourselves."

—Vaishnavi Patel, bestselling auth[ ]

"Crackles with vivid fury, passion, and strength. A powerful, thought-provoking portrayal of a fascinating and complicated woman framed in beautiful prose. I loved it"

—Jennifer Saint, bestselling author of *Ariadne* and *Atalanta*

"Rivals *House of the Dragon* in conspiracies and feminine brutality. Here is a complex and courageous woman, all flesh and blood, simmering with passion. Facing the grimmest of betrayals, Clytemnestra's ruthless desire for revenge powers a thrilling plot. This is an electrifying read that shocks and fascinates in equal measure."

Liz Fremantle, author of *The Honey and the Sting*

"A heroine of fierce spirit caught in a world ruled by men, finding a way through with a sharp, unquenchable courage. With the fire and spark of Madeline Miller and the depths of Mary Renault, *Clytemnestra* will keep you reading well into the small hours, and your dreams will be of worlds where women reach for the gods."

—Manda Scott, bestselling author of *A Treachery of Spies*

"What a pleasure to fall in love with Clytemnestra through the mind of Costanza Casati, who renders a singularly vibrant Greece, populated by familiar characters and absolutely alive with emotion and suspense. Casati reveals a Clytemnestra we've never met before: fiercely intelligent, passionate, and loving—and willing to do anything to avenge the ones she loves."

—Naomi Krupitsky, *New York Times* bestselling author of *The Family*

"Savage, passionate, and absolutely spellbinding. Costanza Casati's recreation of Sparta is astonishing—you feel you are with Clytemnestra, completely immersed in the brutal world she inhabits with her siblings, whose complex relationships are drawn with skill and tenderness. Clytemnestra's rage, her heartbreak, and her determination radiate off the page—I was utterly gripped."

—Elodie Harper, bestselling author of *The Wolf Den*

"Bold and elegant, Costanza Casati's debut bursts onto the page in flashes of light. This book deconstructs Clytemnestra's infamy and then, with tremendous empathy and wisdom, reconstructs her into an enthrallingly complex figure filled with passion and spirit. This fiery tale of revenge and desire really is the stuff of legend—Casati's unflinching storytelling is irresistible."

—Sarah Priscus, author of *Groupies*

"Powerful and sympathetic, *Clytemnestra* shines a light on Helen of Troy's overshadowed sister. Crafted with page-turning suspense, Casati spins a mesmerizing story of an ambitious warrior queen who must use all her skill to protect herself and those she loves from men who view women not as equals but as pawns to be sacrificed upon the altars of lust, greed, and fame. An ancient and intriguing tale made fresh for today's twenty-first century battles."

—Liz Michalski, author of *Darling Girl*

CLYTEMNESTRA

A NOVEL

COSTANZA CASATI

sourcebooks
landmark

Published by Sourcebooks Landmark, an imprint of Sourcebooks
P.O. Box 4410, Naperville, Illinois 60567-4410
(630) 961-3900
sourcebooks.com

Originally published as *Clytemnestra* in 2023 in Great Britain by
Michael Joseph, an imprint of Penguin Random House. This edition
issued based on the hardcover edition published in 2023 in Great
Britain by Michael Joseph, an imprint of Penguin Random House.

The Library of Congress has cataloged the hardcover edition as follows:

Names: Casati, Costanza, author.
Title: Clytemnestra : a novel / Costanza Casati.
Description: Naperville, Illinois : Sourcebooks Landmark, [2023]
Identifiers: LCCN 2022028704 (print) | LCCN
  2022028705 (ebook) | (hardcover) | (epub)
Subjects: LCSH: Clytemnestra, Queen of Mycenae--Fiction. | LCGFT:
  Mythological fiction. | Novels.
Classification: LCC PS3603.A835 C59 2023 (print) | LCC PS3603.A835
  (ebook) | DDC 813/.6--dc23/eng/20220708
LC record available at https://lccn.loc.gov/2022028704
LC ebook record available at https://lccn.loc.gov/2022028705

Printed and bound in the United States of America.
LSC 10 9 8 7 6 5 4 3 2 1

For my parents, for everything.

FAMILY OF TYNDAREUS

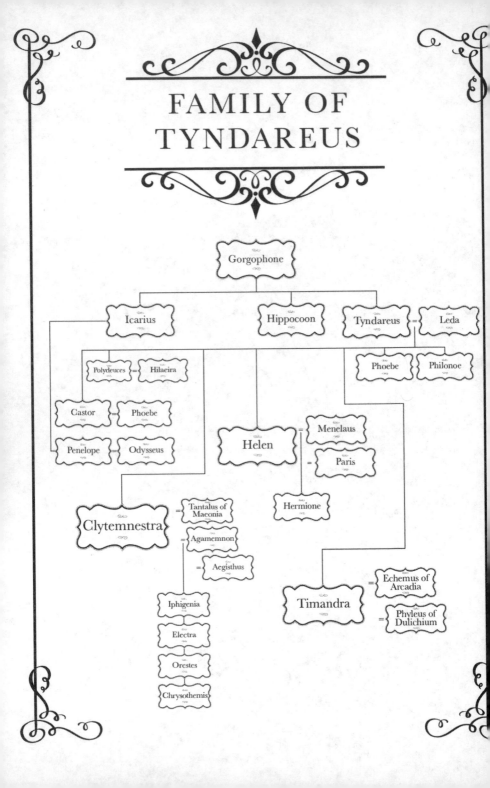

FAMILY OF ATREUS

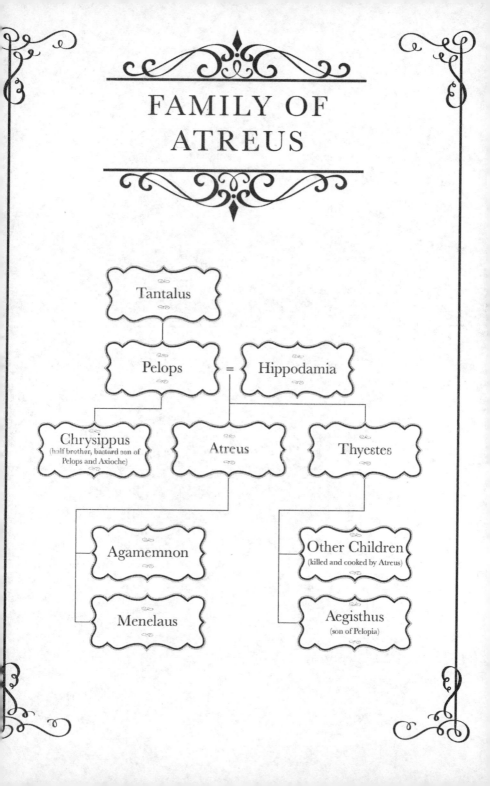

Tantalus

Pelops = Hippodamia

Chrysippus
(half brother, bastard son of
Pelops and Axioche)

Atreus

Thyestes

Agamemnon

Menelaus

Other Children
(killed and cooked by Atreus)

Aegisthus
(son of Pelopia)

Cast of Characters

HOUSE OF TYNDAREUS

Tyndareus: king of Sparta, son of Gorgophone, husband of:

Leda: queen of Sparta, daughter of the Aetolian king Thestius, mother of:

- **Castor** and **Polydeuces**: twins, known as Tyndaridai (sons of Tyndareus) and later as Dioscuri (in Roman mythology)
- **Clytemnestra**: princess of Sparta and later queen of Mycenae
- **Helen**: princess and queen of Sparta. Later known as Helen of Troy. According to the myth, Helen is the daughter of Leda and Zeus, who in the form of a swan raped the queen.
- **Timandra**: princess of Sparta and later queen of Arcadia
- **Phoebe** and **Philonoe**: minor characters in Greek mythology, youngest daughters of Tyndareus and Leda. Unlike their sisters, they didn't commit adultery against their husbands.

Icarius: king of Acarnania, brother of Tyndareus, husband of Polycaste, father of:

- **Penelope**: princess of Acarnania and later queen of Ithaca

Hippocoon: Tyndareus and Icarius's half brother, killed by Heracles

Aphareus: another of Tyndareus and Icarius's half brothers, father of:

- **Idas** and **Lynceus**: princes of Messenia

Phoebe and **Hilaeira**: Messenian princesses known as Leucippides ("daughters of the white horse"), promised to Lynceus and Idas, "stolen" by Castor and Polydeuces

HOUSE OF ATREUS

Atreus: son of Pelops and Hippodamia, king of Mycenae. Older brother of Thyestes and half brother of Chrysippus. The story of his house is unrivaled in Greek mythology for cruelty and corruption. Atreus is the father of:

- **Agamemnon**: king of Mycenae, "lord of men," husband of Clytemnestra, commander of the Greek fleet during the Trojan War
- **Menelaus**: king of Sparta, husband of Helen

Thyestes: king of Mycenae after killing and seizing the throne from his brother. He had three sons, who were all killed by Atreus. After an oracle advised him that if he had a son with his own daughter, the son would kill Atreus, Thyestes raped his daughter, Pelopia, and became father of:

- **Aegisthus:** murderer of his uncle Atreus, cousin of Agamemnon and Menelaus, lover of Clytemnestra

Aerope: daughter of Catreus, king of Crete; wife of Atreus; lover of Atreus's brother Thyestes

OTHER CHARACTERS

Theseus: Greek hero, abductor of Helen, king of Athens

Pirithous: prince of the Lapiths and friend of Theseus

Cynisca: one of the Spartiates

Chrysanthe: Spartan, lover of Timandra

Tantalus: king of Maeonia, first husband of Clytemnestra

Calchas: seer of the Greek armies

Leon: protector and adviser to Clytemnestra in Mycenae

Aileen: Clytemnestra's servant and confidante in Mycenae

Polydamas, Cadmus, Lycomedes: elders of Mycenae

Eurybates: one of Agamemnon's warriors in Mycenae

Kyros: Eurybates's son, later made warlord by Clytemnestra

Erebus: a merchant

Cassandra: Trojan princess, priestess of Apollo, daughter of Hecuba and Priam. After the Trojan War, she becomes concubine of King Agamemnon.

Odysseus: prince of Ithaca, son of Laertes, "the man of twists and turns," husband of Penelope

Ajax the Great: prince of Salamis, son of Telamon, cousin of the hero Achilles

Teucer: cousin of Ajax

Ajax the Lesser: hero from Locris

Nestor: king of Pylos

Philoctetes: prince of Thessaly, famous archer

Menestheus: king of Athens

Diomedes: king of Argos

Idomeneus: prince of Crete

Ephenor: hero from Euboea

Machaon: son of Asclepius, expert in the art of healing

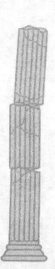

PART I

There is no peace
for a woman with ambition

No love
for a woman with a crown

She loves too much
she is lustful

Her power is too strong
she is ruthless

She fights for vengeance
she is mad

Kings are brilliant
mighty
godlike

Queens are deadly
shameless
accursed

1

Prey

CLYTEMNESTRA LOOKS DOWN at the steep ravine but can see no trace of dead bodies. She searches for cracked skulls, broken bones, corpses eaten by wild dogs and pecked by vultures, but nothing. There are only a few brave flowers, growing between the cracks, their petals white against the darkness of the ravine. She wonders how they manage to grow in such a place of death.

There were no flowers down there when she was little. She remembers crouching in the forest as a child, watching the elders drag criminals and weak babies up the trail and throw them into the gorge Spartans call Ceadas. Down the cliff, the rocks are as sharp as freshly cast bronze and as slippery as raw fish. Clytemnestra used to hide and pray for all those men whose deaths would be long and painful. She couldn't pray for the babies: the thought made her restless. If she walked closer to the edge of the ravine, she could feel a soft breeze caressing her skin. Her mother had told her that the dead infants lying at the bottom of the Ceadas spoke through the wind. Those voices whispered, yet Clytemnestra couldn't grasp their words. So she let her mind wander as she looked at the sun peeping through the leafy branches.

An eerie silence looms over the forest. Clytemnestra knows she is being followed. She descends quickly from the high ground, leaving the ravine behind, trying not to trip on the slippery stones that form the hunting trail. The wind is colder, the sky darker. When she left the palace hours ago, the sun was rising, warm on her skin, and the grass was wet against her soles. Her mother was already sitting in the throne room, her face glowing in the orange light, and Clytemnestra slipped past the doors before she could be seen.

There is a sudden movement behind the trees, and the sound of crunching leaves. Clytemnestra slips and cuts her palm against the sharp edge of a rock. When she looks up, ready to defend herself, two big, dark eyes are staring back at her. Just a deer. She clenches her fist, then wipes her hand on her tunic before the blood can leave tracks for her hunter.

She can hear wolves howl somewhere far above her but forces herself to keep going. Spartan boys of her age fight wolves and panthers in pairs as part of their training. Clytemnestra once shaved her head, like a boy, and went to the gymnasium with them hoping to prepare for a hunt. When her mother found out, she didn't feed her for two days. "Part of the training is to starve Spartan boys until they are forced to steal," she said. Clytemnestra endured the punishment—she knew she deserved it.

The stream leads to a spring and a little waterfall. Above it, she can see a crevice, an entrance to what looks like a cave. She starts to climb the mossy rocks at the sides of the spring. Her hand throbs and slips on the surface of the cliff. Her bow is slung over her back, and the dagger hangs loose from her belt, its handle pressing against her thigh.

At the top, she stops to catch her breath. She tears off a piece of her tunic, douses it in the clear water of the spring, and wraps it around her bleeding hand. The crowns of the oaks blend with the darkening sky, and everything is blurred to her tired eyes. She knows she is too exposed on the ground. *The higher you climb, the better*, her father always says.

She scrambles up the tallest tree and pauses astride a branch to listen, holding her dagger tightly. The moon is high in the sky, its contours clear and cold, like a silver shield. Everything is silent, except for the water of the spring below her.

A branch cracks, and two golden eyes appear in the darkness in front of her, studying her. Clytemnestra remains still, blood pulsating in her temples. On the tree opposite her, a silver shape slips away from the shadows, revealing a coat of thick fur and pointed ears. A lynx.

The beast jumps and lands on her tree. The impact makes her lose her balance. She clutches the branch, but her nails break, her palms slip. She falls and lands on the muddy ground. For a second, she is blind and her breath is gone. The animal tries to jump down on her, but her hands are moving fast to her bow and arrows. She shoots and rolls onto her side. The lynx's claw scratches her back and she screams.

The animal stands, its back to the narrow crevice that leads into the cave. For a moment, woman and lynx stare at each other. Then, swift as a striking snake, Clytemnestra throws her dagger into the animal's shoulder. The lynx shrieks, and Clytemnestra runs past it, toward the blackness of the cave. She barely passes through the crevice, grazing her head and hips, sinks into the darkness, and waits, praying that the cave has no other entrance and no other visitor.

Slowly, her eyes become accustomed to the gloom. Her bow and most of her arrows are somehow intact and she sets them aside. She removes her bloodied tunic and rests her back against the cold rock. Her panting echoes in the humid air as if the cave itself were breathing. Can the goddess Artemis see her now? She wishes she could, though her father has always told her not to bother with gods. Her mother, on the other hand, believes that forests hide the gods' secrets.

Caves to her are shelters, minds that have thought and lived the lives of the creatures they have hosted over time. But maybe her father is right: this cave sounds as empty as a temple at night. There is only the moaning of the wounded lynx, which moves farther and farther away.

When it dies, Clytemnestra drags herself closer to the crevice and peeps out. Nothing moves on the muddy ground. She slips back into her tunic, flinching when it sticks to her wound, then leaves the cave, her hips brushing against the smooth rocks.

The lynx lies close to the spring, its blood spreading on the orange leaves like spilled wine. Clytemnestra limps closer to it and retrieves her dagger. The animal's eyes are open, reflecting the bright shape of the moon. Surprise is still etched on them, and sadness. They are not so different from a dead man's eyes. Clytemnestra ties the animal's paws to her quiver and starts to walk, hoping to be home by morning.

Her mother will be proud of her hunt.

2

One Girl Wins and the Other Loses

"Slow down, Clytemnestra! Artemis will shoot me if I am second again!"

Clytemnestra laughs, and the sound echoes like birdsong across the plain. "She won't. Mother told you that to make you run faster!"

They are racing between the rows of olive and fig trees, their hair catching the leaves, their bare feet stepping on fallen fruit. Clytemnestra is faster. Cuts and bruises cover her arms, and her eyes show her determination to reach the river first. Behind her, Helen pants, calling to her sister. Whenever the sunlight catches her hair, it glows as brightly as the ripe fruit around her.

Clytemnestra jumps out of the grove onto the sunbaked earth. The ground burns her feet, so she hops onto the yellow grass. She stops only when she gets to the river to look at her figure mirrored in the water. She is dirty, disheveled.

"Wait for me," Helen calls.

Clytemnestra turns. Her sister has stopped at the edge of the grove, sweat pouring down her tunic. She is glowering at her. "Why must you do everything in a hurry?" Helen asks.

Clytemnestra smiles. To their people, Helen of Sparta may look like a goddess, but truly, she follows her sister in everything she does. "Because it's hot," Clytemnestra says. She throws aside her tunic and plunges into the river. Her long hair dances around her like seaweed. The fresh breeze of the early morning is making way for the summer heat. Along the banks of the Eurotas river, between the dry plains and rough mountains, a few bloodred anemones struggle to grow. Not far from the banks, the thin strip of fertile soil with olive and fig trees stretches shyly, like a ray of sun in a clouded sky. Helen is lingering by the bank, the water up to her thighs. She always walks slowly into the river, wetting herself with her hands.

"Come on." Clytemnestra swims toward Helen and hugs her waist.

"It's cold," Helen moans, but she keeps walking into the water. When Clytemnestra tries to let go of her, Helen clings to her sister's warm body, pressing as close as she can.

"You are no Spartan woman," Clytemnestra says with a smile.

"Not like you. If you were a man, you'd be among the strongest fighters in Greece."

"I'm already among the cleverest in Sparta," Clytemnestra says, grinning.

Helen frowns. "You shouldn't say these things. You know what Mother says about hubris."

"*The pride that comes before a fall*," Clytemnestra recites, bored. "But Father always says he's the bravest warrior in Sparta, and no one has punished him yet."

"Father is king. We aren't, so we shouldn't anger the gods," Helen insists.

Clytemnestra laughs. Her sister, moving through the world as if life were all mud and murk, always amuses her. "If you're the fairest woman in all our lands and beyond, I might as well be the cleverest. I don't see why the gods should be angry with that—they'll always be cleverer and more beautiful anyway."

Helen thinks it through. Clytemnestra swims toward a patch

of sunlight glistening on the water, and her sister follows. The two remain floating in the river, their faces like sunflowers, always following the light.

They reach the gymnasium in time for their daily practice. The sun is strong, and they hurry under the shade of the trees that surround the courtyard. On the sand, young girls are already practicing, running around the square fully naked. Here the Spartiates, daughters of the best and noblest warriors of Sparta, train with commoners, and they will continue to do so until they start a family. Their bodies are covered with oil, old scars pale against their tanned skin.

Clytemnestra steps into the yard, Helen close behind her. The sand burns under their feet, like a heated blade, and the air is thick with the smell of sweat. The master—one of her father's warriors—gives them a discus, then a spear, and corrects their posture as they throw again and again. The sun grows higher, and the girls jump, race, and run, their limbs hurting, their throats sore in the dry, hot air.

At last, there is the dancing. Clytemnestra catches sight of Helen smiling at her; the dance is her sister's favorite moment. The drums start beating and the girls begin. Bare feet thud on the sand, pulsing through the sunlit air, and the dancers' hair moves, like tongues of flame. Clytemnestra dances with her eyes closed, her strong legs following the rhythm. Helen's movements mirror her sister's but are more composed and graceful, as if she were afraid of losing herself. Her feet light and precise, her arms like wings, she looks ready to take flight and soar high, away from the others' eyes. But she can't rise, so she keeps dancing, relentless.

Clytemnestra dances for herself; Helen dances for others.

The water of the bath is cold and pleasant on the skin. Only Helen, Clytemnestra, and the Spartiates are allowed to share the small room in one corner of the courtyard. Most of the other athletes, commoners and girls who can't claim to be native Spartans, are washing away the sweat in the river.

Clytemnestra rests her head against the stony wall, watching Helen as she rises out of the pool, golden hair plastered to her shoulders. At sixteen, their bodies are changing, their faces growing leaner, firmer. It scares Clytemnestra to witness it, though she doesn't speak of it. It reminds her that at their age, their mother had already married their father and left her homeland.

Leda had come to Sparta from Aetolia, the arid land of mountains in the north of Greece famous for its wild beasts, nature gods, and spirits. Like every Aetolian princess before her, Leda was a huntress, skilled with the ax and bow, and she worshipped the mountain goddess Rhea. King Tyndareus loved her for her fierceness and married her, even though the Greeks called the tribes of Aetolia "primitive" and spread rumors that they ate raw meat, like animals. When Leda, a strong woman with raven hair and olive skin, gave birth to Helen—a light-skinned girl with hair the color of honey—everyone in Sparta believed that Zeus was Leda's lover. The god was famously fond of beautiful young women and enjoyed taking different shapes to ravish them. He had been a bull to abduct the Phoenician princess Europa, a shower of golden rain to touch the lovely Danaë, a dark cloud to seduce the priestess Io.

So he did with Leda. Disguising himself as a swan, he found her sitting alone on the bank of the Eurotas, her hair black and shiny as a raven's feathers, her eyes lost and sad. He flew into her arms, and when she caressed his wings, he raped her. Rumors indulge in details, so the Spartans talked of how Leda fought as he seized her, his beak wounding her, his wings keeping her still. Others spoke differently: the union was so pleasurable, they said, that she was left flushed and breathless.

"Of course, she must have liked it," Clytemnestra heard a boy say in the gymnasium once. "The queen is different... Her people are more *barbaric*." Clytemnestra hit his face with a rock but didn't tell her mother. Such rumors spread out of jealousy: Leda was beautiful, and the Spartans distrusted her. But wicked voices are hard to ignore, and even the king came to believe that Helen wasn't his child. He saw nothing of himself in her as she grew to become passionate about music and dancing and cried when she saw a wounded soldier.

But Clytemnestra knows Helen is her sister. She knows that even though as a child Helen seemed frail and gentle, her will is as strong as Clytemnestra's. When they were little, Helen would stand next to her and compare every tiny part of their bodies until she found a similarity and was satisfied. After all, as Helen used to say, their eyelashes were thick, their fingers skinny, their necks long. And when Clytemnestra replied that her own hair was darker, the color of dirt, Helen would scoff.

"The boys will be here soon."

Clytemnestra looks up. The other girls have left, and Helen is gazing at her, her head tilted like that of a curious doe. Clytemnestra wants to ask her if she too is scared of the future, but somehow the words don't come, so instead she stands. "Let's go then."

Tonight there are no men in the dining hall. The room is lively with the women's laughter and the smell of roasted meat. When Clytemnestra and Helen walk in, their mother is seated at the head of the table, speaking to a few servants, while Timandra, Phoebe, and Philonoe, Clytemnestra's younger sisters, fill their plates with flatbreads and olives. They smile as they chew, their hands and cheeks greasy with fat from the meat. Helen and Clytemnestra take the two empty seats at their mother's sides.

The hall is large and bare, its tall windows opening onto the plain. There are only a few old weapons hanging on the walls and a long table, dark wood scratched and faded, where men and women usually eat together.

"Make sure no one has stolen from the grain stores," Leda is telling the servants, "and leave some wine for the king when he comes back from his journey." She dismisses them with a wave of the hand, and they slip out of the room, as silent as fish moving through water.

Phoebe wipes her hands on her brown tunic and leans toward her mother. "When *will* Father be back?" she asks. She and Philonoe are still little, with their mother's deep-green eyes and olive skin.

"Your father and your brothers will return from the games tonight," Leda says, savoring her cheese. Clytemnestra's uncle has been hosting races in Acarnania, and young men have gathered from every Greek city to participate.

"It will be as boring as an elders' meeting, Sister," Castor had told Clytemnestra before he left. "You will have more fun here, hunting and helping Mother to run the palace." He had brushed his lips against her forehead and Clytemnestra had smiled at his lie. He knew how much she wanted to come.

"Do you think Castor and Polydeuces have won anything?" Philonoe asks.

"Of course they have," Timandra says, her teeth sinking into the

juicy pork flesh. She is thirteen, with stark, uninteresting features—
she looks much like her father. "Polydeuces is stronger than any
Spartan, and Castor runs faster than the gods."

Philonoe smiles, satisfied, and Phoebe yawns, slipping a piece of
meat under the table for the house dogs.

"Mother, why don't you tell us a story?" she asks. "Father always
tells the same ones."

Leda smiles. "Clytemnestra will tell you a story."

"Do you want to hear of the time Castor and I killed that wolf?"
Clytemnestra asks.

Phoebe claps her hands. "Yes, yes!"

So Clytemnestra tells her stories, and her sisters listen. Blood and
death don't frighten them because they are still young, growing up in
a world of myths and goddesses, and they don't yet understand the
difference between what is real and what is not.

♛

Outside the window, the sky is orange-flushed. Someone is singing in
the village, and the air is hot and sweet.

"Timandra is so like you," Helen says, ready for bed. Their room
is at the very end of the *gynaeceum*, the women's apartments, and has
walls painted with simple images—red flowers, blue birds, golden
fish. There are two wooden stools where their dresses are neatly
folded, a water bowl, and a bed of Egyptian ebony—a gift from the
Athenian Theseus to Helen when she was fourteen.

Clytemnestra lifts a handful of water to wash her face.

"Do you think she looks like you? Timandra?" Helen repeats.

"Hmm. Yes."

"She is mischievous."

Clytemnestra laughs, wiping her forehead. "Are you saying I am mischievous?"

Helen tilts her head, frowning. "That is not what I meant."

"I know." Clytemnestra lies down on the bed next to her sister, looking at the ceiling. She sometimes likes to think it is painted with stars. "Are you tired?" she asks.

"No," Helen whispers. She hesitates, taking a breath. "Father will come back tonight, and tomorrow he'll tell you and Timandra all about the races. He loves you very much."

Clytemnestra waits. She feels for the scar on her back, touching its jagged ends.

"It must be because I have never killed anything," Helen says.

"It is not," Clytemnestra says. "You know it is because he thinks Leda had another man."

"Well, did she?"

How many times have they had this conversation? Clytemnestra sighs, ready to repeat what she always tells her. "It doesn't matter. You are Leda's daughter and my sister. Now, let us rest awhile."

No matter how many times she says it, Helen listens as if it were the first. She gives Clytemnestra a small smile and closes her eyes, her body relaxing. Clytemnestra waits until she hears Helen's rhythmic breathing, then turns to her. She looks at her sister's perfect skin, smooth as an amphora ready to be painted, and wonders, *When did we start lying to each other?*

The next morning is wrestling day. The servants brush and flatten the sand in the gymnasium, then carry a high-backed chair under the shade of the trees. The Spartiates gather in one corner of the ground.

Some are restless, picking up handfuls of sand, while others stand quietly, touching old bruises. Clytemnestra stretches her arms while Helen ties back her hair so that the strands don't fall into her face. Her sister's fingers on her head are gentle.

Up on the hill, the palace bathes in the hot sun opposite the river and mountains, which are cool and shaded. The exercise yard is quiet, half hidden by rocks and tall grass. Often in spring and autumn, the girls come here for their music and poetry classes, but it is too warm now, the sun high overhead, hot air sticking to the skin like wet sand.

A small group of men appears on the dusty path that runs from the palace. The servants move away from the courtyard, crouching behind the trees, and the Spartiates fall silent. Clytemnestra watches the warriors take their places around the yard as her father sits on the high-backed chair. Tyndareus is short but strong, his legs stiff with muscles. His eyes linger on the girls, bright and sharp as an eagle's. Then he clears his throat. "You live to honor Sparta and your king. You fight so that you may have strong, healthy children and rule your houses. You fight to prove your loyalty to the city. You fight to belong. Survival, courage, and strength are your duties."

"Survival, courage, and strength are our duties," the girls say in unison.

"Who will start?" Tyndareus asks. He casts a quick glance in the direction of Clytemnestra. She looks back at him but remains silent. It can be foolish to challenge the other girls straightaway—her brother has taught her that. She has wrestled the Spartiates for years, yet there are always new things she can learn about them, secret moves they haven't shown her yet. It is important that she observe them first.

Eupoleia steps forward. She chooses her adversary, a thin girl whose name Clytemnestra doesn't know, and so the wrestling begins.

Eupoleia is slow but violent. She shouts and tries to grab the other by the hair. The girl looks scared and edges around slowly, like a stray cat. When Eupoleia aims at her head once again, the girl doesn't jump far enough, and Eupoleia's fist meets her jaw. The girl falls and doesn't stand. The game is over.

Tyndareus looks disappointed. He doesn't come often to watch them train, and when he does, he expects a good fight. "Someone else," he says.

Cynisca steps forward, and the other girls make space, like frightened dogs. Daughter of an army comrade of Tyndareus, she is tall with a beak nose and strong legs. Clytemnestra remembers when Cynisca tried to steal her toy, a painted clay figure of a warrior, years ago at the marketplace.

"Who are you fighting, Cynisca?" Tyndareus asks.

Something in Cynisca's eyes stirs Clytemnestra's blood. Before she can volunteer to fight her, Cynisca speaks: "Helen."

The girls gasp. No one has ever challenged Helen before, because they know the fight would be too easy, and there is no honor in that. They are afraid that Tyndareus might intervene in favor of his daughter, but Tyndareus doesn't favor anyone. Everyone looks at him, waiting for an answer. He nods.

"No," Clytemnestra says. She takes her sister's arm.

Tyndareus frowns. "She can fight like any other Spartan."

"I will fight," Clytemnestra replies.

Helen pushes her sister aside. "You are shaming me." She turns to Cynisca. "I will fight you." She ties her hair back, her hands shaking. Clytemnestra bites the inside of her cheek so hard that she tastes blood. She doesn't know what to do.

Helen walks to the center of the ground, and Cynisca follows her. There is a moment of stillness, when the sand glimmers and a soft wind blows. Then Cynisca strikes. Helen leaps aside, graceful and quick as a deer. Cynisca steps back and moves slowly, thinking. The most dangerous kind of wrestler, Clytemnestra knows—one who thinks. Cynisca prepares to strike again, and when she does, Helen moves in the wrong direction and is punched in the neck. She falls sideways but manages to grab Cynisca's leg and drag her down with her. Cynisca jabs her fist at Helen's face, again and again.

Clytemnestra wants to close her eyes, but that is not how she was taught. So she watches, thinking of how she will hurt Cynisca later, in the forest or by the river. She will take her down and make her face purple until the girl understands that some people must not be touched.

Cynisca stops punching and Helen crawls away, her face swollen, her hands bloody. *Fly, fly away*, Clytemnestra wants to shout, but deer have no wings, and Helen can barely stand. Cynisca doesn't give her time to compose herself. She strikes and kicks again, and when Helen tries to hurl her backward, Cynisca leaps on her and snatches her arm from under her.

Clytemnestra turns to Tyndareus. He is watching the fight, his face expressionless. He will do nothing, she is sure of it.

Helen cries out, and Clytemnestra finds herself running to the center of the ground. Cynisca turns and her mouth drops open in surprise, but it is too late. Clytemnestra takes her by the hair and hurls her aside with all her strength. Cynisca raises her head from the dirt, but Clytemnestra puts her knee into her backbone, because the dirt is where the girl belongs. She hooks an arm around her head and pulls, aware of Helen, lying half conscious in the bloody sand a few inches from them. It is over, Clytemnestra thinks, but Cynisca takes her leg and twists her ankle, hard. Clytemnestra trips, and Cynisca takes a moment to breathe, her eyes bloodshot.

"This is not your fight," Cynisca says, her voice hoarse.

You are wrong. Her leg hurts, but pain doesn't trouble her. Cynisca lunges at her. Clytemnestra moves aside and shoves her to the ground. She stands on Cynisca's back so she won't rise anymore. When she feels the body give in, she limps away. Helen is barely breathing, and Clytemnestra lifts her from the sand. Her sister wraps her arms around her, and Clytemnestra takes her away, her father's angry stare following her like a hound.

Clytemnestra's ankle swells. The skin grows purple; the foot slowly becomes numb. A servant dresses the wound, her little hands quick but gentle, her eyes downcast. Helots, people like her are called, former inhabitants of the valley, now slaves since the Spartans took their land. They are everywhere in the palace, their faces dull and sad in the torchlight, their backs bent.

Clytemnestra rests her head against the wall, rage twisting inside her. Sometimes her anger feels so real that she wishes she could cut it out with a knife. She is angry with Cynisca for daring to touch her sister; with her father, for letting Helen be beaten; with her mother, who never intervenes when the king's indifference hurts her daughter.

"It is done," the girl says, checking Clytemnestra's ankle. "You should rest now."

Clytemnestra springs up. She needs to check Helen.

"You can't walk," the servant says, frowning.

"Bring me my grandmother's stick," Clytemnestra orders. The girl nods and scampers away toward the king's quarters, where Tyndareus keeps his family's things. When she comes back, she is holding a beautiful wooden cane.

Clytemnestra never met her grandfather Oebalus; she knows only that he was the son-in-law of the hero Perseus. Her grandmother Gorgophone, on the other hand, is well marked in her memory. A tall, strong woman, she married twice, something unheard of in her country. When her first husband died—a king of Messenia whose name Clytemnestra doesn't remember—Gorgophone married Oebalus, even though she was older than him. She outlived him anyway, and Clytemnestra remembers when Gorgophone, wrapped in sheepskins before she died, told her and Helen that their family was a dynasty of queens.

"You girls will be remembered longer than your brothers," Gorgophone claimed in her deep voice, the lines on her face as dense as those of a cobweb, "just like me with my dear brothers. Alcaeus, Mestor, Heleus…good men, brave men, but does anyone remember them? They don't."

"You are sure of this?" Helen asked. She was only twelve, yet her face was as serious as a woman's.

Gorgophone stared at them, her eyes clouded but alert. "You are fierce and loyal, but I see wariness inside you too. I have lived among kings and heroes for so long, and they all grow too proud. When men grow proud, they become too trusting. Sooner or later, traitors cut them down." She was mumbling, though her words had clarity and wisdom. Clytemnestra felt compelled to listen. "Ambition, courage, distrust. You will be queens soon enough, and that is what you will need if you want to outlive the men who'll wish to be rid of you." Gorgophone was dead a few hours later, and Clytemnestra had turned her words over and over in her head, savoring them like drops of honey left on the lips.

Her ankle is now throbbing. Leaning on her grandmother's stick, Clytemnestra walks past the stony halls and corridors. The lit torches on the walls cast shadows that look like black figures painted on amphorae. She reaches the *gynaeceum*, gritting her teeth against the pain in her leg. Here the windows are smaller, the walls painted with bright patterns. Clytemnestra walks to the baths, where Helen is meant to be resting, and stops outside for a moment. She can hear voices, loud and clear.

"I will not tell you," Helen is saying. "It is not fair."

"It is not fair that she fought you. You know how things are. If one can challenge you, others will." It is Polydeuces. Her brother's voice is sharp, like an ax blade. Helen keeps silent. There is the sound of water and of Polydeuces's impatient steps, back and forth, back and forth.

"Tell me, Helen, or I will ask Clytemnestra."

"There is no need," Clytemnestra says, entering the room.

Helen is lying in a painted clay bath. The wounds on her arms are dressed with herbs; her face is broken and battered. Her lips are swollen, and one of her eyes is half-shut so that the light-blue iris is hardly visible, like a glimpse of clear sky on a cloudy day. Polydeuces turns. He is slender like Clytemnestra but taller, and his skin is the color of honey. At twenty, he will soon stop training and go to war.

"It was Cynisca who challenged Helen," Clytemnestra starts. Polydeuces is about to leave, his face twisted. She grabs his arm. "But you will do nothing. I dealt with it."

Polydeuces looks at her leg. There is a spark in his eyes that Clytemnestra knows too well: her brother is like a flame, always ready to pick a fight. "You shouldn't have," he says, shaking her away. "Now Father will be angry."

"With me, not with you," Clytemnestra says, knowing how much her brother hates disappointing Tyndareus.

"She protected me," Helen says. "The girl was killing me."

Polydeuces clenches his fists. Helen is his favorite, always has been.

"She had no choice," Helen continues. She speaks slowly, in pain.

Polydeuces nods, opens his mouth as if to say something, but then leaves, his steps light on the stony floor.

Helen closes her eyes, rests her head against the edge of the bath. "I am ashamed," she says. Clytemnestra can't tell if she is crying. The lights are dim and the air smells of blood.

"At least you are not dead," Clytemnestra says. Neither Tyndareus nor any other Spartan would agree that a life with shame is better than a glorious death, but Clytemnestra doesn't care. She would rather live. Glory is something she can earn later.

She finds her father in the *megaron* speaking to Castor and Leda. The great hall is large and beautifully lit, and she limps past the frescoed walls toward the throne. Next to her, the painted figures are running, hunting, and fighting, the colors as brilliant as the morning sun, frightened boar, rabid hounds, and heroes with spears, their long hair like ocean waves. Flocks of geese and swans fly over the shimmering plains, horses galloping beneath them.

Tyndareus sits on his throne near the hearth, holding a cup filled with wine, and Leda, beside him, occupies a smaller chair draped with lambskins. Castor is leaning against one of the columns, his manner relaxed as usual. When he sees Clytemnestra, he smiles. "You are always in trouble, Sister," he says. Like Polydeuces's, his face is already sharp with manhood.

"Cynisca will recover soon," Tyndareus says.

"I am glad," Clytemnestra replies. She is aware of her brother's amused stare behind her: there is nothing Castor enjoys more than trouble and the sound of someone else's scolding.

"We were lucky it was a girl," Tyndareus continues. Clytemnestra knows this already. A king's children can burn down houses, rape, steal, and kill as they wish. But hurting another noble's son is forbidden.

"Cynisca offended your daughter," Clytemnestra says.

Her father frowns in annoyance. "You offended Cynisca. You didn't give her a fair fight."

"You know the rules," Leda adds. "When two girls are wrestling, one wins and the other loses." She is right; Clytemnestra knows it, but matches aren't always that easy. Leda has taught them that there are winners and losers in every fight, and nothing can be done to change that. But what if the loser is your loved one and you have to watch her fall? What if she doesn't deserve to be beaten and turned to dust? When Clytemnestra asked these questions as a child, her mother would always shake her head. "You are not a god," she said. "Only gods can intervene in such matters."

"Cynisca would have killed Helen." Clytemnestra repeats what her sister said, even though she knows this isn't true. Cynisca would have just hurt Helen badly.

"She wouldn't have killed anyone," Tyndareus says.

"I know Cynisca," Castor intervenes. "The girl is violent. She punched a helot to death once."

"How would you know her?" Leda mocks him, but Castor doesn't flinch. They are all well familiar with his tastes anyway. For a few years now, Clytemnestra has started hearing moans and whispers from behind closed doors. Servants and the daughters of noble warriors have been in her brothers' beds and will continue to be so until Castor and Polydeuces decide to marry. When she walks around the palace, Clytemnestra watches servant girls pouring wine, cutting meat, and scrubbing floors, and she wonders which among them have slept with Castor. Most, probably. But then it is easy to pick out those who have been with Polydeuces. They are the ones who look like Helen, fair hair and skin, eyes like water springs. Not many.

"Father," Clytemnestra says, "I did only what soldiers do in war. If they see a friend dying next to them, they come to the rescue and fight."

Tyndareus tightens his grip on the cup. "What do you know of war?" He lets the words linger in the air. "What do you know of anything?"

"Finally someone gave Cynisca what she deserved," Castor says cheerfully as they leave the *megaron*. He carries his sister on his shoulders, and Clytemnestra looks at his hair bouncing as he walks. She remembers when they used to do this as children, Clytemnestra on Castor's back and Helen on Polydeuces's. The two boys raced each other carrying their sisters, tumbling and laughing until their faces hurt.

"I wanted to kill her," she replies.

Castor laughs. "Well, you've always been bad-tempered. *And* you always cared more about others than about yourself."

"That's not true."

"You know it is. Not that you care about everyone, of course. Just your family."

They reach the stables, close to the lower part of the palace, where the ground is more even and less rocky. Some young men are training; others are feeding the horses.

"Come," Castor says. "Let us ride awhile." They share one sturdy stallion, named for Ares, the god of war, and ride into the plain, toward the Eurotas. They pass the fig trees, the scorched earth dotted with yellow and red flowers, closer and closer to the river. Ares's hoofs raise a cloud of dust and sand until they finally splash in the water of the river. Castor rides fast, whistling and laughing, and Clytemnestra clings to him, her ankle hurting, her face warmed by the sun. When they stop, Castor helps her down and they sit on the riverbank. Grass and flowers grow here, but sometimes corpses can be found too, putrid and rotten.

"You know Father is right, though," Castor says, lying on his back. "Cynisca had every right to beat Helen."

"She didn't. Helen is different."

"We are all different in our own way."

Her eyes meet his. "You know what I mean."

Castor smirks. "You are wrong in protecting her too much. You underestimate her. If Cynisca kept beating her, Helen would have fought harder the next time."

"And what if she had died?"

He lifts his brows, amused. "People have always challenged each other. The strongest rise and fall, the weaker come and go. But some keep standing." He plays with a blade of grass before ripping it out. "You inherit Father's and Mother's strength, but Helen has strength of her own. She may be sweet and frail, but she is crafty. I wouldn't be surprised if she outlived us all."

His wit warms her like a sun-hot stone. This is how her life has always been: pleasure and misery, games and races, her brother always next to her ready to unravel the mysteries of the world and laugh at them.

For a moment, she wonders what it will be like when he is gone.

3

A King

EVERY TIME A stranger arrives in Sparta, the palace turns into a house of whispers. News travels as fast as sea breeze and the servants make every surface shine like gold. In the late afternoon, when the light is thinning and the air scented, they call Clytemnestra for her cleansing. "An important man will be here for dinner," they twitter.

"A warrior?" asks Clytemnestra as they walk toward the baths in the darkness of the corridor. Her ankle hurts less every day, and soon she will be able to run and exercise again.

"A king," they say. "Or that is what we heard."

In the bathroom, Helen is already cleaning herself in the painted clay bath, the old wounds on her arms dressed with herbs. Her face is smooth, luminous again. Only one bruise remains, on her left cheek, where the bone was broken. Two more tubs are ready beside her, filled to the brim with water, and behind them an old servant woman is preparing soap. It is made from olives, and it smells rich and fruity.

"Have you heard?" Helen asks.

Clytemnestra takes off her tunic and climbs into her tub. "It's been a while since we had any guests."

"It was time," Helen says, smiling to herself. She always enjoys it when visitors come to the palace.

The door opens. Timandra rushes into the room, breathless, and leaps into the cold bath. Her feet and hands are dirty, her hair messy. She has already started to bleed but her body is still lean, without any trace of feminine curves.

"Clean yourself, Timandra," Clytemnestra says. "It looks like you've been rolling in the dirt."

Timandra laughs. "Well, that is what I was doing."

Helen smiles and her face glows. She is in a good mood. "We can't be dirty for a while," she says, her voice lively with excitement. "A rich king is coming."

The servant starts combing her hair, her brown spotted hands untangling Helen's locks as if they were spun gold. Timandra feels for knots in her own dark hair. "I can be dirty," she says, eyeing Helen. "The king must certainly be for you."

"I am sure he doesn't come for marriage. It must be some economic proposition."

Clytemnestra feels hurt. Why must Helen be the only one ready for marriage?

As if she's read her mind, Helen says, "Maybe he will court Clytemnestra." Her words are as silky as cream, but for the first time, something underlies them, something Clytemnestra can't quite tell.

"I hate kings," she says carelessly. There is no reply, and when she turns to her sister, Helen is looking at her, her eyes dark and fierce.

"No, you don't," Helen says. "You will marry a king."

Clytemnestra wants to say she doesn't care about marrying a king as much as becoming a great queen. But she can see that Helen is hurt already—the same hurt that creeps in every time Clytemnestra dismisses her—and knows it is a useless argument. Let the men be proud and quarrelsome. She reaches out her hand and touches Helen's shoulder.

"We all will," she says.

Helen smiles and her face brightens, like the ripest fruit.

They sit together in a large room close to the dining hall for their *mousike* class, a chest filled with flutes and lyres in front of them. Their tutor, an older noblewoman who often performs poetry at dinner, is teaching them a new tune, plucking the strings of her lyre. Helen's brows are furrowed in concentration. Timandra is scoffing, looking at her feet, and Clytemnestra nudges her.

It is a song on the wrath of Artemis, on the wretched fate of the men who dare to challenge the gods. The teacher sings of the hunter Actaeon, who saw the goddess bathing in a spring on the mountains and called the rest of his party to join him. But no man is allowed to watch Artemis without witnessing the goddess's rage. *Thus the hunter became the hunted*, the teacher concludes, *and as Actaeon fled deeper and deeper into the woods, Artemis turned him into a stag.*

When it is their turn to perform, Timandra forgets half the words. Helen's and Clytemnestra's voices blend together like sky and sea— one light and sweet, the other dark and fierce. They stop singing and the teacher smiles at them, ignoring Timandra.

"Are you ready to impress the foreigner at dinner?"

They turn and Castor is standing by the door with an amused smile.

Helen blushes and Clytemnestra puts down her lyre. "Do not be too jealous," she tells her brother. "I am sure he will have eyes for you too."

Castor laughs. "I doubt it. Anyway, your lesson is over, Clytemnestra. Leda is waiting for you in the *gynaeceum*."

Outside her mother's room, the corridor is full of noise—women's whis-pers, hurrying feet, the clatter of pots and pans—and the smell of spiced meat drifts from the kitchen. Clytemnestra opens the bedroom door and closes it quickly behind her. Inside, it is as quiet as a tomb. Her mother is sitting on a wooden stool, staring at the ceiling as if praying to the gods. Slivers of light from the small windows touch the walls at intervals, illuminating the white flowers painted against a bright red background.

"You wanted to see me?" Clytemnestra asks.

Leda stands and smooths her daughter's hair. "Do you remember when I took you to the sea?"

Clytemnestra nods, though she can only recall glimpses: Leda's skin, wetted by the crystalline water, the drops tracing paths on her arms and belly, and the shells, scattered among the pebbles. They were empty. When she had asked why, Leda had explained it was because the animal that had been living there was dead and its body had been eaten by another.

"I told you about my marriage with your father that day, but you were too little to understand."

"Do you wish to tell me again?"

"I do. Do you know why marriage is called so by the Spartans?" *Harpazéin* is the word she uses, which also means *to take with force*.

"The man kidnaps his wife and she needs to put up a fight," Clytemnestra says.

Leda nods. She starts plaiting Clytemnestra's hair and her hands are rough against the back of her daughter's neck. "A husband needs to show his strength," she says, "but the wife must prove herself a worthy match."

"She must submit herself to him."

"Yes."

"I don't think I can do that, Mother."

"When your father came to take me to his room, I struggled but he was stronger. I cried and shouted but he wouldn't listen. So I pretended to give in, and when he relaxed, I put my arms around his neck until he choked." She finishes her daughter's hair, and Clytemnestra turns. The green in Leda's eyes is dark, like the evergreens on the highest mountains. "I told him I would never submit. When I let him go, he said I was worthier than he had expected and we made love."

"Are you saying I should do the same?"

"I'm saying that it is hard to find a man who is really strong. Strong enough not to desire to be stronger than you."

There is a knock on the door, and Helen steps inside. She is wearing a white gown and a corset that barely conceals her breasts. She stops when she sees her mother, afraid to interrupt.

"Come in, Helen," says Leda.

"I am ready. Shall we go?" Helen asks. Leda nods and takes her hand, guiding her out of the room. Clytemnestra follows, wondering if Leda has already told her sister what she has just vouchsafed to herself.

The dining hall looks different tonight. Wooden benches have been draped with lambskins, and tapestries are hanging in place of the bronze weapons. Royal hunts and battle scenes with bleeding men and godlike heroes now cover the walls. Servants move quickly and silently, like nymphs around streams. Tyndareus has ordered more oil lamps hung up, and they cast flickering lights on the large table where a few noble Spartans and the foreign king are eating.

Clytemnestra can't take her eyes off the stranger. The man looks young and different from every other guest. His hair is as black as obsidian and his eyes turquoise, like the most precious gems. Tyndareus introduced him as the king of Maeonia, a land in the east, far across the sea. Men like him are called *barbaroi* in Greece, people ruled by despots, who live with neither freedom nor reason. Clytemnestra wonders if kings fight their own battles in Maeonia, as they do in Sparta. It doesn't seem so, for the stranger's arms are smooth, quite different from the scarred bodies of the Spartans around him.

The table is laid with rare delicacies—goat and sheep meat, onions, pears and figs, honeyed flatbreads—but Clytemnestra doesn't want to eat. The king of Maeonia is talking to Helen, who is seated beside him. When he makes her laugh, he stares straight at Clytemnestra.

She looks away as her father speaks, addressing the stranger over the loud chatter. "Tell me, Tantalus, are the women in your homeland as beautiful as they say?"

Is Tyndareus trying to arrange a marriage? Sparta rarely has guests from such faraway lands, and the king of Maeonia must be very wealthy.

Tantalus doesn't blink. He smiles, and two small lines appear at the corners of his eyes. "They are, but nothing like the beauty you find here in Sparta." He looks at Clytemnestra once more. This time she stares back, her heart racing as though she were running. She can almost feel Castor smirking at the other end of the table.

"Your women possess the most precious beauty of all: strength of body and character."

Tyndareus raises his cup. "To the women of Sparta," he says.

Everyone echoes his words, and the golden cups shine in the light of the lamps.

The sun sets late in summer. Standing on the terrace in front of the main hall, Clytemnestra looks at the mountains to the west and the east. Their peaks are perfectly outlined against the orange sky, then slowly become blurred, melting into the growing darkness. When she hears steps approaching behind her, she doesn't turn. Tantalus appears next to her, as she hoped he would. She wanted him to follow her, but now she doesn't know what to say. So she waits. When she turns to him, he is staring at the golden earrings that graze her neck and shoulders as they swing. They are in the shape of big anemones.

"Do you know the origin of windflowers?" he says, breaking the silence. His voice is warm, his skin as dark as oak.

"We call them anemones," replies Clytemnestra.

"Anemones," he repeats. "They were created by the goddess Aphrodite from the blood of Adonis, the boy she was in love with."

"I know what happened. Adonis was slain by a wild boar."

Tantalus frowns. "The boy dies but the goddess's love for him remains. It is a reminder of beauty and resistance in times of adversity."

"That is true, but Adonis is dead, and no flower can replace him."

Tantalus smiles. "You truly are a strange woman."

I am not strange, Clytemnestra wants to say, but she keeps silent, her breath held.

"Your father says you are as wise as a mature woman can be, and when I ask your sister about you, she says you always know what you want."

Clytemnestra tilts her head. "That would be enviable, even for a man."

Tantalus's smile disappears and she fears he will walk away from her. But then he reaches for her hair. He touches her plaits, finds her neck. His hand on her is like a flame, yet she wants more of it. She takes one step forward, close enough to feel his heat. Desire runs through her, but she can't come closer. He is a stranger, after all. They are still, the world moving around them.

The shadows grow longer on the terrace. Everything around them is soft, fading, as the skies merge with the earth, and their faces dissolve, like fleeting breath.

4

The Tales of Tantalus

IT IS EARLY morning, and Clytemnestra is sitting next to her father's throne in the *megaron*. The room feels hot and the frescoes seem to be melting. She can smell Tyndareus's sweat while her brothers argue over a Spartan warrior who claimed a fellow comrade's wife as his own. Soon people will flood the *megaron* with their daily requests, and she will have to listen, but all she can think of is the feel of Tantalus's hand on her neck. It was like being touched by a star.

"The warrior needs to pay," Polydeuces is saying, his voice raised.

Clytemnestra rubs her eyes and tries to focus.

"You are always too vengeful, my son," Tyndareus says. He is eating some grapes out of a bowl, juice staining his beard. "Terror doesn't rule alone."

"We are talking about a man who stole another's woman!" Polydeuces replies sharply.

"Maybe she went with him willingly," Castor smirks. "Make sure he pays the other comrade in gold. Then let the men be."

"If it is just money that the man has to give as punishment, what will stop him the next time he wants to fuck someone else's woman?" Polydeuces asks. "But if you take his child, his wife, show him that he too can lose the ones he loves, he will obey. He won't *ask* for forgiveness. He will *beg*."

"The man has no wife," Castor points out. "He's a widower."

Tyndareus sighs. "What do you suggest, Clytemnestra?"

She sits up. "Summon the woman. Ask her what she did and why."

Her brothers turn to her quickly. "And then?"

"Then act accordingly." When no one says anything, she continues, "Are we in Sparta or in Athens? Do we not take pride in our strong, free-willed women, or do we lock them into the house so they grow fragile and useless?"

Castor frowns. "And if the woman claims she went with another man willingly?"

"Then she will have to ask for her husband's forgiveness with the man. If he raped her, he will apologize to her, not to her husband."

Tyndareus nods, and Clytemnestra's face grows warm with pride. Her father rarely listens to anyone else.

"See this woman, then," Tyndareus orders Castor and Polydeuces. Clytemnestra moves to stand, but her father stops her. "Stay."

When her brothers have disappeared, Tyndareus offers her some grapes. His hands are large, calloused. "I want to ask you about the king of Maeonia, Clytemnestra."

She takes the ripest grapes and swallows them, keeping her face as expressionless as she can. "What about him?"

"The agreement for which he has come here has been discussed. He can return home. But he tells me he likes spending time with you." He stops, then continues. "What do you want?"

Clytemnestra looks at her own hands, long fingers covered with tiny cuts, palms smoother than her father's. *What do I want?*

"Many men of Sparta will soon ask for your hand," Tyndareus says. "You are loved and respected."

"I know."

Because she doesn't speak further, Tyndareus asks, "And yet you wish Tantalus to stay?" He waits for her answer patiently, popping grapes into his mouth until the bowl is emptied.

"Yes, Father," she says finally. "I want him to stay a little longer."

She becomes obsessed with Tantalus. She aches for contact when he is around, and when he is not, her mind drifts, and she finds herself thinking about his eyes and lean body as she has never done with anyone else.

Helen doesn't understand, but how could she? Clytemnestra knows very well that she herself is her sister's greatest obsession. To Helen, all men are the same—strong, violent, excited by her beauty, but nothing more. They feel no challenge to conquer her heart; they see her only as a prize, the most precious one, but a prize still, as a cow or a sword might be. Tantalus, though, has seen something in Clytemnestra that he loves and wants, and he seems willing to do anything to have it.

"He is no different from all the others," Helen tells her as they hurry down the narrow street of craftsmen's workshops and stores around the palace. The street is a shortcut to the square where textile manufacturers and dyers run their errands.

"I believe he is different, but we will see," Clytemnestra replies, missing some steps on the cobbled street.

"Slow down! Why are you running?" Helen pants.

Clytemnestra knows Tantalus is in the stables and hopes he will still be there when they come back.

"We need to collect Mother's tunic before sunset. Hurry!" she says, stumbling from the darkness of the narrow street to the light of the square. The end of summer is near but the sun is fierce, blinding. Clytemnestra stops abruptly, and Helen bumps against her.

"Oh, come on," she says. "You want to go back to see Tantalus."

She takes her sister's arm and guides her across the square. She stops in front of the perfume makers' store to look at the fruit trees and herbs planted in an inner courtyard. Clytemnestra pushes her forward, past the dyers' shops, animal skins hanging by the doors, and toward a smaller shop in one corner. It sells textiles, domain of spinners and weavers. Inside, the space is large and well organized, women working on raw wool and linen.

"We are here for Leda's new *chiton*," Clytemnestra says, her voice loud and clear.

A woman with black hair and pale skin comes forward, leaving aside the wool she was working on. "Welcome, princesses," she says. She leads them to the back of the store, where older women are working on tall looms. "Wait here." She disappears behind a curtain.

"When will Tantalus leave?" Helen asks. "Guests never stay so long."

"Maybe he won't," Clytemnestra says.

Behind them, the women are whispering. Clytemnestra turns, trying to catch the words, and they stop immediately, focusing on their looms. Helen is blushing, her eyes downcast.

"What did they say?" Clytemnestra asks.

"It doesn't matter," Helen whispers. Before Clytemnestra can insist, the woman comes back holding a crimson tunic.

Clytemnestra takes it from her and turns to her sister. "Let's go. We must get back."

Helen mumbles something, but as soon as she speaks, the women are whispering again. She and Clytemnestra hurry out of the shop, the women's eyes following them.

Outside, in the square, Helen walks ahead of Clytemnestra. She seems troubled, so Clytemnestra leaves her be. She can't wait to leave the tunic by the palace door and run to the stables.

"You really didn't hear that word, did you?" Helen asks suddenly. She is still walking ahead so Clytemnestra can't see her face.

"No."

"Those women called me *teras*." The word is cutting on her lips. *Portent*, it means, like a rainbow that appears over the clouds, but also *freak*, like a gorgon, the monster with snakes as hair. "They've been saying this in the gymnasium too."

Clytemnestra is angry. "Why? Why would they say that?"

Helen turns. Her cheeks are crimson, her eyes full of tears. It is painful to watch her face, the sadness it shows. "They think that Tyndareus isn't my father. That I was born after Zeus raped Leda. They believe this, but they don't say it to my face."

Clytemnestra takes a deep breath. "Let's go back to the shop." Her brother is right: some people must be taught a lesson.

"I thought you were in a hurry to see Tantalus," Helen replies, her voice bitter.

Then she is walking, almost running up the cobbled street that leads back to the palace. Clytemnestra stays in the blinding light of the square, her mother's tunic crumpling in her hands. She wishes the light would scorch her so Helen could see her pain.

Back in the half-deserted stables, Tantalus is feeding a chestnut stallion. She walks to him slowly, as if she hadn't run the whole way. When he sees her, he gives the horse a last handful of hay, then turns to her. "I have just heard that you were recently injured in a fight," he says.

"It was nothing. I sprained my ankle."

His eyes are a bright blue, like a gemstone catching light always in a different way but safe, like the crystal clear water of the shore, never too deep, never too scary.

"Do you fight?" she asks.

"Yes, but not like you. We fight with weapons."

"What happens when someone attacks you and you have no weapon?"

Tantalus laughs. "There are guards around us."

"There are no guards now."

He smiles, opens his arms. "Fight me, if you want. So we shall see if we *barbaroi* earn the name you have given us." He doesn't speak with anger or contempt. "But I warn you, I am afraid I am no match for you."

She is surprised. She doesn't know any man who speaks like this. "Maybe we should fight with weapons then."

Tantalus moves forward, one, two, three steps. "Oh, I am sure you would be stronger still. I have heard that you always fight to win."

"And you don't?"

Tantalus is close now: she can see the little lines around his eyes. "I never had to fight to earn anything in my life. That is my condemnation, my weakness."

Again, surprise. The men Clytemnestra knows don't speak of their weaknesses. She considers what he said. A life like that is hard to imagine.

"I can see that with you it must be different," Tantalus adds, "so I will try again and again, if you will have me."

"And if I will not?"

"Then I will go back to Maeonia. And I will have learned how painful it is not to have what you desire."

"That would be good for you."

"I am not so sure."

Clytemnestra leans back, even though she wants to touch his face. She wants to feel his smooth skin under her hand, to press her body against his. But all good things must wait. So she leaves him empty-handed.

♛

They start going together to the river, day after day. They walk under the sinking sun of the late afternoon, when the earth is still warm beneath their feet. As they sit with their legs dangling in the water and the reeds tickling their backs, Tantalus tells her stories of the people he has met and the lands he has visited, of the gods he worships and the myths he enjoys. He tells her about the Hittites, with their war chariots and storm gods. He describes Crete, its mighty palace, each wall covered with rich colors and patterns warmed by the sun. He tells her about the first ruler of Maeonia and his proud daughter, Niobe, whose seven sons and daughters Artemis killed.

"Niobe wouldn't stop crying," Tantalus says, "so the gods turned her into stone. But even then water kept streaming on the rock."

He tells her of Colchis, the wondrous land of Aeëtes, son of the sun, and the spells he conjures to terrify his people. "Dust warriors fight for him, dragons too. And now he has a daughter, Medea. They say she is dangerous. They say she is a witch, just like her father."

"Maybe she won't be dangerous," Clytemnestra points out.

"Maybe," Tantalus says, "but children usually grow up to be like their parents."

"And what about your parents?"

Tantalus speaks of the rulers of Maeonia, the fathers of gold and silver coins. Clytemnestra can see he likes to tell these stories. She doesn't care much for myths—she has grown up with her father and brothers, who look at the world with no enchantment or illusion. But Tantalus is a gifted storyteller, so she listens.

As he speaks, she is stricken by how wonderful and scary it is to hang on his every word and to wish she could listen to him forever. It is like jumping over the edge of a cliff and falling, her heart racing, yet always longing for more.

In the next few days, Clytemnestra watches her parents as she has never done before.

When commoners walk in the *megaron* with their pleas, Leda speaks and gives orders, but only when Tyndareus asks for her opinion. At dinner, when he glances at the servant girls—carelessly enough for his wife to see—Leda drains her wine in silence, though there are sparks in her eyes as if she were ready to catch fire. Clytemnestra sees that her mother challenges her father and that he likes her for it, but only up to a point. Play with the wolf too much, and he'll rip off your arm.

As Clytemnestra watches, she feels like a weaver, spinning each thread, eager to see the final tapestry. She sees that her mother can be two different people and that the best version appears when her father isn't around.

Is this what happens when one falls in love and marries? Clytemnestra wonders. Is this what a woman gives up? All her life, she has been taught courage, strength, resilience, but must those qualities be kept at bay with a husband? But it is also true that her father listens to her when she speaks, and Tantalus looks at her as if she were a goddess.

The thoughts burn and flicker, and she tries to drown them.

It doesn't matter what Leda or Tyndareus does. Her grandmother told her she will be queen, and so it will be.

She will bow to no one. Her destiny will be what she wants it to be.

Her brothers must leave. A heroic expedition, to the rich land of Colchis. A messenger arrives to give the news at dawn, sweat pouring through his tunic after the long trip. Clytemnestra watches him from the terrace as he dismounts from his horse and meets Castor and Polydeuces at the entrance to the palace. They haven't had any visitors since Tantalus's arrival, and she is surprised to see that the man lingers by the door to speak to her brothers rather than hurrying inside to meet the king.

Later, Castor brings her to the riverbank. He seems lost in thought, and his eyes are dark in the morning light.

"That envoy was for you and Polydeuces," Clytemnestra says.

He nods. "We are going to Colchis. We have been called to join a crew of young Greek men."

"Tantalus told me about Colchis," she says. "A wicked king rules there."

"Aeëtes, yes," Castor replies.

"He is skilled in potions. He uses herbs that grow in the woods to work changes upon the world."

"How do you know such things?"

"Tantalus says everyone knows about it in the East."

"What do these herbs do?"

"They heal animals and people alike, bring them back to life. But they also cause pain."

Castor doesn't reply. He is watching a group of boys racing each other in the distance.

"When will you leave?" Clytemnestra asks, dipping her feet into the water.

"Soon. In ten days."

"For how long?"

Castor sits next to her. "I don't know yet. It will be one of the greatest expeditions ever. They will talk about it for years to come."

"So you will stay away for a long time," Clytemnestra says.

Castor ignores her. "Jason from Thessaly leads us. The crew will be forty men or more."

"Jason?" She remembers the women of the palace speaking about the boy, son of the rightful king of Iolkos. It was one of those stories that people loved to tell over and over again: a power-hungry ruler eager to eliminate all threats to the throne and a mother desperate to save her child. When Jason was born, his uncle Pelias ordered him dead, so his mother and her attendants clustered around the baby and wailed as if he had been stillborn. Then she slipped out of the palace in the night and hid her son in the woods, praying that someone would rescue him. No one has heard of him since.

"He is alive," Castor says, "and will take back his kingdom. But first, he needs to go to Colchis."

"What is he after?"

"A golden fleece." Clytemnestra raises her eyebrows, skeptical, and Castor explains. "King Aeëtes is rumored to keep the fleece of a ram with golden wool. Many have tried to steal it, but no one has ever succeeded. Jason's uncle wants him to find it and bring it to him. If we do that, he will give him the throne of Iolkos."

"Why do you follow him?" Clytemnestra asks. "It is not a fight that concerns you."

"Every man worth anything will be there. Anyone who wants to be remembered."

And what about me? Shall I be forgotten? But she remembers her grandmother's words. *You girls will be remembered for longer than your brothers.* She walks into the water, feeling mossy rock under her feet.

"You like this king, this Tantalus?" she hears Castor ask.

She laughs but doesn't answer.

"He wants you, I believe," Castor adds.

"I believe it too."

"Will you marry?"

"Maeonia is far," Clytemnestra says.

Castor tilts his head and looks at her, serious. "Colchis is far too. So what? Do we stay in Sparta and rot for the rest of our days?"

Clytemnestra can feel Helen panting behind her. She reaches for her hand to help her up the forest path. Leaves crunch under their feet, and the sun filters through the trees. Along creeks and fallen trunks, wild strawberries glow bloodred in the shade.

The atmosphere in the gymnasium was unbearable, with groups of Spartiates whispering behind Helen's back as they trained. As soon as the dancing ended, Clytemnestra had taken her sister's arm and led her up the trail that takes them to the top of Mount Taygetus. She knew she couldn't have controlled herself if she had stayed there any longer.

They climb to the peak, where the air is cold and wet and trees pierce the sky like spears. Clytemnestra stops to sit on a large rock, and Helen kneels at her side, her golden hair sweaty and scattered with twigs. From up there, the valley is brown and smooth, the patches of dry yellow land like scars on a warrior's back.

"Do you know about Castor and Polydeuces?" Helen asks.

Clytemnestra nods. Polydeuces must have told her.

"Are you worried?" Helen asks.

"No," Clytemnestra says. An eagle flies over their heads, a dead mouse in its beak. Clytemnestra watches it until it disappears, diving from the sky into the depth of the forest.

"I wish I could leave too," Helen says. "I wish I could leave with them."

"And go to Colchis?"

"Why not?"

Clytemnestra shrugs. "I want to see Knossos, or the Phoenician colonies. Or Maeonia."

"Maeonia," Helen repeats.

Clytemnestra squats on the rock, aware that Helen is staring at her.

"You want to marry Tantalus?" Helen asks. There is no jealousy or anger in her voice, just surprise.

Why surprised? Clytemnestra thinks. *She thought I would marry some common king or a Spartan? No… I want to be with someone who is different, someone who makes me look at the world with pleasure, who shows me its wonders and secrets.*

"I can see how you change around him," Helen says.

"Is it a good or bad change?" Clytemnestra asks.

Helen looks away, smoothing her tunic. Beneath her poise, she may hide sadness and fear, Clytemnestra knows. But her sister has learned to keep the darkness beneath the surface, just as weeds hide under the sea.

When she turns to Clytemnestra again, Helen smiles. "I think good."

At dinner, Castor and Polydeuces announce their imminent departure. Tyndareus and Leda kiss them. Spartan nobles applaud them.

"We will leave when word arrives that Jason is ready in Iolkos," Castor declares, and everyone beats their cups against the table, cheering. Servants bring wine in golden jugs and platters of bread, meat, figs, and cheese.

"Help yourselves to food, kin and clansmen of Sparta," Tyndareus says. "Tonight we celebrate my sons' expedition!" Another round of applause and cheerful shouts. Helen sips her wine quietly as Polydeuces whispers in her ear. Clytemnestra watches them.

"Are you sad?" Tantalus asks her.

Clytemnestra turns to him.

"I can see you are sad because they are leaving," he says. He is staring at her, waiting, as if ready to hold her feelings and secrets in his hands.

"They will be happy there," she says. "They were born for this."

"For what?"

"To be great fighters. Heroes."

"And you?"

"I wasn't born to be in some other man's expedition."

"What were you born for, then?"

She waits a moment before replying. "My grandmother once said I was born to rule."

Tantalus smiles. "All rulers must learn how to follow before they can lead."

"Have you spent a long time following others? Before you were king?"

He laughs and takes her hand. Her skin burns under his touch. Then he lets go and eats while the room fills with drunken chatter.

When the sun sinks into the dry land, the hall grows quieter. The house dogs are eating the leftovers on the floor. Dirty plates, bowls, and cups half filled with wine litter the table. Leda and Tyndareus have already disappeared to their quarters, and now the last drunken nobles are stumbling away, dragging their wives with them.

It is dark outside, but the high-roofed hall is still lit. Castor hands Tantalus a golden jug, a mischievous smile on his face. "Drink some more."

He takes it. "If you're trying to get me drunk, you will find it hard."

"Do you drink much in Maeonia?" Helen asks. She is lying on the wooden bench, her head on Polydeuces's lap.

"We drink to death," Tantalus replies. Castor and Clytemnestra laugh. She is walking around the hall, in and out of the brightness of the torches. Tantalus's gaze follows her.

"Then we can't let our sister come with you," Castor says. "We don't want her to die from drinking too much wine."

Clytemnestra's cheeks burn, but she smiles. "You shouldn't worry, Castor. You know very well that I can fight you even after two jugs."

Castor leaps closer to her and tries to lift her, jokingly, but she takes his arm and bends it behind his back. He laughs, pushes her away.

Helen yawns, and Polydeuces stands. "I'm going to bed," he says. A dark-haired servant steps into the room, looking at him hopefully, as if she were waiting for him to take her. He ignores her, holding out his hand for Helen.

"Well, I am going too," Castor says, walking in the servant's direction. "It seems I might have company tonight after all."

Helen lingers by the door, looking at Clytemnestra and Tantalus. She opens her mouth as if to say something but closes it and takes Polydeuces's hand. They leave together, Helen's head turning one more time before they disappear beyond the door.

Clytemnestra leans against the wall, Tantalus's eyes on her. Now there are only the two of them, facing each other. She waits, still under the light of a torch, and he comes to her. When he is close enough to touch her, he speaks so softly his words feel like a breath.

"Tell me what you want, Clytemnestra." She bites her lip, quiet, so he adds, "I will go too, if that is what you wish."

He understands that she likes power, and he is giving it to her. She wonders if it is a trick, a game he is playing. But even if it is, she doesn't care. She is good at games, and she can play this one.

"Stay," she says.

She has been with a man already, a boy not much older than her. It was during a village feast, a summer night. The stars covered the sky vault and illuminated the villagers as they danced and jumped on the yellow grass. Helen, Clytemnestra, Castor, and Polydeuces had watched the dance, captivated by the thud of feet, the paint on the villagers' faces. Then Helen was clapping and singing to the rhythm, and soon the four were dancing, holding each other's hands, laughing.

Afterward they drank until the stars were spinning and the paint on the villagers seemed like a dream. Helen and Polydeuces continued dancing together, while Castor vanished with the village beauty, an older girl with big eyes, like the goddess Hera. A boy with dark curls took Clytemnestra's hand, and they ran and hid among the tall grass, their bodies light with excitement.

After, as they shivered beneath the silent moon, pleasure slowly fading, the boy asked if he could see her again. She shook her head. She could smell the odors of fig trees and mud, jasmine and sweat. The boy fell asleep quickly, and she left him there, dreaming under the trees.

She walked around the village, eager to find her siblings. Helen and Polydeuces were gone, but she found Castor sitting alone in the orchard, a small smile on his lips. She lay down next to him, her head on his lap, bright fruit hanging above her like small suns. The familiar feel of Castor's hand on her head soothed her. She slept curled up next to her brother until dawn came and the villagers woke them.

She wakes in the darkness of a room she doesn't immediately recognize. No tapers are lit, and the thin curtains dance with the gusts of wind. She lifts herself onto her arm, and a lock of her hair falls onto Tantalus's face. He smiles without opening his eyes. Still, Clytemnestra feels he can see her.

"You don't sleep much," he says.

"I like to think."

"You like to observe."

Clytemnestra wonders how to reply. She is usually good at answering, but he seems to be even better. *It must be because he talks about me and not about himself.* She looks at his dark eyelashes, even thicker than her own. He opens his eyes, and they gleam like the ocean under the moonlight.

"So tell me," he says, smiling. "What do you see?"

She lies down again and stares at the bare ceiling. "A stranger who doesn't feel like one, and a Spartan who feels like a stranger in her own palace."

Tantalus laughs and kisses her neck, her cheeks, her collarbones.

A king is always a king, even when far from home, thinks Clytemnestra. What about a queen? What makes a girl a queen? Surely she is a woman who can protect herself and her people, who gives justice to those who deserve it and punishes those who betray her.

Her head is heavy with sleep. Tantalus smells of spiced wine and tastes like mint, the one used in the kitchen to add flavor to insipid food. His head resting on her shoulder, she feels as if she is flying, a bird diving in the dark-blue sky.

For a moment, she thinks about Helen, alone in their room. Of all those nights they have lain awake together, wondering about being with a king.

She pushes away the thought and presses closer to Tantalus.

5

The Clever Cousin

THE WEDDING IS to be celebrated quickly, before Castor and Polydeuces leave. Tyndareus's permission is easily given. Leda is the only reluctant one.

"Tantalus isn't strong," she says, eating ripe apricots in the *megaron*. Phoebe and Philonoe are running around her, playing with sticks. Their feet are crusted with mud, their hair messy. Rays of sun caress the frescoes, making the colors sparkle, like raindrops on grass.

"He has a different strength," Clytemnestra replies. "He is clever and curious." Leda raises her eyebrows, and Clytemnestra knows she is wondering how curiosity can equal strength.

"Do you think he would be a suitable father?" her mother asks.

"Much better than any Spartan."

Leda frowns but keeps silent. She calls Phoebe and Philonoe and they come quickly, their tunics stained with apricot juice.

"Go and have a bath. Tomorrow is an important day," Leda orders. "Your sister is getting married." Phoebe claps her hands, delighted, but Philonoe couldn't have cared less. Marriage is far away from her. "Go, hurry," Leda repeats.

The girls run away. Before Phoebe disappears beyond the door, she turns, sullen, as Philonoe pulls her hair. Clytemnestra winks at her.

"Not many people will come tomorrow," Leda says, "but your father says his brother and your cousin Penelope will arrive tonight."

"I like it better without many people."

"I know you do. It was the same for me when I was your age."

Clytemnestra kneels by the throne and rests her head on her mother's lap. "You are not sure about this union," she says, "but trust me, Mother."

Leda sighs. "When you are this stubborn, it is no use trying to contradict you."

After dinner, her uncle King Icarius and his daughter arrive from Acarnania, a northern land of green hills and glittering rivers near Aetolia. Clytemnestra and Helen can hear Tyndareus welcoming them in the hall, urging them to rest after the journey. They have been instructed to wait in the *gynaeceum* for their cousin Penelope, where they have saved flatbreads and honey for her.

Penelope is about Clytemnestra's age, seemingly mild and delicate, yet clever and stubborn, like the climbing rose vine that grows on the palace walls. When they were little, they spent much time together. Penelope was more like Helen, a well-behaved child, quiet, yet both found a way to say what they thought, to claim their own space. Clytemnestra respected that.

"Welcome, Cousin," Helen says when Penelope arrives wrapped in a dark-brown cloak, a light veil arranged around her face.

"I am very happy to see you." Penelope sits on the wooden stool Clytemnestra offers her and draws off her veil, revealing brown-streaked hair, like a lynx's coat. She has changed since the last time they saw her. She is still short, her face almond-shaped, her eyes gentle, but her body has developed soft, adolescent curves.

Helen pushes the bowl of flatbreads in her direction and Penelope takes one slowly, as if she isn't hungry. As she tears off a piece, she sets her mild eyes on Clytemnestra.

"Congratulations. You are marrying a foreigner, I heard."

"I am. King Tantalus of Maeonia."

Something flickers in Penelope's eyes, like the sudden sparkle of silver under the torchlight. "You are leaving then."

"Yes, but not soon."

Penelope nods, her face impassive. Clytemnestra knows that expression well. When they were children, Penelope was always following her around, trying to discourage her hasty choices. When she couldn't, she made excuses for her cousin to the elders. She was a very good liar.

"You disapprove?" Clytemnestra asks.

Penelope smiles. "I never thought you'd be the first to marry, that's all. But I am happy for you."

"You must be tired," Helen tells Penelope.

"A little," Penelope says. "But I haven't seen you in too long. We have a night's worth of stories." She stares at them, her face thoughtful. Then she takes Clytemnestra's hand. "So tell me about Tantalus. I want to know everything."

On the wedding day, dawn shines bright and golden. Outside the windows, trees are yellow and orange, and the banks of the Eurotas are muddy. In the *megaron*, tables are laid with bowls of geese and ducks, quail and wild boar, figs and cakes, onions, grapes and sweet apples.

Vases of fresh flowers are everywhere, and the door and windows are wide open to make sure the light does justice to the frescoes.

The room fills quickly with rich Spartan families. Tyndareus and Leda welcome them, offering wine. Most ask what Sparta gains with this new marriage, which economic propositions the king of Maeonia offers. Clytemnestra pays no attention to any of it. She lingers by the largest window, Helen and Penelope by her sides. Penelope looks pretty in her lapis-blue dress, while Helen wears a simple white tunic, her long hair glowing around her shoulders; she has tried her best not to outshine her sister. Clytemnestra is wearing the earrings she had on the first night she met Tantalus, and her own white dress is bound with a thin golden belt.

"Our cousin Penelope has grown," Castor says as he approaches the girls with Polydeuces and a few other Spartan youths. Smiling, Penelope accepts her cousin's kiss. She lets her eyes linger on the other boys, her stare as bright as the moon in a starless night.

"Soon you will marry too, I presume," Castor says.

"Not before I find a man who truly respects me," replies Penelope. Castor opens his mouth, but Penelope is quicker. "And what about you, Cousin? Is marriage still far off for you?" Her voice is wise and mild. She doesn't sound as though she is looking for an argument as Clytemnestra often does.

Castor laughs. "Why settle down when there are so many Spartan women? Look at this room. It swarms with them."

"Haven't you already slept with them all?" Polydeuces snorts.

Castor narrows his eyes. "Not yet, I think." The men around him laugh, and Penelope smiles. "Now, if you'll excuse us…" He turns in the direction of a group of Spartiates, and the other men follow.

Clytemnestra turns to the window. "I feel strange," she says. It's as if her life, as she knows it, is over.

Penelope takes her wrist. "Don't." Then, as if she has read her mind, she adds, "We are taught that marriage is the end of fun and childhood, but it is just the same. Nothing changes much in your life."

"How do you know?"

"I am sure of it. It is one of those things men say to make sure we feel *responsible*, while they can be children forever."

Helen laughs. "I wish I could remember everything you say, Penelope. Did Uncle Icarius teach you any of this?"

Penelope shakes her head. "Father doesn't teach me much. Mother did, though, before she died. She liked to talk, to me especially, less to Father."

Clytemnestra searches Penelope's face for a hint of sadness, but she seems calm. Her mother, Polycaste, had been a frail, gentle woman who died of a bad fever years before, when Penelope was still little. Since then, she has been the one running everything in her palace. Penelope, as Clytemnestra knows, has a talent for making people listen to her, and she can be, at the same time, a very good listener. One day, she will make a just queen.

Five young men take out flutes and drums. As soon as the music is playing, girls and women leap to the center of the *megaron*. They whirl and toss their heads, their hair waving, like branches in the strongest winds. The large windows spill sun on them. Helen takes Clytemnestra to the center of the room. She obliges, moving her wrists and ankles to the rhythm, the jewelry twinkling. Soon the men join them. Clytemnestra sees Castor jumping and beating his hands, and Polydeuces, eyes closed, head bouncing while several girls watch him, giggling.

They stop only when sweat is running down their backs. They all feel drunker now, happier. Clytemnestra takes a handful of dried fruit and sips more wine; she feels almost feverish. Someone begins to sing, the musicians accompanying. They sing of conquered cities and successful hunts and raids. Of warrior women and monumental fights.

"Is it just me, or do men look stupid when they sing?"

Clytemnestra turns to face her brother. Castor looks drunker than her, his olive skin reddish on the cheeks. This makes her laugh.

"We look like animals," he repeats. Sure enough, as she glances around, she sees the men's faces red with laughter, hands tight around their wine cups. Every verse they sing is more obscene than the last, which is not shocking to her—it has always been like this—but they seem almost grotesque now.

She walks around the room, suddenly in need of quiet. As she moves toward the door, she bumps into a tall girl. Cynisca. Clytemnestra takes a step back as Cynisca stares at her, sullen.

"Congratulations," Cynisca says. Her beak nose is weirdly crooked, and there are fading bruises on her arms.

Clytemnestra wonders if they linger from their fight. "Thank you," she says. She tries to step around her and grab a wine cup, but Cynisca moves to stand in the way.

"Loved, honorable, brave," she says. "What a queen you will make."

Clytemnestra keeps silent, unsure of what to say. As always, Cynisca's expression unsettles her.

"I would be careful if I were you. The lucky always fall."

"Many men are lucky and loved and still live happily." Even as she says it, Clytemnestra knows it isn't entirely true.

Cynisca smirks. "Ah, that is your mistake. You think yourself a man, but you aren't. Lucky women never get past the envy of the gods."

Clytemnestra could have her whipped here and now if she wanted to. But Cynisca isn't worth her anger, so she just stares at her coldly.

As she walks away, toward her loving Tantalus, she smiles. *Better to be envied than to be no one.*

In the night, while Tantalus sleeps quietly beside her, she feels restless. They have made love, drunk and excited, and the sheets now smell of their bodies. She turns onto her left side, staring at the bare wall. On the other side of the palace, sheltered by the bright frescoed patterns of the *gynaeceum*, Helen must be sleeping in their bed next to Penelope. Clytemnestra feels a pang of jealousy.

There is no way she will fall asleep tonight. She moves the sheets aside as silently as possible and walks out of the room. Tiptoeing along, feeling the warmth of the lit torches as she passes them, she reaches the *megaron*. The room should be resting, empty and quiet, but Penelope is standing there, admiring the frescoes with a torch in her hand.

"What are you doing here?" Clytemnestra asks. Her voice echoes on the walls, feeble, like the sound of bats' wings.

Penelope turns quickly, holding the torch in front of her. "Oh," she says, "it's you."

"Can't you sleep?"

Penelope shakes her head. "These are marvelous. We don't have as many in Acarnania." She steps back and forth, amazed by a painted flock of birds. "They are so bright—it makes you wish you'd painted them yourself."

Clytemnestra has never thought of this. She looks at the warrior women tossing their hair as they attack a boar and remembers when she spent hours staring at them as a child, wishing to be like them.

As usual, Penelope seems to read her mind. "But you probably just thought of hunting and fighting like them, didn't you?"

"I did."

"We are so different, you and I. I like to see the world from its edges while you wish to be in the center, taking part in the action."

"Why do you want to stay at the edges?"

"I just like it better there. Maybe I am scared."

Rain is pouring outside. They can hear the droplets hammering on the roof and the horses neighing in the stables.

Penelope tightens the pale cloak over her nightdress. "I heard something today, at the wedding," she says. Her dark eyes have a golden look in them, like the burning torch she is holding. "A rumor."

"A rumor," Clytemnestra repeats.

"Yes, about Helen's birth." Penelope speaks without flinching.

Clytemnestra stares at her clever cousin. "What did people say?" she asks. "That Zeus seduced Leda as a long-necked swan?"

"No. They say she was raped."

Clytemnestra grinds her teeth, biting her tongue. "You know how people are," she says, "always eager for vile gossip."

Penelope looks at her, head tilted. "So? Who is Helen's father?"

Clytemnestra walks closer to her. For a moment, she considers lying, but her cousin isn't easily dismissed. "There was a man at court when Leda was pregnant," she says. "A foreigner. My brothers told me that. Castor, actually, because Polydeuces claims he doesn't remember."

"I see."

"I don't know where the man came from, whether or not he was a king. I just know what Castor remembers, which is that Leda often disappeared around the palace with this man and that he left before she gave birth."

"Ah," Penelope says. Then, unexpectedly, she smiles. "I see you have inherited your mother's interest in foreigners."

Clytemnestra doesn't smile back. The air is dusky, as if fog is creeping inside the room, blurring everything. "I am tired," she says, turning to leave. When she reaches the door, her back to Penelope, she adds, "You will speak of this to no one, not even Helen."

She can hear the menace in her voice and hopes Penelope will hear it too.

Word arrives that Jason is ready to leave, that he awaits his men in Iolkos. Rain keeps falling, swamping the banks of the Eurotas and drenching the helots working the fields. Clytemnestra runs to meet Castor in the stables, her sandals splashing in the puddles, her hands hurting with cold.

"I was just thinking about you, Sister," he says with a smile.

"I want to come with you," Clytemnestra blurts out.

Castor frowns. "To Colchis?"

"No. To Iolkos, to say goodbye."

Castor wipes his hands on his tunic. "It is too far. It will take days to ride there." He stares at her, and she knows he is feeling it too—that they won't be together for a long time. "I will be back, I promise," he adds.

"How can you be so sure?"

"Jason is strong. We will be safe with him."

Clytemnestra snorts.

"You are skeptical," Castor says.

"Of course I am. Jason has been stupid enough to believe his uncle Pelias. Even if you come back, Pelias won't give him any throne. He just wants to see Jason die trying. Does Pelias sound like a ruler who keeps his promises? He usurped the throne from its rightful ruler!

And does Aeëtes sound like the kind of king who leaves his treasures unprotected? The kind of king a bunch of warriors can defeat?"

"I have gone away a hundred times," he says. "You know I always come back."

"This is different. Colchis is far away and dangerous."

"And you are married and will soon be in Maeonia." He comes closer to her. "Our lives are about to change," he says, "and we should let them."

Rain hits the stable roof, and the horses neigh, restless. Before every journey her brothers made, as soon as she was old enough to walk, Clytemnestra would always come here to say goodbye. And Castor would always reassure her. "Some things never change," she says.

He smiles and takes her hands. "You are right," he says. "They don't."

Her skin feels warm in his palms. She takes a deep breath and draws away, walking back to the palace as quickly as she can.

They all leave at dusk, Uncle Icarius and Penelope riding to the west, Castor and Polydeuces to the east. The land is dark with the thick layer of rain, and on the terrace in front of the main hall, Helen and Clytemnestra watch as they gallop out of the city, past the Spartiates' houses, the gardens and orchards, past the helot villages. They look tinier and tinier, dwarfed by the dark mountains and the growing blackness, until rain and fog swallow them and they disappear.

Clytemnestra hides her hands in the sleeves of her tunic to warm them. For a moment, her brothers' departure hits her hard and she feels pain inside, as if two trees were suddenly uprooted and left large holes in the ground of her heart.

When she turns to Helen, her sister's eyes are on the place where Penelope vanished.

You will speak of this to no one, not even Helen, Clytemnestra had told her cousin, and she is sure Penelope hasn't betrayed her trust. And yet as she looks at the shadows on her sister's face, she can't help feeling that she is holding a delicate shell in her hands and that she is about to drop it.

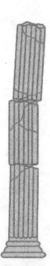

PART II

Any man's fortune, kept straight on course,
can strike a hidden cliff.
—Aeschylus, *Agamemnon* 1006–7

6

In the Eyes of the Gods

FALLEN LEAVES COVER the wet sand of the gymnasium. A few helots collect them in large baskets. In their scarred hands, the leaves glow red and golden, like gems. The Spartiates are waiting in the shade of the trees, their bodies covered with oil. They are to fight with spears today, and Clytemnestra is polishing hers in a corner, trying to keep focused.

Last night, the blankets twisted around their naked bodies, Tantalus asked her why Spartan women train. "To bear healthy children," she replied. "And to be free." Her answer left him confused, but he didn't press her. She had let her long hair fall around him, and he had kissed her, his lips soft on her eyelids.

She puts down her spear and looks up. A woman is watching them from a corner of the courtyard, eyes black and sharp like sea rocks. She wears a white tunic that leaves her breasts exposed in the style of Artemis's priestesses and listens as a girl named Ligeia tells the others about a helot revolt.

"They came in the night and killed two Spartans," Ligeia says while the other girls gasp around her. "I heard the screams—we all did."

"Did they catch them?" a tall girl asks.

"Yes," Ligeia says. "My father and a few others took them away."

"The Ceadas waits for them!" the girls shriek.

The priestess intervenes. "Not before they've been whipped on Artemis's altar. Murder is the worst of crimes for a slave." Her voice is hoarse and unpleasant, and the girls look down, afraid to contradict her.

Clytemnestra feels nauseous. She remembers the times the priestess had her whipped, and her brothers. Timandra has been the last of Tyndareus's children to be punished like that, flogged on the altar on the priestess's order after Timandra had disobeyed her father. Like Clytemnestra before her, she kept silent while blood trickled down her back and wetted the stone.

Later Tyndareus told her never to trust godly people, though Clytemnestra knew that even he could do nothing against a priestess's wish. Priests and priestesses can't be hurt—their gods won't allow it—but others can. So after Timandra was flogged, Clytemnestra and Castor followed the man who had acted under the priestess's order. When the night became dark and quiet, they hunted him, like shadows, until he stopped to piss in a tiny moonlit alley close to the helots' shacks. He had a dagger tied to his belt, and Clytemnestra suspected he was there to kill a few helots for sport, as she had often seen Spartans do. She felt a sick pleasure in knowing she was about to hurt someone who wanted to hurt others, as though she were straightening something crooked. Castor had stepped silently behind the man while Clytemnestra kept watch. *Make sure you are not seen* is one of the first rules Spartans learn as children. You may steal, you may kill, but if you are caught, you will be punished. So Clytemnestra stood guard while Castor sliced the man's calf. Then brother and sister ran together into the night, leaving the man screaming behind them.

"Are you feeling well, Clytemnestra?"

The priestess is staring at her. Her hair is thick against her face, her hands as white as bone. For a moment, Clytemnestra fears she can read her mind. "Yes," she says.

"You look weak," the priestess insists.

How dare she? "I am not weak."

The priestess narrows her eyes. When she speaks, her voice hisses, like a heated blade quenched in water. "Everyone is weak in the eyes of the gods."

Clytemnestra bites her lip to keep silent. She feels her sister's touch on her arm and turns.

"We are ready," Helen says. The priestess gives them one last look, then walks away. Helen waits until her figure has gone, then says, "Maybe you shouldn't practice." She is staring at Clytemnestra, frowning. "You are sweating."

"I feel fine," Clytemnestra lies.

The girls group together on the sand, some carrying bronze and wooden shields, others just the spear. Leda and a broad-shouldered man step in the shade of the trees—Lysimachos, one of Tyndareus's most trusted warriors. Clytemnestra looks away from them. Whenever Leda comes to watch her train, she does her best to impress her mother, but today she feels sick, her stomach rattling, her hands shaking. She clenches her fists to make them stop. All are given a *xiphos* by Lysimachos, a short sword with a slightly curved blade. Clytemnestra ties hers to the belt around her tunic.

"Split into groups now," Leda orders. "And start practicing with the spears. For those of you who have a shield, remember you can also use it as a weapon."

Lysimachos starts pacing around the group while the girls gather in threes and fours to fight. Clytemnestra finds herself with Eupoleia, Ligeia, and a short girl who resembles a stray cat. She is relieved to notice that Cynisca carefully avoids her, as one does a poisoned blade.

They start with target practice. They draw little circles in the sand on one side of the courtyard and gather on the other to throw their spears toward the goal. They jump, their right arms bent over the shoulder, and launch the spear toward the ground with all their strength. All except Ligeia reach the target in Clytemnestra's group. But Spartans leave no one behind, so they keep practicing until Ligeia has also thrown her spear inside the circle in the sand.

Then comes combat training. Taking turns, each group pushes one of the girls to the center of the ground while the other three attack her. Eupoleia is first. She holds her shield up so that it covers her from chin to knees while the others come forward. Ligeia moves her spear with precision while the short girl jumps quickly around Eupoleia, looking for a weak spot. When Clytemnestra throws herself against Eupoleia's shield, the short girl is quick to take Eupoleia's spear in her arms and thrust it aside. Together, they take Eupoleia down and start rolling and fighting in the sand.

"Use your *xiphos*," Lysimachos reminds them. "Aim for eyes and throat."

Clytemnestra grabs her short sword and points it at Eupoleia's throat while Ligeia kicks Eupoleia hard in the face.

"Well done," Leda says.

They stop. They help each other up, patting Eupoleia on the back. Ligeia doesn't last long when it is her turn against the other three. The short girl, on the other hand, manages to remain standing for a surprisingly long time, using her spear so fast to fend off the others that they struggle to anticipate her movements. Eventually, Eupoleia takes the girl's spearhead into her own hands, blood dripping down her fingers, and Clytemnestra breaks the cornel wood in two.

"Good," Lysimachos says. "But you need to last longer. You need to find better tactics to push back your opponents. Use your legs to balance yourself. If you lose balance, you are lost." He points at the broken spear on the sand. "Someone takes your weapon from you? You do not falter. You find a new balance."

It is Clytemnestra's turn. Eupoleia wipes her bloody palms on her tunic and picks up her spear. The short girl takes a new one. Ligeia blows her black hair from her face and grabs a shield. The girls attack as one, jumping forward like a three-headed snake. Clytemnestra spins away while her spear darts forward. Eupoleia slashes at it, but Clytemnestra avoids her. Ligeia grunts under the shield's weight. Clytemnestra thrusts again, and bronze screams on metal as the spearhead scratches the round shield.

It goes on for longer than any other fight. They move across the courtyard in spirals, jumping back and forth, while the girls' spears flicker in and out, aiming at Clytemnestra's head, throat, and hands.

"Take her down!" Lysimachos yells. "Take her down!"

But Clytemnestra keeps dodging cuts from the others' spearheads. She kicks Ligeia's shield so hard that the girl loses her balance and stumbles. Clytemnestra takes advantage of it and throws the shield aside. The short girl hurries to help Ligeia to her feet as Eupoleia takes the shaft of Clytemnestra's spear. For one moment, the two remain still, each pulling the spear. Then, Clytemnestra lets go with one hand and draws her short sword, cutting Eupoleia's cheek. The girl steps back, her hands leaving bloody fingerprints where they held the spear. Clytemnestra prepares to attack again. Her grip tightens around her sword, when, as sudden as thunder, a sickness takes hold of her. She stumbles, feeling suffocated as if she were lying under a slab of stone. Eupoleia's *xiphos* flashes in the air, and Clytemnestra feels pain on her cheek. She slaps Eupoleia hard in the face and tries to regain ground, but she is shaking now, her head spinning. The three girls close in on her while she throws up on the sand.

"Stop!" Leda orders.

"What happened?" Lysimachos asks, but Leda is kneeling next to her daughter.

"Stand. We are going back to the palace," she orders Clytemnestra. She tries to help her up, but Clytemnestra feels her gut boiling, her stomach rattling. She has only ever felt like this before when she saw the corpses of rotting horses on the riverbank after a fight between the Spartans and some rebellious helots. She pukes again, vomit spreading on the sand. Ligeia steps back, disgusted. The girls are all watching her, curious. For a moment, there is silence, like the silence near the altar stone after an animal has been sacrificed, when blood is dripping and birds are fluttering away.

"I said *stand*, Clytemnestra," Leda repeats.

Clytemnestra opens her eyes. She grabs her mother's arm and pulls herself up.

"Have I been poisoned?" she asks.

Her mother shakes her head. "Come with me."

Leda brings her to the palace kitchen. Her sickness seems to be getting worse, but her mother drags her along the corridors without letting her stop.

Helen walks close behind them. "Do you wish me to call Tyndareus, Mother?" she asks, but Leda ignores her.

In the kitchen, two women are slicing reeds and fruit. Almonds, hazelnuts, and small quinces are piled on a large wooden table. In one corner of the room, under the golden light of the torches, a helot no older than thirteen is crushing small dark olives in a mortar. The room smells of oil and ripe apricots, even though there aren't any in sight.

Leda pushes Clytemnestra forward. "Check her," she orders the women. They stop cutting the reeds at once and walk closer to Clytemnestra. They have dark hair, but one's is dry and dirty, the other's shiny and vigorous, with waves like the ocean at night. They grab the hem of Clytemnestra's tunic and lift it over her head. She stumbles and sits on the floor, seized by a headache so strong it momentarily blinds her. The women pinch her breasts, hard. When she opens her eyes, Helen is gazing down at her, her small hand on her sister's arm.

"How many times have you slept with Tantalus?" the women ask.

Clytemnestra tries to think. "You mean—"

"How many times was he inside you?"

"I don't—"

"When was the last time you bled?"

"It's been a while." She vomits again, next to the sacks of wheat stacked on the floor. The women scowl.

"Call Tantalus, Helen," Leda says. "And then tell your father your sister is pregnant."

Helen's small feet disappear from Clytemnestra's sight. She hears her sister running along the corridors, faint like the flutter of wings. Leda strokes her hair as if she were a frightened dog while whispering to the women. Clytemnestra tries to catch the words, but their voices are too low, her sickness too strong. Next to her, the helot girl is cleaning her vomit.

"Drink this," Leda says, holding a small cup to her lips. It smells disgusting and Clytemnestra tries to jerk away her head, but her mother keeps her still. She drinks and suddenly feels very tired, her eyelids drooping against her will. She rests her head on the wheat sacks, her limbs numb. *I am pregnant*, she thinks. *My training in the gymnasium is over.*

Sitting on the bed, she feels sicker than ever. Leda has given her herbs, to crush and mix in her wine, but she doesn't like the numbness.

Servants moved her things to Tantalus's room after the wedding, and now she stares at the bare wall, willing the world to stop spinning.

"I will have to go back to Maeonia for a little while," Tantalus says. He keeps pacing the room, a cloak wrapped around his lean body. He ran to her in the kitchen as soon as he heard the news, his eyes sparkling like snow under the sun. She had never seen him so happy.

"Why?" she whispers. Her voice feels like a crow's croak.

"To announce the coming of an heir. Also, I haven't been back for months. I need to make sure everything is in order and safe for us to return. I've left my most trusted advisers to rule in my stead, but I am careful every time I go back. It is unwise to let a man who isn't king sit on a throne for too long."

She shuts her eyes in a useless attempt to ease her headache.

"It isn't winter yet," he adds, walking to her, caressing her face, "so the weather shouldn't delay us. I will be back in spring, before the baby is born."

"Take me with you," she says.

"We will go together after the birth. Once we leave, you won't come back here for years. Your brothers have just left. I am not sure your family is ready for another of you to go so soon."

He is right, she thinks. Just a few more months here. Besides, her parents need to see their grandchild when he is born. They need to check that he is strong and healthy—she can't take that away from them.

"The people in Maeonia," she says feebly, "they will think I am different from you."

"You *are* different." He laughs. "They will love you because of it, just like I do."

He rests his head against her heart, and she lets him hold her.

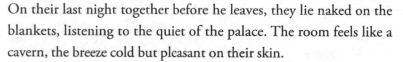

On their last night together before he leaves, they lie naked on the blankets, listening to the quiet of the palace. The room feels like a cavern, the breeze cold but pleasant on their skin.

He tells her that in Maeonia, there is never silence. There are birds singing at night and torches always lit in every street and corridor, servants and guards outside every door. But there is quiet to be found too, when you walk in the gardens and the shaded colonnades, the air scented with roses, the palace walls painted with griffins and other legendary creatures.

Her body is curved into his arm, and his sweet breath tickles her head.

"And our baby?" she asks. "Will he train and grow into a strong warrior?"

At least if she is carrying a boy, she won't have to give him up for training, like every Spartan woman.

"You will train him," he says. "You will be queen and free to do as you please."

She kisses his chest, tasting the spices in the oils he uses. He cups his hands around her face and pulls her closer. His heart beats against her skin. She lets desire flood her veins, lets her heart grow heavy with longing. Outside the windows, the moon shines pale and luminous, bathing their bodies in light as if they were gods.

When she wakes, the bed is cold with Tantalus's absence and the room feels too still. Sickness rises in her. To try to stop it, she thinks of happy times.

She remembers playing hide-and-seek with her brothers and sister. Once, trying to hide from Polydeuces, she and Helen had sneaked into a helot village far from the palace. The hovels where the helots lived were made of wood, their foundations muddied; the streets were narrow and littered with filth. Stray cats and hungry dogs scavenged while pigs and goats rested behind fences. Helen looked apprehensive but she kept going, her hand in Clytemnestra's. A few children, tiny and bony as the dogs around them, were sitting in the mud, playing with the pigs. They gazed at Helen and Clytemnestra, their eyes large and gleaming, their bodies frail like the skulls of babies.

"Let us find somewhere to hide," Helen said, pity on her face. Clytemnestra kept walking until she found a stinking granary. She hurried inside, dragging Helen with her. The floor was covered with dust and animal droppings, and the heat was unbearable.

"He will never find us here," Clytemnestra said, satisfied. Light filtered through the wooden beams, striping the girls' faces. To pass time, they started looking for white stones.

"I don't like it here," Helen said after a while.

"One who risks nothing is nothing," Clytemnestra recited. It was something her father often said.

"But this place is awful," Helen retorted. "And if the priestess finds us here…"

Clytemnestra was about to reply when she saw it—the head of a snake hiding in the darkness. It was gray with stripes on its back.

"Stay still," Clytemnestra ordered.

"Why?" Helen asked, turning. She froze. "Is that venomous?" When Clytemnestra did not reply, Helen persisted, "I think it is. It is not brown and yellow—"

Several things happened at once. Clytemnestra stepped back toward the entrance of the granary. Helen shrieked. The snake struck as quickly as a sword, but before its fangs could reach Clytemnestra's arm, a spear pierced its head. Then Polydeuces entered the granary, breathless. He took back his spear, checking the spike covered with the snake's venom. He turned to his sisters, kicking the dead reptile with his foot.

"I found you." He smiled. "You lose."

Helen laughed and Clytemnestra shook her head, in awe of her brother's swiftness. *Lizard killer*, Spartans call the spike at the end of their spears.

Later, when they were walking back to the *gynaeceum*, Clytemnestra took Helen's hand in hers. It was warm and smooth. "I am sorry. You were frightened and I didn't leave."

Helen shook her head. "I wasn't," she said. "I was with you."

The memory has a strange taste in her mouth. She and Helen were each the other's world back then. But nothing can ever stay the same. You can't step twice into the same river.

Her belly grows; the skin feels stretched on her breasts. The sickness slowly gets better. At times, it returns in waves, like a high tide, but then it goes away again, as quickly as it came.

Tantalus's absence is like a shadow—she can feel it, yet whenever she turns to look at it, it is gone. She decides to stop looking and spare herself useless pain. In a few months, he will be back, and the baby will be born, exposed to the elders and introduced to her family. Then she will move to the east and become the queen of people whose customs will be alien to her.

The servants from the kitchen come to cut her hair. They make her sit on a stool, brush her long, brown mane, then slice it off with a sharp knife. Clytemnestra remembers looking at the other women of the palace as they passed from girl to woman, from daughter to mother. After it was cut, their hair covered the floor like a carpet and she and Helen would step on it, letting it tickle their soles.

When the servants show her her reflection in the water bowl, she touches the ends of her short hair and thinks that the cut suits her better: it enhances her eyes and cheekbones.

The priestess also comes, her pale, chill hands touching Clytemnestra's belly.

"The gods watch us all," she says, her voice screeching like a seagull's cry. "They bless those who are loyal and punish those who aren't." She doesn't say whether Clytemnestra will be blessed or punished, but Clytemnestra doesn't care. The child she is carrying will be heir to the throne of Maeonia, and there is nothing the priestess can do about it. So she lets her speak her dark words until it is time for her to go back to her temple.

"Are you scared of leaving?" Helen asks. They are standing together in front of the tub, staring at the water as it sparkles under the torches. The light of the sunset pours in from the small window, illuminating their skin with pink and orange. From up there, Sparta looks nothing more than a group of small villages, scattered across the Eurotas, like a herd of brown goats. Tantalus has often told Clytemnestra that the valley makes a poor show compared to his own homeland. Yet she will miss the view of the mountains, their peaks wrapped in white clouds.

"You will soon leave as well," Clytemnestra says, removing her tunic and stepping into the tub. Warm water laps at her skin.

Helen starts washing her, the soap perfumed and oily on her fingers. "Why do women always have to leave?" she asks. She still thinks Clytemnestra has the answer to her every question, as she did when they were children.

Why do women always have to leave? Clytemnestra repeats the words in her head until they lose meaning. She doesn't know the answer. She knows only that leaving doesn't feel like punishment to her but rather a blessing. Life at this moment is like being at sea, open waters all around her and no coastline in sight, the world brimming with possibilities.

Helen keeps silent for a while. There is a strange light in her eyes as she gazes at her sister's body. They have seen each other naked a thousand times, but now it is different. Arms, legs, hips, neck, everything that Helen is touching has been touched by Tantalus, and they can't ignore it. His mark is deep inside her, not visible yet, but it is there, and soon Clytemnestra's body will transform because of it—it will become ripe, swollen. Helen's eyes are shiny with wonder, though there is also anxiety in the way she clings to Clytemnestra's shoulders as she scrubs them, an eagerness she puts into wringing out her sister's hair.

Clytemnestra lets her be, listening to the sound of dripping water. She understands her sister's pain. Helen will be forced to sit and witness her biggest fear: Clytemnestra's body slowly becoming different from hers, until there are no similarities to hold on to.

When the water has cooled, Helen stands and takes a step back from the tub. Her eyes are shining, eager for her sister's attention.

"Mother told me that two brothers will soon be here," she says, "the sons of Atreus, coming from Mycenae. They have been exiled and have asked Tyndareus for help."

When Clytemnestra says nothing, Helen adds, "Atreus, the man who murdered his brother's children and fed them to him! Castor used to tell us about them, remember?"

Clytemnestra sets her eyes on her sister. "You won't have to leave if you don't want to. Your future can be as you want it to be." She offers her words as reassurances, rolling them out clearly and carefully, though they seem to fade in the dim room.

Helen looks down with a sad smile. "Maybe for you it can be that simple. But not for me." Then she leaves, back to the room the two of them have shared all their lives.

As the sun sinks behind the mountains and the pale blue sky becomes the color of silver, two tiny figures ride across the valley, following the serpentine shape of the river. Agamemnon and Menelaus ride alone, their horses galloping as if being chased. The night is silent and the valley looks like an empty shell, soon to be filled with the echo of violence.

7

The Sons of Atreus

SHE IS STANDING by the doors of the *megaron*, hidden behind one of the columns. Her hands are clasped, her breath held as she listens to the sons of Atreus speak to her parents.

Agamemnon has strong, scarred arms and greedy, intelligent eyes. His face is asymmetrical, all sharp lines and edges, and there is something unsettling about the way he stares, as though he is searching for weakness in the people around him. Menelaus's features resemble his brother's but remotely, like a lynx resembles a lion. He is leaner, handsomer, and his face lacks the cunning that shows on Agamemnon's face.

They arrived late in the night, their horses wearied to the point of exhaustion. Servants clustered around the columns at the entrance to the palace, eager to see the exiled brothers, doomed offspring of the king of Mycenae. Tyndareus welcomed them, though there was still blood on Agamemnon's sword, fresh cuts on Menelaus's face. They had ridden for their lives, and it was Tyndareus's duty to let them stay in his palace. A guest is always sacred in their lands, no matter his deeds and crimes.

"Mycenae was taken with force and deceit," Agamemnon is saying to Tyndareus. "Our cousin Aegisthus murdered our father and now rules with our uncle Thyestes."

"But the people despise father and son," Menelaus adds.

"Deceit runs in your family," Leda says coolly. "The house of Atreus is doomed."

Agamemnon takes a step forward, as if to attack her, and Clytemnestra almost does the same. When her mother looks in her direction, she hides behind the column. Tyndareus ordered everyone to steer clear of the *megaron*, which only made Clytemnestra more eager to eavesdrop.

Menelaus takes his brother's arm, as if to hold him back. Agamemnon keeps still.

"We will take back Mycenae," Menelaus says. "And we will rule."

A short silence follows. Tyndareus stares at them quietly, then asks for more wine. A servant girl springs up from her place at the foot of the throne and hurries outside. When she walks past Clytemnestra, they look at each other for a second, two girls in the shadows, unnoticed by everyone else, their eyes gleaming. Clytemnestra puts a forefinger to her lips, and the servant hurries away.

"Didn't your grandfather plan the murder of his host and father-in-law in a chariot race?" Tyndareus asks.

"He did," Menelaus says. Agamemnon keeps silent, tense beside him.

"And your father, Atreus… Didn't he murder his half brother Chrysippus?"

"He did. And he was exiled for it. Banished to Mycenae."

"So Mycenae didn't always belong to the Atreidai," Tyndareus says, using the name for Atreus's bloodline. "Who ruled the city when your father was exiled there?"

"King Eurystheus," Menelaus says. "But he was away, fighting, so our father ascended the throne uncontested."

Tyndareus opens his mouth to speak again, but Agamemnon

is quicker. "The people of Mycenae respect us. And Mycenae is a powerful city, destined for greatness. King Eurystheus died far away, fighting, and never proclaimed an heir. Our father took what was his to take. Our family is doomed for our predecessors' deceit, not for our ambition." He lays out each word slowly and clearly, his voice steady and bold.

Something shifts in Tyndareus's face. It is an expression Clytemnestra doesn't know, and she doesn't like it. Leda moves forward to speak, but Tyndareus stops her.

"Sons of Atreus," he says, and his voice is different, warmer somehow, "our country honors the bond between host and guest, and I will not be the one to break it."

Agamemnon kneels, and Menelaus follows suit. For a second only, Clytemnestra sees her mother cast a look of utter surprise in her father's direction. Then, before the brothers can rise and notice her, Clytemnestra leaves the room as silently as she can. Anger is rising inside her, burning her chest, but she doesn't understand it.

The palace changes in Agamemnon's presence. Servant girls quickly grow wary of him, falling quiet when he approaches, hurrying along the corridors when they have to pass him. They avoid him as best as they can, but some—those who prepare his bath and tend his room—are carrying small bruises on their arms and faces. At dinner, as they pour his wine and he stares at their breasts and faces, they keep their eyes down.

The men, though, seem to respect him. Agamemnon and Menelaus start visiting the gymnasium when Spartan warriors are training. Soon, all the boys can talk about is how the sons of Atreus challenge young men and win every wrestle. It is something unheard of in Sparta, where guests and visitors usually steer clear of the training ground.

It is a strange change to witness. Halls and corridors remain the same, with their bare walls and dark corners, but a new light is shimmering beneath the surface, a new promise of violence. It makes Clytemnestra think of the sky when it is gray and sullen, endless clouds never breaking into rain. Just a tiring, never-ending threat.

"If you keep fighting thinking you can win, then you'll keep losing, Timandra."

They are on the terrace, Clytemnestra standing over her younger sister, keeping her down with her foot. Now that she is pregnant, she isn't allowed to train in the gymnasium, so she finds other ways to keep fit while her belly expands—wrestling her sister, riding, shooting arrows and spears in the evening, when the training yard is quiet. It keeps her mind off Tantalus's absence.

Despite the cold winter breeze, the sun glows bright and the ground is warm under their feet. Helen is sitting in one corner, laughing at Timandra's efforts to beat her sister. When Clytemnestra lets her up, Timandra pulls a face and tries to punch her.

"Don't let others see you are angry when you lose," Clytemnestra says. She trips her, and Timandra falls again, keeping her face as expressionless as she can. Still, her cheeks are red, and Helen laughs again.

There is the sound of scurrying feet, and a servant girl walks onto the terrace to bring them bread and honey. She kneels next to Helen to pass her the bowl, careful to avoid Clytemnestra and Timandra as they wrestle.

"Wait," Helen says, grabbing the helot's arm. The girl stops, her hands placing the bowl down carefully. There is a big bruise on her cheek, the kind that comes from contact with the handle of a dagger. Behind them, Clytemnestra takes Timandra's arm and pretends to twist it—"See?" she is saying. "You have to slide this way."

"Who did this to you?" Helen asks. The girl doesn't speak. "Answer," Helen orders.

The helot whispers inaudibly, her eyes fixed on the ground.

Clytemnestra stops fighting Timandra, her body suddenly tense. "What is this about?" she asks.

"Show her your cheek," Helen orders. The helot obeys, her skin sweaty and bruised under the light, as if rotten. Timandra, bored, is tugging her sister's arms.

"It was Agamemnon, wasn't it?" Clytemnestra says.

The servant nods. The bruise is turning green at its edges.

"Did he force himself on you?" Clytemnestra persists, her voice cracked with anger. Timandra stops tugging, alert, scanning her sisters' faces.

The helot shakes her head. "He isn't interested in servants," she mumbles.

"Why did he strike you, then?"

The girl shrugs.

"You can leave now," Helen says softly. The helot casts one scared look behind her shoulder, as though checking that no one has overheard, then walks away, her dark hair around her head like an oily rag.

"We should tell Mother," Helen says. "This isn't the first time it has happened. Have you seen those poor women who prepare his bath?"

"Why do you think he doesn't sleep with servants?" Clytemnestra asks. She has seen Agamemnon grabbing girls, and she knows Menelaus often takes servants, the prettiest ones, to his room.

"I am not sure," Helen says, "but I think he wants only power, that above all else."

In the sky, clouds gather like sheep in a clear meadow. Clytemnestra is beginning to feel sick.

"Maybe we should go back inside," Helen suggests, looking worried.

Clytemnestra touches her belly and feels her stomach rattling. Then she pushes Timandra, hard. "We haven't finished here."

Timandra recoils, readying her fists. She lunges, heat sparking in her, and Clytemnestra moves aside to avoid her. As they punch and wrestle, there is an edge to them. They are angry and afraid, violence crawling under their skin like maggots.

Above them, the clouds grow dark, black and blue bruises scattered throughout the sky.

They find Leda in the *megaron*, sitting on Tyndareus's throne. She is sipping wine from a large cup, a golden circlet gleaming in her hair. Philonoe is huddled in her lap, and her raven hair falls on her forehead in smooth strands.

"What is it?" Leda asks. Her voice sounds hoarse, as if she were half-asleep. Helen and Clytemnestra walk closer to her, and the smell of wine grows stronger.

"Your father's hunting," Leda says. Philonoe shifts on her mother's knees, searching for a more comfortable position.

Helen clears her throat. "We were looking for you, Mother."

"Hmm," Leda mumbles.

"Agamemnon beat another servant girl," Clytemnestra says in as clear a voice as she can.

Silence. Then, to the sisters' amazement, Leda laughs. Her voice echoes in the hall, like a war drum, then fades to nothing. Philonoe startles.

"I am not surprised," Leda says finally. "Are you?"

Helen and Clytemnestra exchange a quick look.

"We should send him back to—" Helen starts, but Leda interrupts.

"Your father won't send him away." Her voice is cold, sharp. She drinks more wine, making her lips purple.

"He won't?" Helen asks.

Leda shakes her head, caressing Philonoe's hair.

"Which god is more skilled with the bow, Artemis or Apollo?" Philonoe asks, lost in her own train of thought.

"Both," Leda replies lazily.

"I want to be an archer, like Artemis," Philonoe says.

"Then go and practice."

"I am tired now," the child complains.

"Do you think Artemis is ever tired? Do you think she complains?" Leda raises her voice, her cheeks flushed. She is quite drunk. Philonoe scoffs and jumps down from her mother's knees, hurrying out of the *megaron*. Leda pours herself more wine. "Your father won't send the Atreidai away because they remind him of himself when he was younger."

Clytemnestra opens her mouth in protest, but Helen is quicker. "Tyndareus is nothing like them."

"He was, once. He and Icarius were exiled by their half brother Hippocoon, just like Agamemnon and Menelaus are exiled now."

"I didn't know any of this," Clytemnestra says.

"You weren't born. When your grandfather Oebalus died, Tyndareus became king of Sparta. But Hippocoon was jealous and cruel. He used to challenge men in the gymnasium only to punch

them to death. Your father always said he was like that because he was
not loved as Icarius and he were. He was not Gorgophone's son, you
see. Oebalus had him from another woman."

Clytemnestra casts a quick glance at Helen, who is staring fixedly
at her feet.

"As soon as Tyndareus was king, Hippocoon overthrew him."

"But how?" Clytemnestra asks. "Surely Father was loved by the
Spartans."

"Hippocoon already had many sons from many women, most of
them slaves. He had them young, when he was no more than fifteen.
When your father took the throne, Hippocoon's sons were of age and
ready to fight for their own father, their own inheritance. Icarius and
Tyndareus were exiled and Hippocoon took the throne for himself,
slaughtered everyone who tried to rebel and sacrificed some helots to
the gods to gain their favor."

Helen looks shocked. Clytemnestra bites her lips. There are many
things she doesn't know about her father, about her land. Living in
Sparta sometimes feels like being stuck in a swamp, the bog sealed
around her feet, her eyes free only to watch for imminent dangers
around her. But as soon as she tries to look beyond, the bog swallows
her.

"So your father asked Heracles for help," Leda continues.

"The greatest of Greek heroes," Helen whispers, and Leda nods.

"Why did Heracles fight for Tyndareus? What did he care?"
Clytemnestra asked.

"Hippocoon hadn't welcomed Heracles when he needed shelter in
Sparta. So Heracles killed Hippocoon and his sons, and your father
took back his throne."

Clytemnestra understands now. Tyndareus hadn't repeated
Hippocoon's mistake and turned away two warriors in need. Still,

how can he not see that Agamemnon and Menelaus are cruel? That they lack honor? Her father has always been a good judge of character.

"Anyway, your father is angry today," Leda says, interrupting her thoughts. "That is why he went hunting."

There is an edge to her mother's voice that makes Clytemnestra brace herself as if she is about to be hit. "Why?"

"The priestess just delivered a new prophecy."

"Father doesn't believe in prophecies."

"Well, this time, he is annoyed."

"Because he knows it is the truth," a hoarse voice behind them says. Clytemnestra turns so quickly she almost strains her neck.

The priestess is walking toward the throne, her black hair parted in the middle, her feet moving as silently as leaves carried by a stream. Leda is sitting straight in her chair, revulsion plain on her face. It is no secret that she hates the priestess. *A cruel woman, leeching off the strengths of others*: that was what Leda called her when Clytemnestra asked her why she always left when the priestess entered the palace to speak to the king.

"Did someone summon you to the *megaron*?" Leda asks.

The priestess stops a few feet from them, her pale hands poking out of her sleeves like claws. "I came here to deliver the prophecy to your daughters."

"Then no one summoned you," Leda remarks.

The priestess ignores her. "Aphrodite is angry," she tells Helen and Clytemnestra. "Your father never sacrifices to her."

"Aren't you supposed to be worshipping Artemis?" Clytemnestra asks.

The priestess glares at her. When she speaks again, her voice screeches like a blade against stone.

"*Leda's daughters will twice and thrice wed. And they will all be deserters of their lawful husbands."* She sets her eyes on them, the same look she gives her beasts before a sacrifice. "That is the prophecy."

Clytemnestra stares at the priestess. Deserter of her husband? How can the priestess even think such a thing?

"It is the will of the gods," the priestess says. "You will be despised by many, hated by others, and punished. But in the end, you will be free."

Helen turns to her mother. She looks confused. The priestess has never delivered prophecies to them, much less about them. Leda puts a hand on Helen's shoulder as if to protect her from the priestess. "You have spoken your prophecy," she says. "Now leave."

"You cannot give me orders, Leda, as you know," the priestess retorts. Her eyes linger on the empty wine cup on the floor, and distaste runs over her face.

Leda stiffens. "You are not welcome in the palace. Go back to your temple." Anger contorts her features, and her hand runs to the jeweled dagger she keeps at her waist, though she doesn't draw it.

The priestess is not intimidated. She raises her chin and says, "You are the stranger here. Remember, I was in your husband's bed long before you fell for that foreigner—" Her eyes settle on Helen.

"GET OUT!" Leda shouts, losing all self-control. "OUT! OR I WILL KILL YOU MYSELF. DO YOU UNDERSTAND?"

The priestess smirks. Leda closes her fingers around the handle of her dagger, and the priestess lingers as if to challenge her. Then she walks away, her feet bare and pale as the moon, her long tunic fluttering behind her. Leda storms down from the throne and follows her to the door, her eyes bloodshot.

"I DON'T CARE IF YOUR GODDESS IS ANGRY. SHE IS NOT MY GODDESS AND NEVER HAS BEEN!" she shouts after her.

The priestess disappears beyond the door, and Leda turns, breathless. Clytemnestra and Helen still stand by the throne, frozen.

"You two also leave," Leda orders. "Now."

"You always said anger was something to keep under control," Helen says, defiance in her eyes. The priestess's words are sinking in.

"I don't care what I said. *Leave.*"

Clytemnestra takes her sister's arm and drags her out. When she turns to look back, her mother has fallen to her knees, her head in her hands as if she is afraid it could break at any moment.

Leda doesn't appear at dinner, and Helen and Clytemnestra don't inquire. Helen eats slowly, lost in thought. Clytemnestra stares at the meat spread on her platter, though it makes her feel sick.

The evening is bright and cold. The last rays of the winter sun light the hall, and through the window, the mountains are sharply outlined, their peaks covered with sprinkles of snow. Timandra has been to the gymnasium during the day and is telling Phoebe and Philonoe all about the wrestling.

"Menelaus is so fierce he almost broke Lycamede's head! Without weapons, just his fists! I saw it." She shovels food into her mouth as she speaks, her face brimming with excitement. "Agamemnon waited until the end, then challenged the strongest man. I think he wanted to see them fight first so he could choose."

"He's as strong as a Spartan but smarter," Tyndareus says. He cuts the pork on his platter into big, irregular shapes, then sticks his knife into a piece of meat.

"Why, Father?" Clytemnestra asks.

Tyndareus chews slowly, thinking. "He's afraid of death," he says and puts more pork into his mouth.

"How does that make a man smarter? The gods envy us because we're mortal," Helen says. Tyndareus ignores her and Helen looks down, her cheeks flushed.

Clytemnestra takes her hand across the table. "Agamemnon didn't fight his cousin Aegisthus when he had the chance, even though Aegisthus had killed his father and usurped the throne of Mycenae. He ran away and took refuge here. That was a clever move—a guest is always sacred in Greece."

Tyndareus nods. "He has patience, a quality few men possess. I'm sure he will have his revenge."

The respect in her father's voice annoys Clytemnestra, but she tries to ignore it.

"What about Menelaus?" Helen asks.

This time, Tyndareus acknowledges her question. "Menelaus is a powerful man, only eclipsed by his brother. Soon they will rise as heroes and gain their thrones."

Clytemnestra sits back in her chair. If Agamemnon eclipses Menelaus, does Helen eclipse her? The most beautiful woman of all their lands: that is what Helen is called throughout Greece, while no one knows about Clytemnestra. But in Sparta, it is Clytemnestra who is most loved and respected. And when Tantalus had the chance, he chose her, not Helen. "Your sister is pretty, it's true," Tantalus told her once, "but something in her is tamed. You both have fire in your hearts, but she pours water over hers, while you add more logs to yours. *That* is beautiful."

When she looks up, Helen is staring at her, her face changing in the firelight. Guilt seeps into her. She wonders if her sister can hear her thoughts, because Helen stands, her chair scraping.

"I am tired," she says. "I will rest."

The next morning, Clytemnestra decides to watch the Atreidai fight. Outside the palace, the air is as cold as a bronze blade pressed to the skin, and the bare trees look like arms stretching toward the sky. When she gets to the gymnasium, Leda is already there, sitting in a high-backed chair in a corner of the yard. Next to her, Timandra is polishing a spear, her knees and elbows muddy. When she sees her sister, she jumps up.

"Look," she says. "They're about to fight."

On the wrestling ground, Agamemnon and a young Spartan boy are walking in a circle. They look like a lion and a wolf, Agamemnon with his long, wavy hair that falls onto his broad shoulders, the boy with his skinny, hairy body. And a lion is always stronger than a wolf—Clytemnestra knows that well. It fights alone, while a wolf needs its pack.

"That one is smart and quick," says Timandra excitedly, pointing at the boy. "I've seen him fight."

"When you are fighting a much stronger animal, intelligence isn't enough," Leda replies.

The Spartan boy is waiting for Agamemnon to go straight at him, walking around to catch him in a moment of imbalance. He has a lean face, dark and sharp-eyed. Agamemnon tries to grab him, but the boy jumps to his right. In a second, before Clytemnestra's eyes can trace the moves, Agamemnon tips the boy over. The Spartan falls facedown and makes a strangled sound. He starts to crawl, but Agamemnon jumps onto his back. He grabs the boy's neck, his large, scarred hands closing in. The boy's face sinks into the sand; blood gushes from his nose. He wriggles, desperate to breathe, but he is choking on his own blood. There is the cracking sound of ribs breaking, and Clytemnestra can't help but think of the sound of criminals' bodies crashing against the rocks of the Ceadas. She turns to her sister, but Timandra doesn't flinch. She too knows the sound well.

Leda runs onto the wrestling ground; her feet sink into the wet sand. She seizes Agamemnon's arm and pushes him backward, shielding the Spartan with her own body. For a moment, Clytemnestra thinks Agamemnon will strike her mother, but he only looks at her, surprised. Behind her, the Spartan boy emits a low, painful sound. He is alive.

"Stand," Leda orders.

Agamemnon brushes the red sand off his hands against his thighs. Then, without a word to Leda, he walks straight toward Clytemnestra. He comes into the shade of the trees and takes her arm gently, surprising her. Out of the corner of her eye, she sees Timandra tighten her grip on her spear.

"I hope you enjoyed the fight, my queen," Agamemnon says. It is the first time he talks to her. His expression is hard as rock and his features too sharp, as if carved by a careless sculptor.

"Leda is your queen," says Clytemnestra. Agamemnon ignores her. He lets go of her arm, and Clytemnestra feels her skin burning where his fingertips touched her.

"I've heard that you're good at wrestling," he says. "Women aren't trained like men where I come from."

"I'm sorry for them," Clytemnestra replies.

His jaw tightens, but he doesn't answer. His quiet is frustrating. She wishes she could strike him or run away as he studies her, his eyes peeling off her skin. But she stays where she is. When he finally turns to walk away from the gymnasium, she joins her mother on the wrestling ground. Timandra drops the spear and hurries behind her. Together, they stare at the broken body of the Spartan boy.

"Timandra," Leda says, "find the physician. And bring some opium."

Her daughter scampers away, quick as a cat. Leda glances at Clytemnestra, then at the portico where Agamemnon had been seconds before.

"He likes you," she says finally. Her green eyes have a flat look, like aging copper.

"Can't he see that I'm pregnant?"

Leda shakes her head. "Some men want only the things they cannot have."

Clytemnestra walks back to the palace alone. The water in the Eurotas is the color of silver and the land around it is like liquid bronze. She thinks about Leda and the priestess, facing each other in the *megaron*. Her mother was right but shameless. She was the one who had taught Clytemnestra there are always better ways to treat your opponents, better ways to humiliate them. But all she had done was humiliate herself. Why hadn't she sent away the priestess? Perhaps she'd tried but Tyndareus hadn't allowed it. The thought is painful, like a sharp cut on the throat.

Rain is falling. She hurries along the path, her sandals muddied already. When she gets to the stables, she stops, catching her breath, taking shelter next to a mare and her foal. She pats them, listening to the raindrops pounding the ground.

Then she hears another sound, somewhere to her left. She listens more carefully, hiding behind the bales of hay. It is a soft cry—she can hear it clearly now. She steps closer, and behind a large stack of hay, she sees Agamemnon's back. His tunic—still stained with the boy's blood, Clytemnestra notices—is rolled up above his waist, and his hands are on a young woman's hips. The girl is moaning and crying but Clytemnestra can't see her face. She steps forward, thinking of the bruised helot.

"Leave her alone," she says, her voice loud over the rain.

Agamemnon turns quickly, his hand flying to the knife dangling from his tunic. The girl stands, not bothering to cover her naked body, and smiles at the sight of Clytemnestra. It is Cynisca.

"What do you want?" she asks. There are scars wrapping around her strong legs, like snakes. Her breasts are small, her nipples large and brown. There is a big birthmark on one breast, which Clytemnestra has never noticed in the gymnasium. She turns to Agamemnon, whose hand is tight on his knife. It is different from Spartan daggers, more like the kind of blade men use for gutting pigs.

"Put that away," she orders.

He doesn't. "It was you who interrupted us."

"This is my palace."

"And I am your guest."

Cynisca puts on her *chiton*, which she covers with a longer cloak. "Go back to the palace, my lord," she says. "I will come soon."

He turns to her with his hard look but doesn't seem annoyed. He leaves without looking at Clytemnestra, his figure quickly swallowed by the darkness and the rain.

Cynisca bends to tie her sandals. "You can't always have everything, you know," she says.

Clytemnestra frowns. "Do you really think I would want someone like him?"

Cynisca looks up at her. Suddenly she laughs. "You thought he was *raping* me."

"I didn't know it was you."

"Or you wouldn't have stopped him?"

Clytemnestra hesitates.

"Never mind," Cynisca continues. "Now you know he doesn't force me to do anything. Anyone would be lucky to be with a man like him."

"I don't think so."

Cynisca laughs, scornful. "That's because you don't see power when you have it in front of you."

She has finished tying her sandals. She gives Clytemnestra one last triumphant look, as though she has just won a wrestling match, then walks away.

When Clytemnestra finally reaches the palace, she is drenched and shivering. The corridors smell damp and musty, and the torches are burning out. She hurries to the *gynaeceum* and knocks on the door of the bedroom she used to share with Helen. It opens straightaway. Her sister stands against the jamb, a thick woolen tunic wrapped around her.

"What is it?"

"Can I sleep here tonight?" Clytemnestra asks.

"Of course." Helen gives her a feeble smile. "I don't sleep much when I am alone anyway."

"Neither do I." Clytemnestra sits on the wooden stool next to the bed, and Helen gives her a warm woolen tunic.

"Cynisca was in the stables with Agamemnon," Clytemnestra says when her teeth have stopped chattering. "He was inside her."

"How do you know?"

"I saw them. Just now."

Helen shrugs. "Cruel people always find each other."

Clytemnestra wraps her feet in the tunic, feeling for each toe. "There is something different about him," she says.

"Yes," Helen agrees.

"I don't like being near him."

Helen gives her a little smile. "Perhaps because he scares you. The only people who frighten you are those whose motives you can't see."

She sits on her stool and pours some diluted wine for herself. On the table, next to the wine jug, there is a golden necklace with petaled rosettes. Clytemnestra has never seen anything so beautiful. "Where did you find that?"

Helen looks at the necklace absently, her golden hair loose around her shoulders. The two of them look so different now that they barely seem blood-related. "It doesn't matter," she says.

Clytemnestra is ready to argue, but Helen is quicker. "What do you think it means?" she asks. "The prophecy." She lifts her head, her eyes burning as they always do when she wants answers from her sister.

Clytemnestra catches her breath. Her face feels suddenly numb. "I don't think it means anything."

Helen stares at her. "You don't believe in it."

"When have we ever believed in prophecies?"

Helen doesn't answer. Her face is as naked as it was when she was a child, before she had learned to hide her weaknesses. She touches the necklace, feels each golden flower under her fingers. For a moment, Clytemnestra thinks she will let it go, but then Helen asks, "Did you know about Tyndareus and Leda?"

"What do you mean?"

Helen raises her eyes and there is something cold in the light blue, like a frozen river. "You know what I mean."

"I didn't know about Father," Clytemnestra says. She sees her sister's expression change, her soft features hardening. She can do nothing to stop it.

"You knew about Leda, then. You knew she lay with another man."

Clytemnestra doesn't move. She can feel anger blistering under her skin and something else too, cold and slippery. Fear.

"You knew and you didn't tell me," Helen repeats.

"I only heard what Castor told me, but he wasn't sure."

"So who is my father?" Helen asks, clenching her fist around the necklace.

"I don't know. I just knew Leda fell for a foreigner who left the palace before you were born."

Helen turns away from her. Clytemnestra feels as if she has been slapped.

"Why did you lie to me?"

"I didn't lie."

Helen shakes her head. The space between them is growing like a whirlpool, sucking them into its blackness. "What about Polydeuces?" Helen asks.

"What about him?"

"Does he know about any of this?"

"He always says he doesn't remember and refuses to say anything."

Helen laughs, a cold sound Clytemnestra doesn't recognize. "Because he loves me."

"I love you," Clytemnestra says.

Helen turns to her again. Her eyes look strange. "No, you don't. You lied to me. Now please go away."

It is worse than being kicked, worse than being stabbed. Physical pain can be healed, Clytemnestra has learned that, but what about this? No one has taught her about this. She stands quickly, walks out, and closes the door behind her. She feels faint, emptiness sucking her from the inside. She brings her hands to her face and feels the wetness on her cheeks. It only makes her angrier. On the other side of the door, she hears her sister punching the stool or the table. She wants to go back, but somehow the door seems impossible to open again.

8

The Most Beautiful Woman

WHEN HELEN WAS fourteen, the hero Theseus had come to Sparta for her. Word of his great deeds had been spreading throughout their lands for years—the fights against bandits around the dangerous roads to Athens, the killing of a king at the holy site of Eleusis. There was no greater honor than to catch the attention of such a man, so Tyndareus said.

"What does he want from me?" Helen had asked Leda. "I am too young to marry."

"He wants to look at you, that is all."

"He thinks himself the son of a god," Polydeuces snorted, "so he wants a *divine* wife."

Helen frowned. "I am not divine," she said. Then she repeated, "And I am too young to marry."

Theseus arrived in Sparta accompanied by his friend Pirithous, prince of the Lapiths, a northern mountain tribe. Theseus was handsome like a god, even handsomer than Polydeuces, while Pirithous had a thick beard and skin raw from the sun. They liked to speak of their adventures together, of how their friendship had formed after they had stolen a herd of cattle, of all the girls they had seduced. They laughed at the memories, and the people in the palace laughed with them, as though those girls had been dull and useless. Theseus truly believed that all women wanted to please him, Clytemnestra realized. As for the rest of the world, it either bored or annoyed him. Only Pirithous made him laugh, made his eyes glitter with excitement.

"Men who find solace only in other men are to be distrusted," Castor told Clytemnestra and Helen one morning as they were watching Theseus and Pirithous fight in the gymnasium. "They don't respect anyone else, let alone a woman."

Theseus filled the Spartan halls with gifts—among them, the bed made of Egyptian ebony—yet he never asked for any marriage. Soon everyone forgot why he had come to the palace. Then, one summer day, Theseus claimed he was ready to go back to Athens and succeed his father on the throne.

The night before he was to leave, while the servants slept and Pirithous prepared the horses, Theseus broke into Helen's room and kidnapped her, as silent as air. Clytemnestra woke in the early morning in the empty Egyptian bed. She screamed and ran to her father, her heart beating so fast it hurt. Castor and Polydeuces hurried outside, gathering servants until they found a helot who had seen Theseus riding east.

"They are taking Helen to the small town of Aphidnae, my lords," the helot said when dragged to the *megaron*. Clytemnestra didn't know where Aphidnae was or what that meant. Polydeuces punched the painted wall and stormed out of the room. Castor and Clytemnestra followed. At the stables, Castor stopped her.

"You stay here," he said.

When Clytemnestra ignored him and took a horse, Polydeuces shouted, "Didn't you hear your brother? *You stay here!*" They spurred the horses and were gone in a cloud of dust.

Forced to wait without any news of the person she loved most, Clytemnestra took refuge in the temple of Artemis. There, near a spring at the foot of the mountains, she sat between two wooden columns and prayed. She was not very good at it, because she was impatient. She gave up quickly and wandered around the mud-brick walls until she found Tyndareus talking to the priestess.

"I don't understand why your sons went to fetch her, Tyndareus," the priestess was saying. "It would be an honor for any girl to lie with Theseus. Helen is ripe for marriage, and she is still a virgin." She had flowers in her hair and a long thin dress that showed her sharp-edged body.

"I want Helen back," Tyndareus said. Then he turned, feeling watched, and saw Clytemnestra. He walked to her, leaving the priestess, and said, "Let us pray together for your sister's return."

Her brothers came back at nightfall. Helen was slumped over Polydeuces's horse, her head resting against her brother's back, her arms scratched. Clytemnestra was still in the temple with her father when she saw them coming. She had never prayed so much in her life. She sprang up and ran to the palace.

Two servants left Helen in the *gynaeceum*, while Castor and Polydeuces spoke with Tyndareus and Leda.

"Theseus was already gone when we got there," Castor said, "but we found her. Two farmers told us where she was hidden."

"What did he do to her?" Leda asked.

"She needs to rest. And I am going to ask the women in the kitchen to bring the goose fat to her room."

Leda covered her face with her hands. Clytemnestra didn't know what it meant then, but goose fat mixed with crushed herbs was helpful for women who were in pain after lying with a man.

"We'll go back tomorrow," Polydeuces said, "now that Helen is safe. I'll take ten of our best men and we'll sack Aphidnae." He looked wild, distraught.

Tyndareus shook his head. "Theseus is now king of Athens. Athens is powerful, and we can't go to war against it, not for such a reason."

Such a reason. Clytemnestra wanted to tear out her hair, but Polydeuces preceded her.

"Your daughter was *raped* by this man for his entertainment. He didn't even ask for her hand in marriage!"

"That is good for Helen," Castor intervened. "Something tells me she wouldn't want to marry him."

Tyndareus waved a hand. "Theseus is a hero, and he does what heroes do. Do you know how many other girls like Helen there are? Do you think their brothers went to war over it? They didn't, because they aren't fools."

That was the end of it.

Back in their room, the air was stinging, suffocating, but Clytemnestra endured it. It was her fault Helen had been taken: if only she had woken, if only she had seen Theseus...

When she sat on the bed, Helen seemed already asleep, so she lay down in the dark and pulled the covers over her.

"They played dice," Helen said suddenly, her voice so low that Clytemnestra barely heard her. "They played dice and Theseus won. So he had me for himself."

Clytemnestra stayed silent. She rolled over to Helen's side and put an arm around her. She forced herself to stay awake all night. When dawn came, she collapsed, her arm numb but still wrapped around her sister.

The day after their fight, Clytemnestra doesn't know where to go. She paces the room, eager to scream or break something. But all she seems able to do is walk, her restless feet stepping back and forth, back and forth. There is a buzz in her head, and she can't think clearly. She splashes her face with cold water and leaves the room to find her sister.

As she passes the busy servants and sweaty boys coming from practice, her mind twists. Maybe Helen isn't angry any more. Maybe she has understood that it isn't Clytemnestra's fault. Maybe she has spoken to their mother, who has explained why she kept Helen's father a secret. The possibilities are like broken rafts, barely keeping her afloat in a stormy sea.

Under the trees that surround the wrestling ground, a wounded boy is sitting at the physician's feet. The man is cleaning the boy's temple, where the skin is swollen, a hard dark lump protruding like a sea rock. Next to them, Helen is grinding herbs, her brow furrowed in concentration.

When she sees her sister, she stops grinding but doesn't walk away from the physician.

"Helen," Clytemnestra says, unable to find any other word.

Her sister shakes her head. She is looking at her but not really seeing her. Her eyes are blank. Clytemnestra winces, feeling denied. Helen has never looked at her like that, not once. She is usually watching her, intent, as a hunter watches the trees for the slightest movement.

"Can we—?" she starts, but Helen interrupts her.

"You should have told me the truth," she says coldly.

She is right, and Clytemnestra has nothing to say to that. She considers replying "I did it to protect you," but that would sound foolish.

She feels all happiness flowing away from her, as water drips to the ground when a soaked tunic is squeezed. She turns her back to Helen and walks away.

Days pass. Winter becomes colder and windier. The water in the Eurotas freezes, and children play on it. The days are dark and the trees are bare.

Clytemnestra has never felt so alone. She yearns for her husband. He must have arrived in Maeonia by now, sitting on his gilded throne, announcing his marriage and heir. Clytemnestra imagines the faces of the men around him, their reactions. She can see their glittering clothes and jewels, precious fabrics and perfumed oils. Then she thinks of Tantalus's hands on the back of her neck, his arms around her belly, and her stomach tightens with longing.

Timandra is the only one who gives her solace. She often accompanies Clytemnestra to the *megaron* now, sitting with her and Tyndareus as commoners make their requests. In the high-roofed hall, she listens, learns, and often whispers in Clytemnestra's ear, eager to speak her mind and make her own suggestions.

"You are too young," Clytemnestra says.

"I am only three years younger than you," Timandra reminds her. Though her body remains lean and athletic, like a child's, her face has grown older, more mature. Her eyes are dark as a starless night, her hair brown like hazel bark.

"Just listen for now," Clytemnestra orders.

"But you never listen when others tell you to keep silent," Timandra points out. Clytemnestra laughs and even Tyndareus smiles, amused by his daughter's remark.

It is late afternoon and they have been listening to the people's requests for hours. The fire of the hearth smokes thickly and the hall is too warm.

It is then that Menelaus comes in, alone. The sunset light falls on him, on his flaming red hair, the color of fire sparks in the darkness. He places his bronze sword aside on the floor, a sign of respect, and walks closer to the throne. Clytemnestra bites her lip. She is wary of his kindness, of the way he always bows to Tyndareus. He reminds her of Theseus when he first arrived in Sparta—handsome and violent, arrogant but respectful.

"I was not expecting you, Menelaus," Tyndareus says mildly. "I thought you would be in the gymnasium."

Menelaus smiles. His eyes are golden brown, like Agamemnon's, but the look in them is not as hard. "I have come to ask for your help."

"And your brother?" Tyndareus asks.

"He will be here soon. I have two requests, and one is best made by myself alone."

Tyndareus nods and calls a servant forward. "Bring us water and food," he orders. Then to Menelaus, "I will listen to your requests, son of Atreus, but let us also eat something. The day has been long." The servant disappears from the hall and runs back again shortly after, a silver basin in one arm, for the rinsing of the hands, and a platter with meat and cheese in the other. Timandra, who was standing and untangling her hair, restless, sits quietly on the stool next to Clytemnestra.

Tyndareus grabs a piece of fat loin and asks, "Tell me, Menelaus, what do you want?"

Menelaus doesn't hesitate before speaking. "Your daughter."

Timandra gasps, and Clytemnestra instinctively lifts one hand to her stomach. Tyndareus turns to her, chewing, then back to Menelaus. "Which daughter?" he asks.

Menelaus frowns. He looks at Clytemnestra and Timandra, as if only just realizing they are here as well. Then, with a tone that suggests the obvious, says, "Helen."

"I see." Tyndareus spits the bone onto the platter.

"I hear she is ready for marriage and I would make her the queen of Mycenae, which, as you well know, is among the richest of cities."

"I see," Tyndareus repeats. He brings a hand to his temple as if easing a headache, showing the wrinkly scar on the back of his hand from when, as a young man, he was training, fighting wolves in the forest.

"What do you say, Tyndareus?" Menelaus asks.

"In Sparta, it is women who choose their husbands as often as not," Tyndareus points out.

Menelaus seems taken aback, though he quickly composes himself. "I have heard that. But I don't think it would be a problem."

"She would never choose you," Clytemnestra says before she can contain herself.

Menelaus lets his eyes rest on her. Timandra bends toward her as if to whisper something in her ear, but Clytemnestra stops her with a gesture of her hand. She wants to listen to the men.

"Even if Helen wanted you," Tyndareus says, "her beauty is known throughout our lands. Many suitors, all over Greece, are waiting for the moment she is ready for marriage."

"Summon them all, then," Menelaus says, "and let Helen choose."

There is silence. His words echo in the back of Clytemnestra's head. Here he stands, believing himself superior to anyone else, believing he can have Helen. She almost laughs. Again, Timandra leans toward her, eager to speak, but Clytemnestra squeezes her sister's hand, telling her to know her place.

"I will do that," Tyndareus concedes. "I will send word that Helen is ripe for marriage and ask all suitors to come to Sparta. But even then, you would have no lands or riches to offer. When you first came here, you told me you had a plan to take back Mycenae. You have been my guests a whole season, and Mycenae is not yours yet."

"You are right," Menelaus says. "This brings me to my second request."

Before he can speak further, Agamemnon enters the hall. He looks at the sword his brother put down but keeps his own hunting blade at his waist. He was eavesdropping, Clytemnestra realizes. As he takes his place next to Menelaus, she forces herself to look up, into Agamemnon's hard eyes. He ignores her presence.

"Ah, Agamemnon," Tyndareus says wearily. "Help yourself to some food."

The servant walks out of the shadows once again, holding the meat platter out to Agamemnon, who picks up the bone Tyndareus spat out earlier, moves it aside, and swallows a piece of cheese. "It is time to take back Mycenae," he says. "We cannot wait any longer."

"I agree," Tyndareus says. "It must be done before the people get used to their new king."

"Thyestes is no king," Menelaus points out, but Agamemnon silences his brother with a look.

"You have been a generous host, Tyndareus," Agamemnon says. "And it pains us to ask for one more favor, but I assure you that we will pay you back ten times more."

Tyndareus lifts his eyebrows, waiting. When Agamemnon doesn't speak further, he says, "I can't give you my army."

Agamemnon shakes his head, a cold smile on his face. "All we need is your blessing and ten of your best men."

The plan is ingenious—even Clytemnestra is forced to admit it. Agamemnon chooses ten warriors, the best and fastest climbers. With the Atreidai, they will ride to Mycenae, hide the horses far enough from the citadel, and climb the city walls. The entrance to Mycenae, the Lion Gate, is impossible to penetrate without raising the alarm, as Menelaus explains, but once inside the walls, they will run in the narrow streets of the lower part of the city, where the people live. They will slaughter the guards who hide in the alleyways, then climb to the higher part of the citadel, up to the palace. When Clytemnestra mentions that the people might raise the alarm, Agamemnon shakes his head. "The people hate Thyestes," he explains. "They will be faithful to us."

"And if they are not?" Tyndareus asks.

"We will kill them before they can run."

Clytemnestra thinks about his words. It shocks her that, for the Atreidai, one life is worth the same as another. In Sparta, she has grown up knowing that equality is a product of nature and that some men and women are *homoioi*, the same, while others are not. It has been hard for her to watch Spartans kill helots for offenses no greater than walking past them, but she endured it, thinking it was the only possible way of life. But Agamemnon and Menelaus speak of killing men without regard to their status and origin. No life matters to them, apart from their own.

She walks the twisting corridors of the palace, her hands on her belly, her legs sore. *They will leave*, she tells herself and the baby. *They will leave and never come back.* A small smile breaks across her face. She feels the soft curve under her hand: soon it will start to show through her tunics as well. And the more her baby grows, the closer she is to Tantalus.

She steps into the dining hall, eager for a drink. The room is empty except for Timandra, who is sitting with her feet on the table, gobbling bread and salted fish.

"If Leda sees you like this, she'll have you whipped," Clytemnestra says.

Timandra swallows a big bite of fish, taking a bone out of her teeth. "I doubt it," she says. "Besides, she does the same when she is in here alone."

Clytemnestra takes a cup and pours herself some diluted wine.

"Can I tell you now?" Timandra asks.

"Tell me what?"

"I tried to speak to you in the *megaron*, but you wouldn't let me."

"It was important to listen to what Menelaus had to say."

"Yes," Timandra replies. "But I saw something the other day." She takes a fig and bites into it, the dark flesh opening under her teeth. As she does so, she casts a look at Clytemnestra, a look that suggests she enjoys having a secret, something others long to know too.

"What did you see?" Clytemnestra asks.

"Helen with Menelaus."

Clytemnestra chokes on the wine. Timandra laughs but then, catching her sister's expression, turns serious quickly.

"They were together near the orchards outside the palace," she adds.

"Did you hear what they were saying?"

"Menelaus said that as soon as he took Mycenae back, he would give her a rich purple-dyed cloth, something from Crete, I think."

Clytemnestra stands, even though her body is hurting. "And what did Helen say?"

Timandra shrugs. "I don't remember. It was cold and I was in a hurry—I had to meet someone else." Clytemnestra sees the disappointment in her sister's eyes when she doesn't ask about her meeting. She turns to leave but Timandra says, "I am telling you this because I think Menelaus is right. Helen might choose him."

Clytemnestra nods, even though she doesn't understand or believe any of it. She needs to talk to her sister.

For a long time after Theseus took her, Helen would wake up screaming. For a few moments, before she understood that she was safe in bed
with her sister, her body would twist and struggle as if she was being
tortured. Clytemnestra never left her side. She held her wrist, feeling
her pulse climbing, and lifted her hands to her sister's cheeks.

"He has come again," Helen would always say. Clytemnestra could
see that her mind was somewhere else, still imprisoned in her dream.
"I fight, but he finds a way to knock me down."

To keep the pain at bay, Clytemnestra would dream of taking
down Theseus. How handsome he looked, how gifted, yet for what?
Heroes like him are made of greed and cruelty: they take and take
until the world around them is stripped of its beauty.

"Something bad will happen tomorrow," Helen said when she was
back with her sister. "It always does when I dream about him."

Clytemnestra shook her head. "Dreams are dreams. They don't
become real unless you give them power." So Helen would fall asleep
again.

But one night, the dream felt so real that Helen woke and ran
outside, leaving the palace behind. Clytemnestra followed her, bare-
foot, the wet grass dirtying her soles, the moon pale and shy in the
mournful sky. Helen darted across the plain until she reached the
temple of Artemis, sobbing and panting. There, close to the spring
spilling water, like a cascade of tears, she sat down and hugged her
knees. Clytemnestra watched her, thinking of the priestess's words, "It
would be an honor for any girl to lie with Theseus." All lies.

"What happened? Has someone hurt you?"

Clytemnestra turned and Polydeuces was there, fear dancing in his eyes, a spear in his hand. He must have heard them running outside.

"It's Theseus," Clytemnestra said. "He comes to her in her dreams."

He sighed with relief and put down the spear. "You mustn't cry, Helen. Theseus is gone." He never used that patient tone with anyone else.

"It still hurts," Helen whispered, and Clytemnestra knew she was speaking neither of the memory nor of the dream. It was her body that still hurt.

Polydeuces knelt next to her. "I understand—"

"No, Polydeuces," Helen snapped back, a flicker of fury in her bright eyes. "You don't. How could you?" *You're a man.*

She didn't say it, but Clytemnestra heard it. Sometimes she could feel Helen's pain in her own body, her sister's sadness wearing her down. It was as if their hearts were beating together, as if they'd learned to keep in rhythm after all this time spent side by side.

Polydeuces clenched his fists, then pressed his hands to his face as if trying to erase the thought of Helen's pain from his mind. Clytemnestra lowered herself next to him. They exchanged a look, then reached out to their sister. Helen's skin felt thin and precious under their touch, like a butterfly's wing. She looked up at them, face streaked with tears.

"Helen," Clytemnestra said, "you're safe now because we are with you." *And we love you.* She didn't need to say it, because she knew her sister could hear her too.

♛

She knows where to find Helen now. She walks to the temple of Artemis, and there is her sister, standing close to the spring at the foot

of the mountains, her eyes closed. Is she praying? As soon as she hears
Clytemnestra's steps, she looks up. Around her neck shines the golden
necklace that was in her room, each rosette perfectly outlined against
her pearly-white skin.

"Who gave you that necklace?" Clytemnestra asks. For a moment,
with her newly short hair and swollen body beside her luminous sister,
she feels ugly. She remembers she had felt like this when she was a
child. A warrior visiting from Argos had told Tyndareus that Helen
was the fairest girl in all their lands. "Her hair is like honey," the warrior said, "and her neck like a swan's. She will marry a king favored by
the gods." He had said nothing about Clytemnestra.

Helen ignores her question. She fixes her eyes on Clytemnestra's
with a challenging stare.

"It was Menelaus, wasn't it?" Clytemnestra asks.

"And what if it was?"

"He is not a good man, Helen."

"You know nothing about him."

"And you do?"

Helen shrugs. The air is cold and the wind blows drops of the
spring water in their direction, sprinkling them.

"Father will send word that you are ready for marriage,"
Clytemnestra says, trying to keep her voice even. "Many men will
soon come to claim your hand, and you will be free to choose."

"He is not my father," Helen says.

"He has been such to you. You have grown up here, in this palace,
with your brothers and sisters."

With a jerk of her head, Helen seems to flick off an annoying fly.
"You don't understand," she says. "I can make decisions for myself. I
do not wish to live in your shadow any longer."

Clytemnestra's face stings. "How can you say that when you have always been the most beautiful, ever since you were a child?" She is speaking with resentment now, and she doesn't hide it. "The Spartan people sing of your beauty during feasts, and everyone thinks you are a daughter of Zeus, just because of your looks."

"I do not care about looks!" Helen cries. "What good are they? You know what my *beauty* got me. You remember Theseus, don't you?"

"What do you care about, then?" Clytemnestra asks, but Helen continues, her voice lower and lower, yet each word sharper, more painful.

"*You* have always been the center of attention. 'Helen is beautiful, but Clytemnestra is clever and charming, strong and wise,' and so many other things… *You*'ve always had Tyndareus's love and, more than anyone else, *you* have the respect of the Spartan people. Whatever you do, you excel. Whatever you put your mind to, you accomplish." Jealousy, which Clytemnestra always thought would be strange to her sister, easily finds its way onto her perfect features. "And there I am, next to you, your beautiful, weak, dull sister, who has nothing interesting to say. I am only interesting to look at."

Clytemnestra stands fixed in her painful understanding. She forces her voice to be as low as her sister's, as colorless as the gray sky above them. "You only see what you want to see. You don't understand how it is for me."

Helen rolls her eyes. "And how is it for you?"

She wonders what would hurt Helen most. Something tells her that shouting and pleading would do nothing. "It doesn't matter," she says. "You only care about your own suffering." She wipes away a water droplet from her cheek. "Do what you wish with Menelaus. Marry him, if you desire jewelry and rich clothes." She sees the shock on Helen's face but doesn't stop. "But do not fool yourself. He doesn't see you or love you for what you are. He is among those who only find you interesting to look at."

She clenches her fists as she walks away, frost crunching under her feet, the sky merciless above her.

The next day, Agamemnon and Menelaus leave. Lysimachos is chosen for their mission, and Cynisca's father. Cynisca stands at the gate to say goodbye. She hugs her father and kisses Agamemnon's hand, but he is not looking at her. He stares at Clytemnestra, his face dark, his eyes drinking her in. Helen stands next to her mother, her hair plaited around her head like a golden wreath. She is still wearing the necklace, the rosettes cold against her collarbones.

The priestess is waiting outside the stone gate, a goat limp at her feet. When the warriors are ready, Tyndareus gives her a large golden bowl. She takes the bronze knife tied to her cloak and cuts the animal's throat. The body kicks as blood spurts and pours into the basin. Clytemnestra watches the red spot spreading on the priestess's cloak.

The priestess turns to the soldiers. She looks taller and dangerous in her gravity. "You may go," she says. "Mycenae will be yours in five days, before the night falls."

Menelaus mounts his horse. Around him, the other men do the same, swords and axes glinting and clanking at their sides.

Agamemnon turns to Tyndareus, his face sharp and cold. "Thank you for your hospitality, king of Sparta. We will send gold from Mycenae soon."

Without another word, he gallops away, his brother and soldiers following. Darkness swallows them, and all that remains is the sound of hoofs beating on the frosty ground.

👑

They gather in the dining hall, their hands chapped from the wind outside. There are no nobles and warriors tonight, only Clytemnestra's family, and the servants set out bowls of pears and apples, cheese and nuts. The hall feels cold, and a helot lights a small fire; the flames cast shadows on the weapons hanging on the walls.

"This morning, I sent envoys to the most powerful cities across Greece," Tyndareus says. "Kings and princes who wish to court Helen have been summoned here to Sparta." He says Helen's name as though she weren't in the room. Phoebe looks at her sister, saddened by her father's behavior.

"Thank you, Father," Helen says without looking at him. Her tone is slightly mocking, but not enough for Tyndareus to notice it.

"Warriors will come from as far as Crete," Leda says. She stops for a second when Phoebe whispers excitedly, "Crete!" then continues, "It will be an honor to have them here." For a moment, Clytemnestra can't help but think of how the priestess had deemed lying with Theseus "honorable."

"Do you know who will come?" Timandra asks.

"Ajax, cousin of the great Achilles, will be here," Tyndareus says. "He is no older than thirty and in search of a wife."

"Isn't he a brute?" Clytemnestra says. "You once said so."

Helen looks at her and their eyes lock. Clytemnestra remembers how they laughed when their mother described Ajax in the past and how they spent an entire night doing impressions of him. The memory makes her stomach burn.

"Chiron trained him, and the hero Telamon is his father," Leda says. Helen looks away, focusing on the cheese on her plate. "Though he was a brute when your father met him, I am sure that he is grown now and would be a good catch."

"If he was trained by Chiron," Helen says, "then he is good in the art of healing, I suppose."

"He is," Leda says. Turning back to Timandra, she continues, "Then the king of Argos might come, Diomedes, and even the archer Philoctetes."

Phoebe giggles, delighted. Each day, she is growing more beautiful. Though she isn't as skilled in wrestling and training as Timandra and Philonoe, she is a gifted archer. "Since so many men will come," she says, "maybe one of them will marry me."

Tyndareus raises his thick eyebrows skeptically. "You have plenty of time to be courted and to decide, Phoebe," he says. "But Timandra may begin to think about it."

"Marriage disgusts me," Timandra says, bored. "Sometimes I wish I were a boy."

Tyndareus laughs. Phoebe glares at her sister. She thinks Timandra wanted to offend her. "Is that why you were with that girl the other day?" she asks.

Timandra blushes, her fists suddenly clenched. Clytemnestra remembers Timandra's words: *It was cold and I was in a hurry. I had to meet someone else.*

"What is this?" Leda asks, frowning. "Which girl?"

Timandra kicks Phoebe so hard under the table that everyone hears the loud thump.

Phoebe lifts her chin, defiant. "I saw her with a girl from the gymnasium, one that always fights with her. They were near the orchard."

Timandra stabs the wooden table with her knife. Everyone is looking at her now.

"What were they doing?" Tyndareus asks, staring at Timandra.

"They were close," she says. "They were talking and—"

"And what were *you* doing there, Phoebe?" interrupts Clytemnestra. "Aren't you ashamed of spying on your sister like that?"

Phoebe looks down, her eyes wet with shame. Timandra seems on the verge of tears too, but nothing comes out of her eyes. Spartan girls never cry, let alone for such a reason.

"Dinner is over," Leda says before her husband can speak. "Away, all of you."

Timandra knocks over her chair and runs outside. As she does so, her mother shouts, "And behave yourself! You are women now—you are expected to behave, not to do as you please!"

In ten days' time, an envoy arrives at the palace. He is taken inside quickly and meets Tyndareus, Leda, and Clytemnestra in the *megaron*. His tunic is ragged and his skin covered with sweat and dirt.

"My king," he says, panting, "I bring news from Mycenae." His voice is cracked: he must have ridden fast without stopping.

"Bring him some water," Tyndareus orders.

The messenger looks up at him gratefully, and when a servant girl gives him a cup of diluted wine, he drinks it all.

Tyndareus leans forward. "Speak."

"The city has fallen back into the hands of the Atreidai. Lord Thyestes has been executed. His son Aegisthus has fled."

Clytemnestra watches her father, but his face is impenetrable.

"Very well," Tyndareus says. He turns to the servants, dutifully waiting by the door. "Bring this man to the tubs, wash him, and give him a warm tunic."

"Thank you," the envoy says, bowing.

When he has left, Tyndareus relaxes against the back of his chair. "I knew they would take the city back."

"You said so," Leda says.

"They are great warriors."

Leda turns to Clytemnestra, then back to her husband. "You know we disagree on that."

Clytemnestra feels the baby kicking and brings a hand to her belly to soothe him. *It is over*, she tells herself. *You will never see them again.* But the more she repeats it, the more she feels this is not the truth.

9

The Flaming-Haired and the Many-Minded

A WOMAN IS riding along the twisting shape of the Eurotas, alone. Two Spartan guards follow her from the palace, their eyes fixed on the face hidden behind a veil, on the cloak flapping in the wind. She passes the yellow patches of burned grass, the hard ground surrounding the fields, and the rocky terrain at the foot of the palace. There, close to the gate, Clytemnestra is waiting for her. The woman sees her and dismounts the gray horse. She walks closer to Clytemnestra, her steps slow and steady. Finally, she draws off her veil, revealing brown-streaked hair and clever dark eyes.

"Welcome back, Penelope."

Penelope smiles, her eyes on her cousin's pregnant belly. "Did Uncle Tyndareus send you here? He knew I was coming."

"I came of my own accord," Clytemnestra says, holding out a hand to her. "Come. You must be tired."

She takes Penelope to the *gynaeceum* to wash and rest before dinner. They walk along the dark corridors, deserted at this hour of the afternoon, until they reach the baths. Two clay tubs have already been prepared by servants. Both women start undressing, the torchlight caressing their bodies, one darker and swollen, the other paler and softer. Penelope lets her cloak and tunic fall onto the cold floor, then reaches out to touch Clytemnestra's belly. It ripples as the baby kicks.

"Not long until he is born," Penelope says.

"A couple of months."

Penelope peers down at herself as if looking for changes. But her skin is still pale, her curves soft. She feels the temperature of the water with her fingertips. "Have any of the kings come yet?" she asks.

Clytemnestra can't help but think of Helen, always pulling back from cold water. "No. Most of them will arrive tomorrow."

"You know why Icarius sent me here?"

"To find a husband, I presume."

"Yes." Penelope smirks. "He wants me to marry a man who comes to Sparta to court another woman. Isn't that pathetic?"

"It is," Clytemnestra agrees. She sinks into the water, the ends of her hair tickling her shoulders.

"The palace seems quiet without your brothers," Penelope says, wetting her arms and face. "I imagine they won't be back soon."

"Many things have changed since you left."

Penelope gazes at her. "Like the fact that you and Helen are not speaking?" Her sweet face is sharper in the shadows of the torchlight. "You were always together before," she adds.

They are silent for a while, the water in the bath cradling them.

"She wants to marry the son of Atreus, Menelaus," Clytemnestra says finally.

"That would be unfortunate," Penelope says. "The family is cursed, their crimes bloody and unforgivable."

Clytemnestra doesn't say anything. She already knows this.

"Do you think Menelaus will come and court her?" Penelope asks.

"I am afraid he will, yes."

"Let me talk to her," Penelope says, confident. "I will persuade her."

Clytemnestra thinks about it. She hates to admit that her own sister would listen to Penelope rather than to her. But it is for a good cause. She gives a small nod, and Penelope smiles.

Kings start arriving the next afternoon. A thin layer of snow covers the plain; it is one of the coldest days the valley has ever seen. From the terrace in front of the main hall, Clytemnestra and Penelope watch mules and horses travel to the palace, their packs heavy with gifts.

Nestor and his son Antilochus are among the first to arrive. They recognize the man from his thin white beard—he is old and his wisdom whispered to be legendary. His son seems no more than twenty, and his skin is brown like copper. Their city, the sandy Pylos, is washed by the sea, with burned yellow grass and water as blue as a cloudless sky.

"And that is Diomedes," Penelope says, pointing at a small group of men barely visible on the other side of the valley. They are ten soldiers, their armor glistening, all gathered around a man on a black stallion.

"How do you know?" Clytemnestra asks. She squints but can't see the man properly.

Penelope shrugs. "I guessed. Argos is in that direction."

They spend all afternoon on the terrace, looking left and right, jumping excitedly whenever they spot a new crew. They see Menoetius and his son, who looks no older than a child; Ajax the Lesser from Locris; Menestheus, king of Athens, a long column of soldiers behind him.

And then, traveling from the port, Ajax the Great and his cousin Teucer from the island of Salamis; soldiers escorting a Cretan prince, their shields with the symbol of a double ax engraved on them; Ephenor from the large island of Euboea, an important source of grain and cattle, the crucial junction between Greece and the East; a man traveling with only two guards coming from what Penelope recognizes as Ithaca, a small island of rocks and goats to the west.

"Who is the king of Ithaca?" Clytemnestra asks.

"I don't think I have ever heard of him. Laertes, maybe? But he is too old now surely. His son may have succeeded him."

Clytemnestra thinks of Ithaca, so small that others don't care to remember it. It must be horrible to live on a forgotten island until you are old and wrinkled. Laertes's son must crave the honor of marriage to the daughter of Tyndareus.

The last to arrive are the men from Thessaly, a land far north, farther than Delphi even. Among them are Machaon, expert in the art of healing, and the archer Philoctetes, an old man with thick gray hair, like sheep's wool. They sway on their tired donkeys, their bags of food almost empty after the long journey.

As the sun sets, the servants call for Penelope and Clytemnestra. When they finally leave the terrace to ready themselves for dinner, their hands are chapped, their eyes watering in the cold.

The dining hall has never been so loud or full. Servants have dragged two more tables inside and lit only half the torches. The fire already smokes thickly, and the room grows warmer by the second.

Tyndareus sits at the head of the table on one side, old Nestor on the other. Most kings and princes are gathered around them, and their soldiers and guards fill the other two tables, seated on benches draped with lambskins. Clytemnestra is sitting between Helen and Penelope. Helen glows like the summer sun in her white dress embroidered with gold, her perfumed hair tied in long plaits; Penelope's and Clytemnestra's dresses are of a dark blue, like the sea at night. Opposite them are Philoctetes, his long hair brushed and his wrinkled face shaved clean, the king of Argos, Diomedes, and the man of Ithaca, whose name Penelope didn't know. They eat eagerly, sinking their knives into the roast goose, cheese, and onions, their goblets filled to the brim with the best wine from the kitchen.

"Are all these yours?" Diomedes asks Tyndareus after he has swallowed a piece of meat. He is talking about the women. He has an ugly scar on his arm and a thick beard.

"Helen and Clytemnestra are my eldest," Tyndareus answers, his tone warm and polite. "Timandra, Phoebe, and Philonoe are younger." He gestures to the three girls, standing by his side. "Penelope is my niece, the daughter of Prince Icarius."

"It is a long way from Acarnania," Diomedes says to no one in particular. Is he afraid to address Penelope directly? Clytemnestra has heard that women in some Greek palaces don't dine with men.

"Did you travel to Sparta all by yourself?" the man from Ithaca asks. He doesn't seem to share Diomedes's awkwardness and stares directly into Penelope's eyes. He lifts his cup and drinks.

Penelope stirs. "Yes. I rode here alone."

The man smiles. There is bright interest in his gray eyes. "Aren't you afraid of riding alone?"

Clytemnestra frowns, but Penelope speaks with a friendly tone. "Would someone ask you the same question if you left Ithaca alone on a boat?"

Some soldier on the other table finishes telling a dirty joke and everyone around him roars with laughter, slamming their cups onto the table. The man from Ithaca snorts as though annoyed by the interruption, then refills his cup before a helot can do it for him. Perhaps he is not used to servants in his poor palace among the rocks.

"I am afraid I haven't introduced myself properly," he says, grinning as soon as he has emptied his cup again. He has a handsome smile and his eyes are clever, conspiratorial. "How foolish of me. Here we are, courting the most beautiful girl in all our lands," he says as he nods to Helen, then he smiles at Penelope and Clytemnestra and adds, "in the presence of other wonderful women, and I haven't even given my name. I am Odysseus, prince of Ithaca, but you won't have heard of me."

Penelope turns quickly to Clytemnestra with a small smile. Something in the way he talks reminds Clytemnestra of Tantalus, though she can't say what it is.

"Ah, son of Laertes, you are too humble," old Nestor says from the other side of the table. "They may not know your name, but everyone has heard of your cunning. They certainly don't call you *polutropos* for nothing." He uses the word for a man who is beyond ingenious, one who is clever and scheming. Clytemnestra suddenly recognizes the name. *The many-minded*, his brother had referred to him in the past. She studies Odysseus with more care, but as soon as she does so, he catches her stare, as one does with a disobedient child. She looks away.

Diomedes laughs scornfully. "What use are brains? The gods favor the strong."

Odysseus's smile doesn't drop. "The gods favor whoever amuses them. And I can assure you that clever men, and women," he adds with a quick nod to Penelope, Helen, and Clytemnestra, "are more appealing than brutes."

Clytemnestra laughs. Diomedes turns red and sticks his knife into the goose as though to pierce a warrior's chest.

"Are you insulting the strong, son of Laertes?" says a tall man sitting close to Nestor, his voice deep like the echo inside a cave. Clytemnestra recognizes Ajax the Great, the hero from Salamis. His cousin Teucer stiffens next to him.

"I would not dare to do that, Ajax, but the gods bestow on each of us different gifts, and we do what we can with them."

"Wise words from a clever man," Tyndareus says. Odysseus smiles at him, like a cat would.

"Speaking of the strong," Diomedes says, his face still red, "I thought the sons of Atreus would be here."

Clytemnestra turns to Helen, who is spreading honey on her cheese with too much care, her cheeks flushed.

"They will come tomorrow," Tyndareus says. "They have recently retaken Mycenae, as you probably know, and have been busy putting things back to the way they were in the city."

"What of their uncle, Thyestes?" Philoctetes asks. News travels slowly to Thessaly, it being so far north.

"He was executed," Tyndareus answers, his face expressionless, like a slab of smooth stone. "But their cousin Aegisthus lives."

Odysseus laughs. Most kings turn to him quickly.

"Does something amuse you?" Diomedes asks. He seems ready to strangle Odysseus.

"Forgive me, king of Sparta," Odysseus says, "but from what you say, it almost seems that Aegisthus lives by the grace of the Atreidai." He winks at Tyndareus, and Leda almost chokes on her wine. "And yet," he continues, "from what I've heard, Thyestes was burned alive and Aegisthus fled with the help of a servant—who was later burned too, I expect—and now lives in the woods, homeless, planning his revenge after he was forced to hear his father's screams echoing throughout the valley."

Clytemnestra sees the horror on Helen's face and feels a kind of satisfaction. It is like winning a match, only the son of Laertes did it for her.

"These tales are not fit for a dinner such as ours, Odysseus," Nestor says. "We do not wish to upset the women."

"Very little upsets the women of Sparta, my friend," Tyndareus says quietly.

Clytemnestra leans forward. "Besides, the prince of Ithaca says nothing we don't know already."

"Ah," Odysseus says and smiles. "The princess of Sparta doesn't like the sons of Atreus."

Clytemnestra smiles back. "We share that, I am sure."

Diomedes finishes the food on his plate, like a lion pulling the meat off its prey's bones. Then he turns to Clytemnestra.

"You are famous for your wrestling skills, even in Argos." The sentence is a statement, and Clytemnestra doesn't know how to respond.

Tyndareus intervenes. "She takes after her mother. Leda hunted lynxes and lions in the forests of Aetolia when she was younger."

Leda smiles but seems unwilling to speak. Clytemnestra suspects she has been drinking again, and sure enough, she sees Helen take the cup from her mother as soon as she tries to have it refilled.

"In Salamis, all women do is moan and giggle," Ajax the Great says. Perhaps that is what his comrades like, because Teucer cackles next to him, but few others, apart from Menoetius, Ephenor, and Diomedes.

"They do not fight?" Clytemnestra asks.

"Fight?" Ajax laughs, slamming a clenched fist on the table. "Women aren't made to fight."

"They weave and dance," Teucer says, still cackling, "and fuck every once in a while." This makes the men laugh more.

Diomedes's face is red again, this time with amusement. "My

father didn't even see his bride until the wedding day," he says. "She had never left the house." Again, a roar of laughter.

Clytemnestra doesn't understand the joke. Though she has grown up among vulgar warriors, she has never heard men speak like this. They usually joke about fucking goats and pigs or challenge each other out of nothing. Tyndareus doesn't join in with the laughter, but he does nothing to stop it.

"How old was she?" Penelope asks politely.

"Twelve." Diomedes shrugs. Timandra stirs next to Tyndareus, suddenly aware of her own age.

After a while, the fire burns out and the lights flicker feebly, like stars in a cloudy sky. Leda seems asleep on her chair, and Helen has to help her out of the room when the dinner is over. Helen doesn't reappear from her mother's room, so when the soldiers start leaving the hall, their foreheads greasy and their eyes tired, Clytemnestra and Penelope go to sleep together. When they reach the entrance to the *gynaeceum*, Penelope mumbles something about forgetting her cloak and runs back to the hall. Clytemnestra waits for her in the room, opening the windows to let in some air. The wind is colder than a blade, cutting her skin, but she enjoys it after hours spent in the crowded hall. She takes off her blue dress and curls up under the thick blankets.

Penelope bursts in, panting. She is holding up her tunic to avoid tripping, and the fabric is now crumpled around her waist.

"What is it?" Clytemnestra sits up.

"Prince Odysseus was talking to your father—I heard them," she says, breathless.

"What about?"

"About me, but I couldn't hear properly." She frowns. "I think they were making a kind of agreement."

"An agreement?"

Penelope shakes her head. She paces the room briefly, then jumps onto the bed next to Clytemnestra.

"I like that prince," Clytemnestra says.

Penelope chortles. "I do too. He sounds like your husband."

"You think so? He gave me the same impression."

"Yes, they are different from the others. They have something dark about them, though it's hard to say what." She thinks for a moment, then adds with a smile, "Talking to them is like entering a cave."

Clytemnestra knows the feeling—moving in the darkness and feeling each stone, finding each secret with your hands, step by step.

"They draw you in with questions about yourself," Penelope continues.

Clytemnestra laughs. "That is Tantalus's specialty."

Penelope moves closer to her, warming her feet under the blankets. She has goose bumps on her arms. "And what did you think of that man, Diomedes?"

"Disgusting," Clytemnestra says. "Even worse than Menelaus."

"I thought so too."

"And Ajax the Great. He looks like an oversized boar, hairs and all."

Penelope laughs. "He does! And when he talked of women moaning—"

"If I hadn't been pregnant, I would have challenged him to a wrestle, right there in the hall."

"Oh, I wish you had. You would have kicked the arrogance out of him."

They keep laughing as they go through all Helen's suitors, huddled close in the bed, and Clytemnestra's baby kicks, giggling with them.

The morning is even colder than it was the day before. In the *gynaeceum*, servant girls hurry around, whispering to each other while helping the women dress. Penelope has already disappeared to find Helen and convince her to choose the right suitor. Clytemnestra stands by the window while a servant does her hair. She feels the girl plaiting two short strands backward, pulling the hair away from her forehead. A myrtle crown lies on the stool beside them, its golden leaves sharp to the touch.

Last night, she dreamed of Tantalus again. He always comes to her in her dreams, with his warm skin and bright blue eyes. *The people are ready.* He smiled. *They know a Spartan woman is soon coming to be their queen. I've told them that you are fierce and that you are not afraid to fight for what is right.* When she opened her eyes, the moon was as small as a fingernail, and the bed was empty.

"Princess Clytemnestra?" the servant says.

Clytemnestra looks out the window. In the frost-covered valley, Menelaus and Agamemnon are riding to the palace. Just in time.

"Are those " the helot starts.

"The Atreidai, yes," Clytemnestra says sharply.

The girl falls silent and works on the last touches. Two small earrings to match the diadem. A white tunic, smooth and thin. A lynx's skin to cover her shoulders. The servant brings a basin of cold water, and Clytemnestra plunges her face into it.

She is ready.

When the servants open the wooden doors of the *megaron*, suitors fill the room like locusts. They are all wearing their best tunics, gold, silver, and crimson, the symbols of their islands and cities visible on their cloak pins and daggers. Tyndareus sits on the throne near the hearth, his beard trimmed, a thin golden crown on his gray hair. Next to him, Leda looks beautiful with anemone earrings dangling down her neck and lambskins hanging over her shoulders. Clytemnestra smiles. It is like looking into a clear stream and seeing herself in twenty years.

Helen is already seated on a chair, draped with brown cowhide, on a small dais positioned in front of the painted wall. There is a veil around her head, covering her golden hair. She is quite still, so that the colorful frescoes of dancing women frame her perfectly. She could be part of the painting, and indeed, exposed like that on the dais, she looks more like a fading fresco. Feeling her sister's gaze on her, she turns and their eyes lock. Clytemnestra wants to run to her, grab her, and take her away from this, to the tall reeds of the river or among the trees that grow on the mountains. But then Helen looks away.

"They should have let her sit next to your father," Penelope whispers in Clytemnestra's ear, suddenly at her side. Clytemnestra didn't even hear her coming.

"Did you speak to her?" she asks quietly.

"I did," Penelope says. She has also plaited her hair, and the style enhances her soft lips and gentle features.

"And?"

"She seemed convinced. I praised Idomeneus, who is quite handsome," she says, turning quickly to her left, where the Cretan prince stands, "and Machaon, because Helen has an interest in the art of healing, does she not?"

"She does," says Clytemnestra, impressed by her cousin's attentiveness. She cranes her neck to see Machaon. He has calloused yet gentle-seeming hands and long, curly hair. Clytemnestra tries to picture her sister next to him, her gleaming beauty clashing with his coarse looks.

As the men stand in the center of the room, their servants holding precious gifts, Clytemnestra notices the son of Laertes leaning casually against one of the columns, his hands empty and his servants nowhere to be seen. How does he think to woo Helen without a gift?

Leda beckons to Clytemnestra, and she approaches the throne. Phoebe and Philonoe stand next to their mother, each wearing a thick cloak adorned with a golden pin. Tyndareus seems annoyed.

"What is it?" Clytemnestra asks.

"Find your sister Timandra," Leda says. "She is not here."

"Be quick," Tyndareus orders. "The Atreidai are coming, so we will start soon."

Clytemnestra nods and walks out of the hall. A few servants are standing outside in a line, flattened against the walls in the shadows, ready to answer Tyndareus's orders.

"Have you seen Timandra?" Clytemnestra asks.

A young boy blushes, but the older helot next to him answers, "She was just here—"

"Your sister is on the terrace."

Clytemnestra turns. On the opposite side of the corridor, wearing a crimson tunic, Agamemnon is walking in her direction, his brother behind him. It has been two months since they last saw each other, and now he is staring at her large belly, distaste spread over his hard features. She resists the urge to cover it with her hands.

"You'd better fetch her before she does something stupid," he says.

"What my sister does doesn't concern you," Clytemnestra replies.

Menelaus snorts. He is holding another wrapped tunic in his hand, the fabric woven with wonderful figures, though Clytemnestra can't see it properly. She turns to Agamemnon. "You have not brought any gift."

"I am not here to claim your sister."

"Come, Brother," Menelaus says, clapping a hand around his

shoulder. Together they walk toward the *megaron*, their steps heavy on the stone floor.

Clytemnestra hurries to the terrace, her heart beating fast, her palms damp. She stops just by the door that leads outside.

Dressed in a long lilac tunic that hides her lanky figure, Timandra is whispering into someone's ear. Clytemnestra takes a step closer. It is a girl, with curly black hair that flows down her back and eyebrows shaped like a gull's wings. The girl laughs at whatever Timandra is saying, then kisses her lips. Timandra kisses her back, her mouth opening with pleasure, her hands cupped gently around the girl's neck.

"Timandra," Clytemnestra says.

The girl jumps back and Timandra turns. She opens her mouth, and her hands tremble. Clytemnestra tries to keep her composure. "We are late," she says.

Timandra nods, clutching one hand with the other to stop the shaking.

"Leave us," Clytemnestra tells the girl, who runs away, terrified.

Because her hands won't stop trembling, Timandra bites one. Clytemnestra reaches out and takes it into her own before walking her sister back inside.

"People can see you here," she says.

Timandra opens her dark eyes wide. "Has anyone—"

"The sons of Atreus just passed."

Timandra gasps in horror. "Please!"

Clytemnestra tightens the grip on her hand. "Don't be sorry. If they say anything, you deny it. I will protect you." They are at the entrance of the *megaron* now, the voices in the hall loud and clear. "But be careful, Timandra. You are not a child anymore."

Before Timandra can nod, Clytemnestra drags her inside. The

servants close the doors behind them, and Clytemnestra takes Timandra to one corner where Penelope is standing by herself, partially hidden by a column.

"Ah, here are my daughters," Tyndareus says, his voice loud in the high-roofed hall. "We shall begin."

The room suddenly falls silent, and the men turn to him, waiting.

"You will offer your gifts to Helen," Tyndareus starts. Many kings whisper in confusion. They probably expected to present their gifts to Tyndareus, the king, not his beautiful daughter. "But before you do that," Tyndareus continues, "I have been told that this gathering may cause some trouble."

Diomedes scoffs. Ajax and Teucer frown, flexing their arms menacingly. Menoetius mutters, "We have been deceived," a little too loudly. Agamemnon looks at the throne, his face indecipherable, while Menelaus whispers in his ear.

Tyndareus ignores them. "It is only fair that before each of you gives his precious treasure to court my daughter, you accept that she will choose only one man."

Some princes look back at Tyndareus as though he were stating the obvious, but the faintest trace of understanding is now spreading over Agamemnon's face. Clytemnestra understands too. Her father is trying to avoid a war against the rejected suitors.

"But surely, king of Sparta," the old Nestor says, looking around, "you trust these heroes?"

"I do," Tyndareus says calmly. "But I have been told that last night there was a fight after someone boasted he would be Helen's husband. Nothing serious," he adds as everyone cranes their neck to see who it might have been, "though it suggested that many of you may not accept rejection."

Ajax's face is purple with fury. Next to him, Menestheus, king of

Athens, a short man with beady eyes, is staring at Tyndareus as though ready to slice his throat.

"I do not wish to give grounds for a quarrel, so I offer you an option. If you want to stay here and present your gift to my daughter, you will also swear an oath."

"An oath?" Idomeneus asks, frowning.

"Yes. An oath that you will accept Helen's choice and that you will support and defend her husband should he need help in the future."

Nobody moves. Suddenly the air feels suffocating and the room hums with unspoken violence. Then Menelaus steps forward. His flaming red hair glows as he bows to Tyndareus. When he looks up, Tyndareus nods, and Menelaus walks to the dais where Helen is sitting.

"I will swear the oath," he says, staring at her with his golden eyes. "I will respect your choice." Helen blushes but manages to keep her face still. "This is my gift for you, princess of Sparta." As Menelaus shows the tunic, Clytemnestra can't help but admire the figures woven on it: King Minos and Queen Pasiphaë of Crete in their palace of dancers and traders, their daughter Ariadne kneeling beside them. Penelope casts a worried look at Clytemnestra.

The other suitors move forward.

One by one, they walk to the dais and bow, swearing the oath and presenting their gift: golden bowls, a shield decorated with copper leaves and flowers, a double-headed Cretan ax.

"That was a smart move," Clytemnestra whispers in Penelope's ear as the suitors keep pledging their allegiance.

"Making them swear an oath?"

"Yes. I wonder who suggested it to Father."

"That would be me."

The two women turn. Odysseus is behind them, a half smile on his face.

"You?" Clytemnestra asks, more angrily than she wants to.

"Yes," Odysseus says, his voice low to make sure others don't hear.

"Why would you suggest such a thing if you have to swear an oath yourself?" Penelope asks.

"Ah," Odysseus says. "But I am not swearing anything as a suitor. You see, Agamemnon is not the only clever man here." He stops because Clytemnestra snorts. "He *is* clever, as much as you hate him." When she shrugs, he goes on. "I have no wish to risk everything just to court one woman, especially when the world is full of them."

"So?" Clytemnestra frowns.

"So what?"

"What's in it for you? What do you gain by telling Tyndareus this?"

Odysseus grins, shaking his hands. They are ruined, fit to work in the fields, not the hands of a prince.

"I have asked Tyndareus for something in return, but he told me it was not his decision to make."

"Well, what is it?" Clytemnestra asks. She is getting impatient, as the line of heroes courting her sister is about to end. Idomeneus is now kneeling in front of Helen, his painted face almost touching the floor.

Odysseus steps closer, positioning himself between Clytemnestra and Penelope.

"It is you, Penelope," he says. As he says her name, his voice is warmer for a second, soft. "I wish to marry you."

Penelope stands silent. Her face has a stubborn look that Clytemnestra knows too well. "You wish to marry me, yet you came here to court another woman?"

Odysseus waves his hand casually. "I never intended to marry Helen. I did not even bring a gift and did not think I stood a chance. My land is barren and my property smaller than any of these kings'."

"Why come, then?"

Odysseus shrugs. "I wanted to see what everyone was talking about. But as you may have noticed, I am not interested in beauty, if it comes alone. I wish to marry you because you seem a clever woman."

Penelope stares straight ahead. "I will think about it, son of Laertes. But this is neither the right time nor the place. The suitors are done."

She is right. The room is silent again. Leda seems tired, Tyndareus agitated. Next to Helen is a high pile of gifts, bronze, gold, and painted amphorae glistening under the torches.

"You have all sworn," Tyndareus claims, standing. "Now, Helen, choose the man you desire as your husband."

Clytemnestra feels a flutter of panic in her chest, but Penelope's unflinching gaze reassures her. She has just taken a deep, calming breath when Helen speaks.

"I choose Menelaus, son of Atreus."

After that, everything is very quiet. Menelaus steps forward again, at the foot of Tyndareus's throne, a triumphant smile widening on his handsome face. Tyndareus rises from the high-backed chair and pats his new son-in-law on the shoulder while the other suitors stare, rage boiling beneath the skin. Clytemnestra watches them, angry figures thrumming with brutality. A sense of repulsion takes hold of her as she sees the men clench their fists and their teeth. They have the look of predators when another takes their meat right before their eyes.

"Silly girl," Clytemnestra hears Odysseus say quietly. For once, he doesn't seem amused. Penelope is gaping at Helen, incredulous. Clytemnestra has never seen her so shocked.

"Thank you for your many gifts, kings and princes," Tyndareus says. "Sparta will not forget them."

Kings can recognize a dismissal. One by one, they walk away, emptying the hall of its violence, until only fear remains. Clytemnestra turns to watch Helen, though the sight causes her unbearable pain. She is pale, like someone who has taken poison and is waiting for death.

Menelaus walks to her, beside the frescoed hunters and their dying prey, and takes her hand. Feeling an old instinct stuck to life, Clytemnestra almost wants to step forward, but her father and Agamemnon are staring at her, so she wipes all expression from her face and walks away, past the hearth and the columns, the painted swans and deer. Out of the hall, she casts a glance over her shoulder, but Agamemnon has already closed the door behind them. Her sister is beyond her help now.

10

Sweat and Blood

WEEKS PASS AND the winter ice melts. The air smells of the earth as kings and princes leave the palace of Sparta, and the sun grows warmer. Philoctetes and Machaon are the last to ride away, their donkeys swaying under the weight of bread, cheese wheels, and other food supplies.

The suitors leave, but Odysseus and the Atreidai remain. The son of Laertes spends much time with Penelope and Clytemnestra, wandering around the palace, laughing and telling stories. He doesn't press Penelope about the marriage, and she doesn't give him any answer. But she studies him, her gentle eyes always on him, never missing a move.

When they walk to the edge of the forest, Odysseus shows them which plants have moist roots and which berries are venomous. When they visit the craftsmen's workshops and stores around the palace, he teaches them carpentry, which he enjoys at home in Ithaca. He tells them everything about goat's milk, cheese, and butter, how to make and store it. Penelope listens eagerly and Clytemnestra relaxes, thinking of her husband and his wonderful myths. Odysseus and Tantalus tell different tales, but they both speak clearly and passionately, and they have the gift of making interesting to others whatever delights them.

For a few weeks, the three are inseparable. They collect wood for fires as the sun sinks beyond the mountains and the rooms of the palace grow cold. They touch Clytemnestra's belly and speak to it, telling her child stories while she feels him kicking softly, eager to participate.

Her stomach has grown so large it is difficult to sleep. She spends the nights staring at the cold moon, thinking about her baby. She imagines dark hair and ocean eyes like his father's and a voice so sweet it makes her heart melt. Tantalus must be on his brightly painted ship by now, coming to take them with him. Each night she waits, and each morning she goes to the *megaron* to see if messengers have brought any news.

She knows Helen is always watching her. When her sister is not caring for Phoebe and Philonoe, she follows Menelaus around the palace, a sad expression on her face. Sometimes she lingers by the terrace and stares at Clytemnestra, Penelope, and Odysseus from afar as they walk by the river, holding each other's hands and trying not to slip on the muddy banks. Clytemnestra wonders if she thinks them happy.

♛

She is cutting salted meat in the dining hall when Timandra enters. Penelope is resting, and Odysseus has gone hunting with Tyndareus, Agamemnon, and Menelaus. Apart from a servant boy dusting the weapons that hang on the walls, she is alone. When she hears her sister, Clytemnestra turns. Timandra's features are changing. Her chest is still flat and her hips narrow, but her face is leaner, her dark eyes bigger. "You look different," Clytemnestra says, smiling.

Timandra frowns. "How?"

"Older. Prettier."

Timandra flushes. She fixes the animal fur around her shoulders. "I won a match today," she says, her voice strangely expressionless.

"Good," Clytemnestra says, then notices that Timandra isn't smiling. "What is it?"

"I had to fight my friend. Father forced me to do it." Her voice cracks. Clytemnestra remembers the girl with curly black hair, her lips on her sister's. "We were always a team before," Timandra adds.

Clytemnestra casts a glance at the servant boy. He seems buried deep in his work and uninterested in the girls' conversation.

"Is your friend hurt?" she asks quietly.

Timandra looks down and her brown hair falls around her face, covering her shame. "Yes. I had to."

"I understand. Did you hurt her so that Father would think you do not like her?"

Timandra nods. When she looks up, her eyes are as dark as a well.

"You should go to her," Clytemnestra says. "You should go now. I will cover for you."

Timandra falters a little. "But you know it is not right."

"I don't know what is wrong and what is right. How could I? We are young. But if you want to go to her, then go. Do it while you still can. You know you will have to marry one day."

Timandra nods sadly. "If Father learns of this, he will punish me."

"He will. So ask yourself, is it worth it?"

"Yes." Timandra speaks with no hesitation, her voice bold, eyes wide.

Clytemnestra smiles. "What is her name? Your friend."

"Chrysanthe," Timandra says, and her gaze sweetens suddenly, like a peach under the sun. *Golden flower*, the name means.

"It is beautiful," Clytemnestra says. "Now hurry."

Timandra is out of the hall in a flash, silent and quick as a breath of wind. Clytemnestra resumes eating, thinking of the curly-haired girl, Timandra punching her on the wrestling ground. She can see her sister's fierceness—she is among the strongest warriors of her age—and Chrysanthe's helplessness, Timandra's anger and Chrysanthe's pain. The images taste of sorrow. This is the life she has always known: an endless chain of brutality, with strength, pride, and beauty only bursting from the blood that someone else has spilled—nothing precious can ever blossom on a barren earth. Maybe that is why she chose Tantalus. His world seems much more hopeful than what she has always been forced to believe. And if everything he told her about Maeonia is true, her baby won't have to be beaten to learn, to be whipped if he disobeys.

The servant boy is done with the cleaning. He bows to Clytemnestra as he leaves. She stands to follow him, but Odysseus is by the door, leaning against the jamb. There are fresh cuts on his face, and he is still holding his hunting blade.

"I thought I'd find you here," he says.

"Is the hunt over already?"

He shrugs. "We killed a small boar. I brought it back. The others wanted to go on hunting, but a storm is coming. Soon they will be drenched and the forest will be a mud lake." He comes to the table and sits. Clytemnestra looks outside, and sure enough, the sky is gray and the air already smells of rain.

"Do you want to wake Penelope?" she asks.

"No. I wish to speak to you alone." He gives her his handsome smile, and his gray eyes twinkle.

"Speak, then."

"Your sister Timandra has interesting tastes," he says.

Clytemnestra pours herself some wine. "Like everyone else."

"I don't think so, no."

Clytemnestra stares at him. It is useless to hide meanings in her words with Odysseus: best to cut straight to the point. That always bothers and amuses him. "You are right. She has interesting tastes. What do you care about it?"

"I don't, really. I just think she should be more careful. Other men wouldn't approve."

"And do you approve?"

He sits back in his chair, leaning on the carved arm. "Young men often lie with their companions," he says. "Why shouldn't women do the same?"

"I agree. But surely you have not come here to talk about Timandra?"

"No." He sighs. He watches her sip some wine, then says, "I have to go back to Ithaca before the spring rains. I am not happy to leave. I have enjoyed my time here." He takes a cup of wine for himself, then looks up at Clytemnestra with a weird expression. "Do you think Penelope will come?"

"Yes," she says. "I am sure she will."

He relaxes and his expression shifts back to the usual amusement. "Good… Maybe in another life, I would have married you," he adds carelessly.

She watches him, but his smile is impenetrable. "You wouldn't have been able to handle me," she says. "I am too fierce for you."

He laughs. "And your husband?"

"He likes the fire. He isn't afraid to burn." She says it lightly, with a smile, but she knows it is true. Odysseus strikes her as a man who is fascinated by fierceness but also repulsed. He values himself too highly to come close to anything that might harm him.

He passes a hand through his hair. "I wish I could have met him."

"You would have liked him."

"I know I would." He stands, rubbing the cuts on his face. "I will wake Penelope before those brutes come back from the hunt." She smiles. He knows how funny his stories about his fellow soldiers are. He comes closer to fix one strand of hair behind her ear, then walks out of the hall.

The sun is rising to the east, and in a matter of days, the winds will ripen into spring rains. Clytemnestra and Penelope sit on a large rock at the edge of the forest, watching the river in front and the mountains behind them. Helots are already at work in the fields, their hands crusted and their backs bent under the weight of large baskets.

"Odysseus came to talk to me yesterday," Clytemnestra says.

"He did?" Penelope asks. Her soft brown hair is plaited, and she has dark circles under her eyes. Last night they slept together, and Clytemnestra felt her stirring beside her in the bed, restless.

"He will leave soon," she says. "Will you go to Ithaca?"

Penelope keeps silent for a while, clasping her hands to her chest as if to hold her heart. After what feels like a long time, she says, "I will go, yes."

"But something is holding you back," Clytemnestra says.

Penelope hugs her knees, drawing her cloak around her legs as birds do with their wings when resting. "Remember when I told you that Odysseus reminds me of your husband? Well, I still think that, only there is something darker about him, something slippery…" She stares at the rocks on the ground, lost in thought.

"I know what you mean," Clytemnestra says. "It is like trying to catch the leaves when the wind makes them dance. One moment you have them, and the next they fly away."

Penelope laughs. "We used to do that years ago, remember? Running around the plain, flying leaves all around us."

Clytemnestra nods, smiling. She would always catch the most leaves, but Penelope would grab the beautiful ones, bright red and pale orange.

"But yes," Penelope says, "Odysseus is like that. He is a man with secrets."

"And yet you like him."

"Very much." Penelope's face is luminous. "My father used to tease me and say that I would marry some forgotten king on a forgotten island."

Clytemnestra nudges her. "Well, you are."

Penelope laughs. "Who knows about Ithaca? Who will remember Odysseus?"

"Probably no one. The clever ones are always forgotten."

"That is why there will be no songs about you and me but plenty about Diomedes the brute."

They laugh together while the wind starts to smell like spring, and life goes on around them, undisturbed.

Clytemnestra sits alone in the *mousike* room, looking at the flutes and lyres in the baskets lining the wall. The space is small with a low ceiling, the walls covered with chalked drawings—images they used to draw as children. There are Helen's lyres and Clytemnestra's lynxes, Castor's spears and Timandra's dogs. In one corner of the wall, a noble girl has scribbled *Polydeuces is handsome like Apollo.*

"Your brother sounds like a charmer."

Odysseus appears at the door. He moves like a cat, so that even she, who is trained to listen for the slightest sounds, never hears him coming.

She takes an *aulos*, the double-reeded flute, Polydeuces's favorite. "Do you play?" she asks.

"Yes," he says. "Though I can't say I have that kind of talent." He takes the flute from her hands. "Ah, this is beautiful. Libyan lotus plant? It's so light." He looks at her with a smile. "I imagine Helen was the most gifted in this class."

She smiles back. "I was gifted too."

He holds up his hands. "Of course."

There is a moment of awkward silence in which he puts the *aulos* in the basket and leans back against the wall. Then, "I must say, Helen doesn't have much luck with men. I have heard how she suffered with Theseus...poor girl." He shakes his head, mortified.

"That was different. She chose Menelaus," Clytemnestra replies.

He tilts his head. "Did she really have that choice? In my experience, some men—kings and heroes, men loved by the gods—always get what they want. Call it power, obstinacy, or simply unwillingness to accept failure."

"You got what you wanted too," she says. "You will marry Penelope."

He stares at her as if confused to be compared to powerful men. He hides it quickly and leans forward until his face is only a breath away from her ear. "I am not the only one who has made a deal with Tyndareus."

She steps back. "Who else?"

"I know nothing for sure, but keep an eye on Menelaus."

"Menelaus already has Mycenae and Helen. What else does he want?"

"As I said, I know nothing for sure, but you have grown up in

Sparta. You know what it means to look out constantly for danger as if you were surrounded by wolves." He winks, as he often does before leaving. "In that, you and I are alike."

Odysseus's warning follows her like a snake, creeping behind her, showing its fangs whenever she turns. She cannot pretend it isn't there.

One afternoon, when Penelope is resting, Clytemnestra ventures to the far end of the guests' quarters, where she knows Menelaus shares a room with Helen. There is no one around and she moves slowly, her belly vast and heavy. The walls are bare, the windows small, close to the roof. They spill little seeds of daylight and long shadows. This place once felt to her like a dungeon. Tantalus must have thought the same when he first came here, because his room is at the opposite end of the guests' quarters, close to the *megaron* and its beautifully lit corridors.

Two voices float from the end of the hall, and Clytemnestra creeps closer, her bare feet careful as if on a road of pebbles. She stops outside the door, her breath held.

"I heard your cousin will marry the son of Laertes."

"I have heard so too." Helen's voice is soft and shy compared to Menelaus's, like a bee-eater's call after a hawk's. "I think they will be happy. They are quite alike."

"Have you spoken to her?"

A small, delicate moment of silence. Clytemnestra can almost feel Helen's sadness.

"No," she says.

There is a clinking sound, as if Menelaus is playing with a knife. "Her looks aren't pleasing," he says, "but she is gentle, though my brother believes she is crafty."

"He is right," Helen says. "Penelope is clever."

Menelaus scoffs, and for a while, there is silence. Clytemnestra imagines his lips on her sister's, his hands on her shoulders. She feels sick.

"What were you discussing with Tyndareus?" Helen asks. She sounds scared, and Clytemnestra hears her effort in trying to steady her voice. "You were in the *megaron* for a long time."

Helen gasps and Clytemnestra moves slightly, peeping. She sees Menelaus step forward while Helen steps back. The movement is elegant, like a wave, but there is danger in it. It seems as if he could hit her, but he doesn't. He takes her small hand into his and says, "You are always asking about things that don't concern you, Helen."

She bites her lip and says nothing. Menelaus watches his wife, then adds, "We were just speaking of Mycenae and of the gold we owe to Sparta. We made a pact with Tyndareus, and pacts must be respected."

Clytemnestra feels her body relaxing, her fear ebbing away. Odysseus's words fade, and all that remains is a noise in her head, a faint note of warning.

She feels the baby kick and takes a step back. Once, she would have walked into the room and shielded her sister. She would have protected Helen against anyone and anything. But now she can't.

She wanted this, she thinks bitterly. *She chose this man out of spite, and now she must have him.*

Penelope and Odysseus's departure a few days later leaves Clytemnestra alone once more. That night for dinner, they are joined by Cynisca, her father, Lysimachos, and a few other Spartan nobles. To avoid the empty place next to Agamemnon, Clytemnestra sits beside Helen, who looks up at her, surprised. She smells her sister's scent, honey, crocus, and almond from the trees that grow near the stables. They stare at each other for a moment. Then Menelaus takes her small white hand in his own, and Helen looks away. Clytemnestra feels colder where her sister's eyes touched her. She wonders why they haven't gone back to Mycenae yet.

The servants are bringing platters of onions and cheese, the smell trailing behind them, while Tyndareus talks about his last hunt. Cynisca often intervenes, boasting about her own hunts, looking at Agamemnon with a longing that disgusts Clytemnestra. Helen barely touches her food.

"So the son of Laertes is traveling with your niece?" Lysimachos asks Tyndareus.

"He is," Tyndareus answers.

"That seems a good match," Agamemnon says.

"You like Odysseus?" Cynisca asks him, sipping her wine.

Agamemnon doesn't blink. "I don't like him. I respect him. He is clever."

"Some say he is the cleverest man alive, a man of endless tricks," Leda says.

"Tricks don't make heroes," Menelaus says.

Clytemnestra scoffs and turns to her cheese. She is ready to retort if anyone insults Odysseus again, but her father changes the subject.

"What news from the East?"

"Not much," Agamemnon says. "The city of Troy still challenges the Greeks at sea, but no one will fight it."

"Many say the city is impenetrable," Leda comments.

"Where is Troy, Mother?" Philonoe asks, her voice shrill in the hall.

It is Agamemnon who answers. "On the other side of the Aegean Sea. Farther north than Maeonia"—he turns to Clytemnestra quickly—"where your sister's husband lives."

"Farther than Lesbos even," Leda adds, and Philonoe nods, going back to her onions, which she selects one by one and savors like sweets.

"No city is impenetrable," Agamemnon says. "If the Greeks united their armies and fought together, Troy would fall."

Lysimachos scoffs. Spartans don't fight others' wars. "That seems unlikely."

Something flickers in Agamemnon's eyes, but he speaks no more of it.

When the moon appears in the sky, Tyndareus calls for entertainment. Wooden blocks are set on one side of the hall for guests to throw knives at. Tantalus has told Clytemnestra that in Maconia, such distractions are common. Whenever he holds a feast in his halls, there are musicians who play lyres, jugglers, and dancers. Acrobats and exotic animals are among his favorite performers. Once, a striped hyena—Clytemnestra had never heard of it—had escaped its trainer and roamed in the palace before it was caught. Tantalus described the hyena's cry, which sounded like cackling laughter, and the two of them started laughing together.

Cynisca stands, knife in hand, still stained with meat fat. She throws it at the block, and when it sinks close to the center, everyone applauds. Leda urges Phoebe and Philonoe to try, and Agamemnon gives them suggestions. Clytemnestra looks away. She focuses on a small dog eating the leftovers at her father's feet. He swallows quickly, avidly, and when he is done, he looks up to the table for some more.

He is not so different from the men, she thinks. Their faces are shiny and hungry under the light of the lamps, their shadows sharp. They keep throwing their knives, fighting for food and wine, as servants clatter back and forth on the floor, which is sticky with spilled juice and fat.

Clytemnestra stands and excuses herself. She moves through the hall, eager to escape, just as Agamemnon throws his dagger. It hits the wooden block right at the center.

In her room, Clytemnestra stares at the ceiling, remembering when she and Helen talked of the stars twinkling in the sky and the gods watching over them.

"Do you think they see us now?" Helen always asked.

"No," Clytemnestra said. "They are too busy watching others. How could they watch everyone at the same time?"

For the first time in weeks, she falls asleep lulled by such thoughts.

It starts with pain, as if someone were cutting her open with a sharp blade. Clytemnestra wakes up and falls off the bed, gasping. There is no blade. Out of the fur blankets, it is cold. A shy light is waking in the east; it must be dawn. She tries to stand but the pain returns, stronger than before. The baby is ready to be born. She tries to call for help, but no sound comes. Her hands are clutched; her breath seems gone. She kneels, then stands, gritting her teeth, trying to focus on other times she has felt a pain as severe: when she fell down a ravine, tearing her shoulder; when Castor had woken a bear during a hunting trip and she had jumped into a thorn bush while running away; when a girl had stuck a spear blade above her hip in the gymnasium; when the lynx's claws scratched her back.

She manages to stumble out of the bedroom and onto the main corridor of the *gynaeceum*. She catches her breath when the next pain comes and hurries to her mother's room. It is cold and she is wearing only a thin tunic, but sweat pours down her forehead. *Breathe.* She bumps into someone on her way to Leda's quarters and raises her eyes. It is Helen.

"What is it?" Helen asks, preoccupied. She is pale and her eyes are red, as though she has been crying.

"The baby is coming," Clytemnestra whispers, her voice strangled. She leans against the wall because the pain is worse.

Helen's eyes open wide. "I will call Mother…"

Clytemnestra shakes her head. "Take me to the midwives. It is coming now." She makes a rasping sound when another pain makes her hunch over. Helen lets her sister lean against her and drags her to the kitchen. Clytemnestra feels her sister's cold skin against her own, the smell of fruit and oil coming off her.

"Does it hurt too much?" Helen asks. They are almost running now, Clytemnestra breathing hard and holding Helen's arm tightly.

"I have felt worse," Clytemnestra manages, and her sister gives her a feeble smile.

Downstairs, near the servants' rooms, there is no light. Helen takes a torch and storms into the empty kitchen. "Where are the women? Where are the midwives?" she cries. There is no one. "Wait here," she tells Clytemnestra and hurries out of the room.

Clytemnestra falls onto a chair, screaming. Putting a hand between her thighs, she feels dampness.

A woman hurries into the room, her black hair tied back. "It is all right," she says. "Your sister has gone to call your mother and the elders. Your husband is also coming."

"Tantalus," Clytemnestra croaks.

"His ship arrived in the port last night. He is riding to the palace now." The woman makes her squat and tells her to breathe. In and out, in and out.

Tantalus is coming, Clytemnestra thinks. *He is almost here.* She stares at the ceiling, at the sacks of wheat piled in the corner, at the midwife's pale face. The pain reaches its peak. Clytemnestra shouts and overturns a table. Berries and reeds roll on the floor around them.

"I can feel its head," the woman calls, and suddenly there are more people in the room: Helen, Timandra, and her mother.

Leda crouches next to Clytemnestra and holds her hand. "It is almost done, Clytemnestra. Push hard now—*push!*"

She pushes and screams, sweating. The midwife is praying to Eileithyia, goddess of childbirth, but Leda shouts angrily, "Help her! You can pray later."

Clytemnestra's breath catches in her throat. She makes a choking sound and then she sees it. Her baby.

"It's a boy!" The midwife is holding it in her white hands, a fragile lump of mucus and blood.

"Give him to me," Clytemnestra orders, shuddering, exhausted. The woman takes a clean kitchen knife and cuts the cord. Then she hands the baby to his mother. Clytemnestra feels the wetness, the softness. She looks at the minuscule hands, each as perfect as a petal, at the head that fits into her palm. She stares at her son, and feeling her presence, he opens his eyes, light and blue as the morning sky.

11

Nightingale

HER SON AND Tantalus: there is nothing else.

Outside, spring awakens. The plain grows greener, and the trees share the first buds, soft and frail. The days are longer, the sun warmer. Snakes and lizards come out of their holes, resting and sunbathing on the dark brown earth. The midwives gut the fish and hang them up outside to dry while servants wash skins and tunics in the river.

Inside, the baby cries and screams, screams and cries. He never sleeps. Clytemnestra complains and Tantalus laughs.

"What did you expect?" He smiles. "*You* never sleep." He is making a sling to carry the baby, his warm, long fingers expertly tying together pieces of leather. How handsome her husband is. She rests her head on his shoulder, the baby in her lap.

Clytemnestra has noticed that the baby sleeps better with his father. She sings and hums to him, she gives him Leda's soothing herbs, but the baby stares back at her, delighted and a bit defiant, his tiny hands reaching for her face. And when he gets tired, he cries. But when Tantalus rocks him, when he kisses him, he relaxes.

The elders welcomed him soon after he was born. They took him naked as he was and brought him to Mount Taygetus. The baby kicked and wailed but he was safe. Safe because he was healthy. The elders checked him and found him perfect, strong.

She walks for hours, carrying him in her arms. He is a curious child. She shows him flowers, takes each petal and holds it to his face. Crocuses, laurel, lilies, anemones. She tells him stories about them. The Phoenician princess Europa was lured into Zeus's arms when he breathed a crocus from his mouth; the nymph Daphne turned into a laurel tree to hide from Apollo, who desired her; the goddess Persephone was abducted by Hades, king of the underworld, while picking lilies in a meadow. The baby likes the anemones most, so Clytemnestra tells him of Adonis slain by a boar and Aphrodite who loved him, remembering when she and Tantalus spoke of the myth on their first night together.

Leda loves the baby very much. She takes him in her arms when Clytemnestra is too tired and lets him play with her earrings, shiny miracles in his eyes. She becomes the woman she was when Phoebe and Philonoe were born, when she would spend her days singing and talking to them, their small heads in her hands. It is a joy for Clytemnestra to see her mother like this, to see the softness behind the strength, the eyes shining with purpose.

When Timandra touches the baby's feet, Leda whispers, "Be careful. Babies are fragile."

When Clytemnestra has fed him, Leda tucks him in a blanket and traces his tiny features with her finger: eyes, nose, lips, ears.

Tantalus starts planning their trip to Maeonia. He sends a messenger to the port to carry the news to the other side of the Aegean Sea. An heir is born and the king is ready to return, the queen at his side.

She is sitting in a corner of the town square, lulling the baby under the shade of an oak. She has escaped the dining hall in an effort to avoid

Agamemnon and Menelaus; she doesn't like the way they glance at the baby, with a mixture of coldness and distaste. Sometimes it looks almost like pity.

"We are leaving soon," she tells him, and he opens his eyes wide, smiling. "We are going to your father's land."

It is quiet here. Two young women are passing, jugs filled with water on their shoulders, a dog following them, licking their ankles. A man is gathering baskets of olives and onions outside his door. The smells dance in the air, filling the square, and a child peeps out a window, a hungry look on his face.

Clytemnestra lifts her eyes. Helen is walking toward the square, stepping slowly in her direction as if she's nervous to approach her. When she is close enough, she pulls her mantle back and comes under the tree. Silence stretches between them until the baby coos, and Helen smiles. "He looks like you," she says.

"He reminds me of his father."

"He has Tantalus's eyes and hair," Helen concedes, "but the way he looks around, that is you."

Clytemnestra savors the warmth of her sister's words, like a bite of a sweet apple. Across the square, the man counts the olives in his basket, and a boy comes to sit on the ground next to him in the warm sunlight. On the roof of the house, two girls are singing, playing with mud.

"I talked to Mother," Helen says, looking at the girls. "She told me she kept my father a secret so that Tyndareus wouldn't send me away."

"I am glad you spoke to her," Clytemnestra says. She is reminded of Castor's words when they were little. *When the tide recedes and leaves something on the sand, one mustn't worry. Sooner or later, the water will climb again and take it back.*

"You protected me," Helen says.

"What else have I been doing since you were born?" Clytemnestra jokes. Helen laughs, and the girls on the roof stop singing and look at them, curious. Clytemnestra wants to talk to her sister about the life that awaits her in Maeonia, yet she can see a small shadow on Helen's face.

"I was just…" Helen stops, searching for the right words. "We never held secrets between us before."

Clytemnestra smiles. "Everyone has secrets."

Helen blushes, looks down. "I kept no secrets from you."

For a moment, Clytemnestra sees Helen as a child, blond hair falling around her shoulders, a cascade of gold, tiny hands stained with apricot juice. "We're like two halves of an apricot," Helen had told her, holding the fruit out for her. "See? We share the kernel, and in it we hide our secrets."

Clytemnestra rests her head against the oak, the baby's skin soft under her hand. As a child, she refused to see it, but now it is as clear as a mountain stream: they will never be the same. And maybe that is not such a shameful thing.

"What should we call him?" Tantalus asks. They are sitting on the terrace, the baby resting on Clytemnestra's thighs, the sun gentle on their skin. Birds scatter in the sky, and the baby follows them with his big eyes.

"Let us wait until we get to Maeonia," she says. "Let us wait until he meets his home."

A tiny brown nightingale flies to the terrace and starts singing. The baby giggles. He is staring at the little bird.

"That is a nightingale," she whispers to him. "He sings for all those who do not have a voice."

The baby smiles and reaches out to it, but the nightingale flies away.

In the night, there is a storm. They hear thunder and raindrops beating on the roof. Clytemnestra holds the baby close to her heart, though he isn't crying. He listens, eyes wide open, staring at the darkness of the sky.

"Is something troubling you?" Tantalus asks her.

She turns to him, rocking the baby gently. "Yes."

"Are you going to tell me?"

She waits for a roll of thunder to pass, then says, "I wish I could see my brothers one more time before leaving."

"They will come to visit us. And you will be able to come back here."

There is a knock on the door, so quiet she almost thinks she has imagined it.

"Did you hear that?" Tantalus asks.

She nods. They wait until they hear another knock, as quiet as the first.

Tantalus stands, frowning. "Who can it be? It is not dawn yet."

He opens the door. A woman is on the other side. In the darkness of the corridor, it takes them a moment to recognize Helen, shivering in her nightgown, her golden hair loose around her shoulders. She isn't carrying a torch.

"Helen?" Tantalus says, but she jumps forward and puts a hand to his mouth. She hurries inside and closes the door behind her quickly.

Clytemnestra sits up on the bed. "What has happened?"

Helen walks closer to her. Her gown has only one strap, and her left breast is visible, white in the feeble light. "I needed to speak with you." Her voice is drenched with fear. Clytemnestra gives the baby to Tantalus, who rocks him.

"Please, don't let him cry," Helen says.

Tantalus nods. "Where is Menelaus? Does he know you are here?"

"My husband is sleeping," Helen replies. Her words are rushed, one whisper following the next. "He must not wake."

Clytemnestra takes her sister's chin in her hand and forces her to look up, straight into her eyes. "What has he done?" she asks.

Helen turns, showing a small bruise on her neck. "It is nothing," she says when Clytemnestra opens her mouth to speak. "This is not why I am here."

"Why?" Clytemnestra says. Anger is taking hold of her, and as always, she can do nothing to stop it. "Why did he do it?"

"He does it when he is angry, to threaten others." Her tone is matter-of-fact. "But this time I heard him. I was meant to be asleep and he was outside our chamber, speaking to Agamemnon. They said, 'It is time. We must do it now before it is too late.'"

"What did they mean?" Tantalus asks.

"Please, we have to be quiet. I don't know. But this isn't the first time they've talked about it. Tyndareus must be involved too. They speak to him often in the *megaron*, in private."

"They have taken Mycenae with his help. They are bound by a pact," Tantalus observes, but Helen shakes her head.

"This is something else. I have tried to spy on them… But they mentioned you, Tantalus, then said, 'We have to be careful even if Tyndareus approves.'"

"What is this?" Clytemnestra stands, agitated. She walks back and forth a few times, Helen staring at her. "Is this the first time he has hit you?"

"I am not afraid of him. This time he hurt me only because he caught me listening. I…" Helen stops and her eyes fill with tears. "I made a mistake in marrying him. I was wrong." Tears streak her face, like rivers flooding a plain. She covers her face with her hands, shaking silently.

"He will not touch you," Clytemnestra spits out. "Do you understand? I will make sure he doesn't touch you again."

Helen falls to the floor, sobbing at Clytemnestra's feet. "And now you are leaving, and I deserve it. I deserve everything. I married him only because I was a fool… I was jealous of you… And Tyndareus told me to do it. When Penelope came to speak to me, to convince me, Tyndareus told me she was just jealous…"

The baby cries softly. Tantalus quiets him. "You must not be sorry, Helen," he says. "What is done is done."

"I will protect you," Clytemnestra says. "I will speak to them. I will end this." She draws her sister to her, and Helen curls into her arms. She weeps silently, and when she is spent, she wipes her face and stands up.

"I have to go now, or he will notice."

Clytemnestra hurries between her and the door. "You can't."

"I must." Helen gives her a sad smile, her cheeks glistening with tears. "He won't hurt me. He is sleeping."

She rushes out of the room and fades into the darkness of the corridor.

When Tantalus has fallen asleep, the baby bundled in his arms, Clytemnestra goes to the window. The raindrops are hitting the earth as musicians' hands beat the tympanon, the rhythm like a song for gods.

No one has ever hurt her sister without paying the consequences. It is strange that she, Clytemnestra, is so used to pain that it doesn't bother her, as long as it isn't Helen's. Why can she bear her own so well yet can't accept her sister's? It must be because she believes Helen can't take it. She imagines Menelaus raising a hand to her sister and Helen covering herself, like a bird hides under its wings. The thought spreads and festers until she can no longer breathe and her entire body is clenched like a fist.

Helen is lost in a game too powerful for her. But these lies and secrets, these threats and games must stop. I will stop them.

12

The Bird with Crushed Wings

CLYTEMNESTRA WAKES WHEN the sun is already high in the sky, a sense of purpose tightening her body. After the storm, the air is cool and the day bright. She wears a light-brown tunic and ties back her hair. Tantalus and the baby are sleeping together on the other side of the bed. Her family. She shakes her husband gently, and when he opens his turquoise eyes, she whispers, "Stay with the baby today."

"Where are you going?" He frowns, suddenly alert. "Do not do anything stupid, Clytemnestra."

She smiles and turns back to give him one last kiss. "Don't worry about me. Look after our baby."

She walks in the semideserted corridors, her bare feet silent on the stone floor. She passes two older servants carrying dead chickens, and Cynisca, who hurries in the opposite direction without a word. She can hear the loud chatter of the women coming from the village, the pleading of a family trying to enter the *megaron* to speak to the king. She ignores it all and keeps moving, past the baths and narrow storerooms, down a large corridor that leads to the dining hall.

She thought about it last night while she was staring at the ceiling, wide awake and restless. At first, she wanted to talk to Menelaus, but then she understood it would be the wrong move. It is no use to clean an infected wound on the surface if a splinter remains inside, festering. You must cut through the skin and remove it before it cor-rupts everything else. And Menelaus is no splinter: he merely does what his brother tells him to. She must deal with Agamemnon.

She finds him in the dining hall, alone, the light spilling softly from the windows onto his tall figure. He is sitting at the head of the table, her father's seat, sipping red wine from a painted jug. As she walks toward him, he looks up at her. If he is surprised to see her, he doesn't show it. She remains standing, quiet, and for a moment, a feeling comes over her, the need to run back to her baby and keep him safe. But she has never run away from confrontation.

"You have something to say to me," Agamemnon points out, half smiling. Smiles don't look good on his hard face. "What is it?"

"Your brother hurt my sister." Her words are flat, as she has heard her father speak so many times when facing an opponent. "He won't do it again, or he will pay."

He seems amused and picks up some grapes left on the table. "What my brother does to your sister shouldn't concern you. She is his now." He puts them into his mouth.

She looks at the blade he keeps at his waist. "No, she isn't."

"Your father says you can be difficult from time to time. That you do not know your place." The words jar her. Why would her father say such a thing to Agamemnon? He stares at her, coldness in his eyes. "I expect your foreign husband likes that. But that is not how women speak to kings here."

Clytemnestra takes the grapes from his hands and throws them onto the floor. They splatter, purple juice staining the walls. *Let him learn that I speak as I choose.*

"If I see another bruise on my sister's body," Clytemnestra says, her voice shaking with rage, "I will kill and gut you like dead fish."

Agamemnon stares at the juice on the floor. In a second, he grabs his blade with one hand and Clytemnestra with the other, shoving her onto the table. She feels the coolness of the knife against her neck, the overturned jug against her shoulders, wine pouring onto the table, wetting her hair.

She bites his hand. Warm blood trickles through her teeth. He doesn't let her go, so she kicks him in the groin. He steps back and she stands, pushing him to the floor. He doesn't fall but swings, the knife tight in his hand. Clytemnestra grabs the overturned jug and throws it at him. He bends, dodges it. They stare at each other. Then he looks down at his bleeding hand as though the arm didn't belong to him. The sight makes him laugh. She jumps toward him, but he is quicker and grabs her by the neck, choking her.

"You must learn your place among men, Clytemnestra," he says. His words are whips, slashing at her hurting throat. "You are too proud, too arrogant."

She feels her face become purple, air leaving her lungs. "You are the same," she croaks, "if you kill me."

He drops her. She hits the floor, like a dead animal after a sacrifice.

"Kill you?" Agamemnon says. "I never wanted to kill you." He comes closer, kneels beside her. Clytemnestra makes an inarticulate noise, clutching at her throat. She tries to move, but he pushes her back. "Stay down, Clytemnestra. Learn your place."

And he leaves her on the floor, alone but alive in the high-roofed hall.

Maybe I should cut myself and pretend I've been beaten, Timandra thinks. *So Father won't be suspicious when I go back to the palace.*

She is lying on the wet earth of the town garden. Ants pass around her in endless lines, and she can smell the fig and almond trees, their branches thick above her. The silence is delicate, disturbed only by the fluttering of wings and the rhythmic breathing of Chrysanthe next to her. She turns. Chrysanthe is staring at the sky. There is a scar on her shoulder where Timandra cut her during training, and some of her fingers are still broken. She shifts, and her black curls tickle Timandra's shoulder. Desire floods Timandra's heart, as powerful as a swollen river.

"Is your sister covering for us again?" Chrysanthe asks.

"Not today," Timandra replies. "She has to care for the baby."

"Can't servants do it for her?"

Timandra laughs. "That is not my sister. She would never put her child in someone else's arms, let alone a servant's."

"So no one is covering for us," Chrysanthe says.

Timandra caresses her face. Chrysanthe has very clear eyes, like snow-melt streams.

"Don't worry. Clytemnestra protects us. For as long as she is here, we are safe."

Chrysanthe opens her mouth to protest, but Timandra kisses her. They haven't kissed many times. Their lips are clumsy: they are too eager to taste each other. Chrysanthe leans forward and Timandra backward.

"I should go now," Timandra says. Pleasure still frightens her, because she isn't used to it.

"I will go first," Chrysanthe says. "It is better." She stands and races away among the plants and flowers of the garden, toward the square. Timandra rests a little in the shade. *Dear gods*, she thinks, *let me be with Chrysanthe forever*. If Clytemnestra approves, why can't everyone else? Sometimes it seems to her that every Spartan rule was made to keep her unhappy. Why does she have to marry a man? Why does she have to be taken with force after the marriage? Why does she have to be whipped if she doesn't obey? Why does she have to threaten others to make them listen? She spots a small snake hiding in a crack in the earth. It is time to go back. Her knees are muddy as usual, and her hair is full of twigs. She hops around the garden and takes the steep, narrow road back to the palace.

When she turns the first corner, she bumps into Cynisca. A dark tunic clings to her strong body, a veil covering her head. There is something threatening about her. Blood freezes in Timandra's veins. If Cynisca has seen her...

"Timandra," Cynisca says. Her voice is like Tyndareus's when he scolds her.

"Cynisca."

"You can't go back to the palace." Her tone is sharp, but her orders mean nothing to a princess.

"Leave me alone," Timandra says, walking past her. That is her mistake. She feels Cynisca move behind her, but when she turns, it is too late. Cynisca hits her head, and she falls to the ground. Her sight is blurred, her head pounding. She tries to move her arms, but a weight is keeping her down, crushing her fingers.

"It is for your own good," Cynisca adds, banging Timandra's head against a stone. Everything goes dark.

Helen opens her eyes, barely breathing. She was dreaming that she couldn't wake up. Someone was pinning her to the ground—she could feel cold stones under her back and hear a man's voice, laughing. "Stop fighting," he was telling her, and there was scorn in his tone, as though she were a lizard pinned to the earth, uselessly wriggling.

It was Theseus. She hasn't dreamed of him for a long time. Something bad is going to happen, she knows it. She pulls herself up shivering, touching her head where Theseus hit her in the dream.

Menelaus is dressing in a corner of the room. A servant is sitting on a stool at his feet, polishing his sandals. Helen stands quietly and her husband looks at her, as if annoyed that she is up.

"I will be gone all day," he says. He is wearing armor, Helen notices. She feels a tingling in her skin, urging her to run to Clytemnestra. She needs to tell her sister about the dream.

"You will wait here?" Menelaus asks. She didn't expect the question. He never asks about her. She hesitates for a moment too long.

"That was not a question, Helen," Menelaus says.

She grasps his hand, panic fluttering inside her. "I wanted to take some air. I am not feeling well."

Menelaus shakes his head. "You can't. You will have to wait here. Someone will bring you herbs to help you feel better." He goes to the door and she hurries behind him, almost knocking the servant down.

"Why can't I leave?" she asks, her voice drenched with fear.

Menelaus turns and pushes her back. "You need to be safe," he says. "The servant will keep you company." He opens the door and closes it quickly behind him. Helen lunges forward but the door doesn't open. He has locked it from the outside. She hits the wall with her hands, screaming.

"Open it! Let me out, Menelaus!"

She hears him mutter from the other side, "Be quiet, Helen, or the servant will make you." She turns just in time to see the helot boy advancing in her direction. She jumps away and grabs the knife Menelaus has left under his pillow.

"Stay away," she says. "You take no orders from him."

The helot backs down. "I have to make sure you stay here," he mutters. "I have to make sure you are safe, Princess."

Helen spits at him, then throws the table against the door. "LET ME OUT!"

"You are wanted in the *megaron*, my lord."

Tantalus turns and sees two young servants waiting for him by the door of the chamber. Their arms are covered with cuts and bruises, and in their eyes, there is a flicker of fear. Behind him, the baby whines. He hasn't been nursed yet this morning. Tantalus wraps him in a piece of light cloth and puts him in the sling he prepared earlier.

"Who calls for me?" he asks as he makes sure the baby is comfortable.

"The king."

Is it his impression, or was the servant's voice shaking slightly? Since the baby was born, he sees danger everywhere: bees flying around him, dogs roaming the palace, weapons hanging on the walls. It is the impression the palace of Sparta has made on him from the very beginning—a place of violence and danger.

The servants are staring at him, uneasy. There is desperation in their eyes, and Tantalus pities them. "I will come," he says.

He follows them around the winding corridors while the baby keeps whining. Tantalus hushes him. Halfway through, he realizes he has not brought any weapon with him, not even his small knife with glittering rubies, a gift from his late grandfather... He is being too fearful again. In front of him, the servants quicken their pace. Instead of turning right toward the *megaron,* they turn left in a windowless corridor, where a single torch is burning. He stops and takes a few steps back. At the opposite end of the corridor is Agamemnon.

"I thought you were bringing me to the king?" Tantalus asks.

"I am king," Agamemnon replies. "King of Mycenae."

The baby has become silent. He clutches the sling, his wide eyes as he stares around.

"Whatever you want to discuss, Agamemnon," Tantalus says, "we can do it somewhere else."

"Give your baby to the servant, foreigner," Agamemnon orders.

Something wrong is happening, Tantalus thinks. There are no guards around, no one he can call.

"Why should I?"

Agamemnon fingers the handle of his sword. Unlike Tantalus, he is carrying two knives and a long bronze blade. They say he is better trained than most Spartans, that he has defeated men much younger and stronger than him. They say he has crushed someone's skull with one hand.

"Give him to them," Agamemnon orders again. "I want to make this quick."

The servants move forward. Tantalus shoves them away—he is stronger than them after all. Holding the baby to his heart, he runs toward the *megaron*. Agamemnon's steps behind him are loud, heavy blows against the stones. There is an older woman near the entrance of the hall, the servant who always brings food inside. In desperation, Tantalus shoves the baby into her hands. "Take him and go! Run!"

The woman's mouth drops open, but she does as she is told. The baby starts crying. Tantalus turns to face Agamemnon. He is walking slowly toward him, a lion facing his cornered prey.

"Kill me," Tantalus says. "Do not harm the baby." He is aware of the woman hurrying away to his right. He hopes she will find Clytemnestra.

Agamemnon gives him a weak smile. "I cannot."

"Have you no mercy?"

Agamemnon takes a step forward, his long sword in his large hand.

"MURDER!" Tantalus shouts. "BETRAYAL—" The blade flies, bright and sharp, and slashes Tantalus. As he falls on his knees, his hands filled with his own blood, he thinks, *Where is Clytemnestra?*

Leda is drinking wine in the *megaron* when she hears a call for help. The doors of the main hall are thick and muffle even the loudest sounds, but the cry is high enough to reach her. Blood beats in her ears. She stands, dropping the cup. Wine spills on the floor. Before she can stumble forward, Tyndareus grabs her arm.

"Someone called for help," she says.

"Stay," Tyndareus says. He seems agitated, but his grip is firm. She shakes him off and runs out.

She is the first to see. Not far from the door, Tantalus is bleeding on the floor, a long cut slashing his body. Leda screams and walks closer. His eyes are empty, the color of the morning sky without clouds. He has a sling around his torso, but where is the baby? Leda looks around. There is something like a blood-stained bundle not far from Tantalus. Marpessa, the old helot who always brings food from the kitchen, is dead, her ragged tunic around her like a shell. And in her arms, Leda's grandson. Leda collapses next to them. *No. No, no, no, no.* She takes the baby and shakes him, but he is dead. A sudden thought comes to her, and she almost faints right there.

"Clytemnestra?" Her voice comes out as a whisper. "Where is she?"

"She is alive," a voice says.

Leda turns. Tyndareus is standing next to Agamemnon. A knowing look passes between them, like hunting dogs before they maul a deer. She runs to her husband and shouts with all the strength in her body, "WHERE IS MY DAUGHTER? WHAT HAVE YOU DONE?"

When Timandra opens her eyes, her face is full of blood and mud. She can barely breathe. She groans and rolls onto her back. The alleyway smells terrible. Onions and old bread crusts are rotting somewhere on her right. She cleans the mud from her mouth and nose. The blood comes from her head. She touches it, and pain makes her gasp. She finds the stone that Cynisca used to hit her and remembers. She needs to run back to the palace. Her hands sink into the mud and litter and her knees shake, but she manages to stand. Cynisca is nowhere in sight. There are voices far away, close to the square. Is anyone hurt? She stumbles onto the main street, stepping on rotten peaches. The light is blinding, but she follows the voices. People are gathering in the square, craning their necks. Some are whispering, agitated, others pushing and shoving. Timandra stops an old woman carrying a basket of bread. "What is it? Is anyone dead?"

The woman gives her a fearful look. "They say it's the princess's son. The Atreidai murdered him."

Timandra starts running. She can hardly stand and keeps bumping into the walls, blood trickling down her neck, but she doesn't stop. Tears stream down her cheeks and blind her. It is the first time she is frightened for someone else, not only for herself. The feeling makes her choke.

Helen has heard the first scream, then the second, and the third. She has kept her place on the stool, even when she was sure the voice was her mother's. Sounds echo around the corridors of the palace faintly, like the fluttering of bat wings in a cave. The servant boy is staring at her, waiting for a reaction. He doesn't know she has long learned to school her face to dullness. Only the gods know how she is crying inside.

She lets the hair loose on her back, twists her neck, as though easing back pain. She touches the pin of her dress and lets one strap fall. The servant blushes, his cheeks red as apples. He wants to look, but at the same time, he doesn't.

"Come," Helen orders. She keeps her voice sweet and quiet. The servant can only obey. He walks closer, staring at Helen's long neck, her breasts barely visible.

"Closer." She beckons. "I won't bite." She sinks her husband's knife into the servant's knee. He shouts but she silences him, her hand clasped on his mouth.

"What is happening outside?" she whispers. "What is Menelaus doing?" The servant shakes his head, and Helen shows him the blade. "Speak now."

"They were looking for the king of Maeonia and the baby."

Helen lets him go and he drops to the floor, holding his leg. She hides the knife in her dress and climbs out the window onto the adjacent terrace. She fixes her shoulder strap as she runs, corridor after corridor. At last, she arrives at the *megaron*.

She sees the whole thing in pieces. Her mother holding the dead baby. Tantalus's bloodied hands. Timandra, her face baked with mud, trying to hold her sister. Clytemnestra is mad, tearing her tunic apart. She is trying to grab a blade to slash her own throat. Helen jumps forward and joins Timandra. Clytemnestra cries and bites like a panther, but together, they manage to take her down, their beating hearts the only comfort to their sister.

13

The Atreidai's Wives

HER FEET ARE soaked in Tantalus's blood. She can smell it, the pain
that is filling the palace, permeating its walls. Clytemnestra knows
that the smell will never go away; it has entered too deep. Somewhere
buried under the odor of blood, the scent of her husband is fading.
She is losing him as she holds him tight, and the blood streaming from
his chest stains her tunic. She cries. All she can see is the scarlet cut
on Tantalus's body. A sweet voice is talking to her, far away. It must
be Helen's. She can barely hear it as his dead body is carried away
from her, like a puppet, broken and useless. She faints, overwhelmed
with pain, as Helen's voice, like a lullaby, guides her to a place of
nightmares.

For a long time, there is darkness. Her sister never leaves her, not even
when Clytemnestra pushes her away. Helen keeps talking to her about
the wind that can't bend the strongest trees, about the heroes who are
never forgotten, about bird songs carrying the word of the dead. She
keeps talking to Clytemnestra to remind her to stay in the world of
the living.

"Think of all the golden masks made for our heroes. The

goldsmiths will prepare one for Tantalus, as beautiful as his face, and under it he will sink into the most peaceful sleep," Helen says.

All Clytemnestra can think of is the image of Tantalus's body dragged through his own blood, the feel of his lifeless hands, too cold in her own. Agamemnon's stare as he cleaned her husband's blood from his sword. He knew he had broken her, but there was no regret on his face.

Her boy, dead in the arms of Leda. His little body was motionless, his turquoise eyes closed. Clytemnestra wanted to touch him, shake him, wrap herself around him. But arms held her, her sisters', keeping her away, rocking her.

Outside the windows, life goes on, its sounds scratching the sky like claws. Clouds form, then scatter. In the night, the stars twinkle and swim in the sorrowful sky. When Clytemnestra falls asleep, Helen lights the lamps and covers her sister with thick blankets.

Clytemnestra dreams about something that happened a long time before: when she was seven, she witnessed a fight in the gymnasium when a young boy's neck was broken by another Spartan, an accident. The boy was left in the burning sand, like a bird with crushed wings, until his mother came and cried to the gods. He died fighting, Tyndareus said.

Clytemnestra wakes from the dream, sweat and tears streaming down her face. "My boy didn't die fighting," she whispers.

Timandra brings her food, but Clytemnestra doesn't touch it. She is sitting by the window, listening to voices rise and fall from the village. The tears on her cheeks have dried and there is a coldness in her, grief freezing into anger.

"You should eat," Timandra says. Her voice is so soft it doesn't even sound like hers.

"She won't," Helen says from her corner of the room. "I have tried."

Clytemnestra's head sinks into her palms. She doesn't see the point in eating. She doesn't see the point in anything. Nothing she can do will bring back those she has lost.

Timandra steps forward cautiously. "Their bodies have been washed and burned," she says. "Their ashes are safe in the royal tomb. Together."

And there they will rot and be forgotten. The worst fate of all, to fade and wither into obscurity. Clytemnestra wanted to clean Tantalus's body, to dress him in his best tunic, but Tyndareus wouldn't let her out of her room. She feels something tearing under her skin as she thinks of another woman laying out her husband's body, touching him and mourning him. Was it her mother? Was it a servant?

"Agamemnon wasn't alone in planning this," Timandra says after a long pause.

Clytemnestra's head jerks up. She looks at her younger sister. "My own father betrayed me," Clytemnestra says. Helen stirs a little, surprised to hear it.

"He did," Timandra says. "But others supported Agamemnon. Some servants and Cynisca."

"Cynisca," Helen repeats, frowning.

"Yes." Timandra looks tentatively at Clytemnestra before going on. "She followed me in the street. She hit my head and left me unconscious so I wouldn't come to help."

Clytemnestra stands, her palms sweating. She takes the bowl of food and starts eating the bread, slowly. Timandra and Helen look at each other, torn between fear and relief.

"Why would Cynisca do such a thing?" Helen asks.

"She wants Agamemnon," Clytemnestra says before Timandra can speak.

"Yes," Timandra agrees. "I think he has promised her that he will take her to Mycenae with him."

"He would never do that," Helen points out, frowning. "Agamemnon will not settle for anyone less than a princess."

"Cynisca is among the Spartiates," Timandra says. "Her family is rich, her father a renowned warrior."

Helen shrugs. "Outside Sparta, no one cares who she is. Agamemnon will never marry her."

"I hope he will," Clytemnestra says quietly. "Monsters deserve each other." The bread tastes sour in her mouth. She waits a moment, then adds, "Do you know the servants who went to Tantalus and brought him to Agamemnon?"

Timandra nods.

"Good. Bring them to me."

The next morning, Clytemnestra pulls a mantle over her head and follows Timandra to the kitchen. It is still early, and the sun's fingers are cold and shy. The palace is strangely quiet, the corridors empty. Their steps echo softly, the sound floating in the dim light.

"Come back," Helen pleads, hurrying to match Clytemnestra's pace. "Let someone else do it." She has been running after her sisters all the way from the *gynaeceum*, grabbing Clytemnestra's arm, tears swimming in her eyes.

Clytemnestra shakes her away. "Keep guard outside," she orders. "Don't let Tyndareus come." *Or the Atreidai.*

Inside the kitchen, under the feeble light of a single lamp, two servants are kneeling by the sacks of barley, their hands and feet tied. They are staring at the stone floor, bare-chested, shivering. Timandra walks to them and kicks them. They look up, their dark eyes shiny, the skin stretched on their cheekbones. Their faces are already like skulls.

"Where are the women?" Clytemnestra asks. Almonds and nuts are scattered on the wooden table, as if left by someone in a hurry. Overripe apricots in a bowl smell sweet and rotten.

"Gone," Timandra says. Her fingers are tight around the handle of her bronze sword. "I made sure of that."

The servants are staring at her, pleading and fear on their faces. She can see the marks and blood crusts on their arms, and she wonders if Timandra beat them before she brought her here or if it was someone else.

"Tell my sister what you told me," Timandra orders, her voice empty of any warmth. "How you were with the king of Maeonia when he died." She looks strange in the shadows, unnerving.

Clytemnestra stands still. The hatred inside her is growing roots. She can see it on her sister's face, and something else beneath it, blistering. If her brother were here, Timandra wouldn't have to do this, but Castor is far across the sea, following some hero's quest.

"The king gave us the order," one servant whispers. His voice is broken, a croaking sound. "We had no choice."

She should pity them, she knows that, their existence made of orders and suffering, their lives like rafts pushed around by the waves. But it is easy to turn to the weakest when you are racked with pain, to hurt those who can't defend themselves when you are unable to hurt those who have hurt you. This is how the world works, raging gods forcing nymphs and humans into submission, heroes taking advantage of lesser men and women, kings and princes exploiting slaves.

Clytemnestra doesn't want to be like that. She is hateful, but she is not merciless. What good would it be to kick and hurt the helots further, to make their last moments insufferable? Let their deaths be quick.

She looks into her sister's angry eyes and nods. Timandra walks behind the servants, her blade in hand. The men are praying now, their words quick, like shadows shifting on water.

"The gods can't find you here," Clytemnestra says.

They have a moment to look up at her, their mouths open to plead, their hands clasped. Then Timandra cuts their throats.

In the evening, when darkness seems to envelop the valley like a dark ocean wave, Tyndareus sends for her. Rain is falling thickly, the wind thrashing and screeching. Soon the Eurotas will overflow and the riverbanks will be muddy for weeks.

"I will come with you," Helen says, closing the purple tunic on Clytemnestra's back with a golden pin. She has been pacing the bedroom all day, restless, cleaning every stain from Timandra's dress. There was crusted blood under her sister's fingernails, and Helen scrubbed them so hard she might have been trying to flay them.

"I will go alone," Clytemnestra says.

"Father must know it was me," Timandra says, frowning. "Why is he calling you?"

"Maybe he wants to ask for forgiveness," Helen says quietly.

Clytemnestra shakes her head. Her people don't know forgiveness. They know respect, greatness, beauty, the forces that shine like flames, brightening the earth. And next to them, like threatening shadows, shame, dishonor, vengeance, and *moira*, the unbreakable thread between guilt and punishment.

She takes her sisters' hands and feels their warmth. "Wait for me here."

She meets her father in the high-roofed hall, her steps echoing on the paving, her fists clenched. It is painful to see his face after all this time spent in her room. She feels as if she is facing a life that has been lost. The man seated on the throne in front of her now might be a stranger to her, not the father who taught her to walk, to fight, to rule. Next to him is Leda, her black tunic too large for her lean figure. Two-handled jars, wheat bread, and pork on skewers are spread on a large table in front of them. Clytemnestra can smell wine, olives, and fear.

Leda is the first to speak. "The dead helots in the kitchen." She stops to take a deep breath, as if at a loss for words. "Your sister killed them."

Clytemnestra ignores her, staring at Tyndareus. His face is cold, inscrutable. She searches for some hint of affection, some warmth, but his features are barren, like the earth in winter.

"You have made Timandra a murderess," Leda says. Her eyes are red—she must have been crying. "She is only fourteen."

She is a Spartan. If I have made her a murderess, then what of Father, who ordered her to break Chrysanthe's face? What of the priestess, who cut her back with a whip?

As if reading her mind, Tyndareus shifts on his throne. "Timandra is strong enough to bear the burden. But those slaves were following orders, Clytemnestra. Those lives weren't yours to take."

A scream in her head is clawing to get out. She spits each word as if it were poison. "You sit there, telling me about lives that were wrongly taken, after you helped a monster *murder* your grandchild."

"Agamemnon and Menelaus are our guests." Tyndareus's voice is flat. "They must be treated with respect."

"They showed no respect to us," replies Leda. She raises her eyes and meets her daughter's. Clytemnestra tries to understand whose side Leda has taken.

"Agamemnon has shown disrespect to a foreign man, not to us," Tyndareus says. "He is Greek, and this makes him an ally."

"He slaughtered your grandson!" Clytemnestra shouts.

Tyndareus looks down at his hands. When he speaks, his voice shakes slightly. "I wanted to keep the baby alive."

This, for Clytemnestra, is even worse than his coldness. Does he expect her to forgive him now? Did he expect the Atreidai to keep their word?

"You are a king," she says sharply. "If you want something, you demand it."

"You are young still," Tyndareus says, "and do not understand that sometimes you have to compromise. It is my fault; I have failed to teach you this. I have always given you too much freedom."

"I do not need you to give me my freedom," Clytemnestra says. "I am free. But you are not. You are Agamemnon's puppet now, because you are weak."

"Your husband was weak," Tyndareus replies coolly.

"Tantalus was a good man, a kind man. But you can't see that, because in your world, only the brutes can live, and they do so by tearing down everything else."

"That is how life is. The weak have to die so that the rest may survive."

"You disgust me," she says.

Tyndareus stands and slaps her face before she can back away. She feels her father's scar on the back of his hand scratch her cheek.

She looks up into Tyndareus's eyes and sneers. "What kind of father are you?" She turns to her mother, seated in her chair with her head lowered. "And *you* do not fight him. You forgive him. You are no better."

"There are laws to be respected," Leda says quietly.

"You don't seek vengeance because you have become a coward," Clytemnestra says. Her hands are trembling, and she clutches them tightly. "But know this. I will have my justice. I swear it here and now. I swear it by the Furies and every other goddess who has known vengeance. I will stalk the Atreidai and crush everything they hold dear until only ashes remain."

"You will avenge nothing," Tyndareus says.

"What would you have me do?" she mocks him. "Forget? Wish Agamemnon a happy life with that whore Cynisca?"

Her mother shifts uncomfortably in her seat. She opens her mouth, but all that comes out is a choking sound. Tyndareus turns to her, annoyed.

"That will not happen," he says slowly. "That will not happen," he repeats, "because you will marry the man."

Her father's voice feels distant. Clytemnestra tries to catch her mother's eyes, but Leda is staring fixedly at the floor. Without meaning to, she thinks about all the times when she would be seated in the hall and, as her father was speaking, she would catch Helen's or Castor's eyes and bite her tongue trying not to laugh. They would always think the same thing at the same time—how funny this messenger's voice is! How serious Father is! How scared this stranger is! How boring the priestess is!—and later, during dinner, they would tell Tyndareus, giggling, and he would say, "You are not to come to the *megaron* anymore." But then he would let them come.

Helen was right. Agamemnon would never marry someone like

Cynisca. Clytemnestra isn't surprised. She isn't angry. She feels like a fool. Agamemnon has always wanted her for himself.

"I won't," she says, her voice so quiet she can barely hear herself.

"You live to honor Sparta and your king." He recites the words he taught her as a child, when he wanted her to grow into a strong warrior, a free woman. "Or have you forgotten? Your loyalty is to me, not to a foreigner. If you think about yourself and not the good of the city…that is treason."

The words hit her like lashes. Other words come too, words she has heard all her life, peeling her skin away one layer at the time. *No man or woman is allowed to live as he or she pleases, not even in Sparta. Nothing ever belongs to them entirely.*

She fixes her eyes on him, lifts her chin. "What are you going to do about it? Drag me to the Ceadas? Cut my head off?"

There is a long silence. At last, Tyndareus says, "You are my daughter. I won't kill you."

Anger and grief ripple beneath her skin, and she is afraid they might tear it. "I will not marry him," she repeats.

"Yes, you will," her father says. "I will come to your room in two days' time, and you will be ready for the wedding. And if you are not, I will have you dragged out and into the hall."

She grabs her tunic around her waist and squeezes it. When she lets go, the wrinkled cloth stretches like a pressed flower.

"I thought you loved me, Father," she says, then walks away, back to her nightmares.

Agamemnon comes for her when the sun is rising, a gutting blade at his waist and a crooked smile on his face. She wishes she could carve it out. She stares at him, making no attempt to hide her contempt, though it seems not to trouble him. It is hard to face a man who is not touched by anything.

Helen stands quickly and walks in front of her sister, her long dress fluttering around her ankles. Agamemnon looks at her as an eagle regards a mouse. "Leave us," he says.

"How dare you—" Helen starts, but Clytemnestra takes her wrist.

"Go, Helen. I will talk to him." She doesn't want to be left alone, she doesn't want her to go, but her sister isn't strong enough to face a monster, and Agamemnon has already taken too much from her.

Helen hesitates, her hands clutching her dress. She's like a bird scared to leave her cage, waiting for an arrow to fly and sink into her wing. She takes a few uncertain steps toward the door. She is barely outside when Agamemnon closes it, shutting her out. Clytemnestra hears her sister protest, then her hurried steps. She must be running to Timandra for help.

Agamemnon fastens his gaze on Clytemnestra. "Your father has informed you of the marriage."

"Yes."

He seems unsettled by her quietness. "So he also told you of the pact he made with me, of how he betrayed the foreign king."

This is how he operates, she thinks. This is how he turns daughter against father, Spartan against Spartan. Treachery and cruelty are his ways to power.

"My husband, you mean."

His face hardens. "I'm to be your husband now."

She stares at him, silent. This disturbs him. She can see that he expected her rage, maybe even wished for it. But he doesn't know how to react to coldness.

"I desired you from the moment I saw you," he says, tilting his head, looking at her as one looks at a fresco.

"It must be easy to live such a life as yours," she says, "to believe you can take everything you want."

There is a flame in his eyes, though he tries to hide it. "No one has ever given me anything, so I learned to take it."

She laughs bitterly. "You can take people, cities, armies. But love, respect…those can't be taken with force."

He watches her, his eyes glowing. "I won't touch you until we reach Mycenae. You deserve that."

Does he truly believe he will earn her respect like this? She can barely see for the rage she is feeling.

"You may grieve for the foreigner now. But you will soon forget him and learn to love another."

For a moment, she can see Tantalus on the terrace, his body so close to hers she could almost feel his heart. He had looked at her, the heat of his gaze like the warmest blanket in winter, and spoken of Adonis, the young man loved by Aphrodite. *The boy dies, but the goddess's love for him remains. It is a reminder of beauty and resistance in times of adversity.*

She gazes at Agamemnon and says, "I do not forget."

It is late evening when she is called for her cleansing. Two servants come for her and Helen, ordering her sister to go back to her husband and taking Clytemnestra to the baths. The hatred in Helen's eyes as she walks toward the guest rooms is blazing like wildfire, and Clytemnestra clings to it, feeling its warmth as she steps into the bathhouse.

The priestess is standing by the painted clay bath, her slim figure reflected in the water. Her long hair cascades down her back like a heavy cloak, and her eyelids are painted black. Upon seeing her, the helots step back and run away. A flicker of satisfaction burns in the priestess's eyes, and for a moment, Clytemnestra wonders how it must feel to live like that, dodged and shunned like a poisonous blade.

A single torch spills its pale light over the floor, and Clytemnestra steps forward, removing her tunic and climbing into a tub. Strands of her short hair stick to her face, and she smooths them back. The room smells fruity, which makes her nauseous, or maybe it is just the way the priestess is staring at her, as if she were dissecting a dead animal.

"You burn with rage for your father."

Clytemnestra bites her tongue. Rage is not what she feels. It is hatred, raw and relentless, clawing at her heart.

The priestess tilts her head as if listening to her thoughts. "He was blinded by power, as men often are. He formed an allegiance to better the interests of Sparta."

And he tore his family apart.

The priestess moves forward and grabs her arm. Her breasts are white and pointed, like shells, and her hand on Clytemnestra's skin feels like fish scales.

"You are a woman now. The gods have given you a taste of true sorrow. They have taught you loss. It is their divine duty to do so or else you forget you are mortal."

"Your gods are cruel," Clytemnestra chokes out.

The priestess lets her hand fall and shakes her head. Her hair sways gently, like seaweed under water. "Death comes for us all, sooner or later. The moment we forget it, we become fools." She looks outside the windows at the black vault of the sky, the stars glimmering.

"I still remember the first time I had you whipped. You had disobeyed the king's orders and hidden in the temple."

Clytemnestra remembers too. The coldness of the floor, the redness of the columns under her hands. The priestess had found her and dragged her by the hair onto the altar in front of her brothers.

"You were afraid, as everyone is, but you didn't show it. You wanted to make me angry, to prove yourself to your mother, to make your father proud."

It is true. She had bitten her tongue so hard she was afraid she might lose it and had stared at a crumpled leaf on the ground, swirling with the wind.

"You are a strong woman. Whatever opposes you, you will fight it," the priestess says. "It is only death that you can't defeat, and the sooner you understand that, the better."

Clytemnestra leans back, and the priestess stands, the feeble light blurring her features. Her steps fade as she walks away. Clytemnestra remains in the bath for a long time, the water turning cold, the priestess's words swirling in her mind.

Clytemnestra leans back, and the priestess stands, the feeble light blurring her features. Her steps fade as she walks away. Clytemnestra remains in the bath for a long time, the water turning cold, the priestess's words swirling in her mind.

That night, when she is cleaned and perfumed, she walks in the darkness of the corridors, away from the *gynaeceum* and toward the main entrance of the palace. She steps outside into the breeze, her feet bare, and hurries along the narrow path that leads down the hill to the river. A few torches are lit in the guests' rooms—she can see them from outside, dim and flickering in the windows. Feeling each stone and flower under her feet, she runs toward the Eurotas, careful not to disturb the horses in the stables and the dogs in the village. In the shadows of the night, the valley floors are covered with wildflowers, shining under the stars like gems.

On the right bank of the Eurotas, between the rocks and the weeds, an excavated corridor is lined by large, squared stones. At the end, an open door, like an empty eye socket, two painted green columns on the side. The *tholos*, the tomb where royals' ashes are placed, its stones piled up to form a dome. Clytemnestra takes a few uncertain steps toward the entrance. Then, clutching her tunic, she moves from the shadows into the blackness of the tomb. She hasn't set foot in here for a long time, not since her grandmother died. The place is small and dark, the air sad and sodden. Gold cups and jewels fill the spaces between the ashes, the tombs arranged like a beehive. Her husband and baby are here—she can feel their presence.

She kneels. In the utter silence, she can almost hear a breeze, as if the dead were breathing. She presses her forehead to the ground, her arms tucked under her chest, and cries.

She doesn't remember much about the wedding. Her world is opaque, shapeless, as though she were an unburied spirit, doomed to wander in the world of the living, mute and invisible. The only thing that feels real is her sisters' touch on her arms. Before walking outside with her, Helen had said, "You are so strong." Clytemnestra couldn't tell whether her sister meant to convince her or herself.

When the ceremony was over and dinner was prepared in the hall, she ate in silence while everyone around her talked and drank. She despised them all.

Tyndareus raised his cup and shouted, "To the Atreidai and the Atreidai's wives!"

Clytemnestra shattered her own cup against the wall. She stood while a servant hurried to clean the wine spreading on the floor. Everyone fell silent, staring at her.

She looked into her father's eyes and said, "Sooner or later, you will die. And I will not mourn you. I will look at the flames consuming your body, and I will rejoice."

She left the room then and hurried along the cold corridors. There was one thing that she noticed before leaving: Agamemnon's face as she spoke, his lips curled into a smile.

14

Mycenae

ON HER LAST morning in Sparta, Clytemnestra wakes alone. The mountain peaks are shrouded in a sun-glow mist while the valley appears clear with daybreak. Most helots are already working the land, cutting the grass, their backs bent so that, from afar, they are crescent-shaped, like the sickles they hold. Vines are blooming on the walls of the village houses, and beyond the fields, the meadows at the foot of the mountains are tinted with yellow and lilac.

A sudden knock on the door makes Clytemnestra jump, and for a moment, she fears it is Agamemnon. Her muscles tighten. Her hand flies to her dagger when Helen comes in, the earliest sunlight glimmering on her messy hair. The bruise on her neck is fading, like an old fresco. She gets into the bed without a word, and Clytemnestra remembers when they used to lie down together as children, putting their hands next to each other, measuring the length of their tiny fingers.

"I always thought I would leave this place," Helen says, "but it seems I am doomed to live in Sparta forever."

"You should have gone to Mycenae, not me," Clytemnestra says.

"It is already decided. I heard Tyndareus say that with Agamemnon in Mycenae and Menelaus here in Sparta, ready to take Tyndareus's throne when he passes, the strongest alliance between Greek cities will be forged."

Clytemnestra almost laughs. "Sparta has always despised alliances."

Helen nods. "Alliances are for the weak."

"No more, it seems."

"You know how shepherds take their sheep and cows to the market so that everyone can inspect them before buying?" Helen asks. "They check their wool, their hoofs, their teeth."

"Yes." Clytemnestra knows where her sister is going but lets her finish anyway.

"We have been sold like cattle for the Atreidai's stupid alliance."

"We are not cattle."

Helen produces a muffled sound between a laugh and a cry. Clytemnestra moves closer and touches her cheek. She wants to speak but she is afraid she will cry, and she has cried enough already.

We will see each other soon. Our lives are being torn apart now, but we will find a way back to each other, just as water always finds its way around rocks.

She leaves her home a few hours later. Her sisters at her side, she walks to the palace gate, where Agamemnon and his men are waiting, ready to escort her. A breath of wind makes the trees dance, and the scents of olives and figs drift to her.

Tyndareus and Menelaus are standing together, the palace looming behind them. A few steps away, the priestess is staring at Clytemnestra, her hands clutching her thin dress. Clytemnestra stares back, trying to read her face. The prophecy echoes in her mind, as if spoken in the depths of a great dark cave. *Leda's daughters will twice and thrice wed. And they will all be deserters of their lawful husbands.* The memory gives her relief, like cold water on a burn. Twice *and thrice.* She looks at

Agamemnon as he prepares his horse and imagines piercing his skull, squashing the brain. *Oh yes. No man can touch what isn't his to take without being punished. You will keep climbing, trampling everything and everyone, but sooner or later, you'll make a mistake. And you will fall.*

She feels Phoebe's and Philonoe's hands on her arm. They have come to hug her, their cheeks streaked with tears.

"Can we come soon and see the great city of Mycenae?" they ask, their little faces as fresh as drops of water.

Clytemnestra kisses their foreheads. "You will come when Mother lets you." Philonoe smiles and Phoebe nods solemnly. Leda pulls them back to take their places next to their father. Clytemnestra waits quietly for her mother's goodbye.

"You are broken now," Leda tells her, pushing a strand of hair off Clytemnestra's face. "But pain will leave you. I promise. The gods are merciful to those who deserve it." Her face is mournful, her sad green eyes fixed somewhere behind her daughter.

Clytemnestra doesn't say that the pain has seeped in too deep, that it's now in her every limb and muscle, in her every breath. She turns to her sisters, and Helen and Timandra come forward, their arms entwined, their hearts beating as one. They cling to each other until Agamemnon grabs Clytemnestra's arm and shakes her away.

"Time to leave," he says. "We don't want to ride at night."

"Take this," Leda says, her arms outstretched, her eyes shiny like falling stars. She is holding a small jeweled knife. "It was your grandmother's." Clytemnestra touches the point with her finger, and a drop of blood appears on the tip.

"It is very sharp, though no one suspects it. Everyone is distracted by its beauty." Leda gives her daughter a final meaningful look, then turns away. Clytemnestra watches her raven hair bounce on her shoulders as she walks. The soldiers around her spur their horses. The last thing she looks at before leaving is Helen, her light-blue eyes spilling tears like summer rain.

As they move farther from the palace onto the plain, the sun peeps through the mist and blinds her. *Here I am*, she thinks. *I was a princess of Sparta and queen of Maeonia… Now I am married to the man who murdered my family.*

They arrive in Mycenae in the late sunlight, the hilltops colored in violet and purple shades. Shrubs and rocks are scattered for miles and miles on the land around her, and in front of her, the citadel stands on a rocky outcrop, massive. The limestone blocks of the outer walls are bigger than bulls, pale against the dark mountains behind. The road to the citadel is steep and unprotected, each approaching visitor at the mercy of the guards stationed on the walls. Clytemnestra wonders how Agamemnon and Menelaus ever managed to retake the city. It looks impregnable.

The suburbs stretch like cobwebs, traders and other workers running their last errands of the day. As Agamemnon and Clytemnestra ride through, the people stop and kneel. They look filthy and strangely thin, like helots. They are not soldiers, Clytemnestra can tell. Her horse steps on some bread crusts on the pebbles, and guards ride on both sides of her as if to protect her from the people.

Two soldiers are waiting for them by the gate, holding a bright banner—a golden lion on purple. The banner flaps in the wind, and Clytemnestra follows its dance. Behind it, the gate is unlike anything she has ever seen. Perched above the posts and lintel, two carved lions stand on their hind legs, their front paws on each side of a column. Their heads are turned to look straight at her. They bathe in the light, quiet and watchful.

The guards let them through. Inside the walls, they follow streets that become narrower and narrower as they draw closer to the palace. At the summit of the citadel, she can make out a small temple. One of the guards talks to Clytemnestra in a low voice.

"Here on the right is one grave circle," he whispers as they pass a massive stone construction guarded by two soldiers. "Those are warriors' houses." Tall buildings along a paved path. And then a barn. A blacksmith's forge. Bakers passing with loaves. Slaves carrying fruit and meat for their masters. The smell of honey and spices coming out of an orange-painted store. Naked little boys and girls playing with sticks. The stone steps are worn smooth in the fading sun. They climb until they reach the top and the palace—big and glowing, each terrace surrounded by fire-red columns.

Once inside, Agamemnon disappears with some counselors and Clytemnestra is taken along shadowy colonnades and perfectly lit corridors. The windows have been covered, and the light comes from golden torches hung every few steps. They pass hall after hall, each leading to a corridor lined with painted chambers. She glimpses deep-blue ceilings and columns ringed with roaring lions, griffins, and fearful deer. As they reach her quarters, the air feels still, cooler.

Two slaves are waiting for her in her bedroom. The younger one has dark-red hair and wide eyes, the older a crooked nose and a large scar on her cheek. They stand with their arms dangling down the sides of their bodies, staring at Clytemnestra with hesitant eyes. They feel threatened, she realizes. She ignores them as she puts down her things and looks around.

The bed is carved and covered with a lion's skin. Next to it, a painted stand, a chair, and a footstool. The paint of the frescoes on the walls is still wet. The images must be meant to remind her of Sparta. Anemones have been painted around large windows, and a river framed by tall reeds flows in front of her bed. She smells the walls and hears the servants whisper.

"How old are you?" Clytemnestra asks them abruptly, fixing her eyes on them.

"Twenty-five, my queen," the older slave says. "I began serving the Atreidai when I was ten." She speaks with a hint of pride, but Clytemnestra feels sorry for her.

"And you?" Clytemnestra asks the red-haired girl. Her eyes are gray, sad like clouds before they shed their tears.

The older servant answers for her. "Aileen is fourteen."

"My sister Timandra is that age," Clytemnestra says, even though she doesn't know why she should mention her sister. When neither of the slaves reply, she orders, "Leave me."

They don't move. "Lord Agamemnon has ordered us to stay here until he comes back," the older slave says.

"It doesn't matter what he said. Now that I am here, you take orders from me."

The slaves exchange a frightened look, and their eyes shine with uncertainty.

"He will flog us," the red-haired girl whispers, her voice barely louder than a breath.

"I will not allow it," Clytemnestra replies. She makes sure her voice sounds firm. The slaves hurry outside.

When their steps have died away, Clytemnestra finally sits on the bed. Painted trees surround her. Fish swim and jump between the reeds. Above her, stars shine on a brushed evening sky, its color as deep as the open sea. The frescoes of the Spartan *megaron* are nothing compared to this. But then, Mycenae is the richest city of all their lands. There are beautiful carved chests for her clothes, and bowls and tripods. An ax hangs near the window, painted doves and butterflies flying around it.

She looks at every image and bright color, at the lies they tell. *This is my life now. Everything I love is gone.* She will never see Tantalus again. She will never rock her son to sleep. Grief streams inside her, and she doubles over, her hands pressed to her heart. She closes her eyes, her limbs aching with sorrow and exhaustion, and drifts into sleep.

She wakes to the strong smell of meat. Agamemnon is standing in front of the bed, a cup of wine in his hand. He looks drunk: his cheeks are flushed and his eyes slightly unfocused. Outside, it is late night, the stars veiled by thin clouds.

"Eat," Agamemnon says, sitting on a chair by the side of the bed. Clytemnestra stands slowly and walks to the window. On a stool, a plate is filled with bread and goat meat. She considers smashing it on Agamemnon's head.

As she eats, he watches her, sipping his wine. She finds herself looking at his hands. They are big, with thick fingers, and Clytemnestra thinks of Tantalus's light-brown hands, his long, elegant fingers brushing her body like feathers.

When she gobbles the last bite of bread, Agamemnon stands. Clytemnestra doesn't move, not even when he is close enough that she can smell his breath. He unpins her dress and it falls at her feet.

"The slaves said you are to give them orders from now on," he says.

"Yes."

"I didn't give you permission." He seems almost amused, though Clytemnestra can't say why.

"I don't need your permission. I won't take orders from you."

A shadow passes on his face. He takes her hair in his hand and pulls. She takes a step back and he moves with her.

"I know what you think of me, and you are right. I am a bad man. But I don't regret it. Do you know why? Because admitting what you are is the only way to get what you want."

And what do you want? You have already taken everything from me.

He grabs her waist with both hands and pushes inside her. She feels her body resisting, trying to draw back, so she focuses on the torches that brighten the frescoes on the walls, the painted fish and birds. When she feels pain, she tries to imagine being the painted nightingale by the door. She remembers the story of the girl Philomela, transformed into a nightingale after being raped and mutilated by her sister's husband. *But she got her revenge first.* Philomela had killed the man's son, boiled him, and served him as a meal.

She stands with her back against the wall and lets Agamemnon kiss and bite her. As he shoves inside her again and again, she licks away the blood on her lip and keeps looking over his shoulder at the wall opposite.

At last, he grunts and moves aside, breathless. She feels the inside of her thighs wet and wishes she could clean herself. She puts her dress back on, ready to leave, though she doesn't know where to go.

He grabs her arm. "I have chosen you because you are strong, Clytemnestra. Stop being weak now."

She shakes him away. Her nightdress flutters behind her as she walks the lit corridors, leaving her chamber far behind. She reaches a window. The corridor feels hot and close and she climbs out, landing on stairs that seem to run toward a garden. She follows the path, almost running, stumbling in the dark, and stops only in a spot where she can see the entire valley stretching below her, resting in the quiet night. Above her, she recognizes the temple she had glimpsed as they rode into the city, its columns as white as a baby's teeth. Engraved on the stone, the name Hera. The most vengeful goddess, her mother always said.

She feels for flowers under her bare feet, patches of color in the shade. *Stop being weak*, he said. She thinks about the meaning, and suddenly she understands, his words as clear as an ice-fed pool.

He desired her strength because it was a challenge to him. He wished to bend her to his own will, break her. He wanted to show he was stronger by subjugating her. Some men can be like that.

She feels the flowers swaying in the wind, then plucks them.

He will not break her. She will break him.

PART III

So Leda's daughters,
two lethal brides,
will twice and thrice wed.

One will launch Greece in a thousand ships,
her beauty the ruin of her land,
and the men sent to rescue her
will come back ashes and bones.

The other, the queen hell-bent on revenge,
will rise in the house of Mycenae,
loyal to those who revere her,
savage to those who oppose her.

15

The Queen of Arcadia

Fifteen years later

CLYTEMNESTRA'S BACK HURTS, but she doesn't stop riding. Mycenae is far behind her now, and in front of her are the endless hills of Arcadia, lush and bright as ripe pears. She follows hill after hill dotted with yellow flowers toward a plain with clumps of dark-green trees. She has been riding for a day already and hopes to reach King Echemus's palace before dusk falls tomorrow.

When the sun sets, crowning the hills with gold, she stops near some stones that might once have been a temple. The blocks have grown darker, and weeds have found their way through each crack. She ties the horse to a tree and walks in the growing darkness, following the feeble sound of water. She finds a stream hidden by tall grass and flowers and bends to fill her empty wineskin to the brim.

A rabbit hops a few steps from her. She looks up and their eyes lock. How small it is, she thinks, and yet it isn't scared of her. Her hand finds the handle of her dagger and throws it. It sinks into the soft fur around the animal's neck. She grabs it, limp and dead, and walks back to the old temple to clean it. Her horse rests while she prepares a small fire and eats the meat.

Sparks glow around her like fireflies. The wind rises, and she wraps her goatskin around her shoulders. Though summer, it is always cool at night in the hills. She lies down by the fire and closes her eyes, but nightmares are already forming behind the lids, black figures dancing in the flames. They have been following her for years. She imagines fighting them, putting her hand right into the flames until her skin becomes scorched and the figures disappear. But no one can fight fire. It is the element of the Furies, goddesses of vengeance, ancient creatures of torment.

So she thinks of her children—Iphigenia, Electra, Orestes, Chrysothemis—each of them a root that keeps her steady. Iphigenia, with her swanlike neck and golden hair; Electra, with her solemn eyes and wise words; Chrysothemis, with her sweet smile. Even Orestes, who looks so much like his father, is a joy. Agamemnon can't take this from her. She has carried them in her womb, nursed them, watched over them at night, their breath in her ear, their little hands fitting in hers. She has clutched her children one by one, shielded them until they have grown, and in return, they have given her her life back.

Stars dance in the vaulted sky, and Clytemnestra drifts to sleep.

She arrives at the palace of Alea the next evening. It is much smaller than Mycenae—simple wood facades on a base of rough stone—and around it, sheep and goats graze on the land. At the entrance, standing by two tall columns painted crimson, Timandra is waiting for her. Her features seem different, more refined under her regal circlet, but maybe it is just because, for once, her hair isn't in her face. She is wearing a light-blue tunic pinned to her left shoulder, and Clytemnestra can't help but notice an ugly scar at the base of her neck, dark and jagged.

"That was our father," Timandra says, following Clytemnestra's eyes. "One of his many courtesies before he died."

"Don't talk badly of the dead." She can hear the contempt in her own voice and hopes her sister won't.

"You once said that the dead can't hear us," Timandra replies. Her body is still lean, her eyes dark, like the sky at night. With her newly cut hair, she looks much like Clytemnestra. Timandra reaches out and hugs her. She smells of mint and wood, of the strong flavors of the kitchen and the thick scents of the forest.

"Welcome to Arcadia," Timandra says.

They walk inside, where the halls are lined with big painted jars, and the walls look naked and gray without any frescoes.

"It is a small palace," Clytemnestra says.

"Don't say that in front of my husband. It was built by his grand-father Aleus, and Echemus loves to talk about it whenever he has the chance. In fact," Timandra says as she turns to her sister, "he will surely talk about it at dinner. He likes to boast."

Timandra had married only a few months before Tyndareus died. When an envoy had come to Mycenae to give Clytemnestra the news, Agamemnon forbade her to attend the wedding. There were too many embassies in the palace to be dealt with, too many guests and quarrels to be resolved. So Clytemnestra had held audiences and discussed land disputes and army training while her sister married the king of Arcadia.

"You don't like him," Clytemnestra says.

Timandra laughs. "Of course I like him. He is my husband."

"That doesn't mean anything."

"He bores me to death," she admits without bothering to lower her voice. "But at least he lets me do what I want."

They reach a small bedroom, the floor covered with sheepskin rugs. A single bed has been pushed against the wall, where a fresco of a nymph is fading. Clytemnestra sits, her joints aching.

Timandra watches her. "Are you sure you want to do this?" she asks. "Go back to Sparta?" Her hair is a dull brown, not as rich as her sister's, but her eyes are so lively that they make her whole face glow. Clytemnestra knows what Timandra is thinking—of the day when she wished her father dead. *I will not mourn you*, she had said.

"I have to," Clytemnestra says calmly.

Timandra nods. "I will let you rest, then. Be ready for dinner soon."

When the sun has set, servants come to accompany her to the dining hall. Timandra is sitting near the head of the table, men of all ages around her, talking. There are only a few women on the benches, gold circlets gleaming in their hair. A young man with muscular arms and olive skin sits beside Timandra. He stands when he sees Clytemnestra and opens his arms in a theatrical gesture.

"Welcome, queen of Mycenae," he says. "I have heard the most wonderful things about you." His voice is sweet but with a sticky quality, like honey when it is spilled on the table. Echemus motions to the benches, and Clytemnestra takes her seat at her sister's side, next to a woman with curly black hair. Servants move under the light of the lamps, bringing meat and wine, herbed cheese and dried fruit.

"I was sorry to hear of your father's death," Echemus says as the room grows livelier with chatter. "My wife tells me you were his favorite." *My wife* sounds funny in his mouth, as though he felt the need to clarify Timandra's position.

"I was, once," Clytemnestra answers truthfully.

"My envoys report that King Menelaus has organized one of the biggest funerals our lands have ever seen."

"How typical of Menelaus," Timandra comments.

Echemus ignores her. "And you will ride there tomorrow?" he asks. "Aren't you tired?"

"We will leave first thing tomorrow morning," Clytemnestra says, looking at Timandra. "He's been dead for four days already. The ceremony can't wait."

Echemus nods, his expression suddenly grave, and Timandra turns to her right, smiling at the curly-haired woman. Clytemnestra follows her stare and freezes on the bench. Eyes clear as water springs, hair as dark as obsidian… Timandra is faster than her. Before Clytemnestra can speak, her sister's features have tightened into a smile.

"You remember Chrysanthe, sister?"

Chrysanthe smiles, and her cheeks redden. Clytemnestra remembers how the girl had flushed when she had caught them kissing years ago on the terrace in Sparta. "How could I forget?" she says.

Echemus clears his throat. He straightens in his chair and touches Timandra's hand. Timandra looks down as if his finger were a worm but doesn't draw away. "My wife brought Chrysanthe from Sparta as her companion," Echemus says. "She has grown up in a large family and is often lonely here." He speaks as though Clytemnestra didn't know her sister, as though they hadn't spent every day playing and wrestling together in Sparta.

"How lucky you are that Chrysanthe keeps you company," Clytemnestra remarks.

"I am the lucky one," Chrysanthe intervenes, "for I can serve my queen every day."

Timandra smiles and rips a piece of meat from the bone. She doesn't speak, but she doesn't need to. Clytemnestra can see that her sister holds the reins in this palace. She sips some wine from her cup and puts all the sincerity she can into her smile. "Although I am sure that you can manage loneliness, Timandra."

Timandra raises her eyebrows, but it is Echemus who speaks again. "My wife is very lively, always looking for new activities. It isn't easy to tame her." He sounds as if he was talking about a horse.

"Impossible to tame her, I might say," Clytemnestra adds.

Timandra laughs, her voice echoing on the walls. "I take after you."

A few young men enter with flutes and lyres. When Echemus acknowledges their presence, they start playing, their music sweet, like ripe fruit. More wine is set in front of Clytemnestra, and she looks at the image on the amphora, two warriors fighting with spears, their armor beautifully refined.

"Now Mycenae is called our mightiest kingdom," Echemus says, eager to make conversation. "Mightier even than Troy."

"The City of Gold, they call it," Chrysanthe intervenes.

"Yes," Clytemnestra says. "Though Babylon and Crete are mighty as well."

"Crete is not as rich as it used to be," Echemus says dismissively. "King Minos is gone, his crazy wife disappeared. Nothing worthy of attention remains."

"Crete remains crucial for commerce," Clytemnestra says. "They have ships and they have gold. They trade with Phoenicians, Egyptians, and Ethiopians."

Echemus looks like a boy scolded for not learning his lesson. He bites his lip, then starts again, eager to please her. "Did you know that my grandfather King Aleus built this palace?"

Clytemnestra turns to Timandra, but her sister is impassive, sipping her wine. Out of the corner of her eye, Clytemnestra sees Timandra's knee brushing Chrysanthe's. "Of course," she says. "Everyone knows of your grandfather. He must have been a great man." She doesn't mention that he is famous for disposing of his daughter when Heracles made her pregnant.

Echemus smiles. "He was. We worship the goddess Alea, thanks to him." He starts to talk about Alea and the many sacrifices needed in her honor, but Clytemnestra doesn't listen to him. She feels Chrysanthe's stare on her, as cool and piercing as an icicle. For some reason, she feels as if the woman is looking for her approval. Clytemnestra stares back, her limbs like those of a wrestler before a fight. She can't tell her she doesn't approve. She can't tell her to be careful, to avoid being too happy or else feel the wrath of the gods. Sooner or later, even the luckiest fall.

♛

They walk back together to Clytemnestra's room, Timandra whistling a tune, Clytemnestra watching her sister's light, careless steps. As they pass the large windows, they can see the moon, sparkling bright, and feel the breeze of the summer night. Just before they turn into the guests' corridor, Timandra takes her sister's arm and guides her in the opposite direction, into a storage room lined with jars of oil and wine. There is only a narrow window, and it takes Clytemnestra a moment to adjust to the darkness. Slowly Timandra's contours appear—she looks giddy.

"Chrysanthe will come with us to Sparta," she says in a whisper.

"I thought so," Clytemnestra says, even though she hadn't. She hadn't expected her sister to be so reckless.

Timandra searches her face. "What is it?"

Clytemnestra glances out the window, then back at her. "She should not come."

Timandra frowns. "Why?"

"You know why."

"You were the one who helped me stay with her. You covered for me in Sparta. You said it wasn't wrong." Her tone is almost accusatory.

Clytemnestra takes a deep breath. "I said those things when you were a child. Now you are a married woman."

"So you tell me you are faithful to your loving husband? The very same husband who murdered your first child?"

Clytemnestra slaps her. Timandra's head jerks back, and when she looks at her sister again, her cheek is purple and her nose bleeding. She wipes it on her sleeve.

"What I do doesn't concern you," Clytemnestra says.

"And yet you can be concerned about me?"

"As long as you parade Chrysanthe, yes."

"You are telling me I am not free to do as I please, to be with the woman I love?"

The word *love* feels like a bucket of ice water poured over her face.

"Listen to me." Clytemnestra doesn't know how to explain, how to make her sister understand. "You must do what you want, but do it in the shadows. Don't let others see how happy you are."

Timandra is silent. Outside, an owl cries and the leaves rustle.

"Do you know who Achilles is?" Timandra finally says.

Clytemnestra nods. Achilles, son of Peleus, king of the tiny Phthia and blessed by the gods. He is said to be the greatest hero of his generation. Agamemnon often speaks of the man with unease, though he has never met him.

"They say he lives with his companion, Patroclus," Timandra says. "They eat together, play together, sleep together. Everyone knows about them. But this doesn't taint Achilles's reputation. He is still *aristos Achaion*." She uses the words for "best of the Greeks."

But you are not aristos Achaion, Clytemnestra thinks. Instead she says, "They are men, and you are a woman."

"What difference does it make? It didn't change anything in Sparta."

"We are not in Sparta anymore."

Timandra is pacing the room, raising her voice. "You want me to be a *servant* to my husband just because that is what the people expect me to be?"

Clytemnestra waits to find the right words, as if pulling them out of deep darkness. "You were born free and you will always be free, no matter what others tell you. But you must see what is around you and learn to bend it to your will before you are the one who is bent."

Timandra stops pacing. Her dark eyes are inscrutable, but then Clytemnestra sees a flash in them, like a torch that is suddenly lit in the blackness.

"I will not bring Chrysanthe, then," Timandra says.

Clytemnestra sleeps dreamlessly. When she wakes at dawn, the air is rich with the scent of summer, and her mind is filled with memories.

Her father talking to envoys in the *megaron*, offering her fruit and making sure she listened carefully. Afterward, when the men had left, he would say, "Clytemnestra, what would *you* have done?"

Her father watching her first fight in the gymnasium. She was six and shy, but his presence gave her strength. "People aren't always as strong as they look," he had told her. "Strength comes from many different things, and one of those is purpose." She had won the fight, and he had given her a brief smile.

Tyndareus eating next to her brothers, laughing at their jokes, occasionally scolding Timandra for giving too much food to the dogs. Even when he was absorbed in someone else's story, he would always look for Clytemnestra, just for the briefest moment.

Sorrow falls upon her, heavy, like snow. She has loved him, hated him, wished him dead. And now that he is, she has to go back to pray for him.

But gods don't listen to women who curse their father, who loathe and dishonor him. For a daughter like her, there are no gods to pray to.

16

Burning of the Dead

THEY STAND IN front of the pyre, all of Tyndareus's children, together after many years. Behind them, the palace stands against the sky, and around them, the people of Sparta. Menelaus lifts a torch and brings it to the pyre. It lights up like a thunderbolt, sudden and pale against the darkening sky. The wood burns and the flames consume Tyndareus's body, turn it into ash and bone. A priest sings, and the words fly with the sparks, filling the air with colors.

Not many cry. Phoebe's fair face is streaked with tears, but she keeps silent. It is not right to cry when a body is burned. The women have already screamed, torn their hair, and clawed their faces. The men have already howled and mourned.

Leda's face is hard, her hands clasped tight. She stares at the fire as if it were holding her fears and nightmares. Her eyes were already red and her breath had smelled like spiced wine when Clytemnestra arrived. When Leda stood and stumbled out of her chair, Phoebe held her and straightened her.

Timandra stands next to her as the fire heats her face and dances in her eyes. On the way to Sparta, she told Clytemnestra what Tyndareus had done to her when he discovered she was still with

Chrysanthe before marrying Echemus. The priestess had found them in the stables, and despite Chrysanthe's desperate pleading, she had gone to Tyndareus. But Chrysanthe wasn't punished. The king had forced Timandra to fight three other Spartiates in the gymnasium until they hurt her. One sank a spear in the soft place where the neck meets the shoulder, and Timandra almost bled to death before Chrysanthe's and Tyndareus's eyes. But then, before he died, he told her that his children were his greatest pride and that he didn't know how to show them love without violence. Timandra had pitied him.

You hurt me, Father, Clytemnestra thinks. *And I don't know how to forgive.* She looks to her right, where her brothers are standing. Castor gazes back at her. The horse-breaker, their people call him now. His brown curls have grown longer, his face more sunken. The journey to Colchis has wearied him, changed him.

Helen stands with her back straight, her golden hair dancing in the wind, her arms around her child, Hermione, though she is old enough to stand. She watches the pyre until every last ember has gone out. When the priest collects the ashes to place them in a gilded urn, people start leaving, their faces still warm from the blaze, their hair smelling of ash. The torches they were holding are left on the ground, and the land seems painted with a hundred strokes of fire.

Seeing her father walk back to the palace, little Hermione leaves her mother, running to catch up with him. Helen shifts. When she turns to her right, she sees that everyone has gone except Clytemnestra. They look at each other. Sorrow is written on their faces, but they know better than to speak of it. So they take each other's hands and walk away, leaving their father behind.

They take the path that leads to the mountain. Castor and Polydeuces follow. There will be a banquet in the dining hall soon, but none of them care. Menelaus will entertain the people: it is what he does best.

They walk for a while in the shadowy darkness, roots tugging at their feet, red and blue berries growing along the way. Above them, the sky is filling with stars. Polydeuces's hand clasps Helen's arm, guiding her as though she doesn't know the path, though she and Clytemnestra always came here as children. Still, Helen doesn't draw away. When she came to the palace last night, Clytemnestra found her brother in her sister's room, his lips close to her neck as she plaited her hair. Clytemnestra didn't ask or want to know. In her mind, Helen and Polydeuces were always as close as twins, as intimate as lovers. Once, when they were little, Helen had told Clytemnestra that her brother tried to kiss her.

"I told him no," she said, confusion in her eyes. "Because it's wrong, isn't it?"

"I think it is," Clytemnestra said. They never spoke of it again.

As they walk higher and higher on the trail, the air grows colder and the darkness thicker. Castor stops in a small clearing, the ground mossy, and starts to collect wood. Helen sits on a patch of leaves. Their breath is visible in the chilled air, and their hands are stinging with cold.

"He wanted to see you before he died," Helen says, her bright eyes on Clytemnestra. "He said, 'I wish my daughter was here.'"

"You don't know he was talking about me."

"All his other daughters were there."

Castor lights the fire and flames rise. The heat on their faces is welcome, and they move closer to it.

"What he did to you was unforgivable," Polydeuces says, "but he is still your father. Loyalty is a difficult thing."

"It shouldn't be," Clytemnestra replies.

"We should have been here to protect you," Castor says. The pain in his face strikes her, and she wishes she could wipe it away. She has thought about this often, and every time, it has hurt her, made her choke. If her brothers had been here fifteen years ago, would they really have protected her? What if they had taken Tyndareus's side and thought an alliance with the Atreidai was the most fruitful thing?

"You gained your fame in Colchis. It was worth it," she says.

"Colchis was a bloodbath," Polydeuces says. It is what he has repeated since they came home, the words sharp and cutting on his lips.

"But you survived," Helen whispers.

"The gods protected us," Polydeuces replies. Castor scoffs but his brother ignores him. Clytemnestra thinks he will keep silent now, as he always does after mentioning Colchis, but Polydeuces goes on. Maybe it is the darkness—it makes them feel hidden from everything else.

"Aeëtes is a monster. He rules Colchis with terror. He enslaves every ship's crew that dares come to his kingdom and tortures them with fire and chains. Slaves, warriors, women—he cares nothing for anyone. He just takes pleasure in tormenting them."

"What about the fleece?" Clytemnestra asks. She has heard the songs that speak of Jason's courage, how he managed to do what no man before him had done: kill the beast that guarded the fleece and snatch it away before Aeëtes could stop him.

"It was Medea," Castor says. "Aeëtes's witch daughter. She told

Jason every trick to survive his father's tasks, then took the fleece herself. She used drugs to put soldiers and animals to sleep and ran away with us when we left Colchis."

"How is she?" Helen asks. "People say she is beautiful."

Polydeuces shakes his head. "Not in the same way as you. She has hair like spun gold and skin as white as a goddess's. But her features are like those of a hungry lion."

"Our people call her mad," Helen says. "They say she murdered Jason's new wife with a dress steeped in poison."

"She grew up in a place of darkness, with no mother and a tyrant as a father," Castor explains. "When we were leaving Colchis, she begged Jason to take her with us. Who knows what her own father did to her while she was growing up?"

"She saved your lives," Clytemnestra says.

"She did." Polydeuces nods. "She gave up everything for Jason. And in return, he left her for another woman." He is polishing his hunting blade by the fire, his blond hair falling around his head.

Stories of the journey spill from them like snow-melted streams. The women they met on the island of Lemnos, whose husbands were all dead. Bear Mountain, where they had slaughtered all the locals after they tried to attack them. The land where Polydeuces defeated a savage king in a boxing contest. The island of Dia, where they found shipwrecked men, naked and starving, their bones jutting out of their skin. And finally Colchis, where Medea fell in love with Jason and helped them escape from Aeëtes.

Sparks fly around them, and so do Castor's words, filling the air with memories. When silence comes once more, they lie down, staring at the sky, thinking about each other's scars.

"Sometimes I see everything," Castor says. "All those memories lined up in my head when I close my eyes."

I do too, Clytemnestra thinks. *Every single night.*

"What do you do when you see them?" Helen asks. "How do you sleep?"

Castor turns his face to her. "Every day you try to forget, but at night, you dream of the past. This is what dreams are for. To make us remember what we were, to tie us down to our memories, whether we like it or not."

The fire crackles. Clytemnestra takes Castor's hand and looks back at the clear dark sky. Selene is the goddess of the moon and is said to have the power to stop bad dreams. Spartans call her "benevolent." But her brother is right when he scoffs at the mention of gods. They are alone.

They can't avoid banquets forever, so the next day, they gather in the dining hall at the king's request. The place has changed after all these years under Menelaus. There are more torches, more weapons on the walls, more cowhide on the floor, more dogs gnawing at the bones, and more women. They bring spiced meat and cheese to the table without the battered, downcast look of helots; they keep smiling, and they wear bright, clean tunics. Menelaus sits at the head of the table and, around him, Helen and the best of his warriors. Among them there is an ugly man with a thick beard and a broken nose—"Cynisca's husband," Castor says when Clytemnestra asks about him. "You remember her, I am sure?"

She nods. "What happened to her?"

Castor looks as the man laughs and cheers with Menelaus. "Her family is more and more powerful. They are among the few Spartans Menelaus trusts. Cynisca is often in the *megaron*, whispering in the king's ear."

"Where is she now?"

"Resting, I believe. She didn't take Tyndareus's death well."

"Do you know where she lives?"

Castor frowns. "Near the dyers' shops, I have heard. Why?"

Clytemnestra shrugs. "I am just surprised that she isn't here."

A servant pours some wine for Castor, smiling and pressing her body against him as she passes, but Castor ignores her. Clytemnestra remembers all the times she saw her brother sneak away from the servants' quarters after spending the night with a girl there.

"You used to spend a lot of time in bed with servants," she says.

"I took my fair share, yes." Castor grins, and for a second, his face looks like it used to. Then he lowers his voice. "But these girls already have to entertain Menelaus."

Clytemnestra follows the servant with her eyes as she fills wine cups along the table. She leans back every time she passes one of Menelaus's warriors, and when they call for her, she startles. It is true what Tyndareus used to say, Clytemnestra muses. No matter how much kindness you show her, a slave will never learn to love you, for she has known too much pain.

Helen stands and walks away from her husband to sit next to her daughter. Little Hermione is eating figs with Polydeuces, and whenever her hands are sticky, he wipes them carefully with a piece of cloth, as if she were his own child. Menelaus seems not to notice. Hermione has her father's hair, like fire-forged bronze, and Helen's eyes, light as seawater. But where her mother's face is delicate as a pearl, Hermione's is sharp as a dagger. She is an odd beauty.

Meat, cheese, and olives are served as the loud chatter echoes from the walls. Phoebe and Philonoe are discussing the man Phoebe is meant to marry, while Timandra and Castor gobble food and wine.

Leda is chewing a piece of spiced lamb without talking to anyone, and Clytemnestra moves closer to her on the bench.

"Mother," she says, "where is the priestess?"

Leda's eyes are large and foggy. "Why?"

"I want to talk to her about the prophecy she made fifteen years ago."

Leda's raven hair is tied in beautiful plaits, and she touches it absentmindedly. "She is gone," she finally says.

"How?"

"I sent her away."

Clytemnestra remembers when her father used to take a woman, a helot, to his room when she was little. Leda found out and told everyone at dinner that she "sent the servant away." But one day when Clytemnestra was walking to the village, she found the helot's dead body, rotting in the mud.

"When?" she asks.

Her mother's face remains impassive. "Not long after you left."

"What did Tyndareus say?"

"He wasn't happy. But after what he had done to you, after all the pain he caused us, he couldn't give me orders."

"How did you feel?"

Leda frowns. "What?"

"How did it feel to send the priestess away?"

Leda puts down her wine and grabs Clytemnestra's hand. Her eyes are big and dark with grief. "Listen to me. I have let vengeance lead my thoughts and actions. Don't make the same mistake."

"Vengeance is our way of life," Clytemnestra says.

"It doesn't have to be. All the time I hated the priestess, I could have spent loving my Helen. All the time I hated your father, I could have loved his children."

"You do love us."

"Yes, but hate is a bad root. It takes its place in your heart and it grows and grows, letting everything rot."

On their right, Menelaus is laughing at some of his comrades' jokes. Cynisca's husband touches the servant as she brings him a meat platter, and her hands tremble.

"Promise me you won't be as vengeful as I have been," Leda whispers.

Clytemnestra looks away from the servant and into her mother's eyes. "I promise."

At night, when warriors and nobles have gone to sleep, she walks down the narrow streets that run around the palace. The air is hot and moist, but she is wearing a cloak that hides her face. At her waist, she carries the small jeweled knife her mother gave her when she left for Mycenae.

The streets are quiet. The only sounds are occasional barks and howls, soft moans, and babies crying. She passes wagons full of hay and a young man kissing a servant under some leather skins hanging by a window. When she gets closer to the square, she turns left into a side road that leads to the dyers' shops. She slows her pace. She listens to the soft sounds that come out of doors and windows—a woman singing to her child, an old man snoring. Then she looks across the road at the opposite wall and stops. A window is open and she peeps inside—a large shield gleaming near the door, a wooden table and a bench on which a golden cup sits, half filled. And by the flickering light of a lamp, a woman with her eyes closed. She is wearing only a light tunic that barely conceals her tiny breasts, yet the heat is so strong she is sweating. The lamp illuminates her short hair, beak nose, and pointed chin.

Clytemnestra steps cautiously around the outside of the house, watching the inside from the only other window. The woman seems to be alone. She tries the door, but it is locked, so she climbs over the window ledge and lands inside the room as carefully as she can.

Cynisca opens her eyes, suddenly alert, and for a second, the two stare at each other. Then Clytemnestra blows out the lamp. The light flickers and dies, leaving them in complete darkness. "It's been a long time since you and I saw each other," she says. She can feel Cynisca's sour breath somewhere in front of her, the wooden table behind her.

"I knew you were here," Cynisca says. "What do you want?"

Clytemnestra walks around the table, one step at a time. She takes off her cloak and leaves it aside, the fabric slipping between her fingers. She feels Cynisca's stillness in the dark and knows she must act before lines and contours become visible to them.

"When my husband was murdered here, in my home, fifteen years ago," she says, "where were you?"

Cynisca gasps, loud enough for her to hear. She swallows to speak but Clytemnestra interrupts her. "Never mind. I know where you were. You followed my sister in the streets—you hit her with a stone and left her to bleed." She feels the golden cup under her finger, the edge jagged, not smooth like the ones in the palace. "You did that to help Agamemnon. You helped him get what he wanted, but he didn't reward you."

Cynisca stands. "He rewarded me. He protected my family and gave me power in Sparta." Her voice is deep and there is something like pride in it.

"How generous of him."

"He can be a generous man."

"So you say. Although I am sure the best reward for you was to see me fall. To know I lost everything I loved and cared for."

Cynisca doesn't speak. She moves in the shadows, and Clytemnestra knows she will try to reach the shield.

"Can you imagine what it feels like to lose your child? To have him murdered?" Her hand is tight around her knife and she tries to relax her grip.

"I have no children you can take from me."

Clytemnestra ignores her. "It feels like drowning. As if someone is holding you underwater, and as soon as you give up and prepare to die, that person drags you to the surface, makes you breathe, then pushes you down again."

Cynisca stops walking. Clytemnestra knows she is wondering why she is telling her this, but she won't ask.

"You have been in my mind throughout this torture," she continues. "I have always despised people like you, who have nothing good of their own so they try to steal someone else's happiness."

"I never wanted to steal anything," Cynisca says.

"But you did."

Before Cynisca can reply, Clytemnestra throws the knife in her direction. She feels Cynisca jump and take the shield and hears the clang of the knife against it. She moves to the side as Cynisca runs forward and crashes into the table. The cup rolls on the floor and Cynisca stands back up. Clytemnestra bends and takes her knife again. In the dark, she feels the shield flying in her direction a second too late. She manages to move aside but the metal hits her shoulder and she gasps in pain. Cynisca runs forward, but Clytemnestra throws her knife again, and this time it hits the target. Cynisca falls on her knees in front of her, and Clytemnestra takes the knife out of her flank before Cynisca can grab it. The metal feels as cold as ice. She tears away a piece of her tunic and stuffs Cynisca's mouth with it.

"I wanted to kill you before I left, but Agamemnon would have complained," she says. "Now he doesn't even remember you. No one cares if you die."

Cynisca moans and shakes her head. Clytemnestra stabs her again; the dagger sinks deep into her chest. The sound Cynisca makes is like a sigh.

"Your plots and plans haven't worked. I have power and all you have is whispers in a king's ear. I am queen of Mycenae, and you are nobody."

She takes the jeweled knife out of Cynisca's chest and steps back as Cynisca drops to the side, blood pouring out of her wounds. She finds her cloak in the shadows, wraps it around her, and leaves.

Soon people will wake and fill the narrow streets with life. Soon Cynisca's husband will come home to find his dead wife. But no one will suspect Clytemnestra, because no one knows what Cynisca did to her.

She runs in the maze of narrow streets until her hands are shaking and her face is wet with tears. In the shadows of a blind alley, she stops to catch her breath and clean her mother's knife on her cloak. The moon shines feebly above her, dripping light like a bucket of milk filled to the brim. The air is thick and sweet with the smell of ripe figs, but there is something rotten about it too, as if the place is tainted.

"Promise me you won't be as vengeful as I have been," her mother has said. And she sat there and promised, knowing it was a lie, that her words were cracked, like dried mud.

When she was young, she was scared of the Furies, the goddesses who take vengeance on all those men who have sworn a false oath. Leda had told endless stories of how the Furies found their victims and hunted them down like hounds, their scourges as painful as a thousand burning whips. Now she is standing here, a murderer and an oath breaker, yet no one comes for her.

A feeling of loneliness opens inside her, as big as a ravine. She rests her head against the wall as clouds and stars float above her and cries for what her life might have been. Was there ever a chance for her? A human's blood is fertile. Once it is spilled, it breeds new violence, but gods can't bring back a life. They can only take another. Leda must understand this. After all, she has kept secrets; she has lied and killed those who opposed her. She has stood aside as her husband betrayed her daughter.

No, Clytemnestra considers. Her mother can't ask her to keep a promise.

17

The Strongest Rules

MYCENAE APPEARS IN the late-afternoon light, and Clytemnestra spurs her horse. Outside the Lion Gate, the street is thick with people. Thin children move aside as she passes, and noblemen's slaves bend and kneel. She lifts her arm in greeting as her horse moves upward, leaving the gate behind. Inside the walls, women are grinding and weighing wheat in front of the barn, their heads covered to protect their eyes from the sun. Girls bear baskets of olives on their heads, and a group of boys count the pigs in a yard. As Clytemnestra passes them, the crowd opens and closes behind her like a wave.

Outside the palace on top of the citadel, on a big terrace warmed by the sun, a woman with auburn hair runs to meet her.

"It is good to have you back, my queen," Aileen says. She has changed since they met fifteen years ago. If her eyes were once downcast and her hands trembling, now she moves in the world with certainty—Clytemnestra has made sure of that. Many servants have come and gone, but Aileen has been her most faithful.

"My daughters?"

Aileen leads her to the garden, where Chrysothemis is playing with some colored stones. Her bare feet are cooling on the grass away from the heat of the terrace. Behind her, a group of dancing girls moves in and out of the shade of the olive trees. A young man is playing the lyre a few steps from them, his eyes closed.

When she sees her mother, Chrysothemis springs up, a sweet smile warming her face.

"I chose this for you while you were gone, Mother," she says, holding out a blue stone.

Clytemnestra brushes her lips against her daughter's head. "Did you choose some for your sisters as well?"

Chrysothemis shows Clytemnestra a reddish stone and a white one, as smooth as an egg. "This one is for Electra," she explains, holding the white stone to the light. It catches violet and yellow shades, just like the clouds when you look at them long enough. "Because she always dresses in white. And because she is as serious and boring as the goddess Athena."

Clytemnestra wants to laugh but she says, "Don't call your sister boring." Behind them, Aileen chuckles.

Chrysothemis turns to look at the group of dancers. "Iphigenia has learned the new steps—look!"

The women are swaying and swirling. The steps are intricate, and some falter, their eyes flying to the light-haired girl at the front. Iphigenia moves with the grace of a goddess, her lovely face twisted in concentration. Clytemnestra knows that look. It is the fire, the fierce determination that accompanies her daughter's every action. She is wearing a small tiara adorned with amethysts and several gold anklets as rich women in Mycenae do. They swing and glitter as they catch the light of the sun.

Chrysothemis stares at her, clutching the stones, shaking her little head with the rhythm. It has been a while now since she started modeling herself on her sister.

When the boy stops playing the lyre and the dance ends, Iphigenia looks around as if waking from a trance. She sees her mother and flings herself at her. "Mother!" she shrieks, throwing her arms around her. "I didn't know you were coming back so soon! How was Sparta? How is Aunt Helen?"

Clytemnestra cups her hands around her daughter's cheeks, searching her face for any trace of bruises or sadness. But Iphigenia glows like a freshly painted fresco. Behind them, the girls are resting under the trees, pouring water on their sweaty arms.

"Everyone is well," Clytemnestra says. "I saw your cousin Hermione, who is as big as your sister."

"And your brothers? Did they talk about Colchis? Did they say anything about Jason and Medea?"

"They did," Clytemnestra replies, and the light sparkles in her daughter's eyes. "But now is not the time. I must see your father first."

Chrysothemis looks down at her feet, suddenly sad. "Father spent all his time in the great hall with those soldiers from Crete and Argos. We saw him only at dinner. Now the soldiers are gone, but Father is always with the elders."

"He is discussing the war," Iphigenia says. "Every city fears Troy, it seems, but no one wants to fight."

Clytemnestra leads her daughters up the steps to the entrance of the palace. Behind them, Aileen follows, her arms filled with tunics and sandals. When they step over the threshold, the air is suddenly fresher.

"I will see your father now," Clytemnestra says. "Find Electra and prepare for dinner."

The courtyard that leads to the *megaron* is cool and quiet. Clytemnestra half expects to see Electra there, eavesdropping on her father, but there is no one under the shadowy colonnades except the frescoed griffins, sitting proudly by every column.

She can hear the whispers coming from the hall in the anteroom, with its bare walls and stone floor. The air there is moist, the light scarce. An older servant approaches to wash her feet. She stands still as the woman unties her sandals and cleans her in the footbath. When her feet have been wiped with a dry cloth, she steps forward into the bright light of the *megaron*.

The hall is richly adorned. Its walls are decorated with frescoes of warriors and lions fighting, their spears flying, chasing the fleeing beasts. The first time she saw the frightened lions, Clytemnestra laughed—no one who ever hunted lions saw the animals in such a state.

"This speaks of the power of our city," Agamemnon had said.

"It is a lie," she replied.

"It is a story. Stories draw people together; they lead armies and form alliances." As much as she hated him, she knew he was right.

Four guards stand with their backs to the walls, holding spears and shields. Clytemnestra waits by the columned entrance as one moves forward to announce her presence to the king. Beyond the hearth that occupies the center of the room, she can see Agamemnon seated on his raised throne, the steps that lead to it gilded and shiny. A boy is seated at his feet while a group of older men whisper, their voices hissing.

"The queen is here," the guard announces, and the king and elders turn. Clytemnestra walks past the frescoed battles of Mycenaeans against *barbaroi*, the lions, and deer toward the throne. Orestes jumps to his feet about to run to her, then stops, controlling himself. He is olive-skinned, like his mother, with dark curls that fall around his face. The elders kneel, their faces touching the floor at Clytemnestra's feet.

"Please stand," she says. "There is no need." It troubles her to see them so obliging, when all they do when her husband isn't here is challenge and contradict her.

"My queen," one says, straightening. He is a brutal man called Polydamas, whom her husband respects above all. "I hope the journey from Sparta was not too tiring?" His breath smells like fresh flowers, but Clytemnestra knows there is something murky about him, like the mud that hides under the bulrushes after a wet season.

"It was pleasant," she says.

"And how is your sister?"

"Helen is well. She has plenty of time to spend with little Hermione, especially now that King Menelaus has taken an interest in the helots around the palace."

Orestes looks at his feet. *Your father has taught you never to look down in front of his counselors*, Clytemnestra wants to say. She will tell him later. The elders close their mouths, embarrassed.

"Leave us," Agamemnon says, and they nod, relieved. They walk away slowly, their limbs old and knotty as oaks. When they disappear into the anteroom, Clytemnestra caresses her son's curls. He doesn't draw away but relaxes under her touch. Agamemnon steps down from his throne, his eyes wary.

"The merchants I asked you to deal with are complaining again," he says. No greeting or questions, but then she doesn't expect her husband to behave in any other way.

"They want to be paid more in exchange for the losses with Troy," she says. She had dealt several times with a group of angry merchants before leaving for Sparta. They demanded that Mycenae keep exchanging goods with Troy, while Agamemnon was trying to boycott the city.

"Yes. But there is another matter," Agamemnon says.

"Speak."

"They don't want to deal with you anymore."

Orestes looks at his mother, worried.

Clytemnestra wipes any expression from her face. "What did they say exactly?" she asks.

"That you are not fit to give them commands. But it doesn't matter. You will talk to them tomorrow and you will teach them to listen."

"Good," she says. One of the few things she doesn't despise him for: he likes it when she is in charge, when she takes matters into her own hands. He wasn't convinced at first, but when he saw how everything in the city functioned under her command, he was smart enough to let her do the work.

"What of Troy?" Clytemnestra asks. "Will there be war?"

Agamemnon shakes his head. "No Greek king wants to fight. They need a reason to do so. Troy is rich and dangerous to us, but that is not reason enough for them."

She frowns. "You go to war because that is what you are trained for."

"I agree. Still, they will wait until the Trojans are on our doorstep."

"The Trojans will not come. They have gold, they control much of the sea, and they have the mines at the foot of Mount Ida. They have no reason to come to us."

His eyes shine for a moment. He comes closer and kisses her forehead. "So we will go to them," he says. He turns to leave but lingers by the door. "I didn't ask about your family. How are they?"

She is almost surprised by the question and braces herself for the snake hidden among the flowers. "They are well."

"And your stay in Alea was good?"

She doesn't like the look in his eyes. "Yes."

"I imagine Timandra is now fucking Arcadian women."

Orestes gasps next to Clytemnestra, but she doesn't flinch.

"I always liked her best, Timandra," Agamemnon continues. "She is tough, like you. I just wish she would visit more." He gives her a sly leer.

She moves toward him, covering the distance between them in a few steps. She stands on her tiptoes and kisses his cheek. Then she whispers in his ear, low enough for Orestes not to catch the words. "If you talk about my sister again, I will strangle you in your sleep."

She goes to the storage rooms to find her daughter. Dinner is ready—the smells of vegetable soup and fish sauce fill the palace—and Aileen has told her that Electra is nowhere to be found, so rather than washing herself in a cool bath, Clytemnestra takes the corridor that leads to the storerooms. Leaving the frescoed halls behind, she follows the stone steps that go deep into the underground vaults of the palace. There is the faint smell of the earth and the spices and oil that come from the clay vases lining the dark corridors. She reaches a room where a single dim lamp shines feebly. On a shelf, there are old offering bowls and sacrifice knives still stained with dried blood. The shadows they cast on the walls resemble claws and fingers.

Electra is hiding in a corner, her head resting on her knees. Her breathing is rhythmic and quiet as if she is sleeping. Clytemnestra takes a step forward, and Electra's head jerks up. A sliver of light from the lamp touches her cheek. "You always find me," she says.

Clytemnestra sits on the cool floor in front of her daughter. "It is time for dinner. You shouldn't be here."

Electra examines her fingernails and keeps quiet. Finally, in a calm voice, she says, "I saw a dead dog today."

"Where?"

"In the alleys close to the Lion Gate."

Clytemnestra doesn't point out that Electra wasn't meant to be there by herself. Her middle child is always the most difficult to talk to—sometimes Clytemnestra wants to unspool her brain, picking through her mind one thought at a time. "What did it look like?" she asks.

Electra thinks for a moment. "A rag," she says. "It was pushed against the potter's door. It must have died on the street and someone kicked it out of his way."

"What did you do?" Clytemnestra asks, though deep down, she knows the answer.

"I washed it, burned it, and buried its ashes by the back gate."

"But you are still here," Clytemnestra says. "What upsets you?"

"I had never seen a dead thing before," Electra says simply.

This strikes Clytemnestra. A flash of Helen sitting on their bed when they were sixteen comes to her. "I have never killed anything," Helen had said. But still, as innocent as her sister was, she had seen plenty of dead men, women, and animals. Horses rotting by the river, children killed by illness in the helots' villages, thieves thrown down the Ceadas, young boys killed in combat. But that was Sparta. In Mycenae, Electra is twelve and her life is shielded. She hasn't bled yet. She hasn't been touched by a boy. She has never been beaten. And she has never seen a dead body.

As if reading her mind, Electra asks, "You saw dead babies when you were my age, did you not?"

Clytemnestra looks away, the image of her dead son in Leda's arms like a heated blade against her brain. Sometimes Electra says things that make her suffer, and she wonders if her daughter does it on purpose. It seems unlikely, but a thought creeps through her mind, making her restless: What if Electra can be as unkind as her father? What if she is not quiet because she is shy but because she is crafty?

"The first dead thing I saw was a boy," Clytemnestra says. "It was in the gymnasium. He died because of an accident."

Electra's eyes go flat. "What did it look like?"

Clytemnestra tries to think. There was no blood, but the head was bent sideways unnaturally, as if the boy had fallen asleep in an uncomfortable position. "It was bloodless."

"Like a fish when it is caught." This is another thing about her daughter: rather than asking many questions, her sentences come out as statements. Other children find it unnerving.

"Yes," Clytemnestra says. "But fish gasp before dying. The boy didn't suffer."

Electra thinks it through. "Death doesn't scare you."

"It scares me, but less than it scares others, because I am used to it. Does it scare you?"

"Yes. Only a fool wouldn't fear death."

Clytemnestra smiles. "Your grandfather once said something similar."

Electra stands, smoothing her dress. "I don't want to eat in the hall tonight. I am sad and the elders are like spiders, speaking into Father's ear, weaving their webs."

Clytemnestra waits, looking at the light shifting in her daughter's eyes as she thinks of the best way to ask. Finally, Electra says, "Can I stay in the *gynaeceum* and eat alone?"

Clytemnestra stands too. "You can't eat by yourself. You know that." Electra opens her mouth to reply, but her mother says, "I will talk to your father so you and I can eat together in your room."

Electra stays very still, and for a moment, Clytemnestra thinks she will say no. Then suddenly, she smiles, and her serious face is lit, like the first glint of sun on water.

Later, when they have eaten their fish and lentils, they lie down in Electra's room, the frescoed ceiling above them like the summer sky. Clytemnestra had the *gynaeceum* repainted when she found out she was pregnant with Iphigenia, every trace of her home scraped away. Now the walls are covered with frescoes of warrior women and goddesses, their spears sharp and precious, their skin pale and polished, like ivory. And on the ceilings of her daughters' rooms, little suns and stars, like golden tears.

Clytemnestra closes her eyes. The image of Cynisca's body kneeling on the floor, blood pouring through her palms, comes back to her, like balm on her skin. *Did she think I would forget? That I would let her live after what she did to me?* Time had passed and Cynisca had thought herself safe. But vengeance works best when it's aided by patience. And patience is like a child: it must be nursed so it can grow day after day, feeding on sorrow, until it's as angry as a bull and as lethal as a poisoned fang.

Believing her mother has fallen asleep, Electra nestles under her arm, keeping close though the room is hot. Clytemnestra feels her shoulder growing numb but she doesn't move, afraid that her daughter might pull away. She pretends to sleep until she can hear Electra's regular breathing against her neck. When she opens her eyes, her daughter is sleeping with her mouth slightly open, her limbs relaxed as they never are when she is awake. Soon, Electra will wake and her sharpness, her alertness will return. But now, as she sleeps with a half smile on her lips, she looks happy and vulnerable, like a goddess resting among humans by mistake.

She wakes to the sound of her daughters quarreling. Around them, the walls are bathed in light. Electra sits on the edge of the bed as Aileen arranges her *peplos*, fastening the fabric at the shoulders with pins. Iphigenia is walking up and down the room, speaking about a lyre competition Electra doesn't want to take part in.

Aileen and Clytemnestra exchange an amused look. Every day, it is the same. Chrysothemis plays with other noblemen's children, Orestes trains with the boys, while Iphigenia and Electra argue and challenge each other. They are so different that sometimes Clytemnestra wonders how it is possible that they came from the same womb. Fair in appearance, Iphigenia is stubborn, like a flower growing in the desert. Limits and constraints fall apart when faced with her intention, and her cleverness, the brightness with which she does everything she puts her mind to, leaves others speechless and in awe. Electra faces the world without the same confidence. She is never truly happy or satisfied, as if a worm is eating her from the inside, making her constantly fearful and frustrated. She tries to find her peace by shutting herself in the most remote rooms and nooks of the palace, but in the end, she always goes back to Iphigenia. It is as if she needs her sister's fervor to light the world around her, but it reminds her that, without it, her life would be gray and musty.

The merchants don't go to her, so Clytemnestra must go to them. She sets out late in the afternoon with her most faithful guard, a young man with thick dark hair and umber eyes. Leon has served her for a few years, after winning a wrestling game organized by her husband. He had thrown his opponent into the dust, walked to the dais where king and queen were seated, and knelt in front of Clytemnestra. "All I desire is to serve you, my queen," he told her. Agamemnon laughed, but Clytemnestra let him kiss her hand and told him she would be happy to have him as guard. He is the kind of man Castor would like—smart and loyal. She could hear her brother say, "That is a rare combination. Intelligent and devoted as a dog. You will need one of those every now and then."

The streets are busy at this hour and the heat almost unbearable. Children are running, jumping, playing catch-me. Vendors shout in the fly-infested air. Clytemnestra and Leon take a side alley that leads to the back gate, where the houses are so tall that they shut out the sun. There is the stink of piss and fish.

"Are you sure they are here?" Clytemnestra asks as they step aside to avoid an old slave pushing two pigs down the road.

"Yes, my queen," Leon says. "I came here myself once. Artists and merchants drink here every evening."

She lets him show her the way. He turns left into an alley lined with wine barrels where the smell of fish lessens and then into a shadowy room lit by three torches. The space is empty except for a woman with long, wavy hair covering her bare breasts and a man cleaning a shiny cup with a rag. Clytemnestra takes off her cloak and they gasp.

"My queen—" they start, but Clytemnestra quiets them. She can see a door covered with a long piece of cloth at the end of the room and hears voices coming from beyond it.

"No need to announce me." She turns to Leon and hands him the cloak. "You wait here."

"You can't go in there alone," he remonstrates. She ignores him and moves the cloth aside, stepping into the back room.

The heat is strong enough to drown men in their own sweat. Six traders are seated at a large wooden table, cups of wine in hand, some roasted meat in the middle. They don't look up when she walks in. Hearing her footsteps, one man says, "I thought we agreed, girl. It's too hot in here to fuck."

Clytemnestra stands very still. She can imagine Leon on the other side of the curtain fuming, clenching his fists.

"The king told me you don't wish to speak to me," she says, her voice loud and clear. The men turn, their faces bright red. When they see her, they freeze on their chairs.

"Basileia," a small man with beady eyes says. Though he calls her "queen," there is no respect in his voice. "We didn't know you were here."

She walks to the table, takes the jug, and pours some wine into an empty cup. The men stare back at her, unsure of what to do. They look like deer, their heads turned together as they confront a leopard.

"I have paid you in gold as compensation for your trade losses," Clytemnestra says, "yet you have betrayed the king and tried to take advantage of the situation by selling your gold and jewels to Troy. I could have executed you, as my husband suggested, but I paid you more and made you promise to keep Troy out of your trade."

"You have been gracious, Basileia," the small man says. The others nod, looking at him as if for instruction.

"I have. But still, you don't wish to take orders from me. Why is that?" she asks, even though she knows why. She wants them to say it aloud.

A look passes between the men and she watches as they take their time to answer. Their tunics are of fine embroidered cloth but yellow-ish with sweat. Their faces are sun-darkened, lines framing their eyes and necks. They are not strong men, but cunning. "You were taught to fight warriors, but watch out for merchants," Agamemnon once said to her. "They are the most dangerous men."

Because they keep silent, Clytemnestra says, "Speak."

The small man speaks again for the others. "We don't take orders from a woman."

"Why?"

He doesn't hesitate this time. "The strongest one rules," he says.

She smiles. "And who is that among you?" She lets her eyes linger on them, on the flabby stomach of one, on the golden rings of another.

"Merchants have no leader," the small man says.

"And yet you speak for all of them."

An older trader with arms thin as a woman's clears his throat. "He is our leader, Basileia."

The small man grins. He wanted them to say it, Clytemnestra is sure. And now it is too late for him.

"Good. Then I challenge you to fight me, here and now. If you win, you will keep making decisions for the merchants. If I win, you will take your orders from your queen."

He frowns. "Surely you don't want to fight a man as low as me."

"The strongest one rules, you said. So let us discover who is stronger." She downs the wine and places the empty cup on the table. The other traders step back toward the wall.

The small man looks panicked, like a field mouse. A thought crosses his mind and he speaks. "What about the king?"

"The king will never know of this," she says. "He will be spared from your vile behavior."

She has just stopped speaking when the man jumps forward, his fists clenched. She moves to the side without effort. He is slow, unbalanced, weak—a man who has never wrestled in his life. And still he wishes to command her. When he moves in her direction again, she takes his arm and bends it behind his back. He falls to his knees, gasping. She punches his head, and he drops to the floor like a sack of wheat. She turns to the other men. They are wide-eyed, gaping.

"He has lost consciousness," she says. "But he will revive in a moment. He no longer commands you. I do. And from now on, every time you hear someone complain that they have to take orders from a queen, remind them of what happened to the small trader."

They nod. It is hard to tell if they are frightened or just in awe. What is the difference anyway? Her brother used to say that there is none.

18

The Favorite Daughter

IT IS AUTUMN, and the land is painted in yellow and orange shades. Envoys come and go from the palace, bringing news of trade, marriages, alliances. Warriors and villagers ask for an audience in the *megaron*, each with their own request: My king, my son is born a cripple, my wife lay with another man, the merchants wouldn't sell me their wine.

My queen, the neighbor stole my bread, insulted the gods, spoke of treason.

Their words fill the room like songs, and Clytemnestra looks at the painted walls as she listens. Beside her, Aileen sits on a low stool, organizing piles of clay tablets filled with inventories: sheep and rams, axes and spears, wheat and barley, horses and war prisoners. Many commoners come to speak to the queen. They walk into the bright light of the hall, kneel in front of the king, then turn to Clytemnestra with their requests on land disputes and marriage portions. They know that she listens calmly to every plea and that she gives her help to those who respect her.

They also know that it is better to have her as an ally than as an enemy. Everyone in the citadel remembers when a villager's daughter was raped and killed by a nobleman's son after she cried out her defilement. The dead girl's father had come to the *megaron*, a small, broken man, asking for the impossible: that the nobleman's son pay the price. The elders had been appalled. Fathers didn't seek vengeance for their daughters. Kings didn't punish lustful young men—Clytemnestra had learned that a long time ago.

But she is no king. She had the nobleman's son dragged outside under the scorching sun and before the people's eyes. He was whipped until his back was soaked.

As the boy was carried away, barely conscious, Clytemnestra remained in the street, watching the stream of blood run past every door. Agamemnon stayed with her. He watched her with the amusement of a merchant who has made a good investment and now enjoys the fruits of his labor. The smile on his face made her sick.

In the practice yard, Clytemnestra and the army master show the boys different swords, shields, and spears. There are also slings and axes, bows and arrows. It is Leon who teaches the boys to shoot, because Clytemnestra has seen him hunt birds and squirrels, and he never misses the target.

Orestes has come for his first year of training, and Aileen has taken his sisters to the yard to watch. Clytemnestra wanted her daughters to train too, but Agamemnon has forbidden it. "If they start training, other women will want to train too," he said.

"So? You would have a bigger army."

"A weaker one."

"I am stronger than most of your men."

He laughed at that, as if she were joking, and walked away.

The day is sweet and rainless, with a cold breeze that carries birdsong to the yard. Clytemnestra makes the boys fight in close combat. She gives one a short sword and leaves the other without a weapon to teach him how to be quick and disarm with his bare hands. It is a difficult task, but the boys are eager to learn. Orestes is smaller than most, but he is as fast as a hare and manages to disarm a much bigger boy by tripping him. When the master hands him the sword, however, he becomes slow and lets the opponent go unharmed.

"Why did you do that?" Clytemnestra asks.

He gives her a guilty look. "It is not a fair fight."

"And it was when you were the one without a weapon?"

Orestes shrugs. He draws a circle in the sand with the point of his sword.

"So you think war is fair?"

Orestes shakes his head. Clytemnestra knows her boy is weak—she has seen him cry after one of his father's beatings, cower when his sisters yell at him. Out of the corner of her eye, she sees Electra staring at her. She wonders what her daughter is thinking.

"Do our people fight only to defend themselves?" Clytemnestra says. "Do we harm only those who have offended us?"

She can feel the buzzing of Electra's thoughts now. She can almost hear her daughter think, *Would that be such a bad thing? There would be fewer wars.*

But Orestes says, "No."

"Start again then," Clytemnestra says, stepping aside to make room. The boy Orestes was fighting walks to the center of the yard again, his feet unsure. Everyone is watching now, and silence is curdling around them.

Orestes casts one last look in his mother's direction. Then he cuts the boy's face. Blood spurts onto Orestes's tunic, and the army master nods approvingly. When the boy steps forward again, his fists clenched, Orestes cuts his leg and leaves him kneeling on the ground, his palms soaked red.

Leon walks into the yard and helps the boy to his feet to clean his wounds. The other boys' whispers flutter like bats through tree branches. Clytemnestra turns to her daughters. Iphigenia's eyes are wide open, torn between terror and relief; she is holding Chrysothemis's hand, though her sister doesn't seem scared. Electra's face is as dark as the sea.

"Does he hate me?" Orestes has walked to her, blood dripping from his sword. He is staring at the boy as Leon cleans his face with water; the cut goes from the temple to his chin. It is a deep, angry gash, and it will soon swell.

"It doesn't matter," Clytemnestra says. "Next time he will fight harder, and he will defend himself better."

Orestes nods. Clytemnestra doesn't touch him—she can't touch him now, not in front of all the other boys—but she will hug him later and tell him he has been brave. Warmed by the thought, she turns to her daughters once more, but next to Iphigenia, there is only Chrysothemis, frowning as she looks at the wounded boy. Electra has disappeared.

Mousike lessons are in a spacious room that opens onto the inner courtyard. The floor is of the purest white marble from Paros and the ceiling painted a brilliant red. When Clytemnestra walks in, a woman with long, black hair and thick gold earrings is arranging the instruments in front of Iphigenia and Electra. Out of the corner of her eye, Clytemnestra sees Electra frown—her daughter is still angry after the scene in the practice yard.

"Out," Clytemnestra tells the music tutor, lifting the lid of the lyres' chest. "I will teach them a song today."

Iphigenia cocks her head, curious, and Electra scoffs. As Clytemnestra's fingers caress the chords, a shimmering sound fills the room. "Our tutor in Sparta taught this song to me and my sisters," she says. "Do you know the story of the goddess Artemis and the hunter Actaeon?"

Electra scrutinizes her mother, her eyes narrowed.

"He watched her as she was bathing?" Iphigenia says. "And called the rest of his hunting party to watch too?"

"He was driven by lust, as men often are. But Artemis punished him and turned him into a stag." Clytemnestra sets her eyes on her daughters and begins to sing.

> *"Foolish Actaeon!*
> *You thought you could*
> *humble the Unharmed.*
>
> *"Look at yourself now!*
> *The hunter is devoured*
> *by his own hounds."*

Iphigenia shifts uncomfortably on her stool. Electra's eyes are as cold and serious as a raven's. "I love the songs on Artemis," Helen had said when she heard the story for the first time. "She is ruthless, but at least she never gets hurt."

"Maybe those men wouldn't have done anything to her," Clytemnestra says. "Maybe they just wanted to see her body. But have you ever heard of a man who stumbles upon a naked goddess and just walks away?"

Iphigenia shakes her head.

"It is noble to be gentle, to save others from pain. But it is also dangerous. Sometimes you have to make life difficult for others before they make it impossible for you."

In the following days, every time boys are cut, Clytemnestra teaches them how to clean wounds and which herbs to use to stop infection. Leon helps her, and Iphigenia and Electra join the boys as they learn. Iphigenia is especially talented: her fingers are firm and gentle, her memory of the right herbs to use never wavering. She doesn't stop in front of anything, not even the most gruesome head wounds.

One morning Clytemnestra and Leon go to the practice yard to find Iphigenia cleaning a boy's knee. He is disheveled, his knees scabbed and his hair dirty—he must have come from the village outside the city gates. Iphigenia bends forward, swiping some salve onto the injury, whistling a tune to calm him. Her profile is soft in the morning light, and Clytemnestra finds herself at a loss for words, not wanting to disturb her perfect daughter.

Before she can stop him, Leon darts forward. He kneels next to Iphigenia and holds out the herbs she needs. She looks at him with a grateful smile and his face shines, like a flower in the sun.

"Mother, come!" Iphigenia says when she sees her lingering at the edge of the yard. "I found him in the village outside the walls. A dog bit him."

Clytemnestra walks closer. She studies her daughter and Leon's adoring stare as they kneel together on the dusty earth of the yard. Agamemnon once told her that Leon desired her, but he was wrong.

It is Iphigenia he wants. Rage mounts inside her, as it does every time someone wants to take away her daughter.

But then she sees the focus with which Leon hands Iphigenia the herbs, his care in staying far enough from her, his gentle eyes. He won't harm her. He wants only to stay close to her and feel her light, her warmth. Who but Clytemnestra can understand that?

One of Agamemnon's spies is reporting on the recent trades of Troy when the doors of the *megaron* are thrown open. Clytemnestra watches as a bearded warrior drags his son forward, ignoring the guards who invite him to wait by the anteroom. The boy is tall, with the face of an angry dog, and on his forehead, a gash is dripping blood down his cheek and onto the shiny floor. The spy stops talking and looks at Agamemnon, waiting for instructions.

"I imagine, Eurybates, that this is your son," Agamemnon says.

Eurybates bends. He is broad-shouldered, his skin the color of walnuts. "Yes, my king. Kyros. Fourteen years old and the fastest runner his age." As he approaches the throne, Agamemnon's spy moves aside, blending with the shadows of the hearth columns.

"And you interrupt me this morning because your son has been hurt," Agamemnon says with amusement, looking at the gash on Kyros's face as if it were a fleabite.

Eurybates's jaw tightens. "Yes, my king, he has been hurt but not during training or in a boys' fight." He falters. "Two girls did it."

Kyros's face grows purple with shame. Agamemnon stifles a laugh, then shakes his head, annoyance growing on his face.

"Do not bother me with this. Take the girls and flog them." He has just spoken when two men—Kyros's brothers, with the same angry face—bring Electra and Iphigenia into the hall.

Clytemnestra's hand flies to her dagger and the men take a step back, pushing her daughters forward. Electra is staring at the floor, tears on her cheeks, but Iphigenia's eyes are narrowed, focused on Kyros with an expression of pure hatred.

"This is what you get when you marry a Spartan woman. Unruly daughters." Agamemnon's smile doesn't reach his eyes. "You demand punishment, Eurybates?"

"He wanted to rip our clothes," Iphigenia hisses, fire in her eyes. "He chased us in the streets shouting that we would be forced to marry him after he was done with us."

Agamemnon speaks without even looking at her. "Do not interrupt, Iphigenia."

"As you said, they should be flogged, my lord," Eurybates says. He is avoiding Clytemnestra's eyes.

Agamemnon sighs. "Do as you wish. Though if your son can be taken down by two girls, he'll never be a man."

"They pushed him down." Eurybates's words are thick with spite. "One threatened him while the other hurt him with a rock."

Agamemnon opens his mouth, but Clytemnestra is quicker. "It is your son who should be punished, Eurybates. He tried to shame the king's daughters, and they defended themselves. Their bodies aren't his to take. Now leave, and do not come here again."

Eurybates storms out, his sons following close behind. Iphigenia and Electra linger, side by side, unsure of what to do.

"This is your fault," Agamemnon tells Clytemnestra. "You treat them as if they are equal to men."

She ignores him and stares at Iphigenia. "Why wasn't Leon with you?"

"He was training the older boys."

"Go and tell him what happened." *So he'll never let you out of his sight.*

Iphigenia hurries away, but Electra doesn't move. She waits until her sister's steps fade, then says, "It was *her* idea. I didn't want to do it."

"I do not care whose idea it was." Clytemnestra already knows it must have been her older daughter's doing. When Electra was little, Clytemnestra would often leave her by herself, as the other children made trouble and she had to run after them. While Orestes climbed trees and Chrysothemis threw stones, all Electra did was sit and stare, quiet. She rarely asked for help, and when she did, she didn't approach it as a child would but rather with the shame of an adult who struggles to admit his own weakness.

"So you won't punish us," Electra says.

"No."

Electra's eyes gleam with danger. "Would you have done the same if Iphigenia wasn't there?" she asks. "If it was just me?"

"Of course."

Her daughter's face tells her that Electra doesn't believe her. "At least Father treats us all the same," she says and walks away.

Once, a few years before, a Cretan envoy had praised Iphigenia's beauty. They were dining in the hall, bowls of spiced meat and honeyed cheese spread in front of them.

"This is a woman who can make a goddess jealous," he said. Iphigenia's face broke into a smile, and the Cretan turned to Clytemnestra. "I imagine she is your favorite."

"I do not have favorites," Clytemnestra said, rocking Chrysothemis.

Orestes hid his head under his mother's arm, and Electra, a small, dark-haired child with serious eyes, sat rigidly, frowning.

The man smiled as if she had jested, and the precious gems on his earrings twinkled. "Everyone has."

Clytemnestra rests her forehead against the painted griffins in the courtyard. At her feet, the frescoed blades of grass shimmer like snake-skin. The light is pale, wrapping its fingers around her body. Dust hangs in the air, suffocating.

"You cling to things too much," she can hear Castor say in her head. "So when you lose them, you lose control."

"You'd rather she let her daughters be flogged like commoners?" Polydeuces intervenes.

She does this often. Just stands in the courtyard and argues with her brothers in her head. Their voices are shadows, cool and faint, unreal if not for the comfort they bring her.

"We have all been whipped several times," Castor points out.

And what good has it done to us? Clytemnestra thinks. *Look at me. I am drowning in hatred.*

"Your hatred consumes you," Castor says gently. "But it also keeps you alive."

The words make her remember her husband's room, bright with lamps and torches despite the darkness of the night. The way she had stepped inside quietly, unseen by the guards and the dogs, her shadow stark on the walls. Her blade flashed in the light of the lamp, and Agamemnon had opened his eyes, feeling the metal against his skin. He could have pushed her away, if he wanted; he was stron-ger than her, but instead he said, "Here you are, consumed by your ever-burning hatred." His throat was soft under the blade. "But you won't do it. If I fall, the people of Mycenae will execute you." He was right, and she had stood up, hands shaking. He had tilted his head, judged the way to hit her—she had no time to think—then grabbed her hair and slammed her head against the wall. When she could see again, the frescoed lion was red with her blood. "Your life with me has just begun," he said, wiping her nose. The day after, she had woken with the sickness and known she was pregnant with Iphigenia.

These children I cling too much to are the only reasons I didn't rip my husband's head off fifteen years ago.

19

Violent Husband, Vengeful Wife

SOMETIMES SHE FINDS herself thinking about Tantalus and her baby, as much as she tries not to. The way Tantalus spoke, the world's secrets in his words, and the way the baby stared at her at night when he was meant to sleep. How her husband laughed when the baby cried and the smells of spices drifted, curling in the air. Her heart clenches, pain flooding her mind. Is there any greater torment than love in the face of loss?

Memory is a strange thing, vicious. The more one wants to forget, the more one can't help but remember. It is like a rat chewing at the skin, slowly and painfully—impossible to ignore.

"Pray to the gods," everyone kept telling her after Tantalus and her son were murdered. But you don't get rid of a rat by praying to the gods. You must kill it, poison it. And the gods can't help you with that.

"What are you thinking about?"

A voice that drags her out of her memories. Clytemnestra turns, and Iphigenia is looking at her. She is in the garden where she took refuge on her first night in Mycenae. The valley stretches below them, and above, the temple of Hera, silent and white. Clytemnestra rarely goes into it. Priests and priestesses aren't her concern.

"I was thinking about those petitioners," Clytemnestra says.

Iphigenia comes closer. "It's the baby you lost, isn't it? You always come here when you think about him."

Clytemnestra wants to look down but she doesn't. Lying to her daughter is of no use. She starts wondering whether she should ask Iphigenia to cover herself—it is getting colder and they are on the highest point of the citadel—when Orestes runs into the garden. He looks excited, his dark locks bouncing around his head as he hops toward them.

"Mother, I have to tell you!" he says, breathless. He stops when he sees Iphigenia, giving her a meaningful look. She narrows her eyes, suspicious.

"What happened?" Clytemnestra asks.

Orestes lowers his voice in a conspiratorial way. "I saw her with *that* man."

Iphigenia's cheeks are burning. "It was nothing."

"His mouth was on yours!" Orestes says, torn between anger and giddiness.

"Orestes!" Iphigenia says.

Clytemnestra wants to laugh, but she stays serious. "Did Leon kiss you?" she asks.

"How did you—" Iphigenia starts, her eyes wide.

"Yes, he did!" Orestes interrupts. "His hands were in her hair, and he told her she was the most beautiful girl ever to walk our lands!" He speaks as though Leon's words were a crime worth a flogging.

Iphigenia stands and starts to pace, agitated. She seems torn between attacking her brother and explaining herself to her mother.

"What did you do, Iphigenia?" Clytemnestra asks. "What did you tell Leon?"

Orestes sits on a mossy rock. He seems confused. "You are not going to scold her? She was *kissing* a man!" He insists on "kissing" to make sure his mother understands.

"It was wrong to spy on your sister, Orestes."

Orestes's triumph fades, like the colors of frescoes when the torches burn out. Iphigenia stops pacing. "It will never happen again, Mother," she says.

"Do you want it to happen again?"

Iphigenia chews her lip. Out of the corner of her eye, Clytemnestra sees Electra look out from behind a tree at the edge of the garden. She is watching them, trying to catch their words. Who knows how long she has been there?

"Leon is good to me," Iphigenia says. "And he is a great warrior, isn't he?"

"He is," Clytemnestra says. "But you won't marry him."

Orestes's face catches the light, full of mischief. He thinks the argument is back in his favor.

"Why?" Iphigenia asks. She looks saddened, though not too much; she is rarely in a bad mood.

"Because you are a princess of the most powerful Greek city, and he is just a guard."

There is a rustle and Electra comes out of her hiding place.

"Who will we marry, then?" she asks, unable to contain herself. Clytemnestra feels warmth creeping inside her. She loves it when her daughter loses her seriousness and composure, when she can't keep her curiosity at bay and hangs on her every word.

"A king," Clytemnestra says.

Iphigenia walks to her sister and takes her arm with a smile. She has already forgotten Leon and the shame of being seen. Clytemnestra watches as they sit together, Iphigenia talking animatedly about husbands, as if she had thousands of them, Electra listening with a frown. Her daughters may not be able to wrestle, she thinks, but they are not fools. They are fierce and clever, each in her own way, and won't have trouble ruling men and cities. Kings will beg for a chance to marry Iphigenia—boys and men already turn their heads wherever she walks. As for Electra, she will find someone who isn't intimidated by her brooding eyes.

They might not know how to wield a weapon, but it doesn't matter. Words can cut deeper than swords.

Leon is in the armory, counting the arrows in a bronze quiver, his back to the door. The boys he was training have gone home, and the yard is quiet. When Clytemnestra walks in, Leon turns and bows. "My queen."

She rests her back against the wooden wall, swords gleaming all around her. Because she doesn't speak, he frowns. "Are the children all right?"

"Yes." She sees the confusion in his eyes and tries to find the right words to say what she has to while Leon waits, discomfort growing on his face. "A few servants from the kitchen asked for you," she says. "You know the dark-haired girl my husband likes so much? She keeps staring at you at dinner."

He seems angry but says nothing.

She raises her eyebrows. "You should go to her."

"I do not like her," he says.

It is not up to you to decide who you like.

"I see." She touches her hand to the cool metal of a sword. "Though sometimes it is bad for us to go after the people we like. Do you know what I mean?"

He tilts his head. He understands that she knows about Iphigenia, but he doesn't seem sorry for it. Silence stretches between them, long and uncomfortable.

"I am sorry for what he did to you," he finally says. His voice is warm, and there is sadness in it. "I know about your other husband and what King Agamemnon did."

For a moment, she is speechless. She cannot believe he is talking about Tantalus. Nobody mentions her late husband—nobody dares. A woman—the wife of one of Agamemnon's warriors—had spoken of him once, years ago. "Is it true you were married to a *barbaros*?" she asked, disgust spread across her features.

Clytemnestra had whipped her knife under the woman's throat and spoken quietly. "I would cut you, but something tells me it wouldn't even be a good fight. So why don't you bite your tongue and never speak in front of me again?"

She looks at Leon. Is this what he thinks? That she doesn't want others to be happy because happiness was stolen from her? "You know nothing."

"You must have loved him," he says. She imagines sinking her palm into the blade, showing him her pain. He shouldn't dare speak to her like this. He shouldn't dare assume he understands her feelings.

"You know nothing," she repeats and walks away.

After dinner, she orders Aileen to prepare a warm bath. The bath-house in Mycenae is much larger than the one in Sparta, with high windows. As Aileen fills the bath with hot water brought from the kitchen, Clytemnestra looks out at the sunset firing over the palace, sending orange streaks across the sky. From up here, she can't hear the singing of the women or the chatter of the children and merchants that echoes throughout the citadel. The bathhouse is mute and muffles the sound of everyone inside it.

The water is ready, and Clytemnestra steps into the tub. The heat makes her flinch. Aileen washes her hair, gently combing out each knot, and Clytemnestra relaxes under her touch. She remembers how scared Aileen was when she arrived in the palace, a small, red-haired mouse always hiding in some corner. Once, Clytemnestra had found her in the dark corridor outside her room, alone, a platter of meat in hand. She was meant to take it to her but was too shy to do so. "You shouldn't be afraid of me," she had told the girl.

"Why?" Aileen asked.

"Because I am not going to hurt you. You should save your fear for the warriors, for the elders, or for the king."

Aileen looked up then. "And you? Don't you fear them?"

"I do," Clytemnestra said, "but I'm smart enough not to show it."

She is thinking back to that day, staring at the reflection of the burning torch in the water, when Aileen speaks. "King Agamemnon asked for my presence tonight."

Clytemnestra stiffens. Aileen moves to scrub her feet, and Clytemnestra catches her face under the feeble light—her features are calm, just like Clytemnestra taught her, but the wavering in her voice is unmistakable.

"You will not go," Clytemnestra says. "He can find some other servant to entertain him."

Aileen looks relieved but catches herself and tries to keep her face expressionless.

"But who?"

"There are plenty of women in this citadel who would like to fuck my husband."

Aileen nods, and for a moment, they are silent.

"What should I do, then?" she asks, unable to contain herself.

All these years, and she is still scared of him. Clytemnestra can't judge her for that. Aileen told her how Agamemnon's father used to sleep with her mother before Atreus was killed, of how his brother Thyestes would terrorize the servants with burns and floggings, of how, when Agamemnon took back the citadel, he executed all the people who hadn't been faithful. For many nights, after they put the children to bed, Aileen would speak to Clytemnestra of the violence of the Atreidai's line. She had frightened words for all men except one: Agamemnon's estranged cousin, Aegisthus.

"Aegisthus didn't like violence when he lived in this palace. He killed and hurt others only when he had to." In Aileen's whispered words, Aegisthus was a shy child, eager to be loved, and then a watchful young man, silent and slippery. While other men his age brought girls to their room, he never requested any servant's presence, and when his father flogged his enemies and made everyone watch, Aegisthus would later sneak into the prisoners' cells, bringing them food and salves to ward off infection.

"He sounds like an interesting man," Clytemnestra said once, "though harmless."

A shadow passed on Aileen's face. "He wasn't always harmless. He could be cruel too, and dangerous."

And now Aegisthus is out there, somewhere, the Atreidai's last standing enemy. Guards have been looking for him for fifteen years, yet no one has found him. As the elders pointed out in their last meeting, he is probably dead.

"My queen?" Aileen says.

Clytemnestra stands and water drips onto the stone floor. Aileen hurries to bring her tunic and wrap it around her shoulders.

"You will do nothing," Clytemnestra says. "I will deal with it."

She finds Agamemnon in his frescoed bedroom, sitting on a chair lost in thought. The painted trees and happy fish jumping in the river clash with his stark figure. He raises his head when she comes in. His look is hard—he is angry, though Clytemnestra can't tell why. Not that she cares.

"Your red-haired servant won't come tonight," he finally says.

"No."

"You told her not to."

"You will find someone else to fuck," she says calmly.

That makes him laugh; the sound scratches the painted walls. He pours himself some wine from the jug. Clytemnestra does the same, taking the other chair.

"And who would that be?" he asks, looking as she brings the cup to her lips. "You?"

"Hopefully not."

He laughs again and relaxes in his chair. She sees the muscles of his bare arms flexing, the scars wrinkling on his skin.

"For someone who hates me so much," he says, "you have endured this marriage for a surprisingly long time."

She smiles, the wine sour on her tongue. "Did you think I would kill you in your sleep?"

"You have tried, remember? Now you would be cleverer than that."

He pauses, studying her. "But you can't hate me forever. One can't live on spite alone."

On that we disagree. They keep silent for a moment, each staring at their own cup.

"I still want that girl," he finally says. "I am king."

She puts down her cup. "You will never touch her."

"Why?"

"Because if you do, I will gut you, like I did that whore Cynisca."

Shock sparks in his eyes. He plants his feet on the floor and stands. "What did you do?"

She throws back her head. "I found her and stabbed her until she bled to death."

He comes to her, moving the carved chests out of his way. "You know Cynisca was from a powerful family. My brother needs their support like your father before him."

"Menelaus will still have their support. Cynisca's husband remains alive and will continue to counsel your brother. No one knows it was me."

He grabs her neck. She smiles, defiant, even though he is hurting her.

"You are a vengeful woman," he spits out, "disobedient." His hand is closing and she thinks of how easily bones can snap in the neck, of how frail flesh is, easy to hurt, hard to heal. Still, she doesn't move or struggle. She wants him to strike her so she can strike him back. But he doesn't.

"Every day I ask the gods why you refuse to submit." His voice sounds hoarse, though she is the one who is being strangled. When he lets go, he is panting.

She clasps the back of her neck, feeling the pain where he touched her. She swallows, then says, "I'd rather die than submit to you."

She can't tell if he heard her. He has turned his back on her and left the room.

20

The Prophecy

CLYTEMNESTRA IS IN the *megaron* when the envoy breaks in, panting, claiming to have urgent news. It is early morning, and the frescoes burn in the red light of dawn. She has been talking to Orestes about trade; her son pointed to some of the swords and axes hanging on the walls, and Clytemnestra told him where the gold, crystal, and lapis lazuli came from.

"Should I call Father?" Orestes asks as the envoy tries to catch his breath. His hands are purple with cold, and he tucks each into the opposite sleeve in a vain attempt to warm them.

"I have a message for the queen," the envoy blurts out. "From the palace of Alea."

Clytemnestra sits up. Of all the possible news, this is the most unexpected. "Is Queen Timandra safe?" She must look ready to lash out, because the man seems afraid to speak.

He gulps. "Timandra has deserted King Echemus, my queen."

His voice is low, and for a moment. she thinks she hasn't heard correctly. The envoy looks up and, seeing that she isn't reacting, continues, "She was seen riding away in the night. They say she married King Phyleus in secret and now is pregnant by him."

The name tells her nothing. She frowns, trying to understand. "This message isn't from Timandra, then."

The envoy shakes his head. "It is King Echemus who sends me. He claims Timandra went mad after he sent her friend away from the palace." *Chrysanthe.* "He says he wants her back."

"Where is Timandra's friend now?"

"No one knows."

"Is Echemus looking for her?"

The envoy frowns, as though Clytemnestra's questions were missing the point. "Echemus only wants Timandra back, my queen."

Orestes stares at him. Behind the columns near the hearth, Leon is waiting for Clytemnestra's instructions.

"You can rest here tonight," she tells the envoy. "Leon will take you to the bathhouse. Tomorrow you will go back to your king."

"What should I tell him?"

"That I grieve for his loss, but I can't bring his wife back. Timandra is someone else's wife now."

The envoy pulls a face, torn between laughter and gravity. "Yes, my queen," he says, then leaves the room, following Leon.

Alone with his mother once more, Orestes walks to the wall and starts tracing the contours of the painted lions with his fingers. He used to do it all the time when he was a child, touching the frescoes as though they were windows to another world.

"Why did Aunt Timandra go mad?" he asks. There are fresh cuts on his face—he has been wrestling harder in the practice field, like a fighting dog that has learned the only way out of the arena is to take the others down.

Clytemnestra takes a deep breath. "She cared about her friend. And King Echemus sent her away."

"So she left him."

"Yes."

"Why didn't she tell you she would leave?"

"She couldn't tell anyone. You heard the envoy; she ran away in secret."

"You will never see her again, then."

Clytemnestra loses herself in the bright blue of the frescoed sky. It is the same shade as the summer sky beneath which she and Timandra played and wrestled. Of all her brothers and sisters, she was always the most like her.

"I knew this would happen," she says. "A priestess back in Sparta delivered a prophecy to my mother years ago. She said that the daughters of Leda would marry twice." *And thrice. And they would all be deserters of their lawful husbands.* But her son doesn't need to know that. She looks up and Orestes is frowning.

"You always tell me we don't believe in prophecies."

She smiles and goes to him, kisses his forehead. "You are right," she says. "We don't."

From the top of the high wall near the Lion Gate, the land glows bright against the dark of the woods and mountains. Iphigenia is speaking to her father animatedly, and two guards watch over them, a few feet behind. Just this morning, Aileen has taken the women down to the river to wash the clothes, and now Iphigenia is wearing one of her best dresses: light blue, sewn with gold drops and pendants. Feeling her mother's presence, she stops talking and turns.

"You are leaving us again, Mother," she says. Agamemnon turns too. His face is tired—he hasn't slept much. Clytemnestra heard him discussing potential alliances with his men until dark. When they had finally stopped speaking and she had fallen asleep, she dreamed of war and death.

"You heard about Timandra," she says.

He nods. "You are going to Sparta. And this time Leon is accompanying you. So in case you want to *murder* someone…" He lingers on the word, sneering, but Clytemnestra ignores him.

"Timandra is not in Sparta," she says.

Agamemnon meets her eyes without flinching. "Your sister isn't the only one causing trouble. Your brothers are starting a family feud."

Eager to participate, Iphigenia intervenes. "Uncles Castor and Polydeuces have kidnapped two women who were already promised to your cousins."

"Which cousins?"

"Lynceus and Idas from Messenia."

"I don't even know them." She has heard the names, the sons of one of her father's stepbrothers, but never met them.

"They are still your family," Agamemnon says, "and they are angry. Your father was close with Aphareus, Lynceus and Idas's father."

"Was he?"

"Tyndareus told me."

Clytemnestra breathes in, clenching her fists. That was when she started losing her father, as soon as Agamemnon came into her home and slowly made his way into Tyndareus's heart.

"You have to go to Sparta and fix this," he says. "Castor will listen to you."

"And if he doesn't?"

"Then you make him."

She looks down at the houses clustered around the city walls. The people in the streets are so loud that she can hear their laughter and shouts, the sounds of smiths casting bronze and of feet splashing in ponds.

"What about Helen?" she asks. "Surely she can convince Polydeuces."

Agamemnon waits a moment before speaking. "Your sister hasn't been well lately. She shuts herself into her room and doesn't even talk to her daughter."

"What happened to her?"

"Menelaus says she is unhappy."

"What has he done to her?"

He laughs. "You always think us guilty of petty crimes. My brother hasn't done anything. Your sister is spoiled, always has been."

"Menelaus doesn't respect her," Clytemnestra spits out.

"Mother," Iphigenia says, touching her hand, soothing her, "I think you should go. Uncle Castor will do anything you tell him to, and Aunt Helen will be happier as soon as she sees you."

Clytemnestra takes a deep breath, letting in the cold air. Her daughter clearly doesn't know anything about Castor: people can cry, plead, beg, but he will always find a way to do what he wants. But then she thinks of her sister, shutting herself up like a prisoner in her childhood home. It is terrible to be alone like that, when you are surrounded by people but no one can help you. It makes you feel there is no hope.

She needs to go to Sparta.

She says goodbye to her children at dawn and rides out of the Lion Gate with Leon when the citadel is still waking up. Down in the village, filthy pigs are snuffling along the streets while two dogs lick some spilled milk.

When she woke them before leaving, Orestes and Iphigenia yawned and kissed her.

"Tell Uncle Castor of my progress with the sword," Orestes whispered.

"Travel safely, Mother," Iphigenia said. "I am sure Aunt Helen will be so happy to see you." Her hair was the color of ripe grain in the semi-darkness, and Clytemnestra caressed it, putting some stray strands back into place. Then she moved to Electra's bed.

"Is it true that Helen is sick?" Electra asked quietly, sitting up straight on her pallet.

"She is just unhappy."

"I have heard that some women can die of unhappiness."

"*That* is untrue."

Electra sat in dissatisfied silence. When Clytemnestra moved forward to kiss her head, she curled up in her mother's lap.

"Come back soon, Mother," she said, her voice as quiet as a leaf that falls from a tree. Clytemnestra wished it were louder, so she could catch it and keep it close to her.

They ride for three days and nights. The land is silent and cold. The trees are losing their leaves and look stark, bonelike. Every time the sky becomes heavy with rain, they find shelter in a cave or among tumbled rocks. Leon is a good companion: he speaks only when he needs to, and his arrows never fail to provide good meals. Sometimes, as night comes and they warm themselves by the fire, she would like to talk to him about Iphigenia. *You kissed my daughter*, she wants to say. *I know you love her, but you can't be with her.* But then she thinks, *What would be the point? What good would it do to tell a man he can't have what he wants?* So she keeps silent and watches him as he skins a rabbit, his hair falling around his face. Maybe he is luckier in that way, she thinks. Maybe it is good for him never to have what he desires. Then others can't come and take it from him.

They reach the Eurotas just after noon on the third day. The water is frozen, reflecting the dark mountains and the colorless sky. The helots are working the land, cloths wrapped around their hands in an attempt to ward off the cold. Clytemnestra is careful to ride by the side of the fields, and as she passes, the helots look up, their faces all age lines and scars.

By the rocky terrain at the foot of the palace, a bearded man is waiting for them. The wind is so strong that he has covered his ears under his cloak. Still, his hands are chapped and his eyes watery. As soon as Clytemnestra and Leon dismount their horses, the man steps forward. "King Menelaus is waiting for you. You are to come at once." His voice sounds like nails screeching on rock.

"Is my sister safe?"

"Queen Helen is entertaining a guest. You are to see King Menelaus first. That is what he commands."

"Bring me to him, then."

They walk up the stairs, hurrying to match the man's pace. As soon as they cross the threshold inside, the warmth welcomes them like an embrace. The man guides them to the *megaron*, turning every once in a while to check on them, as though Clytemnestra didn't know the way. When they reach the hall, the man motions them to wait outside. Standing by the closed door, they hear him announce them: "Queen Clytemnestra, my king."

"What are you waiting for? Let her in." Menelaus's voice, mocking the man. "Bring food and wine."

The door opens again and a servant runs outside, an empty platter in her hands. She nods quickly to Clytemnestra and disappears in the kitchen's direction.

Menelaus is seated in what was Tyndareus's throne near the hearth. At his feet, two house dogs eat a long bone. The queen's chair next to him, draped with lambskins, is empty. Thanks to the many lit torches that illuminate the frescoes, the room is even warmer than the rest of the palace. Clytemnestra walks toward the hearth, Leon close behind her. She stops by the images of running men, their bodies the color of hazelnut, and waits for her brother-in-law to speak.

For what feels like a very long time, Menelaus keeps silent. He looks at her, pensive. His bronze hair has grown grayer with the years, but his face is still handsome. Finally, the servant comes back to the room, breathless and with a full platter, and Menelaus seems to wake from his trance. "Please, eat," he says, smiling. "I am glad to have you here."

Clytemnestra picks up a piece of goat cheese and accepts the cup of wine the girl is offering her. "And I am glad to be back."

Menelaus smirks, as though her response was a jest. "You have a very strange family, Clytemnestra," he says.

She sips the wine. She doesn't know where he is leading. Menelaus stretches in his throne and she notices the precious rings on his fingers, not the kind of jewelry a true Spartan would wear.

"A sister who fucks women but then deserts her husband for another man. Two brothers who kidnap girls promised to their cousins. My wife, who refuses to talk to her husband." He is not speaking with anger; rather, he seems confused by the situation he is in, like a child who asks his mother why the world works in a certain way. "Phoebe and Philonoe seem to be the only sane members of your family. Married off to useless kings. At least I hear they make them happy." He winks, gulping his wine.

"What about your family?" Clytemnestra asks. "What about your father and your uncle? A son killed and cooked, a daughter raped by her father. Your line is cursed."

Menelaus waves her away, as he would an irksome fly. "We knew the gods cursed our grandfather the moment we were born. But our fortunes have changed. The days of family feuds are over. Mycenae and Sparta prosper, and we have no more enemies."

Clytemnestra laughs. "That is because you killed them all."

"Not all," Menelaus corrects her. "Aegisthus still lives. But he will be found."

Clytemnestra thinks about the elders' whispers in Mycenae— "Aegisthus must be dead. No man can live alone in the woods for so long"—but she keeps quiet.

"And you have to remember," Menelaus adds, "you are family too now."

To avoid speaking, Clytemnestra takes more cheese, dipping it into a small cup of honey the servant offers her.

"The first time we came to Sparta," Menelaus says, "we wanted to see only your sister. She was all everyone spoke about. *Helen the beauty. Helen, who glows like a goddess. Helen, daughter of Zeus.* Then my brother saw you and forgot about Helen. He told me he would have you no matter the consequences. He said that you were different from the others, strong and sharp enough to bear anything. He never tolerated people who showed their suffering."

"That is the problem with your brother," Clytemnestra says. "He thinks only of what he wants. He forgets that there is a world around him, filled with people whose wishes he is not considering."

"Oh, he doesn't forget. He just doesn't take them into account. So he got you, and I married the most beautiful woman in all our lands." He smiles as if trying to convince himself of his good fortune. Then a thought crosses his face and he turns serious again. "But it doesn't matter.

She doesn't love me and never will. Helen loses interest easily and can't seem to be happy unless she has someone's attention. It is strange: she who is such a light is always seeking someone to show her the way."

"She was happy before you came along," Clytemnestra says.

Menelaus laughs. "You know very well she wasn't. That is why she came to me in the first place."

Clytemnestra tilts her head. "Did you summon me here to discuss your marriage?"

"No," he says, and his expression shifts. Now he looks more like his brother: sharper, greedier. "I have to leave for my grandfather's funeral. A ship is waiting to take me to Crete, but I wanted to make sure you were here first. You must keep things in order."

"What *things*?"

"There is an important guest here from Troy on a diplomatic mission." She raises her eyebrows but he continues. "The deal he came for is made, but he is staying longer. Help my wife entertain him. And make sure your brothers return those girls to whoever they were promised to."

She wants to ask if Agamemnon knows about this. But of course he does. That is why she was sent here in the first place.

"You speak of these women as though they were cows," she says.

Menelaus laughs. "Cows, women, goats, princesses, call them as you wish. They are the same to me."

And he wonders why his wife doesn't love him.

She smiles coldly and excuses herself. As she walks along the corridors lined with weapons of former Spartan rulers, she finds herself thinking of her grandmother.

This was once a palace of mighty queens. Of warrior women and daughters of Artemis. Now it belongs to a man who treats his wife as a golden trophy.

After a quick bath, she wears a Persian green dress with a dark woolen cloak and leaves the *gynaeceum*. The servants told her that Helen isn't in the palace, so Clytemnestra takes the path that leads to the temple of Artemis. She has ordered Leon to find her brothers and tell them she is in Sparta so she can speak to her sister alone.

Helen is sitting by the columns of the temple, her hands smoothing her white dress. On her head is a golden diadem, thin but precious, on her shoulders a leopard skin. She looks peaceful. Behind her, the spring at the foot of the mountains pours and rushes. Above them, the sky is blue and bare.

"Helen," Clytemnestra says, and her sister turns. Her cheeks are red with cold but her eyes light, like summer water. Helen jumps forward and hugs her. Clytemnestra feels the warmth of the leopard skin and closes her arms around her sister's waist.

"I knew you were coming, but I didn't know when," Helen says.

"Were you entertaining that Trojan prince?"

Helen blushes, though Clytemnestra can't tell why. "I was."

Clytemnestra searches her face for any trace of sadness or emptiness. But Helen's eyes are lively and her lips are curved into a smile.

"They told me you were unhappy. You look happy to me."

Helen's laugh is crystal clear. "I am not sad anymore."

"I am glad. Is Hermione well?"

"Of course she is. She is only annoyed that her uncles don't play with her much these days." She chuckles. "So she plays by herself. You should see her. She draws the most wonderful things in the sand, and sometimes she makes adornments with feathers."

"So does Chrysothemis," Clytemnestra says. "And Mother? How is she?"

Helen shrugs. "She didn't take well the departures of Phoebe and Philonoe. Phoebe was good with her, especially when Mother drank too much."

"We should hide the wine then."

"I have tried. It just makes her angry. She spends most of her time in her room now, so we visit her." She sits again on the stone floor at the temple's entrance. Her hair is plaited and it makes her eyes look bigger.

"We need to speak to Castor and Polydeuces," Clytemnestra says. "They must let the women go back to the men they were promised to."

Helen's face is amused. "You never change. You've just arrived and are already planning to fix everything."

"If I don't, who else will?"

"With everything that happened to us, we should have learned to let things be. We don't want to end up like Tyndareus."

We don't want to end up like Leda either, Clytemnestra thinks. Their mother has always believed the gods decided for most men, but Clytemnestra never accepted that. To exist in the shivering knowledge that gods could do and undo things as they wished: how could anyone live such a life? No. The gods are cruel and have little time for mortals.

Helen takes her hand. "Besides, our brothers aren't holding anyone against their will."

"What do you mean?"

"Phoebe and Hilaeira came here of their own accord. They love Castor and Polydeuces." She looks down, then adds, "Who wouldn't?"

Clytemnestra draws away. "We can't force Sparta into civil war. These women were promised to the king of Messenia's sons." Helen stares at her, frowning. "I can't stay here and fight a war while Menelaus is away. I have a family, children to take care of."

"We are your family too," Helen says with a sad smile.

"I am not risking a civil war against Messenia," Clytemnestra repeats, "so that Castor can sleep with yet another woman."

Helen stands, shaking her head. "This is different. I will take you to him now if you like. He'll make you understand."

On their way back to the palace, they pass the working helots and the stables, where the mares are resting. By the haystacks, next to a black stallion, a girl is retching, her hands keeping her hair out of her face. She lifts her head to look at them—her face is wet with sweat and sickness.

"Pregnant," Helen says.

"We have all been there," Clytemnestra replies. "She will be happy once the child is born."

"Will she?"

Clytemnestra turns to look at her sister, but Helen's face is unreadable.

Inside the palace, Helen stops just outside the wooden door of Castor's room. "You go in," she says, "Menelaus will be leaving soon, and I must say goodbye." Clytemnestra nods and Helen hurries back the way they came, her shadow following her, long and lean on the stone floor.

There is a shuffle, and her brother opens the door before Clytemnestra can knock. His face is brighter than it was the last time she saw him, and his oiled curls fall jauntily around his head.

"You are always trouble, Brother," she says.

Castor laughs. Unable to be serious, Clytemnestra laughs too. After all the times he said the same to her when they were little, he finally gets his payback.

"You have waited a lifetime to tell me that," he says. He moves aside to let her in. The room is bare, plain stone and simple furniture. On a bed carved of dark wood sits a young woman with auburn hair.

"This is Phoebe, Sister," Castor says.

Phoebe looks at her. There is something unsettling in her gaze, as if her eyes were blades trying to peel off Clytemnestra's skin. "Castor told me all about you," she says. "He says that you too love your freedom, yet you have been married off to a cruel king."

"Did your father promise you to our cousin?" Clytemnestra asks.

"He did. Do you know him?"

"I've never met him."

Phoebe stands and walks to the window. Her hair falls down her back like a cascade of fire. She wouldn't be pretty, Clytemnestra considers, without that hair.

"In my land," Phoebe says, "they call me and my sister Daughters of the White Horse. We love to ride, and our horses are whiter than sacred cows. You don't have horses like that here." She stops, taking a breath. "When my father promised me to your cousin Idas, Idas said that he would kill my favorite horse. He didn't want me to love it more than my husband."

"I am sorry," Clytemnestra says.

"Yet you have been sent here to convince Phoebe to leave, haven't you, Sister?" Castor's last word is nearly a sneer. Clytemnestra looks at him. Her brother has never stayed with the same woman for long before. People have always amused him, like a dancer would, or bored him.

"Lynceus and Idas are angry," she says. "They will come for you both."

"Of course they are angry," Phoebe replies. "They are men. They are used to getting what they want."

"It is too late," Castor says. Clytemnestra can see fever in his eyes, wildness. "Phoebe and her sister can't go back to Messenia." He walks over to Phoebe and touches her belly with the gentleness of a warrior touching the petal of a flower. "They are pregnant. Both of them."

21

Birds and She-Bears

IN THE DINING hall, Clytemnestra looks at the elaborate handles of the bronze swords on the walls—bone, ivory, gold, with inlaid decorations of lions hunting deer, geese flying, dogs running. As the servants prepare the room for dinner, her brothers, Phoebe, and another woman with long hair and a dark-blue dress walk in. Hilaeira has the same burning look of her sister, though her features are more delicate. They take their seats, and the servants carry in the wine jugs. Hermione runs into the hall, climbing onto Polydeuces's lap.

"Where is your mother?" he asks her, caressing her hair.

"She is accompanying the Trojan prince here," Hermione says.

Polydeuces stiffens, his eyes on the door. His fists are clenched, as if he were ready to spring up and fight. Clytemnestra follows his gaze and Helen appears, more luminous than ever. Her golden hair is loose, waves falling on her shoulders. A richly decorated tunic, heavy with golden drops, chimes pleasingly as she moves. Clytemnestra can see the mischief carefully hidden on her face. Even after all these years, she knows her sister as well as she knows herself.

Behind her is a man unlike anyone Clytemnestra has ever seen. His eyes sparkle like gems, and his hair is silky as a fox's fur. As he walks into the hall, the light from one of the torches above him turns his skin the color of gold when it is poured into stone cavities to make jewels.

It is a shocking, almost intimidating beauty, because it is careless. *Is this how gods look?* Clytemnestra wonders. Helen beckons him and he follows, never taking his eyes off her. An adoring servant girl jumps out of the shadows trying to pour wine for the prince, but he takes the jug and pours for Helen.

"Paris," Helen says when they are seated, "this is the sister I have told you so much about."

Paris's eyes land on Clytemnestra as if he has just noticed she is there. "You are the queen of Mycenae."

"And you are the Trojan prince who managed to make peace with the Greeks."

"Ah, I don't know about that," Paris says, smiling. It is a cheeky smile. Helen claps her hands and young men enter, flutes and lyres in hand. They play, each note unfolding quietly like wings in the darkness.

"In Troy, they never eat without music," Helen explains. Paris smiles at her and Helen smiles back. She doesn't touch her food; the honey on her plate spreads, soaking the cheese.

"Has your stay in Sparta been pleasurable?" Clytemnestra asks Paris, because the way the prince stares at her sister makes her uncomfortable.

"The most pleasurable," Paris says. "I have always heard Sparta was no more than a small palace on a rocky mount. It is far richer and its people far more welcoming than I could have imagined."

"Surely it must seem nothing compared to your home," Clytemnestra replies. From what she has heard, Troy is bigger than any Greek city, a huge, impregnable citadel built on a hill in front of the sea. "A palace with walls the color of wheat," an envoy had told her once, "its buildings inside so high that the people there are closer to the gods."

Paris shrugs. "Compared to Troy, yes. Our city has walls and towers higher than mountains. From the ramparts, you can see the land stretching around the city. It is like molten gold."

He pauses, sipping his wine, and a strand of hair falls on his face. "But I didn't grow up in Troy. When I was born, my mother dreamed she gave birth to a flaming torch. A warning, the seer at court said, a sign foretelling the downfall of Troy." He smirks, as if mocking the seer. "He declared that the only way to spare the kingdom was to kill me, and my father believed him. Our people are deeply religious... They would cut off their own arms rather than disappoint the gods."

The music is quieter now, and Paris's voice rolls on it as if he were singing. "My mother couldn't kill me. She couldn't ignore the seer, but she couldn't kill her son. So she left me on Mount Ida, sure that I would die there." A shadow passes over his face, but he quickly covers it with his bright smile.

"But who knows what plans the gods have for us? A herdsman found me on the rocky outcrop where my mother left me. He could have killed me, thrown me into the river, but he took me in as his own."

Clytemnestra gazes at his dazzling face. *He doesn't look like a man who lived among sheep and goats.* Any other prince would be ashamed to speak so, but not him. Paris seems prouder of his upbringing than of his birthright. But perhaps that is his way into people's hearts—not his beauty, not his wealth, but his story.

"If you didn't grow up in Troy," Clytemnestra asks, "why were you sent here?"

"I didn't want to grow old as a shepherd," he says as if stating the obvious. "The herdsman told me the truth when I came of age. I traveled to the city, leaving my life behind. I wanted the king to recognize me as his son."

Clytemnestra can easily imagine him, in a dirty tunic, walking inside the mighty walls of Troy, kneeling in front of the old man. King Priam must have been quick to claim him this time—the gods gave him a chance to mend a past mistake.

"Your father is said to have fifty sons and fifty daughters," Clytemnestra says. "Why did he choose to send you here?"

Helen touches her hand as if asking her to stop questioning the prince. But Paris seems neither annoyed nor affronted. Answers come to him with no hesitation. "I asked to come. I wanted to show my father that I am as worthy as his other sons."

The music stops. On Clytemnestra's right, Phoebe and Hilaeira are telling some story to little Hermione. She is giggling, and Polydeuces smooths Hilaeira's hair, listening to them with a half smile. Castor seems lost in thought, gobbling food and staring at the gleaming weapons on the wall. But as soon as Paris stops speaking, he looks up.

"You, a noble prince, all those years on Mount Ida among herdsmen and shepherds… You must have been desired by every woman there."

Helen clears her throat. As if unwilling to be a part of the conversation any longer, she calls Hermione. Her child leaves her place next to Polydeuces and trots happily to her mother.

"I was married," Paris replies, smiling, "though when I went back to court, I couldn't bring her. She was a mountain girl, unfit for life in the palace."

Castor laughs and keeps asking the prince questions—Were the women of the palace fit for it? Are the warriors in Troy as strong as people say? Clytemnestra isn't surprised. Even after all these years, her brother cannot resist pressing others with questions, pinching them with his tricks. She focuses on the food and lets Castor do the rest of the talking.

"So the priestess was right once more," Helen tells her quietly. She is plaiting Hermione's hair. The music grows louder again, and Paris laughs at Castor's inquiries.

"It seems we underestimated her."

"First you, then Timandra," Helen says. "Soon it will be my turn."

Clytemnestra laughs. "And then we'll all be *deserters of our lawful husbands*. Though I am not sure my experience counts as deserting."

Helen smiles, hopeful. "Maybe you'll have one more husband. Remember, the priestess said that we'll marry *twice and thrice*."

"Wouldn't that be wonderful?"

It is Helen's turn to laugh. She finishes her daughter's hair, and Hermione rests her head against her chest.

"You know Leda once said that our lives are short and miserable, but sometimes we can be lucky enough to find someone who cures our loneliness."

Clytemnestra is not sure her mother's loneliness was ever cured, but she keeps silent. Helen takes her hand. "No matter how many husbands we'll have, we have already been lucky enough to have each other."

For a moment, the torches burn brighter, and nothing else matters for Clytemnestra but her sister's love.

♛

Before bed, she goes to her mother's room, in the deepest part of the *gynaeceum*. Most of the torches have gone out, and Clytemnestra feels the wall under her hand to avoid stumbling.

Inside Leda's chamber, it is warmer and the air smells of spiced wine. She can see her mother's figure lying sideways on the bed, her face turned toward the only window.

"Clytemnestra," Leda says, her voice clear in the utter silence. "Light a torch for me."

"Yes, Mother."

She takes the last, dying torch and brings it to the others in the room. They light and flicker, casting long shadows on the cowhide on the floor. Leda sits up and studies her. "You are more beautiful than ever," she says. "Mycenae agrees with you."

"I wouldn't say that."

Leda smiles. "Come, sit with me."

Clytemnestra covers the space between them and sits on the sheepskins. From up close, she can feel her mother's warmth and detect her faint smell, like the earth after rain.

"What do you think of the girls your brothers love so much?"

She examines her mother's face in search of any right answer, but Leda is just curious. "I like them."

"I knew you would. Phoebe is tough. They were just unlucky." She stoops to pick up a quartz-chiseled cup from the floor. She gulps some wine, then turns to stare at her daughter. "I know you killed Cynisca," Leda says.

Clytemnestra stays quiet. Her mother doesn't seem angry, just sad. The moment of silence stretches between them until it snaps.

"You have always been a bright child," Leda says, "brighter than the rest. And I think you knew that. It gave you the strength to be bold and to speak freely whenever you wanted to." She sighs, resting her head on the pillow. The golden leaves embossed on the headboard frame her head like a crown. "But it didn't teach you to accept defeat and that to achieve what you want from the men around you, you must allow them to believe that they are in charge."

"If that is what a woman must do, I don't want to be one."

Leda sinks lower into the bed. Her hands are more lined than they used to be, veins popping out of the skin like rivers. "You are one. Who else has a spirit like yours? Since the moment you were born, you were your father's favorite. What king prefers a girl to his sons?"

"A good one."

Leda takes her hand in hers, which is warm, almost feverish. "We had hopes for you, ambitions. Your father put too much pressure on you, eager for a powerful marriage. And he ruined you."

The words sting. "I am not ruined."

"But you are unhappy." Leda puts aside the cup, and her head falls onto her shoulder. She is exhausted. "Now I must sleep," she says, her eyes closed. Quickly, her breathing becomes louder and her hand falls limp from her daughter's.

Clytemnestra remains on her mother's bed for a long time. Leda is right. All her childhood, she tried to be perfect, to excel in every challenge and mend every broken thing on the way. She did it because her parents taught her so. But that girl—wild and brave, always testing her own courage, always protecting her loved ones—is long gone.

How can Leda not see that?

♛

The corridors reek of memories.

Someone else might have to focus to catch the smell—it is buried under the oily scents of the baths and the hints of spices from the dining hall. Not Clytemnestra. She wants to go to her room, bury her face under the sheepskins and disappear, but the dead are here, somewhere, desperate to reach her.

The walls are cold under her touch, lifeless. Dark old stones that carry the dried blood of her Tantalus, his last words and breaths. Her son's last cries and tears. He was killed while he was in the hands of a helot—Marpessa was her name. He should have been in the hands of his mother.

She is supposed to mourn her husband and son outside, in the royal tombs, where their ashes and bones rest in gilded urns. But only cold and silence await her there, nothing more.

It is here that their memories are to be found, here that their pain has seeped—in each crack of the wall, every ember of the dimming torches.

It is here that Tantalus and her baby died and here they will be trapped forever, while life in Sparta goes on without them, unconcerned, merciless.

"Did you forgive him before he died?" Clytemnestra asks. She has spent all night pacing the corridors, stomach burning, memories clawing, and now she is back in her mother's room, eager to cry out her grief.

"Who?" Leda asks. Her eyes are foggy.

"Father."

Leda sighs. "It is not our duty to forgive. Forgiveness is in the hands of the gods."

Clytemnestra turns away. "You did nothing. You knew of his plan and did nothing to protect me. You spent all those years lying for Helen, keeping her safe, yet you couldn't find a way to protect me."

Leda shakes her head. "I found out when it was too late. You know this. I found their bodies when they were already dead."

"I am not speaking of their deaths," Clytemnestra says. "I am speaking of my marriage." Leda closes her eyes and her face seems about to crumble, but Clytemnestra continues to talk: she has been keeping the words inside for too long. "You could have warned me, helped me. Instead you kept silent while he sold me to a cruel man."

"This is Sparta. The king's wish is the law. Every man's honor, every woman's life belongs to him. Yes, I was powerful. Yes, I ruled with your father, but I wasn't free. None of us are."

"What about my honor?" Clytemnestra snarls. "You can't begin to contemplate the things I have endured because of the *king's wishes*. There is no honor in being raped, no honor in being beaten. If you think there is, you are a fool."

Leda draws a deep breath. Cold air seeps into their bones, and Clytemnestra waits for her mother to ask for forgiveness, even though she knows it wouldn't be enough.

But Leda says, "I never told you how I came to marry your father."

I do not care, Clytemnestra wants to say. *It is too late for your stories.* But her tongue feels heavy in her mouth, like a stone.

"You remember when I told you about Hippocoon and how he overthrew your father? Before Heracles helped him retake the throne, Tyndareus ran away with Icarius. They begged many kings for hospitality until they were welcomed by your grandfather Thestius, my father. Thestius fed and treated Tyndareus as if he were his own, but he asked for something in return."

"A marriage," Clytemnestra says.

"Yes, a marriage. I was young, disobedient, and my father's favorite. I thought myself hard to love, but Thestius liked that I was rebellious. When he came to me to propose the marriage, I said yes. I thought it my chance to make him proud and happy.

"Our winter festival came, when the girls had to dance for the goddess Rhea. It was my favorite moment of the year—we wore dresses and masks of feathers and ran in the forest where the spirits hide. We sang to the stars, asking for warmth in the winter and rains in the summer. Your father watched me. His skin was dark and warm, and I thought that was a taste of the sunny land he came from. I let him touch the feathers of my dress, and he said I was the most beautiful bird he had ever seen. The forest heard him, because soon nightingales were singing. I followed the sound, leading Tyndareus away from the torches into the thick part of the forest where long branches make everything a secret. The morning after, he asked me to marry him."

Leda doesn't look at her as she talks. Her eyes are fixed outside the window, on the woods in the distance, the trees swaying with the wind.

Clytemnestra looks at her hands. "Your marriage was the result of a political alliance, but that doesn't mean you know how I felt."

"That is true." Her hand grabs Clytemnestra's wrist and she feels the strength her mother once had, the boldness. "If I could go back, I would change everything. I would stand beside you and defy your father." Her eyes brim with sadness. "But if you are truly like me and you find it hard to forgive, I hope you will come to understand that it has been hard for me too."

The sky darkens above them, ready to shed its tears. Clytemnestra watches the birds fly away from the trees, dancing like Leda, looking for shelter before the storm.

👑

"*Artemis Orthia,*
we worship you!"

Clytemnestra stands by the temple as the women around her dance and sing. It is the winter festival for Artemis, when boys and girls bring gifts to the goddess, singing until dawn breaks. Torches are fixed in the ground, swaying with the thud of feet, and the dancers come in and out of the shadows, dressed in nothing but animal skins. A wolf.

A lynx. A leopard. A lion. The youngest are she-bears, and they pray loudest to the goddess.

"I always forget—did a girl kill a bear, or was it the other way around?" Castor licks his lips, a jar of wine in his hand. In the light, the liquid is dark, like blood.

"A girl once teased a tamed bear on this land, and the beast clawed out her eyes," Clytemnestra recites. "Then the girl's brothers killed the bear, unleashing Artemis's rage. So now we atone for the bear's death."

"Artemis can be quite brutal," Castor points out, swigging his wine. Clytemnestra grabs the jug before he can finish it.

"Huntress, archer,
we worship you!

"Goddess willow-bound,
we worship you!"

Helen is standing not far from them, a leopard skin tied to her shoulders, her blond hair in a cascade of plaits. Clytemnestra looks around, but Paris is nowhere to be seen. Her sister's eyes are on the dancers. Polydeuces rests his hand on her arm, as if that was where it should be.

"You know I once saw Timandra kissing another girl during the procession of she-bears?" Castor says. "She looked up at me as if daring me to say anything, then ran away into the shadows."

"And? What did you say to her?" Clytemnestra asks.

"Nothing. Sooner or later, Father would have found out and flogged her anyway. Not that Timandra cared. She has always been unruly."

A cold breeze stirs, and Clytemnestra fixes her lion skin around her neck. "I miss her," she says. "She was never meant to marry. That wasn't the life she wanted."

Castor smirks. "Did *you* get the life you wanted? Did I?"

> *"Mother of the forest,*
> *we worship you!"*

The girls' song feels like a bird's cry now. Their dance becomes wilder. Arms, breasts, hair, legs appear and disappear as they move in circles around the torches, the painted statue of Artemis watching them. The boys are coming out of the shadows of the temple. Naked, slender bodies with masks and horns on their heads, they join the song before running away toward the forest. They will come back at dawn with their offers to the goddess, their bodies spotted with blood.

"I wanted to rule," Clytemnestra says, "and you wanted to go off on adventures."

"You didn't want to marry a brute." He speaks calmly, without the amusement that once was always on his face.

Behind them, the trees are so dark that they are one with the sky. She turns away from the she-bears and cups her hand around his cheek. "It doesn't matter," she says. "I won't stay married to him forever."

22

Helen's Secret

BETWEEN THE TIME with her sister and the dinners with her brothers, her stay in Sparta becomes sweeter. She rides along the frosted hills with Castor and strolls around town with Phoebe and Hilaeira. They pass the gardens and houses in the village, walking in the patches of light and shadows that alternate between each building, and they tell each other stories.

Girls may not learn to fight in Messenia, Phoebe tells Clytemnestra, but they learn other things. They know the secrets of the woods, where each mushroom grows and the deer hide. They know the names of plants and trees, of berries and fruit. And then there are the horses. Boys and girls in Messenia are riding before they can walk, and they prize their horses above anything else.

"Do you miss your home?" Clytemnestra asks as they are walking between the roses in a garden. Phoebe is usually the one who speaks, with her fervent eyes and defiant face, but this time it is Hilaeira who answers.

"There is nothing for us in Messenia anymore." Her words are stiff and clear. Her face is like a stone, perfectly carved, but her eyes are soft, brimming with secrets.

At night, after dinner, they gather around the flames of the palace hearth: Clytemnestra and Helen, Castor and Polydeuces, Phoebe and Hilaeira. Leon joins them, always close to his queen, and the Trojan prince. Around them, the bobbing heads of servants, who listen furtively, curious.

Paris tells many stories, of the beauty of the city of Troy, of his time growing up on Mount Ida, of his first wife and how she loved to play the lyre. Each evening, as the fire dies down, Hermione falls asleep in her mother's lap, and Helen caresses her little head as she listens to the prince. It feels peaceful to be together in this way, like resting under thick warm covers when rain is falling outside.

When Leda joins them one evening, Phoebe tells a funny tale about lustful gods and jealous goddesses. Everyone laughs, and the house dogs rub against their legs, looking for food and affection. Clytemnestra smiles at her mother, and Leda's eyes light up. *See, Mother?* she thinks. *See how happy I am?*

Still, in all that peace and lightness, Clytemnestra can hear a distant rumble. It is like being on a beach when the tide has receded. All is calm, yet everyone knows that soon the water will climb.

And then, on the tenth day of her stay, the tide rises as quickly as a winter storm.

They are lined up together in the *megaron*, Castor and Polydeuces standing at the side, Helen on the queen's draped chair, and Clytemnestra on Menelaus's throne. When she had tried to convince her sister that the throne was for her, Helen shook her head.

"You were called here for a reason, to take care of the family. Do it." Her eyes held urgency, which Clytemnestra had never seen in her before. "Besides," Helen added, "from what the people say about these cousins of ours, they frighten me already." Clytemnestra had no time to ask her what the people said about the princes of Messenia, because Leon announced that Lynceus and Idas were walking into the room.

Now that they are standing in front of her, she understands what her sister was talking about. Lynceus doesn't look like a prince: he's more like a farmer who can handle an ax. He has a thick beard and a wolf skin on his shoulder. Idas's face is shaven to reveal a clean cut on his left cheek and a terrifying smile. Three daggers are tied to his belt, the blades short and thin, the kind a cutthroat would use. Though he is younger, he does the talking.

"Our dearest cousins," he starts, "how good it is to see you." He looks around at the frescoed walls and opens his arms wide. His eyes are flat and cold, of a dirty gray. They remind Clytemnestra of a frozen puddle. "And what a palace this has become. Once, your people didn't care about riches, but now it seems you have more gold and weapons than mighty Crete."

Clytemnestra feels Helen shift in her chair, but she doesn't move. She stares back at Idas, serious. She remembers her father once saying that when a king welcomes a guest in the *megaron*, the more he moves and fidgets, the more terrified he appears.

"Welcome to Sparta," she says, her voice steady.

The smile doesn't drop from Idas's face. It is like the grin of a poisonous snake. "I must admit, I am a bit confused. We came here ready for our women to welcome us with open arms, and instead we find ourselves in front of the queen of Mycenae."

He walks toward the throne until Leon blocks his way. Idas looks at him and chuckles. He takes a step back.

"We all know why we're here," he continues cheerfully. "Return the girls to me and Lynceus, and we will forgive your brothers for abducting them. Rather than treating you as traitors and thieves, we will forget about this." His smile becomes wider, creepier.

"Phoebe and Hilaeira were not abducted," Castor says. "They came with us willingly."

Idas turns to him. "You speak, cousin, yet you don't even sit on a throne. Have you lost your cock by any chance?"

Helen gasps. Castor laughs. The sound echoes against the walls, and when it dies, it leaves behind a faint, evil echo.

"Speak of my brother like that again and I will cut your throat," Polydeuces says.

Idas's eyes find Polydeuces's, and he grins. "I hope you won't do that, *Lizard Killer.* That is what they call you, isn't it? I'm sure you haven't earned that name by being merciful." His tone is mocking. "But you seem an honorable man, one who wouldn't murder a cousin in your own home, not after you have taken his bride."

"Your bride wasn't taken," Castor repeats.

"You are right, Idas," Clytemnestra intervenes. "We wouldn't murder you in our home. We can give you hospitality, food, wine, but not Phoebe and Hilaeira."

Idas smiles again. His front tooth is chipped. "Well, it seems we are at an impasse. We are not leaving without them."

Clytemnestra takes a deep breath. She sees Leon standing tense by the throne, his grip tight on the handle of his sword. Wrong move. Idas doesn't seem like a strong man, but he must be quick. He has the stillness of those animals that strike before you can anticipate them.

"Would you still take a woman who is pregnant by another man?" she asks after a long pause.

Idas's smile drops. Lynceus places his hand on his brother's arm as if to still him, but Idas isn't moving.

"You fucked them, then," he murmurs. His eyes are shining, with satisfaction or rage, it is hard to tell. "Lynceus told me you would, didn't you, Brother?"

Lynceus nods. He looks like a bull with his mean little eyes.

"He told me, 'Don't trust these bastards, Brother. They will bed our women before you know it.' And he was right."

There is nothing to say, so Clytemnestra is silent. She has known cruel men before, she even married one, but Idas looks like someone who would torture people for the sake of it.

"I imagine you enjoyed them," he says, opening his eyes wide. "Phoebe especially is a spirited girl. Did she tell you of our own time in bed together?" he asks Castor.

Castor's face is as cold as a blade. "She did."

"That's it? She didn't comment on it? She didn't mention how she cried when I took her?"

"You will never take her again."

Idas's smile curdles. "We came to ask. If you don't give them back, we'll take them, and that will be worse for everyone here."

"Sparta is more powerful than your father's kingdom," Clytemnestra says. "Offending Menelaus would be bad for you. Half the Greek cities are loyal to him and to my husband."

"I'm sure the king of Sparta would be happy to give back what belongs to us."

"He is not here," Clytemnestra says, "so we decide."

Anger flashes across Idas's face. "If you were my wife, I'd cut out your tongue."

Leon, Castor, and Polydeuces all take a step forward, but Clytemnestra stops them with a movement of her hand. "That wouldn't be necessary," she says. "If I were your wife, I'd murder you in your sleep."

Idas smiles. "Would you? Because you didn't murder your husband,

and I hear he slaughtered your child. So maybe," he says and licks his lips, "you are not as strong as you think you are."

"Leave," Clytemnestra orders, "or I will have you cut to pieces here and now."

Idas looks around, and for a moment, Clytemnestra thinks he will be crazy enough to fight them. But then his brother grabs his arm and a look passes between them.

"Thank you for your hospitality," Idas says. "I am sure we will meet again soon, and then we will have some fun."

He turns and leaves, his brother behind him. The daggers on Idas's belt flash across the hall.

"Should I shoot them as they ride away, my queen?" Leon asks when their steps have faded in the corridors. His voice is firm, though Clytemnestra knows he is as scared as the rest of them.

"No," she says. She turns to Castor, and it pains her to see that he is hurt, sorrow and rage assailing him.

"Did you know about them?" she asks.

"Yes," Castor replies.

"Why didn't you tell me?"

"I didn't want you to turn them away because they're monsters. I wanted you to do it because I love Phoebe, and Polydeuces loves Hilaeira."

She goes to him and hugs him. He puts his arms around her, though his body remains rigid, alert. She understands why her brother loves Phoebe now. Colchis had hardened him, left him empty inside. But with Phoebe, he has a chance to care for something broken, someone who deserves his love. That must give him purpose.

"What if they come back?" she asks.

He stiffens in her arms. "We'll kill them."

Later, Phoebe finds Clytemnestra in the gardens, among the fallen leaves. "You were brave today, facing Idas like that," she says. Her steps were silent; Clytemnestra didn't hear her coming.

"I did what I had to. There was nothing else I could have done."

"You could have sent us back, like Menelaus asked you to."

Clytemnestra feels the tip of her nose redden with the cold. "You said Idas told you he would kill your horse if you married," she says. "Did he do it?"

"He did. And he made me watch while the horse died."

"What else did he do?"

Phoebe lifts her chin. There's something challenging in her face. "Idas did horrible things to me and my sister. No one complained because everyone fears him. He is cruel and perverted. Death amuses him." She adjusts a sleeve of her gray dress. The color doesn't suit her, but Phoebe doesn't look like someone who cares about being pretty. "But I don't want to talk about it," she adds. "Each of us has her own scars, and it's our duty to bear them. I just came to say that I am grateful for what you did."

Clytemnestra takes her arm. "And I am grateful that my brother was lucky enough to find you."

Phoebe nods and her auburn hair falls around her face. Her eyes hold Clytemnestra's, dark and steady.

"Whatever happens, whatever Idas and Lynceus do, I'd rather die than go back to Messenia." Each word is like a stone, heavy. "Your brother knows this."

Then she walks back to the palace.

"I always thought our brothers would marry someone vain," Helen says.

They are in the bathhouse, just the two of them. Helen is resting her head against the painted clay, her eyes closed. Clytemnestra watches her face, tipped up to meet the leaping torchlight.

"What made you think that?" she asks.

"Men are usually so invested in themselves, even more so when they are special. And Castor and Polydeuces are special. I thought they would want someone ordinary next to them."

"You were never ordinary, yet Polydeuces used to love you."

Helen sits up. "We were children. He didn't know it was wrong to love your sister like that."

Clytemnestra feels water lap at her neck. "Do you think he changed his mind, then?"

"People can change their minds, but they can't change their feelings. I just think he knows now what is wrong and right and acts upon it." Helen's cheeks are flushed from the warmth of the room, and the steam blurs her features.

Clytemnestra feels for a scar on her own back, smoothing its jagged ends. When she looks at her sister, Helen is staring at her, eyes wide. "What is it?" she asks.

"I have to tell you a secret," Helen says in one breath.

Clytemnestra almost laughs. As a child when her sister said she had something to confess, it was always a small secret, like stealing a fig, or avoiding Father, or hiding somewhere. Clytemnestra used to make fun of her for that.

But then Helen speaks again. "I slept with the Trojan prince."

The light that creeps from the torch seems suddenly thin and cold. Helen's hair is curling around her face, damp from the bath. "You have nothing to say," she says, her voice quivering.

Clytemnestra sinks deeper into the tub, though the water is turning colder. "No."

"That is not true. You always have something to say."

"Are you happy?" Clytemnestra asks. The question sounds strange on her lips, and she realizes it isn't something she often asks. Perhaps her mother was right after all.

"Yes."

"You know he will leave soon."

"Yes." Helen sounds worried and speaks quickly, eager. Clytemnestra wonders if anyone else knows.

"If Menelaus finds out?"

"What if he does?"

That her husband might be angry and Helen wouldn't be afraid: this is something new.

"I was lost when you left," Helen says. "I was unhappy until Polydeuces came back, but then I had Hermione. She cried all the time—she wouldn't let me sleep. But I couldn't leave her in the hands of others, not after what happened to you…" She looks up at her sister and Clytemnestra nods, her heart snapping into fragments. "And then when she would finally sleep, all I would hear was Menelaus with the other women. He paraded them around, and they all hated me. I knew what they were thinking: Look at you, the most beautiful woman of our lands, you can't even keep your husband. You are no better than us."

"But you are better than them," Clytemnestra says.

Helen shrugs. "I don't know if I am. But then Paris came and everyone adored him. Godlike, they call him."

He is like her, Clytemnestra suddenly considers. How could she not see that? Refused by his father, desperate to please others, the most beautiful of all men. Then she remembers what Menelaus said. *Helen can't seem to be happy unless she has someone's attention. It is strange: she who is such a light is always seeking someone who shows her the way.*

"He understands me," Helen says. She tortures her fingernails for a moment, then asks tentatively, "Do you think I did wrong?"

Clytemnestra looks her straight in the eye. "You didn't. But let's not talk about this anymore or with anyone else."

She almost expects her sister to complain, to plead, to keep talking about Paris. But Helen stands, her body faintly glowing in the pooling light. She wrings out her hair and says, "We should go. It's getting cold."

Clytemnestra rests her gaze on the small round breasts, the long legs, the curve of her hips. She once thought that Helen was delicate like a lamp, something that must be taken care of or it will burn out. But her sister is no longer like that, and maybe she has never been.

♛

That night, they sleep together, curled up one facing the other, just like when they were small. Helen's breaths are slow and calm, her body light since she freed herself of her secret. Clytemnestra lies awake, listening to the branches rustling in the wind.

We will find a way back to each other, she had promised all those years ago. And they have. But they are no longer the girls they were then. How could they be? Those girls were fresh and hopeful, like two trees sharing a root, the trunks and branches so intertwined that they looked like a single plant.

But now they have grown so used to their aloneness that they don't even remember what it felt like to be so close to each other. There are glimpses of that love and harmony, like now, when their chests move up and down together as the night creeps past. But there is no hope for them to go back to the life they had, and deep down, Clytemnestra knows why.

The thought slides into the room, slippery and boneless. The tragedy that befell them started the day Helen chose Menelaus of all the kings and suitors. Her choice set everything in motion, each event like the ring of a heavy chain. It was that chain and the pain it brought that slashed the root that held them together. And now all they can do is keep loving each other, bearing sorrow and anger for choices they can't change.

Castor is the last person Clytemnestra sees before she returns to Mycenae. She sneaks into the *megaron* at dawn to look at the frescoes of hunting men one more time, and he is standing by the wall, his head resting against a column. Clytemnestra walks to him and takes his hand in hers. He opens his eyes, weary but alert.

"I'm leaving," she says. "I don't know when I will come back."

Castor smiles. "Once, it was always me saying goodbye." He walks to the chair draped in cowhide, Helen's chair, and rubs his hands against the skin.

"Do you remember when we used to stay here after Tyndareus had received all the envoys?" Clytemnestra asks.

The weariness disappears from Castor's face. Under it, there is longing and amusement.

"We asked him questions and he would answer. Though he wasn't very patient."

"Sometimes he was."

"Only with you."

She feels pleasure, like fresh water after a climb. Then the familiar fear creeps back in. "There's something I need to tell you," she says.

His head tilts. "It's about Helen, isn't it?"

"You know, then."

"Yes. I saw her."

Clytemnestra shakes her head. "Has she been that careless?"

"She has been careful enough. But you know me, always looking for trouble and secrets."

"I thought you'd changed."

"Some things never do."

She watches him in silence. He plays with the cowhide on the chair, then looks back at her. "So Menelaus comes home and finds his wife has betrayed him with a Trojan prince," he says. "He is furious and wants to tear Paris apart. But *unlike* Paris, Menelaus is a man of reason and knows the alliance with Troy must stand. He also knows that if he murders the prince, a Trojan army will soon be knocking on our door. So he sends him away."

"But he punishes Helen," Clytemnestra says.

Castor laughs. "Do you really believe Polydeuces would let Menelaus hurt our sister? I once saw him cripple a man who made a comment about ravishing her."

There's a knock at the door, and Clytemnestra turns. Leon is standing there, his face still sleepy. "Time to go, my queen," he says. "The horses are ready."

She looks outside and the sky is streaked with the redness of sunrise. She can already feel the cold, clinging to her skin and bones.

Castor walks to her. "Here you go again," he says. She knows he expects her to leave, but she lingers, unable to move her feet.

"Don't worry, Sister," Castor says, seeing her struggle. "We will survive without you." He smiles, but she can see the dark thoughts on his face, growing like weeds. *What if Idas and Lynceus come back and cut us down? What if Menelaus doesn't forgive our sister's affair? What will become of us?*

She draws him to her one last time. "I am sure you will," she says.

23

The War to Come

THE *MEGARON* IS dark and quiet, the fire crackling in the hearth. Clytemnestra watches its sparks fly across the empty room like butterflies. She and Leon came back when the palace was already asleep, each hall silent and moonlit, empty but for its guards.

The door creaks, and a thin thread of light cuts the floor in two.

"The king isn't here." The voice is warm and pleasant, like the sun in winter.

"I wasn't looking for the king," Clytemnestra says. A man is walking toward her, his feet bare on the painted floor. When he comes close enough to the hearth, the fire illuminates his face. Clytemnestra freezes. She had expected a mild, pious man, not the hooded figure in front of her—skin pale and wrinkled with scars, hollow eyes, thin, bloodred lips. Clytemnestra feels her body turn cold where his eyes touch her.

"Do you know who had this hall painted?" he asks. There is a creepiness underlying the warmth of his voice, a meanness.

She forces her own to sound flat. "The king who ruled this city before Atreus took it from him, I suppose."

His lips break into a smile, revealing old teeth. "The hall was bare when Eurystheus was here. No frescoes, no gold, no weapons.

Mycenae might have been any other Greek city. Then Atreus made the palace his home and covered every wall with *this*." He gestures toward the images in the shadows. "Sometimes the cruelest people are capable of the most wondrous things."

He is staring at her in a way that reminds her of snakes.

"You are not from here," she says carefully.

"I have come from Megara at the king's request. He has summoned me as his new counselor."

"My husband has plenty of counselors already."

"None are able to speak the will of the gods."

A seer: that is what he is. A man expert in prophecies, who divines the future from the flight of birds and animals' entrails. Her people call him *oionopolos*. A bird savant. Tyndareus used to mock leaders who relied on one. "What can seers tell me that I don't know already?" her father would say. "That the gods can be harsh? That I will die soon? That there's going to be a war? There's no need to look at a sheep's liver for that."

Clytemnestra lifts a brow. "Agamemnon never paid much attention to divination."

"The Atreidai's line is cursed, but the king of Mycenae reveres the gods, and the gods respect him in turn."

She scoffs. "My husband is an ambitious man. He wants power above all else, not to impress any gods, just for the sake of it."

"He says the same of you."

She regards him. "What is your name, seer?"

"Calchas." It sounds unpleasant, like an overripe fruit. She lets it rot in the air until she feels nauseous.

"Well, you must be a very convincing man to make a king who despises prophecies listen to you." *And very dangerous.* "Sleep well, seer."

The air is soft with the first smells of spring. Someone is singing in the streets of the citadel, and the vendors' shouts are fading as the last sales of the day are made.

"I am hungry, Mother," Chrysothemis says. She is pacing the bedroom, a wooden priestess in her little hand. The doll's hair is painted black, her gown red and gold, and in her hands are two snakes, symbols of the Cretan goddesses. "Can we eat soon?"

They are in Iphigenia's bedroom, the light pouring in from the large windows. The frescoed huntress on the wall is fading, and at her feet, the flowers and bees that Iphigenia sketched when she was little. It is almost dinnertime, and they can hear the bustling of the servants outside their door.

"Be patient," Electra says before Clytemnestra can reply. "We must finish this first." She is sitting on the floor with Iphigenia, using red paint to color other wooden toys for their younger sister: a horse, a chariot, and some spinning tops. Leon carved them during their journey back to Mycenae.

"We will go to the hall when your father calls for us," Clytemnestra says. "Unless you want to spend more time with the seer?"

"No, please!" Chrysothemis shrieks. She goes to sit in a corner of the room, by the table where Iphigenia's jewels are laid out. Aileen kneels behind her, trying to fix her hair in a plait.

Clytemnestra chuckles. Of course her daughter is scared of the seer. Who wouldn't be?

"You don't like the seer," Electra says. The horse she is painting is black with a golden mane.

"It is hard to like him," Clytemnestra replies.

"I don't like him either. He says he speaks for the gods, but the gods haven't been generous with him."

"Is that going to be your new threat, Mother?" Iphigenia asks. She lifts the wooden horse to the light, making sure the paint is dry. "Don't go *unless* you want to see the seer?"

Aileen bites her lip, trying not to giggle. Clytemnestra and Electra laugh. It is a pleasure to hear her voice mingle with her daughter's.

"It is a good threat when you know it works," she says. "Aren't you going to paint that chariot?"

"I will do it!" Chrysothemis says, jumping out of her corner. She stumbles as she hits the table with her flank, and Iphigenia's earrings clatter. Aileen hurries to put them back in place.

"But you will spoil it," Iphigenia says. "The wheels are difficult to do."

"She can do it," Aileen says. "Just be careful with the brush around your tunic."

Clytemnestra is about to join her daughters on the floor when Leon bursts in, panting. His hands are trembling, and his face is red.

"My queen," he says, his voice faltering. Iphigenia looks up at him, her face bright with delight, but Leon doesn't even see her. He is distraught.

"What is it?" Clytemnestra asks.

"Your brother."

Clytemnestra springs up and the blankets fall from the bed.

What?

Leon takes a deep breath, and for a moment, Clytemnestra wants to tear the words from his mouth. Then he speaks, and she wishes he hadn't spoken at all.

"Castor was murdered, my queen. Idas killed him in an ambush."

It was a spear wound, Leon says. It hit him in the neck and sliced it open, like thunder tears the sky. Castor was hiding in a tree, and when Idas struck him, he fell and bled to death among the roots and bushes. It was a lucky death, quick, because Idas is known to torture his victims before giving the final blow.

Her brothers had received their cousins' death threat on the day Clytemnestra left Sparta—two wolves' heads in a sack, the eyes gouged out. Phoebe made Castor swear that he wouldn't leave the palace and search for revenge. But Castor was never good at keeping promises. He left with Polydeuces to slaughter Idas and Lynceus's herd in the night. They had heard that Lynceus loved his animals as if they were sacred and never allowed anyone to touch them. Castor climbed on a tree to keep watch while Polydeuces cut the sheep's throats.

Idas and Lynceus were waiting for them, like foxes stalk their prey. Idas spotted Castor hiding among the tree branches and threw his spear to take him down. As he fell, Castor screamed his brother's name. Polydeuces turned and saw Lynceus run at him with an ax. His dagger sank into the man's neck, and Lynceus fell, heavy as a bull.

Idas attacked him then. The quickest man in Messenia, his men called Idas, but Polydeuces was quicker. He killed him as Idas taunted him about Castor's death. When Idas's body finally dropped to the ground, Polydeuces butchered it until his cousin's face was gone. His men found him the morning after, a bloody bag of bones among the beheaded sheep.

Polydeuces didn't cry as he walked back to Sparta with his brother's body in his arms. He didn't cry as Phoebe ran to him, wailing, touching her lover's lifeless hands. "Castor. Castor. Castor," she muttered.

The women took the body in their arms, falling to the ground with him, beating their fists against their chests. Polydeuces stood there, like a statue, until Hermione was beside him. She wrapped her little hands around his bloodied waist—the waist of the man who is her uncle but has been a father to her, of the man who loves her mother more than he loves himself. Her arms were like the petals of a lily, and only then he broke down. He fell and shook and sobbed as he had never done in his life, his voice echoing in the empty valley. The pain nearly broke him, and he cried out his anger in the arms of a child.

Leon is quiet. Aileen puts her hands on Chrysothemis's shoulders as if to stop her doing something impulsive. Clytemnestra feels her daughters staring at her, three pairs of big eyes waiting for a response. Why is a reaction to loss always expected? Why can't loss be something one mourns in private, away from everyone else? Isn't she mourning if she doesn't tear out her hair, bruise her cheeks?

"Let us ready you for your father's presence," she says. Her voice is cold and detached, and she listens to it as though it belongs to someone else. "He will be wondering why we are late for dinner."

Chrysothemis shakes Aileen away. She takes a few shy steps forward and hugs her mother's leg. Clytemnestra focuses on the Cretan priestess in her daughter's hand. Iphigenia slips into her blue dress and sandals—she is doing everything in her power to be as silent as possible. Next to her, Electra's face is like a flame. Clytemnestra hopes her daughter won't speak. She is feeling rage mounting inside her, ready to lash out.

"Mother," Electra says, "we should pray for your brother first."

Clytemnestra's slap makes her fly sideways. Electra hits the wall and stumbles. When she turns back to her mother, her cheek is redder than blood and her eyes are burning.

Go on, Clytemnestra thinks. *Provoke me again.*

Electra takes her bruised cheek in her hand, narrows her eyes as she has seen her sister do a thousand times, and shouts, "Why do you make others suffer when you are in pain? Why can't you weep and mourn like everyone else? Why are you like this?"

She leaves the room before her mother can dismiss her. Her rage stays behind, razor-sharp.

Clytemnestra walks into the dining hall with her fists clenched, savoring the feeling of her nails sinking into her palms. Iphigenia walks at her side, and behind them Aileen holds Chrysothemis's hand. Are servants whispering as she passes or is she imagining it?

Agamemnon is already seated, sipping wine from a bronze cup. Next to him is the seer, gnarled and scarred, like an old tree, and on the other side, Orestes and Electra. Clytemnestra sits as far from Calchas as possible, keeping Iphigenia close. From the way everyone is sitting, rigid and uncomfortable, it seems they were waiting in silence.

"I am sorry to hear of Castor's death, Mother," Orestes says. He looks at her tentatively, and she gives him a feeble smile. The food on her platter is messily arranged. She moves the roasted fish and bread aside and focuses on her wine. Everyone else starts eating; the plates scrape in the silence.

"Castor's death wasn't the only news that came from Sparta," Agamemnon says.

Clytemnestra's head jerks up. The torch behind him has gone out, and his face is in the shadows. "What else?" she asks.

"You pretend you don't know now?" He is angry: his voice is low and thick, each word pointed. She straightens the knife beside her platter, admiring how still her hand is, how firm her grip.

"I have just learned of my brother's death," she says. "What would I lie about?"

Agamemnon leans forward and slams his hand on the table. She can see his face more clearly now, rutted and hot.

"I have told you to tame your family!" he shouts. "And what have you done? You have let your sister fuck the enemy!"

Clytemnestra flinches. How does he know of this? Keeping her face expressionless, she turns to the seer. He is staring at her, the hollowness in his face sucking her in.

"You are wondering how the king knows of your sister's betrayal," he says.

Agamemnon grips his cup so tightly that his fingers turn white. "Tell her," he says. "Tell my wife how another of her sisters became a whore."

She feels Iphigenia hold her breath. On the other side of the table, Chrysothemis is still clasping the Cretan doll, her face pale and terrified. Clytemnestra wants to tell her to leave, to finish her dinner in the *gynaeceum*, but she is too focused on the seer. His little eyes are cold, shiny like onyx. "Helen left Sparta with Prince Paris," he says. "They are headed for Troy at this very moment."

His voice feels too loud. Everyone's eyes dart to her. She almost cries then, though she is not sad. What she feels is more like satisfaction or pride. She sees herself seated next to her sister in Sparta, laughing together as Paris answered Castor's questions. *Soon it will be my turn*, Helen had said. *And then we'll all be deserters of our lawful husbands.*

"Is this true?" she asks.

"Troy deceived us," Agamemnon says, "and your stupid sister fell for it."

Iphigenia intervenes. "I thought Sparta was finally at peace with Troy, Father."

It is the wrong thing to say. Agamemnon throws his cup in her direction. Iphigenia dodges it, and the bronze thunders against stone. Wine spills, spreading quickly around their feet.

"Take my daughters away, Aileen," Clytemnestra says calmly, "before the king can shame himself."

Aileen jumps up promptly, but Agamemnon spits on the floor. "The children stay here. They need to know your sister is a whore. We are at war now because of a whore who couldn't stay in her husband's bed."

"Your brother can find a new wife," Clytemnestra says. "I once heard him say that women are better when ripe and fresh, like fruit."

"We made peace with Troy," he hisses.

"The peace can stand."

"A prince came into my brother's palace and took his queen!"

"My king," Calchas says, intervening, "this war was meant to happen."

"Good," Clytemnestra says, staring straight at Agamemnon. "You spent the last five years looking for a reason to wage war. Now you have it, and you want to blame someone else."

Agamemnon walks to her. Quick as a serpent, he raises his hand to strike her, but Clytemnestra draws back, grabbing the kitchen knife. His hand slaps the air and his eyes rest on the knife, disbelieving.

"Are you going to kill me in front of our children?" he asks. "Are you going to murder a king?" With a quick sway of his arm, he sweeps the platters off the table. "Go back to your room before I order the guards to drag you! And contemplate your sister's mistake!"

She takes Electra and Iphigenia by the arms and pulls them up from the bench. Somewhere behind her, Aileen grabs Chrysothemis's hand and follows, the child crying softly.

Clytemnestra pants as she runs out of the hall, the torches swaying around her, the smell of fish sickening her. Once safe in the dark corridors, she leaves her daughters and keeps running forward, toward the *gynaeceum* and beyond, out of the palace.

The winter sun is long gone beyond the mountains, and now the sky is the color of the sea at night. She walks the streets of the citadel, the darkness soothing her. Dogs rest in every corner, looking up at her as she passes, and a few men are drinking in the artists' quarter, huddled around a small fire. If she lived in a palace by the sea, she would go for a swim now, scrub herself in the salted water until her skin was raw. But here, in the narrow streets of Mycenae, all she wants to do is set something on fire. A tree, one of those in the main streets, or a granary: the flames would build and build until the fire lapped the sky. Just the thought of it makes her drunk with power.

"You have so much rage inside you," Helen had told her once. "It is like one of those fires for the dead that look like they will never burn out."

"And you don't?" Clytemnestra asked. "Don't you ever feel rage?"

Helen shrugged. They were ten, and a helot was ministering to some wounds on their shoulders, a courtesy of the priestess's whip. Helen winced as the servant cleaned hers, but she kept silent. She never talked about her own anger, yet Clytemnestra knew it was there, hidden under the layers of goodness. She would see it at dinner sometimes, when the men's hands found their way under the servants' tunics as they passed to pour their wine. Helen would look at them as they asked for more mutton, forcing the girls to come back, and Clytemnestra would see a flicker of rage in her sister's eyes. It was always the small things that made Helen angry. A wrong comment, a sharp pinch, an unsaid thought. Clytemnestra, on the other hand, kept her anger for the whipping and the fighting, for the beatings and the executions. If Clytemnestra's rage was a fire, Helen's was a lamp, warm and thin in the darkness but burning if you came too close.

And now Menelaus has made her sister angry, and she has left. Did Helen leave before Castor was killed? How could she leave Polydeuces alone and little Hermione behind? She tries to picture her sister on a ship to Troy with Paris, but the thought slips away like sea breeze.

Some drunken men stumble in the street, walking back to their houses. The trees are one with the sky, and the last sounds of the night are dying out.

"Do goddesses sleep?" Castor asked her once.

She chuckled. "I don't think so. Why?"

"I want to catch one. I want to see what they look like."

"And then what will you do?"

"Seduce her, of course," he said, and they laughed. So that night, when everyone slept, they sneaked outside and walked to the river. There they waited and waited for Artemis to appear until Clytemnestra fell asleep on Castor's shoulder. Artemis never came, and for years after, Castor would make fun of that night spent together shivering, wishing to see a goddess who wouldn't pay them any attention.

Clytemnestra feels her heart clench.

He's gone. He's dead and now you must live with that.

In front of the door that leads to the *gynaeceum*, Calchas is waiting for her. His head looks like a crumpled, sickly leaf in the torchlight. She has the urge to walk past him but instead she asks, "Have you come to give me the news of someone else's death?"

"No," he says. "Your remaining brother and sisters will live for a long time."

"That is good to hear."

He tilts his head as if to study her better. "Do I unnerve you?"

"I am not easily unnerved."

"I thought so. Yet you don't respect me. You should be careful with that. Disrespecting me means disrespecting the gods."

She has never heard such a sweet voice speak such menacing words. It is like drinking mulled wine, savoring it on the tongue before realizing it is poisoned.

"We each serve the gods in our own ways. You kill a sheep and tear open its belly to look at the liver. I rule a city and its people."

"Your husband rules."

"We both do. I am sure he would agree with me."

Calchas sighs. The sound is a hiss. "Power is strange. All men want it, but few achieve it."

"I am sure you have something to say about the gods now."

"The gods have nothing to do with it."

"Then what?" she asks. "Who gets it and who doesn't?"

The light casts moving shadows on his scarred face. One moment, he looks like an ordinary man; the next, he seems monstrous.

"If you ask the people of Mycenae who rules their city," he asks, "what do they say?"

"King Agamemnon," she replies.

"And yet you say you rule the city with your husband."

"There is the truth, and then there is the lie that keeps a kingdom together."

Calchas's mouth twists into a smile. "Yes. And so it is with power. Some men hold it in the open, like a sword. Others hide it in the shadows, like a small dagger. But what matters is that the people believe someone has it and wields it."

Their shadows on the floor are lengthening, two rivers of blackness merging where they meet the wall.

"You still haven't said who acquires power among all the people," she says.

"Ah, that depends. Some people are born into the right families. Others understand that fear can be a key that opens many doors."

"Then there are the ones like you. You see the people's thirst for knowledge, their fear of the gods, and you find ways to quench it."

"Sometimes the truth of the gods is hard to accept. But their will always prevails. There is power in acknowledging that."

The first lights of dawn gleam out of the windows and she shivers. There is no colder moment than the early morning in winter.

"I will sleep now, seer."

She tries to move past him but he catches her arm, his palm sweaty against her skin.

"You have a part to play in the war to come," he says.

She shakes him off, resisting the urge to wipe the arm where he touched her. When he turns to leave, his shadow follows him, like a dog.

Over the next few weeks, the palace sings with the sounds of war. Chariots are fixed and readied, men shout orders, horses are harnessed in the stables.

Clytemnestra makes her way outside, past envoys and men building shields with bull hide and bronze plates. The frost is melting; spring is coming. The sky is a warm white like the top layer of milk, the cream. Down by the armory, Leon is teaching some boys to shoot. Earlier, Clytemnestra asked him if he had to leave too, and he shook his head. "I am your guard and protector," he said. "I stay where you and your children are." The words filled her with calm, though she didn't show it.

Agamemnon is standing under a large oak by the entrance of the palace, speaking with Calchas and two men-at-arms. He is dressed in bronze, his boar's-tusk helmet in his hand, and looks tired. When Clytemnestra walks to them, the men leave. She stares at Calchas as if inviting him to do the same, but the seer doesn't move.

"We are gathering the biggest army the world has ever seen," Agamemnon says.

"How many?" Clytemnestra asks.

"A hundred ships for the Mycenaeans and sixty for the Spartans. Forty more from Locris and Euboea each. Fifty from Athens. Idomeneus's men told me eighty more will come from Crete."

"Everyone who swore to protect Helen of Sparta will have to come," Calchas says.

Clytemnestra freezes. She had almost forgotten the oath. Thirty princes and kings or more—she can't even remember, it feels so long ago—swearing allegiance to Sparta in the case of war. How could anyone predict that Helen's marriage would cause such a thing? Odysseus did.

"So you have sent envoys to everyone who was there," she says.

"Yes. And I have dispatched Odysseus and Diomedes to con-vince…any who need convincing."

"How many ships has Diomedes?"

"Eighty. And he claims that the men of Argos are so well trained they fight twice as hard as any Greek soldier."

"And Odysseus?"

"Just twelve. But I don't need his men. I need his mind."

"You once said you didn't like him."

"I still don't. But I respect him. Do you know what he did when my men arrived on Ithaca to call for him?"

She shakes her head.

"He plowed a winter field, naked and screaming. He wanted us to believe he was mad. But I had told my men to bring him here at all costs and to threaten him with his child. You know that your cousin Penelope has given birth, I assume?"

She knows it well. A year ago, an envoy had brought her the news. The queen of Ithaca had given birth to a boy—Telemachus, she had named him.

"You didn't kill his child," Clytemnestra says, stiffening.

"No. But my men put the baby in front of the plow blade. So Odysseus stopped and his trick was revealed. Threaten the many-minded with his own son, and even he will lose all his minds."

How brave of your men, to put an infant in front of a plow.

"So he is coming," she says. Penelope must be furious. Her big-gest fear was to lose Odysseus. *While all I want is to get rid of my husband.*

"He will serve the army well," Calchas says. "Unlike many others, he sees things as they are. He knows men's true nature and doesn't fear it. He plays with it."

Clytemnestra wishes the seer wouldn't interrupt. It is hard to speak to her husband with Calchas by their side, staring at them with his shiny little eyes.

"We will gather everyone at Aulis," Agamemnon says.

"When will you leave?"

"As soon as I know that Achilles, son of Peleus, will come."

Clytemnestra frowns. "Why?"

"The war can't be won without him," Calchas says.

"Whose liver told you that?" Clytemnestra asks, but the seer ignores her. "Why does Achilles need convincing?" she asks. "Wars are how heroes are made."

"It has been prophesied that he will die in the war," Agamemnon says. "But he will come. I have sent Odysseus to fetch him. Word has it that he is hiding on some rocky island, pretending to be a girl."

"If he is so needed for your victory," she says, "let us hope the great Achilles won't outshine you." She enjoys seeing the flicker of annoyance in her husband's eyes before excusing herself. She can't stand Calchas's presence any longer.

♛

Clytemnestra stands still as Aileen mends her sandals in the sunlight. The air carries a sweet scent, and they enjoy a rare moment of silence— the soldiers seem to be resting.

"Do you fear for your sister?" Aileen asks after a while.

Clytemnestra smiles. "You always ask the right questions, Aileen. Has anyone ever told you that?"

Aileen chuckles. "I also meant to ask if your sister is as beautiful as everyone says, but I thought it might annoy you."

"Helen is a light," Clytemnestra says, echoing Menelaus's words in spite of herself. "Her hair is like liquid gold, and her face carries the secrets of her heart. She is gentle but strong."

"Like Iphigenia," Aileen says.

"Yes."

Clytemnestra looks at Aileen's chapped hands. "I don't fear for Helen. I am glad she left. Now the king will leave too, and I shall rule Mycenae."

Aileen flushes, and Clytemnestra smiles. "I know you want to get rid of him too."

Aileen giggles and soon they are laughing together, their voices floating over the citadel like little suns.

More days pass, and more news arrives at the palace.

The great Ajax, son of Telamon, will come, and with him twelve ships from Salamis. They are not many, but his men are trained by the hero so they are as hard as oak and as belligerent as Spartans.

Old Nestor from sandy Pylos pledges himself, bringing with him his many sons and ninety ships. In the *megaron*, his envoy speaks of the honor Nestor will have as one of Agamemnon's closest advisers. He, with his legendary wisdom, next to the greatest commander of his time. Clytemnestra sees Agamemnon curl his lips as the envoy sings his praises.

And then Tlepolemus, son of the hero Heracles, with his Rhodian forces, and the archer Philoctetes with seven more ships. All kings and princes pledge allegiance to Agamemnon, each one agreeing to have him as their general. It is something unseen before, all these proud heroes willingly fighting under one man's leadership.

Finally, the news arrives that Odysseus and Diomedes have

convinced Achilles to join the cause. Orestes hears it in the *megaron* and runs to his mother to tell her. Clytemnestra is practicing in the armory, and when he tumbles in, she almost throws the spear she is holding.

"How many times have I told you?" she asks. "You can't come in here when I am practicing."

Orestes ignores her. "They are leaving soon! Achilles said he'll come!"

"That is good," she says. She puts away the spear among the axes and maces.

"Can I go too?" Orestes asks, out of breath.

She turns, frowning. "You are ten. It is too young."

"But it will be a short expedition. We will be home by winter!"

"Who said that?"

"Father. I heard him talk to Philoctetes's men today."

Clytemnestra sighs. She ties her hair back, wiping away some sweat from her forehead. "He lied, Orestes. This will be a long war. Troy has never been conquered, and its soldiers are skilled in battle. No matter how big our army is, it won't be an easy campaign."

Orestes huffs. He thinks it through for a while, then asks, "And Aunt Helen will be there, in Troy?"

"Yes."

"Do you think she will come back when the war is won?"

Fear stirs in her like dust. Everyone knows what happens when a city is taken—its goods stolen, its people killed and butchered, its women raped or, worse, enslaved. Even if Helen is no common Trojan woman, still, what will Menelaus do when Troy falls? Will he forgive her? But then, if the Greeks lose, what does it mean for them? Will the Trojans come to take their women, ravage their land, destroy their palaces?

"I hope she will," Clytemnestra says.

That evening after dinner, Agamemnon comes to Clytemnestra's room. She is sitting on a stool, looking out the window at the looming clouds.

"You are leaving tomorrow," she says.

"It is time. We'll catch the spring winds."

"And what do you think of these men, the generals you are going to command?"

"I can trust some of them." He stands next to her by the window. "Like Idomeneus and Diomedes."

"Only a fool would trust Diomedes. He is like a dog, sniffing where the power is."

"Which is lucky, because as long as I have the power, he'll lick my feet."

"And Odysseus?"

Agamemnon snorts. "Only a fool would trust Odysseus."

Clytemnestra nods. "We agree on that."

Outside, they can hear the first drops of rain. Agamemnon touches his hand to the back of her head, and she becomes aware of the shape of her skull, small in his large palm. "I will be away for a long time," he says. "I imagine you will find yourself a lover."

"And you will find yourself some pretty slaves."

He lets his hand drop. The bed is still made, the sheepskin covering it, and Agamemnon lies back on it. Clytemnestra turns away from the window but doesn't join him.

"Do you expect these men to love you?" she asks.

"No. Fear and obedience are the best a commander of such a large army can attract."

"Some men are loved by many."

"Like Achilles," he says. "But he is just a boy. Talented, but still childish in his quest for glory. The others will soon see that."

"And if they don't?"

"Then I will show them."

They are quiet for a moment, listening to the raindrops strengthen.

"If you win," Clytemnestra says, "what of Helen?"

Agamemnon chuckles. "Oh, I am sure my brother will forgive her as soon as he sees her. He is the forgiving type, and your sister can be quite convincing."

Yes, she can.

"Come here, Clytemnestra," he says. It isn't a request. He is looking at her with his hard eyes, and she can't help but think of breaking a stone with a chisel until all the hardness is gone.

She goes to him and feels the bed covers under her hands. He wraps his arms around her, ripping away her tunic. Just one last time, she tells herself.

As he moves on top of her, she thinks of Helen in bed with Paris, right at this very moment, their perfect bodies woven together, moving like a dance.

The army leaves at dawn. Clytemnestra wraps herself in a cloak and goes to the Lion Gate to watch. Orestes is already there, waving to his father, his curls a messy knot on his head. Outside the citadel, the road is thick with soldiers, polishing their armor, soothing their horses. The sky has cleared after the storm, and now the shields are glistening in the warm light.

At the gate, Agamemnon looks up and their eyes lock. Then he spurs his horse, and his men follow, the banners of Mycenae flying like golden swans around them.

Last night, before falling asleep, he told her he would return for her. "You know you can't escape me. I always come back. So be a good wife for once and wait."

Now, as she watches him against the brightening sky, she hopes her husband will die in the war.

24

Aulis

IT HAS BEEN just two weeks since the army's departure when an envoy no older than a boy comes to Mycenae. His hair is as black and shiny as olives, and his tunic is covered with dust and dirt. Clytemnestra receives him in the *megaron*, sitting on her husband's throne. Leon is at her side, polishing his sword, yawning. It has been a boring day so far, filled with merchants' requests and noble women's gossip.

"Where do you come from?" she asks as servants give the envoy bread and water. He takes it too willingly, coughing when he almost chokes himself. He clearly isn't used to speaking to royalty.

"Aulis, my queen," he says.

She frowns. "Who sent you?"

"The king and lord of men, Agamemnon, my queen." *Lord of men*. Her husband has already found himself a pretty name. The boy pants, drinking some more water. "He wants you to go to Aulis and meet him there with your eldest daughter."

"Why would he send you and not a general?"

The boy looks apologetic. He scratches a scab on his elbow. "All the men are preparing for the war, my queen. The generals must stay with the lord of men, Agamemnon. So they found me in the village and sent me."

"And what does my husband want?"

The boy stands straight, proud to give the news. "A marriage, my queen."

"A marriage?"

The boy nods, his eyes shiny with excitement. "Among the generals, there is the greatest warrior who ever lived, Achilles Pelides." *The son of Peleus.* "King Agamemnon wants your oldest daughter to marry him before the troops sail for Troy."

Leon's head jerks up. He stares at the boy with contempt. "Why would Iphigenia marry a man who is about to leave for war?" he asks.

The envoy gives him a perplexed look, then turns back to Clytemnestra. "The army will be ready to sail soon, but King Agamemnon says that the men need to be cheered up before the long war. He says that a wedding is the perfect occasion, and even better, one between the best of the Greeks and the leader's beautiful daughter."

"And if I refuse to come?" Clytemnestra asks.

"King Agamemnon says you won't. He says this would be an important political alliance that will make Mycenae even more powerful." He speaks as though reciting a poem.

"Very well," Clytemnestra says. "Go and rest before you go back to Aulis."

The boy seems confused. "Will you come, my queen?"

"Your job is done, boy," she says. "Rest and go back to your village. You have no more news to bring."

He nods, stuffing his tunic with one more loaf of bread, like a thief. When he leaves the *megaron*, his steps are as light and quick as a bird's.

Leon turns to her. "You will go?" he asks.

She can tell from his eyes that he had meant the words to be an accusation, but his voice is feeble, little more than a whisper. "I must," she says. "I can't turn away from a political alliance."

"But she will marry a man she doesn't even know."

"Don't we all?"

"What if he doesn't love her?"

They say Achilles lives with his companion, Patroclus, Timandra had told her. *They eat together, play together, sleep together.*

Her hesitancy makes him bolder. "Don't you want someone who can love her?"

"Achilles is young, handsome, and the greatest warrior of his generation."

He has grown paler, his eyes shinier. "Iphigenia should choose."

Clytemnestra stands, a weight in her chest. "Which is why I shall ask her now. No one has ever made Iphigenia do anything she didn't want to do."

He shakes his head. It is not his place to say more. And Clytemnestra doesn't need to tell him the obvious. Leon understands many things—that he will never be with her beautiful Iphigenia, that Clytemnestra loves her daughter above all else. But he doesn't see other things. That for Clytemnestra, no one would ever be good enough for her daughter. That whoever Achilles likes or doesn't like, he won't hurt Iphigenia, or Clytemnestra will kill him. That sometimes it is better to be with a man who doesn't regard you than with someone who wishes to wound you.

She takes Leon's arm, slowly and carefully, as if to show him she is sorry. He doesn't look at her, doesn't speak. He stares at the wall, contemplating what he is about to lose. His silence hits the hall like a wave, spreading its grief until Clytemnestra feels as if she is drowning.

Iphigenia is sitting on a bench in the *gynaeceum*, plucking the strings of a lyre. She is learning the song of Artemis and Actaeon, and her brows are furrowed in concentration. Next to her, Electra is looking at some new vases brought from the artists' quarter of the citadel. Aileen waits patiently by her side as she traces the curves of each pattern—octopods with tentacles like sea anemones, hunting dogs, and warrior women. Clytemnestra takes a step forward. "I have news for you, Iphigenia," she says.

Her daughter puts the lyre down, looks guarded. "What is it?"

"We are going to Aulis." She waits a moment. "You are to marry the prince Achilles."

Iphigenia opens her mouth. "Achilles Pelides?"

"Yes, the best of the Greeks. Or so everyone says."

"Isn't he going to war?" Electra asks, her hand still held midair, her fingers outstretched.

"Your father thinks this marriage could be a great political alliance. Mycenae is the most powerful kingdom of Greece, and Achilles the strongest soldier in its army. But," Clytemnestra adds, turning back to Iphigenia, "you don't have to marry him if you don't want to."

Her daughter is silent, staring out the window, as if no one is waiting for her answer, as if there aren't three women staring at her. Then she says, "If I marry him, I'll have to go and live in Phthia."

"Not before the war is over. You can stay here, with us," Clytemnestra says. "Then when Achilles comes back a hero, you'll go with him."

Iphigenia doesn't comment. She stays seated, considering something, studying it.

"Phthia is small but beautiful," Clytemnestra adds. "It's a land between the mountains and the sea."

Iphigenia smiles. "I love the sea." Then she stands and says, very seriously, "I will marry him."

Aileen looks radiant, her hands clasped in delight. Clytemnestra forces herself to smile. Her daughter's voice is calm, sure, and she knows that Iphigenia has made her choice. *I will marry him.* Clytemnestra had once said those same words to her own mother. She had been so sure of her own future.

"Good," she says. "We will leave tomorrow. Now go and find your best tunic with Aileen."

Iphigenia grabs Aileen's hand and runs out of the room, her body light with excitement, her eyes glittering. Their long hair dances behind them, golden and bronze.

"I thought Achilles didn't like girls," Electra says when her sister is out of sight.

"Who told you that?" Clytemnestra asks.

Electra shrugs.

"He will like your sister. She has the best heart and he will see that." As Clytemnestra speaks, she realizes it almost sounds like a threat.

"You will stay here," Clytemnestra adds. "My men will advise you, so listen to them."

"Shouldn't they advise Orestes?"

"You are older. And I trust you more."

A small smile breaks on Electra's lips. "And Leon?" she asks.

"Leon will come with us."

♛

They leave at dawn. As they fit into the chariot, bags are settled at their feet. A length of embroidered fabric spills out of one of the packs, and Iphigenia smooths it with her fingertip. Leon takes the reins, and the horses snort and move. Soon, the Lion Gate and Mycenae's high stone walls are far behind them, bathing in the rising sun.

They ride through the hills dotted with the first colors of spring, the land green and yellow, the early morning sky the color of peaches. The chariot bumps over the rocky path, and Leon sings to pass the time. His voice is warm and lovely. Birds chirp from the trees, and morning gives way to afternoon. They stop only to refresh themselves by a small river and to eat the cakes Aileen has left for them in the bags. Leon does his best to avoid Iphigenia's eyes. When Clytemnestra told him he was to come with them, he looked hurt. "Why me?" he asked.

"Because you swore to protect us."

"You always say you don't need protection."

Clytemnestra almost laughed. "Well, I do now."

In the end, the need to stay close to Iphigenia was stronger than the pain of losing her. Not that he could disobey a queen's order. So now he speaks only when he has to, and whenever Iphigenia asks him something, he answers without looking at her, as if afraid that her light might make his eyes water. But Iphigenia doesn't notice—she is too excited to care about anything other than the marriage. She sways as the chariot rolls on, talking excitedly to her mother.

"Aileen told me that Achilles is the fastest man who ever lived. Did you know that?"

"Since when does Aileen listen to the women's gossip?" Clytemnestra asks.

"And that his mother is a goddess," Iphigenia adds, "and that his men adore him. Myrmidons, they are called, and they all grew up with him in Phthia."

Clytemnestra looks at the landscape around them, rocks and fields with grazing sheep. "You know that everyone in Sparta believed Helen's father was a god when we were children?"

Iphigenia shakes her head.

"That is what the people say when no one knows who the parent is. 'She lay with Zeus,' 'He loved a sea goddess.' But Achilles is no more god than you are."

At last the sea appears on the horizon, sunlight glittering on it, and beyond, the coast of Euboea.

As soon as they step down from the chariot at the edge of the camp, something in the air shifts. The heat clings to their bodies, and their tunics stick to their backs. It is the wind, Clytemnestra realizes—there is none. Leon wipes his forehead with his hand and casts her a confused look, but Iphigenia doesn't notice. She jumps up, her mouth open. "Look, Mother!"

The shoreline is covered with ships of every color and shape, and behind them, a sea of tents that stretches to the horizon, thousands of men grouped around them. There are the vessels of Crete, Ithaca, Argos, and, at the center of the camp, Mycenae, its purple and gold a treat for the eyes. Beyond the cluster of ships, the sea is as flat as a silver blade.

Iphigenia unties her hair, letting it swing down her back, and mounts the chariot again. "Come on!" she says. Reluctantly, Leon takes the reins again, and Clytemnestra goes to stand next to her daughter. Sunlight falls over them, blinding them as they enter the camp.

Inside, it is chaos. Soldiers are moving poles and canvas, pennants and weapons. A few servant women, probably taken from villages the Greeks passed as they rode here, are hanging laundered tunics on poles, filling bowls with food. There is a latrine that stinks like death, flies buzzing around it. A few skinny dogs roam about, sniffing, barking.

As their chariot rolls along, soldiers start making space, opening a pathway that takes them to the king's tent. It is between Agamemnon's pennant and an open space that looks like a marketplace, with a black stone altar. The sun shines on it, merciless, and Clytemnestra imagines putting a hand on it, burning herself.

They get off the chariot. Outside the tent, there is a row of guards, sweat pouring through their thick armor. They bow and show them the way inside. Clytemnestra hesitates, but her daughter rushes in, so she and Leon follow.

Inside, it is spacious and glittering. Wherever Clytemnestra looks, she sees gold: tripods, axes, cups, pins. Even the columns that support the canvas around Agamemnon's throne are gilded. He looks pleased to see her, almost relieved. *Why relieved? You said you knew I would come.*

Around him, other chairs and other kings, though not many. This must be the smallest council, only Agamemnon's most trusted generals. Menelaus is on his brother's right, Diomedes on the king's left. Beside him, Idomeneus with his painted eyes and shiny hair, and Odysseus smiling at her with his catlike grin. He sits in his chair as though it were a throne, leaning on the armrest with a cup of wine in hand. She recognizes other men seated around her: old Nestor, the giant Ajax, the archer Philoctetes. There is also Calchas, standing in the shadows, some dead birds next to him on a table. Achilles is nowhere to be seen.

Agamemnon stands and opens his arms, smiling in a warm way that doesn't suit him. Iphigenia runs into them, and they hug. "Welcome," he says. "I am glad you made it to Aulis."

"And I am glad to be helpful, Father," Iphigenia says. She has spoken slowly and clearly, as though she rehearsed what she would say on the journey. "I am sure a marriage party will cheer all your soldiers."

He lets her go. Diomedes and Menelaus exchange a glance, though what it means, Clytemnestra can't tell.

"My men will escort you to your quarters," Agamemnon adds, "so you can prepare everything for tomorrow."

"And where is Prince Achilles?" Clytemnestra asks.

The silence that follows is painful. For some reason, not one of the generals seems willing to speak. Then Odysseus smiles.

"Our prince is resting. In Phthia, it is customary not to see the bride before a marriage."

Iphigenia almost jumps in delight. Clytemnestra looks back at Odysseus, but his eyes tell nothing more. So she nods and follows Agamemnon's men outside the tent.

In the evening, Agamemnon comes for them. Iphigenia has been caressing the fabric of her wedding dress, smoothing it to perfection. She jumps up when she sees him, putting the dress carefully aside, but Agamemnon stays by the entrance, looking around the tent as though he has never seen one.

"I've come to tell you to rest. You will be up early tomorrow." He avoids Clytemnestra's gaze, smiling feebly in his daughter's direction. "It is good what you are doing, helping us in this way."

"I am only happy to do so, Father," Iphigenia says. "Can you tell me more about Achilles?"

"You will see him tomorrow," Agamemnon says briskly. "Now rest."

He leaves as quickly as he came. Iphigenia remains where she is for a while, half expecting him to come back. When she finally realizes they are alone, she sits on the floor cross-legged.

"Sometimes I don't understand Father," she says.

Clytemnestra finishes her meat, looking at Leon's figure by the entrance to the tent. He has been restless since they came here, peering at every soldier suspiciously. She knows he wants to get a glimpse of Achilles but has ordered him to stay close to Iphigenia. There are too many soldiers in the camp, too many lonely men.

"He acts as if nothing mattered to him," Iphigenia adds. "Not even me."

Clytemnestra puts the bowl down. "You are his daughter. Of course you matter." She feels a pang of hatred for her husband, who can make even her beautiful, generous daughter feel unloved. "There is no one in the world more special than you."

Iphigenia smiles, then breaks into a yawn. All the excitement of the day is waning, and now she is just tired. She lies down on her pallet, stretching her long limbs. "Can you blow out the lamp when you are ready, Mother?" she asks.

"Of course." Clytemnestra caresses her daughter's hair; Iphigenia relaxes under her touch. Then she walks to the lamps and blows them all out. The tent falls into darkness, and Clytemnestra goes outside to think by the sea, under the stars.

The beach is like a furnace, even at night. Because there are no waves, there is no sound. She kicks her feet in the sand dunes, marram grass tickling her soles. The moonlight makes the blades look like desperate arms stretching in the darkness. And then there are the ships, their shapes looming on the water, like seabirds waiting.

"Have you come here in the hope of some breeze?"

She turns. Odysseus is just a shadow behind her, though she would recognize him anywhere—the relaxed posture, the amused voice. He is holding a beautiful wine cup, its gems shining dimly.

"How long has it been like this?" she asks. "Without the wind."

"Since the morning after our arrival. We woke up and the air was so dense that I felt as though dead men's fingers were trying to suffocate me."

"You won't be able to sail until the wind comes."

"Let us hope Boreas will grace us with his presence soon, then." Boreas, god of the wind and bringer of the breeze. They stand side by side for a while, looking at the sea. It is difficult to think in such heat.

"How is Penelope?" Clytemnestra asks.

"Your cousin is good, as clever and beautiful as ever. I still can't explain how she agreed to marry me."

Clytemnestra takes the cup from his hand and drinks some wine. "She will probably say the same now that you are gone."

He shrugs. "Ithaca couldn't be in better hands, with her ruling in my stead. You should see her… That woman knows more secrets than all my spies put together." He smiles to himself. "She doesn't share them, of course. She is as quiet as a tomb. Though I suspect that the people listen to her because they know she could unravel their lives in a moment if she wanted to."

The wine tastes sour in Clytemnestra's mouth but she sips again. Odysseus takes the cup back from her. "If you drink my wine, I am afraid I won't be *polutropos* anymore."

"Well, Agamemnon has other men whose minds he trusts now," she jokes. "Soon you will be set aside."

"And who will take my place? Diomedes? He can't tell the difference between a snake and a lizard."

"Calchas."

"Of course." Odysseus laughs. "But your husband will soon tire of the man's pessimism. Yesterday he told us that the war will be much longer than expected after he looked at some sheep's bones."

"What did the others say?"

"Most of them believe him. They see him as the spokesman for the gods. Others, like Idomeneus or Achilles, are bright enough to nod when he talks. They know that he controls everyone in some way. What if one day Calchas wakes up and announces the gods are angry with them?"

"Do you think Achilles is worthy of my daughter?" Clytemnestra asks.

He passes a hand through his hair, smoothing it. "I would say so. He is young, handsome and, unluckily for us, can also have a soft heart."

"That is no good in war."

"But perfect for a marriage."

His words roll in the thick air, making their way to the sea. Clytemnestra senses something beneath them, like a rotten root that refuses to be seen. She wants to ask him to say more, but he turns to walk away. "If you'll excuse me, I have some planning to do for your husband. You'll see for yourself tomorrow."

His sturdy figure walks back toward the tents and disappears, leaving nothing but the scent of wine.

Clytemnestra wades into the sea. The water laps at her calves, and her toes sink into the sand. Knee-deep in the water, she thinks of Helen and Castor. One gone, the other dead. One in the enemy's city, the other burned. Her mother always told her that the people who die never really leave. Sometimes they watch; at others, they speak. So Leda was taught to look and listen. "They can be in the trees, hidden behind the bark, or in the water, whistling with each crashing wave."

Clytemnestra stands in the warm water, hoping that someone is

watching. But there are no waves and no whispers. She walks back
to her tent.

She is woken early in the morning. Leon is shaking her gently and
she blinks in the darkness. Dawn hasn't come yet, and she hasn't slept
more than three hours.

"Odysseus has called for you in his tent," Leon whispers.

Clytemnestra wipes her forehead with her sleeve. The air is still
damp, sickening. The wind hasn't come. Next to her, Iphigenia
is sleeping, panting slightly in the heat. She kept stirring in the
night.

"You stay here with her," Clytemnestra says, standing and brushing
down her tunic.

"I will come with you, my queen," Leon says. "There are other
guards outside."

"You don't have to."

"I know, but I don't trust that man."

Clytemnestra smiles. "Odysseus is an old friend. Come now. Take
me to him."

On the beach, the fires have gone out. Some soldiers are sleeping
outside, trying to cool down by the sea. No one pays attention to
them as they walk past every tent, their steps muffled on the cool sand.
There are three guards outside Odysseus's tent, half-asleep. They don't
even blink when Clytemnestra throws open the tent door.

Inside, there are two other men, with daggers at their waists.
Odysseus is wide awake, sitting by a table and looking at some maps.
They must have been discussing war tactics.

"Here you are," he says when he sees Clytemnestra. "Hope you managed to sleep." She shrugs. He jerks his head at Leon. "Why did you bring him?"

"Does it matter?" she asks. "Unless you are going to murder me, which I hope you aren't."

There is a flash in his eyes, quick and bright as lightning. It goes as fast as it comes. "That would be far beneath me," Odysseus says.

"And you wouldn't stand a chance," she adds, smiling.

He grins back. "You must be wondering why I have woken you so early." He gestures to another chair, and she takes it, Leon standing stiffly behind her. "As you know, there is some discontent among the men. The heat, the restlessness, the brawls…" He waves a hand.

"I was called here for that reason, remember? To appease the army with a marriage."

"Yes, yes," he says. "But Agamemnon is also struggling with complicated decisions. As you pointed out last night, without the wind, we cannot sail."

She snorts. "Why don't you consult Calchas? He surely has some gods-related insight into the matter."

Odysseus half smiles. "You are right. He has."

"And?"

"Calchas says the gods demand a sacrifice. You know, seers are fond of blood."

Clytemnestra laughs, though she doesn't see what this has to do with her. Outside, dawn breaks. The tent is already becoming warmer.

Odysseus scratches his neck. "Do you know what your husband did to convince me to fight in this war? You probably remember I didn't swear that cursed oath back in Sparta."

"I know what he did," Clytemnestra says, but Odysseus ignores her.

"When he sent his men to Ithaca, I pretended I was mad. I didn't want to go to war. My son was just born, and Penelope, as you well know, has a certain fear of me abandoning her." He chuckles at the thought. "'I am going mad,' my clever wife said, so *I* decided to pretend I was mad to send Agamemnon's men away. I stripped off my clothes, went naked in the cold, and started plowing the stony winter field.

"The first day, the men laughed at me. They almost believed the act. I can be quite convincing. But on the second day, they went into the palace. They took Telemachus from Penelope's arms and threw him into the field, right in front of the plow. The blade almost cut his tender flesh, right here." He touches his hand to the belly.

"So I stopped, picked up Telemachus, and said I would go to war. You can imagine Penelope's desperation, though she kept it to herself, as usual. My wife doesn't like to trouble others with her feelings."

"I am sorry to hear it," Clytemnestra says. She feels the tiredness inside her bones, like a sickness. Her head is spinning: it must be the heat and the lack of sleep. On each side of Odysseus, sweat glistens on the men's necks and arms.

Odysseus shrugs. "We all have to sacrifice something. I sacrificed the time with my wife and son. The chance to see him grow."

"I am sure you will see him again." She stands to take some water, because the warmth is oppressive. One of Odysseus's men almost stands too, but Odysseus stills him with a hand on the shoulder. An odd gesture.

Clytemnestra drinks and cools her forehead. She must check on Iphigenia: the wedding will take place in a few hours.

"I have to go back now," she says, smiling at Odysseus. "Help my daughter get ready."

She waits for his face to break into another of his mischievous smiles, for the lines around his eyes to appear. But Odysseus's face remains blank. He opens his mouth to speak, then something shifts in his eyes. "It is time," he says coldly.

Before Clytemnestra can understand, his men jump up and draw their swords. Instinctively, she snatches for her own, but her hand comes up empty: she has left it in the tent. Leon pushes her behind him, his grip tight on his short dagger.

"Go back to the tent, my queen," he says. She turns to do as he says, slowly, before the men can move—

But the door is blocked. The three guards who were sleeping outside are wide awake now, blocking the entrance. They must have been pretending before. She turns to Odysseus, shocked. He is looking at her.

"There are two ways in which we can do this," he says, and his voice is suddenly emptied of any warmth. "Give up your weapon and stay here—"

"Where is Iphigenia?" she asks.

"Or I am afraid I will have to knock you out."

"Where is she?" she repeats. "Tell me, or I swear I will cut you down."

"You have no blade," Odysseus says matter-of-factly.

Leon lets his dagger fly. It sinks into one man's knee while the other throws him against the table. There is a loud crash and the wood smashes, Leon collapsing on the ground with it. Clytemnestra jumps aside and yanks the sword from the wounded man. The guards are behind her, and Odysseus is in front, unarmed. On her right, his man and Leon are thrashing, moving together on the ground. Leon is choking, kicking the floor.

"Let him go," Clytemnestra says.

The men behind her attack. Their swords close in around her. Clytemnestra keeps them off, swinging hers, but they are too many.

She feels the blade of one cutting her leg and she stumbles. They take her down while she shouts, still waving the sword. Someone's blood spurts on her face. They tie her hands and feet with thick rope. When they try to gag her, she bites their hands and they scream. But soon even her mouth is tied, the knot so tight her head throbs. She can't see Leon. In front of her, the figures of Odysseus's men waver before they walk away, outside the tent. She sees Odysseus's serious face as he kneels in front of her and waits for him to speak, but he says nothing. He places a hand on her knee as though he were soothing a dog, then he leaves too.

She is alone.

The rope cuts into her wrists, and her arms are numb. They must have tied her to the chair, because however she moves, she feels a weight against her back. She tries to think, to ignore the pain, but the heat makes it impossible. The gag in her mouth is so tight that she can't feel any liquid in her mouth. She needs water. She needs something sharp.

When she was young and disobedient, Leda would leave her alone in her room without food or water. When her throat started to scorch, she would convince herself that her mind was tricking her, her body really didn't need water, and thus she would endure.

Now she wills herself to do the same. She must think first, then do something.

Her mistake was to trust. It is always the worst mistake to commit. She trusted a man who is a master of exploits. And he tricked her. *The many-minded*, Odysseus is called, but he is just a traitor. Unless he wanted to keep her here to protect her? But that seems impossible. Where is Iphigenia? Someone must be harming her daughter, or they wouldn't have brought Clytemnestra here, to Odysseus's tent. Iphigenia needs protection, and as long as she's safe, Clytemnestra is safe too. So no. Odysseus has betrayed her, though she still doesn't know how.

Something moves behind her. A pained mumble, then a struggled breath. Biting into the gag, she turns, the chair scraping. Leon is lying on the opposite side of the tent. He seems alive, barely. His face is almost purple, and he is gasping for air. They have tied and gagged him too. Clytemnestra moves in his direction, pushing the weight of her body forward with her legs. A jug lies on the floor. It came down with the table when Leon was thrown against it, but there is still some water inside. And next to it, a kitchen knife. They must have overlooked it when they cleared the space. Clytemnestra looks at the shapes moving outside the tent. There seem to be just two men tasked with guarding them now.

Beyond them, somewhere toward the marketplace, a crowd is gathering. She can hear shouts and prayers, the chanting of soldiers calling to the gods. Calchas must be presiding at the sacrifice Odysseus was talking about. But what of Iphigenia?

She swings forward and gets into a kneeling position, the chair on her back, the sand scraping her skin. She moves on her knees as silently as possible until she reaches the knife. Then she lets her body fall to the side and grabs the handle with the tips of her fingers. She feels the skin bleeding around her wrists. The knife isn't sharpened and the chair slows her, but she manages to cut the ropes around her wrists. The chair falls with them. Her hands freed at last, she unties the gag, gasping for air, then pours the water onto her face, licking the pitcher. The soldiers outside are chatting, but she can't hear anything—the sound is muffled by the rising chant. She saws the ropes around her ankles as quickly as she can. When they come off, she stumbles, trying to stand, the numbness in her legs slowing her down.

For a moment, she considers trying to revive Leon. But that would only give her away. Besides, he looks too weak; he is barely breathing. So she approaches the entrance of the tent alone, the knife in her sweaty palm. The guards are laughing at something, their voices loud and unpleasant.

She throws the tent open and stabs the first guard in the back of his neck. He falls like a sack of wheat, the ghost of laughter still etched onto his face. Before the other man can draw his dagger, Clytemnestra snaps his head to the side. He drops to his knees, unconscious, and she takes his dagger to finish him off. The blade cuts into the skin easily; blood spurts on the sand.

The chanting from the marketplace is growing, each word still in the windless air. It is a sacrifice song, though she can't hear any mooing of cattle. She moves swiftly between the tents on the beach, though it seems that most of the men are gathered in the market anyway. She passes the open ditches where two men are easing themselves and keeps moving toward her tent, keeping the chanting sound to her left.

Then, a cry. Her daughter's voice, fearful and desperate, calling for help. It is coming from the marketplace. Clytemnestra turns to the left, running. She stumbles in her sandals and kicks them away—the sand burns her soles.

When she storms into the marketplace, this is what she sees.

A crowd of men singing with their eyes closed, their faces directed at the sky, as if the gods could hear them.

Prince Achilles—it must be him—frozen in his spot beside the altar, his mouth open as if he would cry, except he is silent. Or maybe he is crying and the sound is buried in the song.

Calchas next to him, his twisted face a mask of utter coldness.

His little black eyes are resting on a group of generals at the edge of the altar:

Agamemnon, Odysseus, Idomeneus.

And Diomedes, his hand on Iphigenia's bright hair, dragging her backward, away from Achilles and Calchas, toward the sacrificial stone. Her robes are covered with dust, her hands scratching, clawing at Diomedes, trying to free herself.

"Father!" she is shouting. "Father, please!"

Clytemnestra moves forward, as fast as a lion. Some men back away, and others come at her, trying to stop her. She cuts them down, one after another. Their bodies wriggle like insects on the ground, useless.

She is almost at the altar stone when Odysseus and Agamemnon turn. They see her. Her husband's knife is flashing in the sun, its gems catching the white light. Odysseus shakes his head.

Clytemnestra jumps forward to cut their treacherous throats, but someone takes her by the hair and pulls her backward. She hits the ground. She tries to anchor herself with her hands, but her fingers break.

"Iphigenia!" she calls, and for a moment, her daughter stops crying and thrashing and turns to her. Their eyes lock.

Then Clytemnestra feels a knee in her back, and she knows she is about to be knocked unconscious.

As her daughter disappears and everything goes to black, she wonders, *How?*

How is someone not killed by such sorrow?

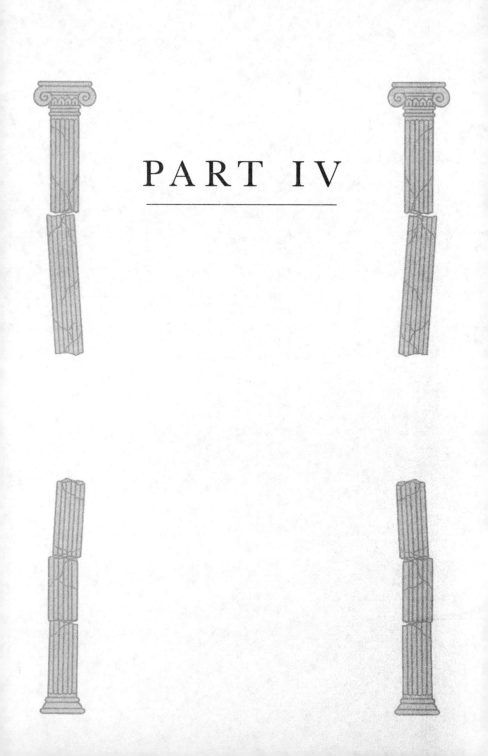

PART IV

My sister Clytemnestra,

They told me you wanted to die, but I didn't believe it. I almost had the envoys flogged in the megaron when they said it. "My sister would never do such a thing," I told the fools. "You do not know her." They told me that you wouldn't eat, wouldn't drink, wouldn't let anyone into your quarters. They said that you wavered between life and death.

If such a thing is true, then you must stop. We grew up thinking we understood death, but we didn't. We would fight in the gymnasium, hunt with Tyndareus, witness the priestess's floggings. Often enough, we would be flogged ourselves. We were starved and beaten, scolded and defeated. And yet we always believed that the strongest would never die, or the most cunning. That was a mistake. Our brother was the most cunning man I knew, yet he was killed by another. Tyndareus was strong, stronger than most men. When he fought in the gymnasium, other Spartans cheered him, and I watched, thinking no one could beat him. And yet he died.

You can do nothing about death, and you can do nothing about pain. The gods follow those who have grown too rich, beautiful, and happy, then grind them down. I told the same things to Helen years ago, when we were riding back to Sparta from that cursed town of Aphidnae. After Theseus had taken her, she wanted to die. She told me that the pain and the shame were too much to bear. I told her she had nothing to be ashamed of and that death was inevitable but she wasn't meant to die then.

So it is with you. Your daughter is gone, but you must go back to life.

There is nothing more powerful than a strong-willed woman. That is what you have always been and must be no matter what others do to you. It is easier for a man to be strong, for we are encouraged to be so. But for a woman to be unbent, unbroken, that is admirable.

Phoebe and Hilaeira send you their love. Castor and Phoebe's child has grown into a skilled boy, and so has my daughter. She looks like Helen, I think, though she has Hilaeira's hair. Hermione misses her mother, but I won't let her hate her, no matter how hard she tries. And now that Menelaus is gone, I will teach her to rule. She might be queen one day.

I know that you will be yourself again when I hear the news that the city of Mycenae is back in the hands of its "single-minded" queen.

Polydeuces

My beloved cousin,

If only you could hear the things the women of Ithaca say when they scrub the clothes by the river, you would shiver. They gather every morning, their arms filled with dirty tunics, and sit on the rocks, washing and talking. Goats climb around them, paying them no heed. Not far from them, little children play, running around with sticks, picking flowers. It would be quite a lovely scene if it weren't for the things they tell.

They tell of the day the Greek troops sailed for Troy, of the brutal sacrifice of your daughter. Agamemnon and Menelaus, they say, gathered their ships in Aulis to launch the biggest armada to Helen's rescue. How unkind the Fates can be—to sacrifice a princess for the rescue of a queen? Is one life really worth more than another? And if so, who is the judge of that?

In Aulis, the wind wouldn't come, so the generals waited for a signal. The men were stranded, the air became unbearable, and the sea was as flat as a silver lid. Then the seer Calchas saw two birds diving from the sky, plunging their claws into a hare and her unborn young. He looked as the eagle kings devoured the hare and said that the army needed a sacrifice to appease Artemis. I haven't met this Calchas, but he sounds like a monster. I always wonder what seers would do if someone told them to sacrifice their own family—would they abandon all their reverence for the gods?

Then these women say that you were tricked into going to Aulis and that my husband helped to create the plan. They say he lured you into his tent and tied you so you couldn't fight. That he left you there in the scorching heat and went to help with the sacrifice of an innocent girl. That Iphigenia *was gagged, lifted, and carried to the altar by Diomedes, that Odysseus and everyone else looked on as Agamemnon cut her throat.*

I do not believe any of this. My husband can be cunning, but he can also be merciful. He sees what needs to be done and always thinks of the best, most efficient way to do it. He surely would have thought of another way rather than sacrifice the general's daughter. I lie awake at night, thinking about it. It can't be, I tell myself, that the man I love betrayed my cousin and massacred her daughter. You understand that I have no other choice. I can't live thinking I have married a man who would do such a thing. What life would that be? A life of truth, I can almost hear you say. But as my mother always told me, in truth, we must suffer. In lies, we can prosper.

The women also say many things about you, things they have heard only the gods know where. They say that you rule Mycenae, that you are growing strong in the palace, that you "maneuver like a man." I find this last one fascinating—as if women couldn't maneuver. I know many more maneuvering women than men. I think of myself as one of them. Besides, you were born to be a ruler.

Odysseus once told me the best thing that can happen to a man—or a woman for that matter—is to be talked about. You might as well be dead otherwise; that is what he believes. I am not sure I agree, but I think you would. You never liked anonymity.

I wanted to come and see you, but if I leave this house, Ithaca's sons will try to take the throne from me. They have already tried. They don't want just a throne; they want a wife too. I sent them away as gracefully as I could, but they will come back. I will think of something to keep them at bay. I will maneuver them.

I know you. You must be angry and thirsty for vengeance for everyone involved in Iphigenia's murder. But do not direct your anger at Odysseus. He loves and respects you, and I am sure he did everything he could to prevent such a tragedy. Be angry with your husband, with the bloodthirsty seer. And try to forget. You have other children. Take care of them.

You are always in my mind·
Your cousin Penelope

My dear sister,

As soon as I heard what they did to you, I almost took a ship, twenty of my best swordsmen, and left for Troy to slaughter them myself—that heartless man Father made you marry, the stinking seer, and the traitor Odysseus. I could see myself cutting them down, carving them into joints.

But something stopped me. You are a woman of revenge. You know how to play this wretched game of retribution. If someone can do justice, it is you. And I am sure you will.

You have done everything for me; I will never forget it. You hid me when the priestess demanded I was flogged, you taught me how to beat other girls when I was weaker, you encouraged me to love whoever I wanted. That is more than anyone can claim of their own sister. And now they have hurt you and I wasn't there to protect you. I must live with this for the rest of my life. Is there any feeling more painful than regret? It spreads like a fever, invisible, and you can do nothing to fight it.

Mother is dead too, so the envoys from Sparta tell me. It must have been the wine. To me, she had been dead for quite a long time. I only remember glimpses of her hunting and fighting when I was little, but I think you, Helen, Castor, and Polydeuces had the best of her. She was tamed after a while.

You should never be tamed. Your men don't bend to you because you are someone else's wife: they do it because they respect your power. So rule them, keep their respect, make sure they are loyal and faithful to their last day. Then you will have a city and an army at your will.

Echemus always told me that some men are destined for

greatness and others aren't. He believed the gods decided that and we had no power in the matter. That is probably why he did nothing to earn his kingdom or the love of his people and also why he will die and wither into obscurity.

Agamemnon, Calchas, and Odysseus, on the other hand, know that one doesn't grow powerful thanks to the gods: they take matters into their own hands and fight to have their names written into eternity. It is no wonder they have survived for so long: they are cruel and cunning. Although they are very different from one another, they have something in common—they believe they are special because no one but them sees the horrible things that need to be done. They believe others shy away from the brutal nature of life but that they are clever enough to see and act upon it. This is also what they tell everyone else: we have no choice, the gods demand it, war is a brutal affair, and we can't win unless we too are brutal. These are all lies. They had a choice. The gods didn't need Iphigenia to die for a whiff of wind. You don't win wars by sacrificing little girls. You do it by killing your opponents. You taught me that.

Your sister Timandra

My dear Clytemnestra,

I am writing these words, which you will never read, sitting by a window in Troy, looking at the battlefield. It is a wasteland of broken wheels, circling crows, and putrefying bodies. Sometimes a severed arm is lying on the muddy ground, detached from everything else, as if it doesn't remember where it belongs.

I can see the battle from here every day, but I can't hear it. It is strange to look at the fighting and dying men. Their mouths are open, but it is as if no sound comes out. Sometimes I think this is how the unburied must feel, wandering around the world, destined not to hear and not to be heard. What a wretched state.

Heroes come and go on the plain, but I haven't seen Castor and Polydeuces. I used to look for their heads among the spears and horses, but I don't do that now. I just pray that they aren't dead.

I am writing and weaving, weaving and writing. I have been doing it for a while now. It keeps me sane. And drinking. Will I end up like Leda, struggling to sit straight at dinner after the endless jugs? There is no one to answer that question. Once, it was you or our brothers who kept me calm. I would come to you with my gnawing doubts and believed everything that came out of your mouths. Now I answer my own questions, but I don't really believe in myself.

Everyone hates me here. Remember how the Spartan women used to call me teras? To them, I was a portent and a freak, a godlike creature and a stain upon my family. Now the

Trojan women call me much worse. I am a husband stealer, a whore, a traitor to my land, a terrible wife, a deadly woman, an undeserving mother. They blame me for everything that happened in my life and their own. Somehow they even found out about the Theseus affair. You should see how they twist that story. How lucky she was to be with such a hero...and yet she was never grateful...she went home to look for a new man...it is never enough for her. I wish I could remind them that Theseus stripped me naked when I was still a child, raped me while I cried, then left, laughing, with his friend Pirithous. But what would the point of telling be? They would not believe me. They won't give me their pity. They want me to be their scapegoat. So be it.

I have come to hate Paris. He doesn't defend me from the gossip, from the spiteful words of his family. And he doesn't fight. This is his war too, yet all he does is train with his bow. When he is done, he comes back to our quarters to make love to me. But it is not the same as before.

Sometimes at night, when he falls asleep, I watch him and think about murdering him, crushing some drug into his cup. I have a few in my quarters—they come from Egypt. They banish pain and sorrow if taken in small quantities, but if you exceed, they kill you. So I put them in his cup, mix the wine, but then I always find myself throwing it away. Paris is the reason I left everything behind. I used to love him with all my heart. Who has bewitched whom?

I think about you a lot. At least I know that Agamemnon is away from you, fighting under this city's gates. So is Menelaus. Maybe they will die in the war, maybe not. I spend *my days looking at the soldiers cutting each other down on the battlefield, their blood spilling into the shape of anemones, and I wonder, What are you doing, Sister? What are you thinking about? Are you happy?*

Your Helen

25

Different Kinds of Wars

Nine years later

IT HAS BEEN nine years since her daughter died. Nine years to the day.

The world has changed, the seasons slipping past her. Flowers blossoming, leaves falling, stars floating. The land has grown dark and fertile, then burned and yellow again. Clouds have come and gone, like sheep in a meadow. Rains have fallen.

She has watched the world shift around her while her heart stayed the same, bleeding hatred. She often thinks of what her mother said all those years ago. *Hate is a bad root. It takes its place in your heart and it grows and grows, letting everything rot.*

It is sunset in the garden, the sky orange as if on fire. The temple of Hera looks pale in the burning light, the columns like bones. She walks by the trees and sits on the grass at the edge of the citadel, listening to the deafening silence. It swallows her, keeping her safe from the world.

She comes here every evening. When the sunlight is gone, she wears her grief like a sling across her chest and allows herself to remember.

She remembers her daughter when she came into the world, a fragile lump of mucus and flesh. Iphigenia had held up her little hands and smiled at her. *This is my chance*, Clytemnestra thought, *my chance of a new life.*

Iphigenia cradling a newborn Electra in her arms. "Why is she so serious, Mother?" she had asked, her eyes wide with wonder.

Aileen washing and tickling Iphigenia's feet and Iphigenia laughing, covering her face with her smooth hands.

Her bare feet beating on the ground as she danced. Her hair moved like a wave, and her earrings dangled around her long neck. She looked so much like Helen that Clytemnestra was afraid her heart might burst.

And then Aulis.

The truth is, she doesn't remember everything about Aulis. Some memories just slid away, like water on a silver shield, and now she can't get them back. All that is left of those dark moments are questions: How did she get back to Mycenae? How did she tell her children?

But other things are engraved on her mind, and the more she thinks, the more details come back to her, as if she were showing a wound to the lamplight and slowly seeing each edge and color, the torn flesh and the festering.

The two men who were with Odysseus in the tent, with their bright armor and sweaty skin. They had looked at her with no pity, no mercy. Just another victim of the gods' plans, they must have thought.

The face of Calchas as he presided over the sacrifice, his black eyes emptied of any feeling. Back in Mycenae, he had told her, "You have a role to play in the war to come." Oh yes, she does. But her daughter's death is not it.

Diomedes dragging her child toward the altar stone. A decent man would treat a goat better than that. And yet he had taken her daughter's precious hair and dragged her as if she were a doll. Dust settled on Iphigenia's dress, the wedding dress she had chosen with such care, and her knees split open, bruised against the hard-grained sand.

Odysseus. She almost chokes when she thinks of him. Every word he had the courage to utter, every smile. All lies. Every night for years, she wished him dead, though she knew very well he wouldn't die, not for a long time. Men like him are hard to kill.

Agamemnon's blade catching the light. Her husband's expression, grave, almost annoyed at her interference with the sacrifice. It was the same expression he wore before he hurt someone in the gymnasium. She remembers the thirst, the pain in her back when they kicked her, the sand on her tongue and in her eyes.

She has done a lot of thinking in the past years. For each painful memory, a thought of revenge. It is as if she keeps burning herself, then plunges her arm into freezing water to keep the pain at bay.

Iphigenia's little hands.

Odysseus tied in his own tent, hurt and alone in the scorching heat.

Iphigenia's big eyes.

Diomedes's throat under her blade.

Iphigenia's hair dancing in the golden light.

Calchas cut down, his lips finally sealed.

Iphigenia smoothing her wedding dress.

Her husband's butchered body.

For a while, this was all she could do, all that kept her alive. She focused on each memory of her daughter and thought of ways to kill everyone involved in her sacrifice.

Then, slowly, those thoughts healed her, as much as one so broken can be healed. She showed her face again. She went back to ruling. She pretended she had moved on. The elders demanded it. If she had stayed isolated for too long, they would have taken over. They would have stolen her crown. A woman can't afford to close her eyes for long. Now she moves around the palace, her heart as dry as a desert, her tongue poisoned with lies. No one will ever come again and take what she loves.

For a long time, she has known there are two different kinds of war. There are the battles where heroes dance and fight, with their glistening armor and precious swords, and there are those fought between walls, which are made of stabs and whispers. There is nothing dishonorable about that, nothing so different from the field. Either way, it is always what she has been taught in the gymnasium: take down your enemies and make them bleed. After all, what is a field after battle if not a stinking lake of corpses?

She will fight her own battle when the time comes. And the palace will be her bloody battlefield.

She is lost in her thoughts when she hears steps behind her. It is late night and stars are scattered in the sky, twinkling feebly. Time has slipped through her fingers.

"My queen," Leon says. His voice has remained low and rasping since Odysseus's men strangled him.

She doesn't turn. She has ordered him never to disturb her when she is in the garden. "What is it?" she asks.

He steps forward, closer to her. "There is a man in the *megaron*. He claims he wishes for your hospitality, but he refuses to show his face."

Clytemnestra turns. The shadows are dark on Leon's face. "Let him wait."

"You want me to tell him to rest in the guests' quarters?"

"Yes. I will see him tomorrow, and he will show his face then."

Leon takes one more step forward and touches his hand to her neck. It is rough but pleasant. She wishes she could close her eyes and enjoy the feeling of being soothed. But she can't afford that. "That will be all, Leon."

For a moment, she fears he will kiss her, as he has done many times in the past, but he nods briefly and walks away. His shadow on the grass is dark, like a starless night.

It was a mistake they both made. She knows she can't blame him alone. When they were back in Mycenae, bruised and wounded, cut and broken, they found comfort in each other.

Clytemnestra was in the garden, a sword in her hand. She had refused to be tended and cleaned and had threatened anyone who came near her. Her hair was still caked in layers of mud from Aulis, her knees and elbows scraped. Her hands were a mass of blood, some nails missing. Leon found her as she was swinging her sword madly. "My queen," he said.

She looked up then. He was standing by the flowers, his throat greenish and swollen, one of his eyes half-shut. They had beaten him again and again back in Aulis until he had fallen unconscious and they had left him for dead.

He took a step forward, his bruised arm extended. She took it but stumbled and fell. Leon knelt next to her and put aside her sword as if she might hurt herself.

They stayed like that for a long time on the grass. Then Leon left, and when he came back, he was holding a soaked cloth. He approached her hesitantly, as you do with a wounded beast. She stayed still while he wiped her face and arms, then her hair and legs, removing all the layers of blood and dirt. His care calmed her, and she gazed into his umber eyes, strong and comforting, like tree bark.

When he had finished, he put down the cloth and started sobbing. His breath came in muffled pants, like a soldier wounded in battle. She had never seen a man cry before. She drew him to her, and his head shook against her shoulder.

"She is gone," she whispered. "She is gone."

He cried even louder, and she thought of how cold his hands were in her lap. The stars were coming out when, at last, he stopped. He looked up at her, his face a mess of bruises and tears. He looked at her as though he didn't see her or as though he saw her for the first time—it was hard to tell.

Then he leaned forward and kissed her. Her mouth opened under his. He was trembling and she tried to hold him still. She grasped his arms as hard as she could, knowing the pain would give him pleasure. She knew it because that was what she wanted too—and he gave it to her. They tore the clothes away from each other's bodies and flinched as they touched each other's wounds. As he moved inside her, she cried, thinking of his half-dead body in Odysseus's tent, one of the last things she had seen before her world had fallen apart.

26

The Stranger

IN THE EARLY morning, the *megaron* is empty and quiet. She wraps her lynx skin around her shoulders and sits on Agamemnon's raised throne, waiting, as the feeble light of the hearth flickers on the frescoed walls.

A man comes forward from the anteroom, alone. He is not one of her queen's guards—he isn't wearing any golden armor or a cap but a long dark cloak. He looks like a fugitive.

Leon appears behind him, grabs the man's arm, and pulls him back. "My queen," he says, "this is the man who refuses to speak his name."

"Let him in," she orders.

Leon stands aside, and the man walks past the footbath and into the hall. He carries a long sword at his waist, and locks of warm brown hair fall out of his hood.

"Clytemnestra," he says. "I come here to ask for your hospitality."

She almost flinches. She hasn't been addressed by her name for a long time. Whoever this man is, he refuses to recognize her status as queen. A thief or a traitor. "Take off your hood," she says.

The man hesitates, fingering the handle of his sword, but then he does as she has ordered. Their eyes meet. His irises are of a cold blue green, like evergreen leaves covered with frost. He reminds her of someone, though she can't tell who. So she waits for him to speak.

He turns to look at the frescoes. His eyes linger on the warriors chasing the frightened lions. The long bodies of the animals glow golden in the feeble light, and the warriors' hair is as dark as ashes.

"I've always found this scene rather false," he says. "Lions don't flee like that."

There is restlessness in the way he stands, as if he is ready to run or strike at any moment. Clytemnestra regards him. *That is what I always thought too*, she wants to say, but instead she asks, "You have been here before?"

"Oh yes," he says, turning back to her. "Many times."

"Then you know how to address a ruler when you are in front of one."

He tightens his jaw. He doesn't look angry, rather like a conflicted boy. "Isn't Agamemnon king of Mycenae now?"

"Yes. And I am the queen."

He gestures to the empty queen's seat next to her husband's throne but keeps silent.

"You come here asking for shelter, yet you do not bend to your queen."

He tightens his jaw again. "I assume you will send me away as soon as I reveal my name. What would be the point of bending?"

"I haven't sent you away so far. The law of hospitality forbids it." She uses the word *xenia*, the respect from hosts to guests that no one can break, not even a god.

"Some laws are stronger than this."

She frowns. "Such as?"

"Vengeance," he says.

She sits back in her throne. She half expects the man to draw his sword, but he is standing still. "Have you wronged my family in any way?"

He looks at her with his strange eyes. In Sparta, children born with such a blue color are considered freaks.

"I have wronged your king in the past," he says. It seems he is waiting, for scorn or punishment, it is hard to say.

"Even if you have wronged my husband, you know I must allow you to stay in this palace."

The man smirks. "I don't want to be killed in my sleep, *my queen*." The words sound mocking in his mouth, yet she likes it.

"You won't be. I give you my word."

He tilts his head and clenches his fists. He doesn't trust her, she can see.

"Leon," she says, "bring Aileen here so we can wash this man's feet and welcome him properly."

Leon disappears, his steps echoing on the stone floor. Other guards take his place by the door, staring at the stranger with suspicion.

"I will have you washed and welcomed," she says, "and then you will tell me your name."

"Yes, my queen." That mocking tone.

They wait in silence as Leon brings Aileen to the *megaron*, staring at each other. The stranger's hair is jagged, as if roughly cut with a kitchen blade. It barely hides the scars on his face: one on the bridge of the nose, the other on his cheekbone, close to the eye. He looks at her with his head slightly bent, as if afraid. She wonders what he is noticing of her.

"We are ready for the cleansing, my queen." Leon stands aside and Aileen enters, a cloth in her hands, her red hair tied back in a long plait. She takes a few steps forward, smiling at Clytemnestra, then notices the stranger and freezes. *She knows him.*

"Wash this man's feet, Aileen," Clytemnestra orders.

Aileen hurries forward and kneels in front of the stranger. As she unties his sandals and cleans him in the footbath, Clytemnestra studies his face for any hint of recognition, but the man seems not to remember Aileen. Still, Aileen has changed since Clytemnestra came to the palace. Whoever this stranger is, he hasn't been to Mycenae in years, or Clytemnestra would know him too.

And then she understands who he reminds her of.

Aileen wipes the man's feet with a dry cloth and ties on his sandals. Then she hurries back into the shadows of the anteroom. The stranger turns to Clytemnestra. "I will tell you my name now, since you have sworn to offer me shelter."

"There is no need," she says, smiling coldly. "You are Aegisthus, son of Thyestes and cousin of my husband."

He starts. His jaw moves, as though he is biting his tongue. Behind him, Aileen stares at the scene, gaping.

"You are clever," he says.

"And you are a fool for coming here thinking to hide your identity."

"I have lived in the shadows of forests and palaces for years. Men never recognize me."

"Well, I am no man," she says, smiling again.

He smiles back, unable to contain himself. The expression is jarring on his face, as though he hasn't done it for years. It shows a different side of him, more childish, less alert.

"You are welcome in this palace, Lord Aegisthus," she says. "No one shall harm you. Now go. I will see you at dinner."

"My queen," he says, bending his head slightly. Then he turns abruptly and walks away. She stares at his back as he passes the frescoes and the columns.

There is a feeling in her she can't recognize, as if a flame has been suddenly lit, burning her from within. After nine years of pain and plotting, this is unexpected. Whether good or bad, she will find out soon enough. In both cases, she holds the sword, and she is not afraid to strike.

By the time she has received all the petitioners for the day, dinner is almost ready. The smells of onions and spices come from the corridors, making her stomach twist. She orders the doors of the *megaron* closed and lets everyone out except Aileen. When the room is empty and quiet, she sits by the fire and invites her servant to join her.

"You once said that Aegisthus didn't use violence like everyone else in his family," she says. "You were scared of everyone except him. And yet he comes here alone with a sword at his waist, refusing to call me his queen. Should I trust this man?"

Aileen looks at her hands in her lap. They are very pale, like milk. "He saved my life," she says quietly.

"You never told me that."

Aileen smooths her tunic; it is wrinkled at the knees. "When Agamemnon and Menelaus came back to retake the city, I was in Lord Thyestes's bedroom, cleaning the torches and folding the sheepskins. I don't know where he was. There was a call from the Lion Gate that the walls had been breached, and I could hear the soldiers arming themselves. I didn't know where to go, so I stayed in there, waiting.

"Then Lord Aegisthus came in. I think he was looking for his father. He asked me what I was doing there and dragged me out of the room. He told me to run behind him and I did. When I stumbled, he picked me up. He took me to the kitchen and ordered me to stay there and pretend that was my duty. 'The servants in the king's quarters will be the first to be executed,' he said to me. Then he disappeared. He took the tunnel that leads to the back gate.

"When Agamemnon and Menelaus infiltrated the palace, the first thing they did was to slaughter all the servants upstairs, just like Aegisthus said. Then Lord Thyestes was burned alive, and everyone else was interrogated on Aegisthus's whereabouts. We heard Lord Thyestes's screams for a long time."

"And yet you didn't say anything," Clytemnestra says.

"No, my queen. I hope you can forgive me."

"He saved your life. There is nothing to forgive."

Aileen nods, with a small, grateful smile.

"Still," Clytemnestra continues, "I can't trust a man like him. You understand why?"

"I am not very good at politics, my queen."

"No one is."

Aileen thinks it through. "He wants revenge on Agamemnon and Menelaus."

"Yes, but both are away now. Yet Aegisthus came to Mycenae today, not when Agamemnon was here. Why?"

"You are in Mycenae. And Agamemnon's children."

"Yes. Do you remember what Atreus did to his brother Thyestes?"

Aileen looks down. "He killed his children, cooked them, and fed them to him."

Clytemnestra stands and paces around the hearth. "Aegisthus hasn't come here to be friends with Mycenae's queen. He either wants the throne his father once occupied, or he is looking for vengeance. Whatever the case, we must be careful."

Aileen looks up timidly. "I don't think Lord Aegisthus wants to murder the children, my queen."

"Why not?"

"Aegisthus is a secretive man. He loathes violence and spectacle. If he had wanted to kill you or your children, he would have done so in the shadows without revealing himself first."

Clytemnestra stops pacing. She can't help smiling. "You say you don't understand politics, Aileen, but you understand people. They are one and the same."

She wears a rich purple tunic for dinner and earrings with precious gems. Her face is more lined than it used to be, her cheekbones jutting under her big dark eyes, but her body stays the same, tall and slender, muscles rippling under the skin.

Orestes is waiting for her outside the *gynaeceum*. "I've come to escort you, Mother," he says with a grin, "now that a stranger and traitor roams free in the palace."

She laughs and smooths one of his curls with her fingers. His eyes are bright and watchful—it is hard to glimpse the shyness, the weakness, they once showed.

"Do not taunt him at dinner," she says while they pass the frescoed chambers. Each corridor is brighter as they approach the dining hall. They can hear the servants behind them and their whispers. Clytemnestra knows they are looking at her son—he has grown into a charming man, and the girls in the palace buzz around him, like bees with honey.

"I never taunt anyone," Orestes replies, though he is smiling. "I am just surprised you welcomed him."

"I couldn't send him away. He is an enemy, and enemies are better kept close. Then they're easier to control."

"Well, I pity the man. He probably thinks himself guest of the king of Mycenae's *harmless* wife."

She takes Orestes's arm. "I can be harmless." He looks at her, eyebrows raised, and they exchange a smile.

In the dining hall, the torches spill light on the meat fat and the golden wine jars. She has ordered ten guards to stand by the walls. Leon has been dining with them lately, but today he is standing near the head of the table, his sword at his waist.

Aegisthus already sits at the end of a bench, Electra in front of him. Her brown hair falls down her back, and her deerlike eyes watch the stranger. Chrysothemis is telling a story, and around her, servants listen as they pour the wine, giggling.

"Welcome to Mycenae, Lord Aegisthus," Orestes says with a dazzling smile as he sits next to Electra. Clytemnestra takes the place at the head of the table.

"Thank you," Aegisthus replies.

"It must feel strange to be back here after all these years," Orestes says.

Aegisthus tilts his head. "I didn't think the queen would accept me."

"My mother is a woman of many virtues," Orestes replies, choosing a piece of mutton. "Strength, wisdom, bravery, generosity. She has them all."

Aegisthus studies him, trying to understand whether he is mocking or not.

"Where do you come from, my lord?" Chrysothemis asks him.

"The forest," Aegisthus replies.

"Did you survive on goat's milk? Did you hunt?"

"Something like that."

"I once heard of a man who lived in the forest for so long that naiads came for him. They left the ponds and marshes and gave him food and shelter. But when he wanted to leave, they held him captive. They were jealous, you see."

There is eagerness in Chrysothemis's voice, as there has been ever since her father left—a constant need to tell stories cheerfully to avoid grief or struggle, any outburst of violence. She is like a blanket of glittering snow: she buries ugliness beneath it until it melts and she must find another cover.

"My daughter knows the most wonderful stories," Clytemnestra says. "Do you want to tell some, Chrysothemis? Perhaps you can entertain our guest."

"Of course." Chrysothemis smiles. "There was the one about Boreas and the stallion…"

She speaks so fast, so excitedly that she forgets to eat. Aegisthus listens, frowning, and barely touches any food. At times, his gaze flickers to Clytemnestra and she pretends to be absorbed in her daughter's story, laughing on cue.

She wants to ask him questions, to spill stories from him and know what lies behind that troubled face. But she doubts he would talk. A man like him probably hasn't talked in his entire life. She imagines his thoughts crawling inside him, like worms in the earth, doomed to stay in the shadows.

Helen would have charmed him with her beauty and subtle cleverness, softening him until he opened like a peach.

Castor would have mocked him, pricked him with words like needles until he talked.

Timandra and Polydeuces wouldn't have tried. "He is dangerous," they would have said. "Better get rid of him." And they would have been right.

He is dangerous, but she can't get rid of him, so she has to find a way to crack him. She must dirty her hands and dig into the earth until she finds those wriggling worms.

She walks back through the corridors alone. The noises of the palace are dying out, fading like sounds underwater. She has ordered Aegisthus to be escorted back to the guests' quarters, and now all she can think about is whether he will be able to sleep. She knows she won't—she must keep cautious and awake.

When she reaches her room, a familiar figure emerges from the shadows. Leon.

"I told you to make sure Aegisthus stayed in his room," she says.

"I left five guards outside. He won't come out without you knowing."

"Good."

She walks past him and opens her bedroom door.

"Shouldn't you send him away, my queen?" he asks.

She turns. "That is my decision, not yours."

"He is dangerous. You know how long the elders have been looking for him. Everyone thought him dead. And now he comes here, after everything he suffered in this place…" He takes a deep breath. "He is like a rabid dog that has been beaten to death but somehow survived. He has made it inside these walls but can bite at any moment."

"He hasn't attempted to harm me or my children so far."

His voice cracks. "You also trusted Odysseus when we were called to his tent."

She strikes him so quickly he doesn't have time to react. When he looks back at her, there is sadness in his eyes.

She clenches her fist, laying each word out as a knife. "You decided to come with me instead of keeping my daughter safe. I asked you to protect her. Instead you chose to protect me, not understanding that my life without her is nothing. Do not speak of it again, or you will be the one sent away."

"Yes, my queen." He has spoken so softly she might have imagined it. Either way, she closes her bedroom door behind her, locking him out.

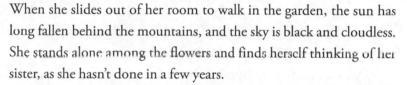

When she slides out of her room to walk in the garden, the sun has long fallen behind the mountains, and the sky is black and cloudless. She stands alone among the flowers and finds herself thinking of her sister, as she hasn't done in a few years.

The last time was three winters ago, when an envoy had come to the palace to give her the news of her mother's death. She couldn't find any tears.

"How?" she asked.

"In her sleep," the envoy replied, and Clytemnestra almost laughed bitterly. Her mother, once a huntress and fighter, dead in her sleep because of all the wine she drank.

Such is the fate of a woman, no matter how shining and brilliant she is, to be crushed like grain under a pestle. And what is left of Leda now? Rumors, myths. The woman who slept with the god of sky and thunder, the queen who was raped by a swan, the mother of the most beautiful woman in the world. But Leda was much more than that.

Clytemnestra spent that night pacing the palace, grieving for the mother who spoke to her about the gods of the forest, about Rhea and her whispers in sacred caves and cypress groves. The woman who ruled Sparta with her husband, who taught her children to fight in the gymnasium, and who sometimes woke her daughters in the night for a secret walk in the moonlight. She held their hands and made them laugh until Helen's eyes shone with happiness.

She didn't grieve for the Leda who stood aside as her father and Agamemnon plotted. That Leda was long dead to her.

Now she tries to picture her sister in Troy, alone in a city of people who must hate her. She has sent two of her best scouts across the mainland to bring her any news of the war they can find, yet they have nothing about Helen. That means her sister is still alive. The comfort she takes in this is strange, for it has a bitter taste in her mouth, like ashes.

Helen lives, Iphigenia is gone. There is some injustice in it, though Clytemnestra has spent her life protecting her sister.

Do you wish Helen had died?

She closes her eyes. She can see them together, swimming in the Eurotas as children, their naked bodies splashing in the clear water, their arms wrapped around each other. It is always difficult to decide if one life is worth more than another. It is also pointless. The dead are dead.

She walks back inside, leaving her thoughts behind. Above her, the pain of Iphigenia's destiny hangs in the sky like an endless prayer.

27

Wolf's Teeth

CLYTEMNESTRA FOLLOWS ELECTRA in the hot summer sun, the market stalls around them. People stream past, their faces sun-darkened, their hands chapped for the work—a man cutting a pig's hocks, his ax and apron stained with fresh blood; a woman hanging plucked chickens by their feet; a dark-haired girl giving apples from a large basket. Clytemnestra stops by a stall displaying diadems, the gems glittering so brightly that sunlight seems to rise from them. Jewels for royalty. The trader bends his head, staring at Clytemnestra's feet. "My queen," he says. "My princess."

Electra caresses a thin golden headdress, each pendant in the shape of a leaf. It would look good against her pale skin, Clytemnestra thinks, but Electra moves on. The people flood the streets like lizards, each looking for a spot under the sun.

Clytemnestra thinks about her meeting with the elders, how arrogant and ungrateful they had been that morning. They insisted that she imprison Aegisthus and that she keep him hostage until Agamemnon returns.

"What use would that be?" she asked. "Aegisthus has no family left. No one will pay a ransom."

"Then keep him in the dungeon until the king decides what to do with him."

"*The king* has been away for nine years," she replied. "During which *I* have ruled this city, kept it safe. And yet you still refuse to trust my authority."

They fell silent. She enjoyed the look of defeat in their eyes.

"Do you think the traitor Aegisthus is handsome?" Electra asks, distracting her from her thoughts. Her cheeks are red from the sun and she is patting a dog as if she had just asked the most innocuous question.

"I haven't thought about it," Clytemnestra replies. That is a lie. She has, in fact, considered what it is about Aegisthus that intrigues her, but she hasn't come up with an answer yet. "Do you?"

Electra lifts the hem of her dress to avoid some fruit left rotting on the ground. "I think he was once. But now he is too scared of himself."

"You don't find him frightening, then."

"No. I just wonder what a man like him thinks. His eyes are like ice—they shut you out." Clytemnestra smiles to herself. It must be hard for her daughter to feel shut out from someone's mind—she, who is always searching people's faces to understand their every move and motive.

They reach the end of the street. Perched on the gate, the sculpted lions are mighty in the sunlight, their gazes empty, indifferent. "The kings of Mycenae are lions," Agamemnon told her once, "preying on the weak." When she pointed out that the relief sculptures were more like lionesses, her husband laughed. Would he laugh now that a lioness sits on his throne?

Clytemnestra starts walking back to the palace, and Electra follows, still brooding.

"I have asked the women in the kitchen," she is saying. "They say Aegisthus was born after Thyestes raped his own daughter, Pelopia.

She was performing a sacrifice in the temple, and he took her in the darkness, then disappeared before she could see his face."

"The women in the palace talk a lot," Clytemnestra comments.

"Pelopia didn't know that it was her father who raped her. She was ashamed and sent the baby away, so he was raised by Atreus, which means Aegisthus grew up with Agamemnon." She has stopped calling him "Father" in Clytemnestra's presence ever since her mother threw a cup at her years ago. Now, all her children call their father "Agamemnon." How they refer to him when she is not there, she doesn't know.

"When Pelopia sent Aegisthus away, she gave him a sword, Thyestes's sword. Only she didn't know it was his. She had snatched it away from him before he left. So when Atreus sent Aegisthus to murder Thyestes, Thyestes saw the sword, recognized Aegisthus as his son, and convinced him to take his side."

Clytemnestra knows Electra is talking to try to understand the man better. Stories are all she has, so she dissects them until she feels in control. After all these years, she hasn't yet understood that women are rarely in control.

"I wonder if he knew his father raped his mother. He must, for everyone else knows. And if he does, what does he think? Does he forgive him?"

A group of women walk past them, their arms filled with figs, grapes, and lemons. The fruit is so bright it looks like flowers.

"Do you know where Pelopia is now?" Clytemnestra asks.

"No."

"She killed herself."

A shadow passes over Electra's face. She looks at her feet, her cheeks bright red. The sun drives higher in the empty sky, and Electra is silent for the rest of the walk.

A product of incest and rape. A child born for the purpose of revenge. Unwanted by his mother, abandoned in the woods, taken by the very man he was meant to kill once he had grown up. How many things has Aegisthus seen? How much pain has he endured? The answers to her questions seem carved onto his face like scars, stitched into his skin like secrets. She can find out by reaching out and touching.

She is told that he spends his time around the practice yard in the late afternoon, so she goes there alone when the boys have finished training. Sunset is painting the sky in dark-red strokes. In the middle of the yard, a torch is thrust into the ground, its light burning strongly.

She can't see anyone at first—maybe Aegisthus has left already. Then a shadow moves by the armory and he comes into the light, a sword in one hand, a spear in the other. Two hunting blades gleam at his waist. She can see the scars running along his bare arms, pink like peaches and jagged like stones.

He casts his spear into one of the trees. The weapon flies faster than her eyes can follow. It sinks into the bark, and splinters fly.

In the stark light of the torch, Aegisthus wields his sword. It flashes forward, like a lion's claws, then back. There is nothing elegant about his movements, nothing graceful. There is a kind of desperation in the way he fights. The sky bleeds above him, then grows darker, angrier.

She holds her jeweled knife tight. She waits as he turns his back to her, making his sword whirl, and then she throws it in his direction. His head jerks back in time. He lifts the sword to his face, and her knife bounces off it.

He looks at her, his face raw with rage. She feels as if she has just discovered a secret of his, something she wasn't meant to see. She moves forward, grabbing a spear from the ground as she walks. In the practice yard, she smiles. A challenge.

"You are good."

He takes a step back, and his figure slips away from the light of the torch. "I won't fight you."

She keeps moving forward. "Why? Are you afraid?"

"You are my queen. And a mother."

And you are a usurper. And a son.

"Fight me," she says.

She lifts the spear and he instinctively moves his sword. The two weapons clash, bronze on bronze.

"I'll put my sword down now," he says.

"Then you will die."

She attacks him again, and this time he pushes forward too, ripping the air, his eyes filled with violence. They fight each other, their feet kicking up dust. When she disarms him, he takes his hunting blades. He is fast with them, much faster, and Clytemnestra struggles to keep him away. She throws her spear at him, and as he wards it off, she grabs a shorter sword from the ground. Their arms move quickly, one blow after another, until they are exhausted, sweat pouring down their backs. They stop fighting together.

His face is twisted, his daggers abandoned in the dust. He retrieves his sword carefully, cleaning it on his tunic. She wonders if it was his father's but doesn't ask. Instead, she picks up her own knife and says, "You look different when you fight."

"So do you." His head is bent, and his profile is handsome in the golden light of the torch. *How do I look different?* she wants to ask, but he is quicker. "Who gave you that knife?"

"My mother," she says. "It is the sharpest blade I've ever touched."

She holds it out for him to see. As he caresses the blade with his finger, she adds, "But you are not afraid of a little sharpness, are you?"

He looks up at her, and she holds his gaze. Leon was right. He is like a wounded animal, ready to bite at the first provocation. But he is no rabid dog—rabid dogs are weak because they are mad. Aegisthus isn't mad. He is strong and manipulative, his rage boiling inside him but always kept at bay. He is more like a wolf, showing his teeth to those who come too close.

He smiles. "Sometimes it is better to bleed than to feel nothing at all."

She avoids dinner and goes to the bathhouse to clean herself. Her tunic is dusty, her hair messy and tangled. The lamps are already lit, streams of light in the quiet darkness. She takes off her *chiton*, brushing her fingers against her stomach, the fading cuts on her arms. There is an edge to her. The water of the bath is cold, and she shivers.

"My queen." A voice chirping in the darkness, like a bird at sunrise. Aileen. Her steps come closer, soft as raindrops. "Lord Aegisthus came to eat and you weren't there," she says, "so I thought I would find you here."

"Warm the water, Aileen," Clytemnestra orders.

Aileen hurries to light the fire, her shadow on the wall small and sharp. The water grows warmer, wrapping Clytemnestra like a sheepskin. Aileen starts scrubbing her with soap. Clytemnestra offers her hands and arms, and Aileen touches the soap to the soft inside of her elbow.

"Chrysothemis couldn't sleep last night," she says. "She has been having bad dreams again."

Clytemnestra looks at her face in the shadows. Aileen never had children of her own, but maybe she should have. Once, Leon suggested she was pretty, his tone casual as if to test how Clytemnestra would feel about it. She discouraged it. Two loyal servants together can't be easily controlled. It is much more useful to pair a loyal dog with a more difficult subject to keep him under control.

"Perhaps she should sleep with you tonight," Aileen continues.

"She is fourteen years old. She is a woman now, not a child, and she needs to behave like one."

Aileen doesn't speak, but her eyes are sad. Clytemnestra knows she disapproves. One night, a year or so after Iphigenia's murder, she had the gall to tell her that she was too cold, too detached from her daughters. "Electra and Chrysothemis need you, my queen," she said. "You don't speak to them. You don't touch them." Clytemnestra wanted to strike her, but she kept silent—she couldn't afford to lose Aileen. She wouldn't trust anyone else to take care of her children.

"I will talk to her in the morning," Clytemnestra adds, keeping her voice as sweet as she can. "But wipe that disapproving expression from your face, Aileen. You are not the goddess Hera."

Aileen chuckles, and as she cleans Clytemnestra's neck, her touch becomes gentler. *There*, Clytemnestra thinks. *That is how easy loyalty is for some. They are satisfied with crumbs.*

Brushed and cleaned, she goes to the dining hall. The smell of meat is strong and inviting, and she looks at the leftovers as servants hurry to take everything away. The house dogs keep close to her, sniffing for scraps on the floor. Leon appears by the door and sends them away with a flick of his hand.

"Bring some wine for the queen," he orders the servants. "You can finish clearing later."

Clytemnestra sits on the chair at the head of the table. She accepts the wine a woman gives her and sips. Leon sits next to her.

"How was dinner?" she asks.

"The elders joined," he says. "They were wondering why you weren't there."

"Did you tell them it was because I didn't want to see their wrinkled faces?"

"No," he says with a small smile.

"You should have." She can almost picture them, staring at Aegisthus like foxes around a chick. She finishes the wine and Leon pours more for her. The servants have all disappeared. The door is closed, and there are only their shadows on the floor.

"I have heard them whisper in the corridors today," Leon says. "They spoke about you and Aegisthus."

"I thought we had enough women whispering around this palace."

Leon plays with the handle of his dagger. "Some said that a woman should not wear a crown. Others defended you."

"What exactly did they say?"

Leon hesitates. She gives him time and drinks more. This is not the first time she has heard the elders' discontent.

"They said that your power is like 'the plague among soldiers.'"

"Who said this exactly?"

"Polydamas."

"Ah, of course." One of her husband's most faithful dogs. Throw him a bone and he'll bring it back, wagging his tail. But he doesn't like women. He keeps his own wife and daughters in the house, never to see the light of day. Clytemnestra wanted to have him killed many times, but she knows that would send the wrong message to

the others. So she has tried to deal with him, however you can deal
with someone else's dog.

"What do you think, Leon?" she asks. "Am I like the plague?"

"No, my queen." He looks at her, then away, at the weapons gleaming on the walls. "But you can be intimidating. You are like the sun.
If one looks too long, he'll be blinded."

She can feel the love, the reverence in his tone. She should reward
him for that. If she pushes away her own loyal servants, why should
anyone follow her?

"Then why do you think the elders might say such a thing?" she
asks.

Leon leans back a little, as he always does when he is thinking. One
of his eyes, the right one, is still half-shut from the beatings at Aulis.
"They see themselves in your place. They think they could do better
what you do. They dream of their own kingdoms, their own crowns."

His answer pleases her. He can be astute when she forces him to
think. He would make a good ruler if it weren't for his common blood.

"And how do you think I should make them understand that their
kingdoms are nothing more than a dream?"

"You can't. I imagine that is a ruler's burden to bear." He stands
and the bench scrapes loudly. "Now I will leave you, my queen. You
should rest."

He bows and walks toward the door.

"Come here, Leon."

He stops. When he turns back, pleasure is plain on his face. He
covers the steps between them and kneels next to her chair. She
touches his hair, draws him to her. His lips on hers taste of home and
sorrow.

"Someone might come," he says, breathless, as he lifts her tunic.

"Let them," she says. "I am queen. I do as I please."

This excites him, the thought like a drug running through his veins. She lets him inside her, her arms around his shoulders, his breathing ragged on her neck.

How wrong this is, she thinks, how unjust. *Does he think of Iphigenia when he looks at me? Does he still remember her smell, the softness of her skin against his?* He never speaks of her, but Clytemnestra feels his pain growing inside him, in every crack and wound, every hollowed space.

He clings to her for a while when he is done, his skin damp on her chest. She lets him, staring at the light thinning as the torches go out. When the room falls dark, she searches for a feeling inside her—grief, safety, anger, pleasure, anything.

Sometimes it is better to bleed than to feel nothing at all.

Is it?

28

Broken People

Outside the windows, autumn is creeping in. The leaves glow bright and red on the trees, and cold nights frost the grass. It makes Clytemnestra think of Aegisthus's eyes. There are no birds singing, no figures moving. It seems as if the land has stopped to rest.

"My queen, we should discuss matters of the throne."

Polydamas's screeching voice brings her inside. In the *megaron*, the elders are sitting around her in a semicircle. Rather than being on her throne, she is standing by the windows. Their presence makes her feel in need of air.

"What is there to discuss about the throne?" she asks.

"If King Agamemnon doesn't come back from the war—" Polydamas starts.

She interrupts him. "Whether the king does or doesn't come back from the war makes no difference. I am queen now, and my son will be king next."

Polydamas keeps quiet. If she hates him when he speaks, she likes him even less when he is quiet. She can hear his mind spinning, weaving plots against her.

"The traitor Aegisthus might pose a problem," Cadmus says. He reminds her of a bruised apple, one of those left on the ground until someone steps on them. At least he tends to favor Clytemnestra on most matters.

"You should send him away or imprison him," Polydamas says. "He has a claim on the throne."

"My husband used to say that it is better to keep your enemies close." That is a lie. Agamemnon never said such a thing. But she has noticed that whenever she mentions him, the elders struggle to contradict her.

"Then imprison him," Polydamas repeats.

"You underestimate me, as usual," she says.

"How so, my queen?"

"You believe I let Aegisthus eat at my table and walk around my palace without having a plan. You do not consider that I might be trying to understand him better, to manipulate him."

"Men don't manipulate their enemies. They force them into submission."

She laughs bitterly. "I thought you served my husband. Who can manipulate better than Agamemnon? The king you so blindly follow has risen to power thanks to his deceits. And what about Odysseus, king of Ithaca?" The name stings on her tongue but she speaks it nonetheless. "Is he called a hero because of his strength or because of his tricks?"

Cadmus nods, and so do a few others.

Polydamas shifts in his seat. "You are mistaken if you think you are the only one ready to manipulate," he says. "Aegisthus will try to do the same. He has come here for power, not to bend to a woman."

"A queen," she corrects him.

"Yes, a queen."

"I will keep Aegisthus under control. And if he tries to hurt me or usurp my throne, he will pay for it."

The elders seem to relax in their seats. They are such cowards that a single man can unsettle them so.

"You will never doubt me again on this matter," she adds, sitting back on her throne. A murmur of assent. "Is there anything else to discuss?"

"We haven't spoken of Troy yet, my queen," Cadmus says.

It is true. She hasn't asked because her scouts keep her well informed, though nothing much has happened. The city hasn't fallen yet.

"A plague has struck the Greek army," Cadmus continues. "Many of our men are dying. They say it is Apollo who must be placated."

She almost raises her eyes to the ceiling. She is tired of hearing about the gods. "Has the king been struck?" she asks.

"No. But the plague is subtle, my queen," Polydamas replies. "It strikes without mercy and without regard for rank and honor."

She caresses the rings on her fingers, enjoying the uncomfortable silence that follows. "It's odd that you should talk about the plague in such terms, Polydamas," she says.

"Why?"

"I thought you said that a woman in command can be like the plague among soldiers." She looks him straight in the eye, placing each word carefully.

He doesn't blush or mumble. He holds his ground. "I said it and I believe it." There is no arrogance in his tone, just a hideous matter-of-factness. The honesty of a man who believes he can say whatever he thinks.

"I am aware that many of you consider you might rule this city better than I do," she says. "That because I am a woman, I should put your counsel before my own. That my husband was a better ruler, more fit."

Some look away from her, uncomfortable. Others blush but keep staring at her, bold.

"Yet Mycenae has grown richer under my command, despite the loss of men and resources at war—a war my husband wanted. So as long as I am on this throne, you will give your counsel and respect my choices."

And if we don't? she can almost hear them think.

Then I will cut out your tongues.

In the practice yard, she finds her son, a ray of sun on a cloudy day. He is teaching the younger boys to shoot, a lion's skin across his shoulders.

"They are learning fast today, Mother," he says when she joins him.

"Are you shooting arrows only?" she asks.

"Yes, for today. But we will work with spears and axes soon."

They take a few steps away from the yard. The cold grass crackles under their feet. She fixes a curl behind his ear, and he smiles as if to tell her, *I am no child now, Mother.*

"You should come to my meetings with the elders more," she says.

"Why? You manage them much better than I could."

"You must learn to manage them too. You will be king one day, and there are still things you need to learn. The elders are like snakes. They creep up behind you and strike you in the back if you are not ready to defend yourself."

"Why don't we simply eliminate them?"

"A city needs its elders. Every queen or king must have counselors."

"You are my counselor," he says.

"I am," she says, smiling, "and now I am counseling you to come and listen to the elders so you can learn to see their lies."

He laughs. "I will come, and I will try not to murder Cadmus when he speaks of the tragedies that await us. Last time I heard him, he was raving about some beggars possessed by the Furies."

"Today it was the plague."

He shakes his head as if to say, *See?* then runs back to the yard. Clytemnestra watches as the boys tear after him, gazing at him in awe. When he was a child, there were times when she feared for him—that he wouldn't be able to face confrontation, wouldn't know how to defeat his enemies. But Orestes has learned that and much more. He has learned how to inspire love and respect, which most princes of his age overlook. *Men are often blinded by power*, the priestess in Sparta had once told Clytemnestra. But not her son. He is still a man, so some things he will never understand—he will never have to—but Clytemnestra has taught him the most important thing of all: that power alone doesn't buy you a kingdom.

On the high stone walls of the citadel, the wind is as cold as snow. Clouds are dropping on the land around her, slowly swallowing the landscape, from the mountain peaks to the lower hills and streams. Helen used to dream of being able to command the clouds. She would lie on the grass, close her eyes, and ask them to move faster, the wind to blow stronger, the sun to burn brighter.

"It won't work," Clytemnestra would say.

"You should lie down too," Helen always replied, tugging at her sister's tunic. "If we can unite our wills, we are stronger."

So Clytemnestra would lie down. When the wind didn't blow and the sun didn't burn, she would take Helen's hand and say, "I think it hears us but doesn't want to listen. The wind can be spoiled sometimes."

Helen would smile. They both knew it was a lie, but it kept them closer and happier.

"My queen."

She turns. Aegisthus is a few steps behind her, watching her. He always gets past the guards—she should tell them to be more observant.

"Your daughter came to talk to me," he says.

"Which one?"

"Electra."

She frowns, surprised. Electra rarely goes to talk to anyone.

"What did she want?"

"She told me that the elders don't want me in the palace and that you are fighting them." He studies her, waiting for a reaction. When she keeps silent, he adds, "But I think she wanted me to tell her why I have come here."

"That is Electra's way, yes. She talks to make *you* talk. You must frustrate her."

"How so?"

"She can't know anything about you. You are an enigma."

He frowns. "Everyone knows plenty about me. Wherever I go, my family's curse precedes me."

"I don't think that interests Electra. She is always looking for what others think or feel, what they fear or desire. Knowledge about your family is something she can easily have, and that is why she doesn't want it."

He comes closer until they are standing next to each other, a sea of gray all around them. He could throw her down the walls now if he wanted to.

"My father used to come here and watch every man, woman, and child in the village," he says after a while.

"Why?" she asks.

"To decide whom he would flog or kill. He would see enemies everywhere."

"I am not your father."

Pain passes over his face, but she doesn't turn away. She likes to see his sorrow because it feels intimate, something he wouldn't show to anyone else. His features are blurring in the thickening mist, and she finds herself wishing she could touch him before he disappears.

"No, I can see that," he says. "You're not cruel and yet you hold a kingdom together. I've never seen anything like it."

One of her warlords dies, so the elders call a council to replace him. Clytemnestra asks Orestes and Electra to stay in the *megaron* with her as the best young men from their army offer their swords to her. One by one, they approach the throne, the watchful eyes of the elders studying them from the shadows, and introduce themselves and their deeds.

I won every wrestling match last year, my queen.

My father gave his life on the Trojan battlefield.

My brother dealt with the villagers' riot two winters ago.

It isn't an easy choice. The warlords must patrol the streets of the citadel, protect Mycenae against foreign invasions, and crush revolts within the city walls. Most of the warriors left with Agamemnon nine years ago, and Clytemnestra has been building a strong army to replace them.

"It would be an honor to serve you, my queen Clytemnestra."

She looks up. The man in front of her is young, with a lean face, like a hunting dog's. He looks at Electra briefly, then back at Clytemnestra.

"I have been beating every other man in the practice yard for years."
He looks at Orestes. "Your son is always there. He can speak for me."

"Kyros is a good soldier," Orestes says carefully. Clytemnestra
doesn't comment, and Kyros feels compelled to speak again.

"We've met before, my queen, although I am not sure you remember. I am Eurybates's son. Your husband respected my father, who died
fighting beside him across the sea."

"I remember you," she says with a cold smile. "The boy who tried
to rape my daughters."

Electra looks away. The elders start whispering, and Clytemnestra
quiets them.

"You wanted to flog me years ago, my queen," Kyros says. "You
were right. I disrespected your daughters, and they showed me never
to underestimate a woman in return. In every mistake, there is always
a lesson to be learned." She can tell he has been rehearsing his little
speech, though he is careful enough to look honest as he speaks.

"How many mistakes does it take to make a decent man?" she asks.

Silence. Clytemnestra stares at the flames dancing in the hearth,
their shadows lapping at Kyros's feet.

"Would you have Kyros next to you in war, Orestes?" she asks her
son. "Can you trust a man who offended your sisters?"

Again, Orestes speaks slowly. "Kyros is a good partner during practice. He always helps a friend in need." Kyros nods to him, grateful.

Clytemnestra sits back, feeling Electra's eyes on her. "Very well.
Then I will have your sword, Kyros. You will fight for me, next to my
son and the other warlords."

Silence again. Then Kyros kneels, his face warm with pride. When
he stands, he and Orestes exchange a glance.

"This is your chance to make your queen proud," Clytemnestra
says. "Do not waste it."

"Thank you, my queen."

When he has gone, Clytemnestra orders the elders to leave her with her children. The hall feels lighter, cooler without them. She asks the servants to bring wine and turns to Electra. Her daughter is standing in the shadows, brooding. She has kept silent throughout the day, torturing the hem of her purple dress as the men tried to win her mother's attention. Clytemnestra knows that she too is remembering when Kyros tried to hurt her, when Clytemnestra sent the boy away and Electra said, "At least Father treats us all the same." But he didn't, did he?

You have become like him, she can hear Electra think. *You think of your throne and kingdom before anyone else now.*

"Are you sure of this, Mother?" Orestes asks. Glints of fire from the torches shine on his handsome face.

"I gave Kyros that position to show the elders that there is a second chance for those who are disloyal." *Besides, his father is dead, so now Kyros's family will be loyal to me, not to Agamemnon.*

"You won't regret it. Kyros is the best warrior among those who trained with me."

"Good. Because he is not a good person."

Orestes smiles and covers her hand with his own. "Do good men make good warlords?"

Once, three or four years ago, Clytemnestra asked her daughters what kind of husband they wanted. It was summer and they were in the garden. The trees were heavy with fruit, and birds were flying from branch to branch, eating cherries, chirping. Their feathers were brilliant in the sunlight.

Chrysothemis considered the question. She was still too little to think about husbands, but she liked speaking to her mother in the garden, away from the trouble of the palace, from the hisses of the elders and the emptiness of the *gynaeceum*. "One who stays with the family," she said after a while. "One who doesn't die."

Clytemnestra laughed then. Of all the things she might have said... Electra laughed too and the birds twittered. Chrysothemis took her sister's hand and asked, "What about you, Electra?"

Electra replied instantly, as if she had thought about it many times already. "I want a man who can get what he wants. One who understands me and at the same time frightens others with his brilliant mind."

Maybe she would have liked Odysseus. The thought filled Clytemnestra with unspeakable bitterness.

Electra is in the courtyard, looking at the frescoed griffins. Her hair is loose on her back, and on her hands are the rings her sister used to wear. Clytemnestra takes a step forward before seeing that Leon is with her daughter, leaning against a red column. She moves back into a corner, next to some jugs of oil lined against the wall, and listens to them as they speak.

"She used to wear more," Leon is saying, touching the rings. "Three or four on each finger." He closes his eyes and rests his head against the column.

"Do you miss her?" Electra asks.

"We all do." He waits, takes a deep breath. "Your mother more than anyone else."

Electra bites her lip, lowers her eyes. "She never talks to me about her."

"It is too painful for her."

The shadows grow longer on the floor, like fingers reaching out for each other, looking for some sort of comfort.

"You love her now?" Electra asks.

Leon doesn't seem shocked by the question. "I've always served her," he says simply.

"She will leave you. You know this."

Clytemnestra doesn't wait for his answer. She comes out of the shadows, and Leon looks at her, surprised. Electra covers her ringed hand with the other instinctively, as if her mother might take away the jewels.

"Leave us," Clytemnestra tells Leon. He obeys, and as soon as he is gone, a cold breeze is blowing, bringing raindrops as small as grains of sand. They scatter on Electra's face, glistening. She doesn't wipe them away.

"You are wearing your sister's rings," Clytemnestra says.

"I polished them first."

"They suit you. You have the same long fingers." It isn't easy to say, but she knows Electra needs this. Her daughter opens her eyes wide, then offers her hand. Clytemnestra takes it, touching the precious stones—onyx, amethyst, lapis lazuli.

"Aegisthus told me of your talk," Clytemnestra says.

"I thought he would," Electra replies.

"Did you find what you were looking for?"

"I can't say I did."

"You should have asked differently, more directly."

Electra surprises her by saying, "I agree."

"Why does he interest you so?" She knows the answer to her question but she wants to hear Electra say it. Here is a riddle her daughter can't solve, so she becomes stubborn.

But Electra says, "Broken people fascinate me."

Thunder rumbles loudly, and rain is flooding the courtyard now. Electra hurries under the portico, hair plastered to her face. Clytemnestra stays where she is: she enjoys watching everything dissolve in the rain, the outlines of objects and people fading.

"Mother, you are soaked," Electra calls, but Clytemnestra ignores her. It's as if her daughter's words have suddenly cleared a murky river and now she is looking at her mirrored feelings. *Broken people fascinate me.*

Is that why she is drawn to Aegisthus? There are no answers in the pouring rain.

Dawn comes, bright and quiet, her rose-red fingers stroking the roofs of the citadel. Clytemnestra sneaks out of the palace, enjoying the thickness of the silence. There is nothing she likes more than being awake when the city sleeps. It gives her a sense of power, an illusion of control.

She creeps out through the back gate of the citadel, a warm shawl wrapped over her *peplos*. The road up the mountain is steep and muddy. Goats and sheep are bleating somewhere on the slopes, where the land is ripe with grapes. Above her, pine and oak trees thicken, casting long shadows on the ground.

She stops to rest by a small rock pool, the water so clear that it looks like a slice of sky. Though it is still autumn, the winter ice has already appeared on the mountains, covering the peaks with white sprinkles. She sits on the rock and touches her bare feet with her palms, warming them a little before plunging them into the freezing water of the pool. Her muscles scream but she keeps still, enjoying the pain.

"I didn't expect to find anyone here."

Her hand flies to her dagger. Aegisthus is standing by a tree, watching her. His hair is held back and the scars on his face are stark in the pale light. She takes her feet out of the cold water and puts down the dagger. "Were you following me?"

Maybe the elders were right and she has underestimated him. She empties her mind of the sudden fear: a man like Aegisthus can probably smell it, as a wolf would.

"I always come here," he says. "I used to come here when Thyestes still ruled."

"To do what?"

"I just stayed away from everyone else. The palace was different then from what it is now."

"How so?"

"It was grayer. And bloodier."

She doesn't like his tone. He speaks as if she couldn't understand, as if she grew up with nymphs, spending her time with combs and pretty dresses.

"How many dead men have you seen?" she asks.

He pauses, and displeasure grows on his face.

"I have seen hundreds," she says. "In Sparta, the elders would take the criminals, and my father and brothers would drag them to the Ceadas. Then they pushed them off the cliff. Most were killed instantly. But others lived for a day or two, moaning, while the birds pecked their broken bodies until they bled to death or died of thirst."

She wills herself to remember. An image of herself as a child, crouching among the bushes and hearing the men's cries, comes to mind. There were other cries too, fainter, but they slip away, like shadows.

Aegisthus comes to sit on the rock beside her. The dagger lies between them, easy for either to reach.

"Atreus used to say that it takes only one to deliver a message," he says. "So he would send his men into the woods whenever a group of envoys came and shoot them until only one remained. Then he would send back the envoy with the heads of the others in a sack. Agamemnon and Menelaus would take part in those hunts, but I couldn't." He must have been punished for it, though he doesn't say.

"And how many men have you killed?" she asks.

He shrugs, and she watches the wind stir his hair.

"There was a boy I butchered once," he says, staring at his hands. "When I had finished with him, his face looked like mud." The water in the pool changes color as it reflects the sky. "How many times have you been whipped?" he asks.

It feels almost like a game now, comparing the scars inside them, waiting to see who crumbles first.

"Twenty. Or more. I can't be sure. The priestess in Sparta hated me. She was worse with my sister, though. She would whip her whenever she could, yet Timandra would still find ways to make her angry. You?"

"Thyestes liked to flog his servants. He would do it until their backs were blood-soaked. He saw traitors everywhere. He was saturated with malice and mistrust, especially after his sons' deaths."

His other sons. He is good at avoiding the answers he doesn't want to give, she considers. His words feel like smoke through her fingers.

"And Atreus?" She knows something of Agamemnon's father already, because her husband told her. Atreus was strong and vengeful. He once killed a boar with his bare hands. He slept with a different servant every night, so the palace was filled with pregnant women.

"Atreus did far worse." He stops there. They both know what Atreus did anyway. "No one was a match for my uncle's cruelty," Aegisthus adds. "No one but his wife."

Clytemnestra frowns. "Aerope?" She doesn't know much about her, except that her affair with Thyestes started the endless chain of violence and revenge between the brothers.

"It was said in the palace that whenever Aerope whispered in Atreus's ear, ten men would die."

"Was it true?"

"I never found out. I kept my distance from her, never talked to her unless she talked to me first. Once she told me that boys born with eyes as cold as mine should be skinned alive."

"Maybe Atreus and Thyestes loved her because she was vicious."

"I believe so. Whatever poison they had in them, she had it too."

They keep silent for a while, their unspoken words like fish that can't be caught. Questions slip into her mind, tickling her like water drops. *How many women have you been with? How many servants? Do you know pleasure or only pain?*

When she turns to him, he is staring at her, motionless. He has the stillness of animals about him. She wants to lean forward and trace the scar on his cheekbone. The desire is so strong that she can almost feel it under her finger—it is like a crumpled leaf.

"My queen," he says. Nothing else. The morning sun falls on his olive skin, makes his eyes glisten like snow in the sunlight.

She is breathless, and she can't bear it. She picks up her dagger and walks away.

29

Lovers

NO MORE FEAR, she decides. No more surprises. It is her turn to follow.

She starts to go after him in secret, in the early hours of the morning, before she meets the elders and petitioners in the *megaron*, and in the late afternoon when he practices. She is careful, for she knows he can easily catch her. He is a watchdog, ever patient.

She follows him in the narrow streets of the citadel and up the hills and mountains. In the practice yard and in the bathhouse. She is always close enough to see what he is doing but far enough to vanish if he turns. And he often turns. He walks as if hunted, casting a backward glance every now and then.

After practice, he dives into the narrow streets of the citadel close to the back gate. It is the busiest time of day, with men passing barrels of grain and wine from hand to hand, dogs sniffing around every corner, older women lining every door like sentinels. Aegisthus moves like a shadow, his figure sharp on the pale walls, and Clytemnestra follows, a mantle pulled over her head. They pass the baskets of onions and apples, the vendors cleaning their hands from the blood of butchered animals, the women with cheap jewels and lined eyes.

After walking in the maze of side alleys, Aegisthus always visits the tavern where artists and merchants eat. He sits in the darkest corner by the wine barrels and drinks by himself. No one pays him much

attention. The tables are crammed with traders singing obscene songs
and men eating bread and meat, juices dripping from their beards.
The little lamps spread around the place burn like embers from a
dying fire.

Clytemnestra watches from outside, a crack in the wooden wall
showing her enough of the room. The people who pass by pay her no
heed, being mainly drunks and slave women. She never stays long,
returning to the streets shortly before dinner.

One night, a merchant catches sight of Aegisthus. He is boasting
about a trade of precious amber that filled his pockets with gold when
his eyes find the corner where Aegisthus is sitting. He studies him as
a hawk his prey.

"Are you the cursed man?" he asks, stumbling down the rows of
tables, visibly drunk. "The traitor Aegisthus?" His voice is loud, and
the other men stop and listen.

Clytemnestra can see enough of Aegisthus's face to witness his
rage. The merchant is a fat man, hairs running thick on his chest
and hands. Aegisthus could knock him down with a slap, yet he says
nothing.

"It is you, isn't it?" the merchant continues with a grimace, stopping in front of Aegisthus. His cheeks are flushed and he is streaming
with sweat. Everyone is quiet now, leaning forward, waiting.

"It is," Aegisthus confirms quietly. His jaw is tightened and his fists
are clenched. Now he will cut the man in two, Clytemnestra thinks.

"You're a marked man," the merchant says, "coming to our city
when the king is gone, living in the palace as a guest after all those
years in hiding. You're either a coward, or you hope to fuck the queen!"
There is a burst of laughter. Then the merchant spits at Aegisthus.

The laughter dies down and the man waits, his smile like a viper's.
Aegisthus stands slowly, wiping his arm. There is anger on his face, but

grief and sadness too. Clytemnestra can almost see the boy he must have been, shunned, teased, and rejected.

And yet he doesn't strike the merchant. He leaves the room, the whispers of the others following him like hungry rats. Clytemnestra watches him hurry in the darkening street until his figure fades in the thinning light and disappears.

When the sun starts setting, dropping from the sky like a burning ball of hay, Clytemnestra runs back to the garden to think about her beloved Iphigenia.

She remembers her cheeks and the curve of her neck. Her sweet voice and clever questions. The way she frowned when she played the lyre, narrowed her eyes when she wanted to learn something new. As always, the peaceful memories are stained by her daughter's calls for help. By her blood streaking the altar stone. The brutal indifference on Agamemnon's face.

Every evening, she uses the thoughts to weave her net of vengeance.

She has been spying on Aegisthus for ten days when something unexpected happens.

Clytemnestra is sitting in the back room of the tavern, Leon at her side. When he found her sneaking out the back door of the palace, he insisted on following her. She let him, knowing he would anyway.

Aegisthus is drinking in the main room, alone as usual, oblivious to their presence. They have asked the old man at the entrance to keep the room to themselves, and he didn't ask any questions. Now they are sitting in the darkness, spying on Aegisthus from behind the dirty curtain.

Next to him, a group of merchants are drinking and singing, thumping the table. Clytemnestra has recognized the small trader she knocked insensible years ago. Beady eyes, voice as sticky as honey, sun-darkened face. They have been drinking like beasts, shouting for more meat and wine. "And not that cheap piss from Kos!" They laugh as the old man prepares the drink in a mixer. "Give us the one from Rhodes!"

As the small man grabs his cup, his arm catches the empty jug. It topples and shatters on the floor, the last drops of wine forming a small puddle. A girl comes out of the shadows to clean. She cannot be older than fourteen, her hair tied in plaits the color of almonds. She picks up the broken pieces, shivering, her eyes staring fixedly at the ground. The small man kneels next to her with a smile. Then, before she can speak, he grabs her hair and drags her to her feet.

"Look at this one!" he shouts. "Look at this face."

The girl reminds Clytemnestra of a rabbit trapped by hounds. The other merchants stare at her, sizing her up, their tongues darting across their lips. One walks closer to her, puts his hands around her hips.

"She is all yours, Erebus," he tells the small man. "No breasts, no hips. If you fuck this one, she breaks in two."

The others laugh, and Clytemnestra feels Leon shaking his head next to her. "We should leave," he says, touching her arm.

"We stay," she orders.

Erebus tilts his head, caressing the girl's hair. Then he tears her tunic and she gasps. Her body is skinny like a starving dog's, her breasts like two tiny figs. "You're right," Erebus says, disgusted. "No breasts. Still, I'll take her."

The girl cries softly, her hands clutching at her dress, trying to cover herself. Leon looks away. The man at the entrance keeps pouring water and honey into a large mixing bowl, though his arms are shaking. He doesn't wish for trouble. *Coward.* Clytemnestra is considering what to do when Aegisthus comes out of his corner. The traders look at him as if they have just noticed him.

"Maybe *you* want her, friend," Erebus hisses, annoyed at the interruption.

Aegisthus shakes his head. Fast, so fast the merchants don't even see it, he yanks a dagger from his belt and sinks it into Erebus's hand, pinning it to the table. Erebus shouts, and blood spurts onto his tunic.

"Do you know how long it takes to bleed to death?" Aegisthus says. He looks like a wild animal. "Not long if you keep losing blood like that."

The traders step back, Erebus's moans a warning.

"You should leave," Aegisthus says to the girl. She nods, her face a mask of fear, and rushes away. Taking advantage of the distraction, Erebus pulls out the knife, blood spattering, and cuts Aegisthus's hand. It is a superficial cut, and Aegisthus looks at it as if it were a fleabite. Then he punches Erebus, knocking him out, and retrieves his dagger.

As he walks away, Clytemnestra touches Leon's arm. "Go and find my daughters," she whispers. "Prepare them for dinner. I will come soon."

She finds Aegisthus in the armory, grunting as he tries to wrap a piece of tunic around his hand. He looks angry and tired.

The wooden door creaks as she opens it, and his head jerks up. She stands there, framed by the door, the light of a torch warming her cheeks. "Why did you protect that girl?" she asks.

He clutches his hand tightly. "You have been following me."

"Just as you followed me up the mountain."

There is a tense silence. The scents of wine and blood come from his skin.

"Did you know her?" Clytemnestra asks. He must be worn out, but she doesn't care. She wants answers.

"Who?"

"The girl you helped."

"No."

"Then why did you protect her?"

He slams his wounded hand on his knee. The light in his face is frightening. "Why do you care so much about her?"

She walks to him, takes a deep breath. "Those men called you weak, cursed, a coward. You walk away from their cruel words, yet you cut them when they try to take a slave girl."

He springs up and grabs her arm. His hand on her is a shock to them both. He flinches as if she hit him and steps back from her. Her skin feels tight, burning where he touched her.

"You shouldn't be so scared," she says quietly.

"You shouldn't be so careless."

He is right, she shouldn't, but she doesn't care. She moves forward and her lips brush his. He tastes like salt. A moment passes, the span of a breath. When she looks up, he is still, barely breathing.

Say something. But he is staring at her. She doesn't like that look: she doesn't understand it. Slowly, she takes a few steps back.

Well then, she thinks as she walks away, *I have made the first move. Now he can either strike back or leave this place once and for all.*

Aegisthus doesn't come for dinner. After platters and cups have been emptied, she waits while her family walks out of the hall, the house dogs licking her hands. Leon lingers, but she asks him to go and rest. The smoke in the hall is suffocating. The weapons on the wall look grotesque, like hungry vultures dropped from the sky. She stands, agitated.

The painted walls seem to sway. The windows spill the light of the moon, white and cold.

She doesn't see the shadow that lurks in front of her bedroom door. When he grabs her arm, she tries to hit him, but he has already covered her mouth with one hand and is holding both of her arms with the other. Together, they move into the torchlight. Aegisthus's eyes look dark, two pieces of dirty ice. Slowly, he lets his hand drop to let her speak.

"Have you come to kill me?" she asks calmly.

She sees the struggle on his face, raw on his bare skin. Her fearlessness confuses him. His grip on her arms becomes tighter, but he doesn't speak.

"I could have you murdered for coming in here," she says.

"And yet you won't."

"No. So what will you do?"

He lets her go. The strength of his desire is plain on his face, and so is his fear. She doesn't like waiting, so she steps into her bedroom, unties her tunic, and lets it fall onto the floor. He follows her, barely breathing, and when his hands touch her again, she shivers for the cold.

They are two knives slicing each other, cutting at the bone and thus giving each other pleasure.

PART V

She is like a lioness,
she stands high on her hind legs,
she mates with the wolf,
when her noble lion is missing.
—Aeschylus, *Agamemnon* 1258–9

30

Loyalty

SO WHAT WILL you do?

She asked the question and watched the answer forming on his face. Still, she didn't know what would happen afterward. She expected wariness, fear, violence, but there is nothing of the sort.

His love for her comes like a flood. Sudden, fierce, overpowering. She should have predicted it: to someone who has spent his entire life unloved, unwelcome, it must feel like a miracle to have someone like her beside him.

When he lies in her bed at night, she can feel him watching. Maybe he thinks that if he looks away, she will disappear. She touches his scars, feels the texture under her fingers, as if to remind him, *I am here*. He never flinches. Pain is a constant for him, a second skin he cannot shed.

He likes to hear her talk, of her memories of Sparta, of her brothers and sisters. She carefully avoids speaking of her life in Mycenae, because she sees that it makes him angry, as though her family here were something he didn't want. Or maybe he simply likes to pretend that she is all his, no one else's. But in truth, she likes that he does that. Seeing the look on his face when she tells him something that makes him feel understood is like watching a new flower bloom among rocks.

"You remember when you wanted to know how many dead men I had seen?" he asks her one night. The torches have gone out, and their faces in the darkness are like clouds.

"Yes."

"You didn't ask about the women."

She is lying down, listening to the rain outside. The sound usually soothes her, helps her drift into sleep, but there is no rest to be found with Aegisthus. Only the ever-present longing for more words, more pleasure, more secrets.

"How many have you seen dead?" he asks.

She lifts herself up, pours herself a cup of wine. She knows he wants to hear about Iphigenia, but that is no memory to share with him or anyone else.

"I didn't see my mother die," she says, "though I heard it was a pitiful scene."

"How so?"

"She died in her bed, with a cup of wine in her hand."

"That sounds peaceful."

"Not for her. Leda was fierce when I was a child." She touches the gems embossed on her cup, a gesture her mother used to make before she sipped. "She once told me that I was unhappy, but I think she was talking about herself."

It is the first time she has spoken of her mother's death. She fears Aegisthus will ask her if she is unhappy, so she keeps talking.

"She believed in gods too much. She told me they were everywhere, in caves and forests, on roofs and in every village alley, so I would always look for them as a child, but I never found them. I thought there was something wrong with me. I thought, if I can't hear them whisper, then maybe they don't like me."

"Atreus would say something similar. Though his gods weren't exactly merciful beings who whispered to children."

She scoffs. "Gods are never merciful. Even in the stories we heard growing up, how much mercy did the gods show? Cronus devours his children to avoid being overthrown by them. Zeus transforms into eagles, swans, and serpents to rape young virgins. Apollo fires his arrows to bring the plague to mortals whenever he is angry."

Aegisthus stands and pours wine for himself. The sheepskin falls off his naked body but he doesn't shiver. "How were your mother's gods, then?" he asks.

"Simpler, less jealous and vengeful. Less like us. She loved them and they loved her back, or so she said."

The rough skin of his side brushes against her. She presses herself closer to him, her warmth against his coldness.

"My mother didn't know such gods," he says. "No one ever showed her any mercy, up until her death." The crack in his voice makes her shiver. "I have seen hundreds of men die in the worst possible ways, yet Pelopia's death I'll never forget."

"She was your mother."

"I barely knew her. She left me when I was born, so she was no mother to me."

"You were there when she died?"

"We were all there, in the *megaron*. Thyestes had been found near Delphi and brought here with force. Atreus threw him in a cell, then sent me to kill him."

"Why you?"

"He thought I was weak. He was always looking for ways to test me. I went to the dungeon and saw my father for the first time. See how cruel the Fates are? I met him moments before I was meant to kill him. I didn't know who he was, but when I unsheathed my sword, Thyestes said it was his. That is how I knew he might be my father. The only thing my mother had left me was the sword of her rapist, whom she didn't know either, because his face was concealed when he took her. His sword was all she had. So I didn't kill Thyestes. I went to Agamemnon and asked him to find my mother, and I told Atreus that I would let Thyestes live only for a while. I needed to know if he was my real father. That was my mistake."

It shocks her when he speaks of his failings and weaknesses. The only other men she has known to do that were Tantalus and Odysseus, but they would do it in a way that asserted their power. They spoke of their mistakes to achieve something, to soften and bend the world to their will. That was what Tantalus had done to win her over. Aegisthus doesn't speak of his failures to gain a reward. His purposelessness appalls her.

"Atreus's men found Pelopia and brought her to the palace. I remember thinking she was too young to be my mother, but I brought her to the *megaron* nonetheless. Atreus ordered Thyestes to be brought there too. Pelopia didn't cry when she saw her father. I showed her the sword and told her it belonged to him. She looked at him, at the sword, then at me. Her eyes were like fire. She jumped forward and grabbed the sword from my hands.

"When she stabbed herself in the stomach, no one did anything. We all stayed and watched as she gurgled and died in her own blood. When I looked up, Atreus was smiling on his throne. The sun was on his face and he was laughing. I hated him then, for all he had done to me. I pulled the sword out of Pelopia's body and thrust it into Atreus's neck."

"What did Agamemnon do?"

"He ran away with Menelaus. He could have stayed and

wrestled—he was always stronger than me—but he knew that not all the guards would side with him after Atreus's death. We took back the palace then, Thyestes and I."

"You gave your loyalty to a man who raped his own daughter." She doesn't mean to insult him, but the words come out as blades.

"I had no one else," he replies.

She touches his head and he closes his eyes. They are silent for a long time, until the rain outside lightens. She traces his jaw with a finger. He has told her his secrets and now it is her duty to carry them, like gems.

And what about my secrets?

"I saw a few dead women too," she says. "Some in the helot village down in Sparta, starved to death. One giving birth. But one I killed myself. She took something from me, so I paid her back. I stabbed her in her home and watched her die."

He opens his eyes. She draws away her hand, waiting. Her words float between them. He will grow angry now, or scared. He will become cold, his face like ice, his eyes distrustful. It is one thing to fall for a fierce queen but another to love a woman who is ruthless enough to deal out death to her enemies.

He will crawl away, like they all do, and hate me.

But he doesn't. He brushes his lips against her forehead and says, "She must have been a fool for thinking she could take something from you."

They come alive at night, when the rest of the palace is sleeping. Servants must suspect that something is happening between them, but even if they do, they are too afraid to speak. During the day,

Aegisthus keeps his distance, wandering in the woods and training alone. It is cold outside, though the winter isn't merciless. Sometimes the sun appears between the clouds, shiny and timid, a promise of warmth and spring.

"A woman in the kitchen told me Aegisthus visits your room every night," Aileen says to her one day. They are in the gardens, Aileen weaving dried flowers into Clytemnestra's hair.

"What did you say?" Clytemnestra asks.

"I didn't know how to reply."

She wonders what it would feel like to be Aileen. So gentle, loyal, true. She is like one of those dogs rescued from an alley, frightened at first but, once you win them over, always loyal to their master.

"Do you think it unwise," Clytemnestra says, "that I sleep with Aegisthus?"

"Maybe," she replies. "He is a broken man."

"And?"

"Broken men are hard to handle." She gives her a small smile as if to excuse her boldness of judgment.

"I find broken men easier to handle," Clytemnestra says.

"Sometimes, yes. But Aegisthus will start to love you, because you are strong and beautiful, and then he will always want to be by your side."

He already does.

"You are saying that I will never get rid of him because he loves me?"

Aileen smooths back her own hair. It is tied in a long plait, but some rebellious strands fall down on her cheeks. She nods hesitantly. Clytemnestra thinks it through while Aileen rests her head back to enjoy the cold sun on her pale skin. Sometimes she glances at her queen, and Clytemnestra can't help but notice how her eyes are like the sky above them and her hair rich like the earth under their feet.

At dinner, she calls for Orestes. The long table is empty—she has ordered everyone to stay away.

"What is it, Mother?" Orestes says. "Did news come from Troy?" He is studying her face, wiping his hands on a piece of cloth.

"I have slept with Aegisthus," she says. Sooner or later, he would know anyway. Better from her than from someone else. She watches the blow fall as he puts down the cloth and fills his cup to the brim.

"Why are you telling me this?"

"Because people will talk soon, and you must not believe them."

"Why did you do it?"

"To control him better," she lies.

He pours some wine for her too. "Whatever you do, Mother, I trust you. I never listen to idle gossip."

"This time you must. I want you to listen to what everyone says in the palace—servants, soldiers, children, elders. If you hear anyone speak treason, you tell me."

Someone will betray her for this, she knows it. And she will have to handle it. She thinks of Leon's hurt, disappointed face when he finds out. *You are the queen. He has no say in deciding whom you sleep with. You owe him nothing.*

Orestes sits back and his voice breaks through her thoughts. "The elders won't like it."

"They don't like me already, so I doubt this will change anything."

"They will have a reason to plot against you now."

She smiles, takes his hand in hers. "Which will finally give me a reason to get rid of them."

When she goes back to her room, Aegisthus is standing by the window, sharpening his dagger against a piece of stone. She kisses his neck from behind, but he stiffens, his muscles pulled taut.

"That servant of yours," he says, "the one with red hair."

"What about her?"

"I think I recognize her. She was here when my father was king, wasn't she?"

Clytemnestra watches as he feels the tip of the dagger with his fingers. "She was."

"I saved her," he rasps.

"She is grateful for what you did."

"I have shown my weakness. When others come to know about it, they will destroy me."

"Aileen is faithful to me and won't speak of the past if I order her not to."

He looks around, the dagger tight in his hand. His body is always tense, his face always shifting. She takes the blade, puts it aside.

"The gods crush those who show their weakness," he says. "Atreus said that when I was young. *Love breeds weakness*."

"You're not weak," she says. Her words are butterfly's wings, folding and unfolding in the semidarkness.

He yanks away from her and sits on the bed. Clytemnestra waits for him to come back to her, for the anger to fade. After a long moment, she moves toward him.

"Do you hear me? You are not weak," she repeats.

The frost in his eyes slowly melts, like ice in spring. He leans forward. She can almost feel his lips on hers when someone knocks at the door. She startles. It is getting dark outside. Something bad must have happened if her men disturb her.

When she opens, Leon is on the other side. He looks at her, then at Aegisthus sitting on the bed. She is aware of her bare arms and loose hair.

"They told me, but I didn't believe it," Leon says quietly.

She stares at him as he grows pale, breathless. She hasn't seen him so agitated in a long time.

"I warned you that he is dangerous," he says, speaking of Aegisthus as if he weren't a few feet from them.

"You did. And I thank you for your counsel."

"You let him in here!" he shouts. "You disgrace yourself."

"You will not speak to me like that," she says. "Or I will doubt your loyalty."

He tightens his fists. "My loyalty… This man *murdered* his uncle so he could rule Mycenae," he spits out. "You believe he won't do the same to you?"

Aegisthus stands but Clytemnestra stops him. "Leave," she tells Leon.

"How can you trust him?"

"I said leave. I will see you in the *megaron* in the morning."

"You are wrong about this. I just hope you will see it before it's too late."

His tall figure disappears in the dim light of the corridor, though his steps echo for a long time.

She closes the door behind her, controlling her movements as one does with the strings of a puppet. She lies down on the bed before Aegisthus can speak to her and pretends to sleep.

The news flows as fast as spring rivers. If no one dared speak of it before, now that the queen's closest adviser has complained, everyone in the palace gathers to comment on the affair. A traitor and a queen. A cursed man and a "single-minded" woman. What will the king say when he comes back from the war? Will he burn Aegisthus alive, just like he did his father? And if he doesn't come back at all? Will Clytemnestra marry Aegisthus? Will Aegisthus have her murdered and take the throne for himself?

The palace whispers, and the whispers reach the elders, flying like little birds. Clytemnestra calls for a gathering in the *megaron* before the elders can call for one without her.

She is sitting in her room, Aileen polishing the gold circlet in her hair, when Orestes comes in. "I have news, Mother," he says, as she hoped he would.

She stands and Aileen wraps a boar skin around her shoulders. Orestes wipes his forehead; his curls fall messily at the sides.

"The servant heard Polydamas speak to another elder in an alley close to the artists' quarter. They were spreading the news that you are unfit to rule. They want to make you surrender the throne."

"To whom?"

He stares at her. "To me."

She steps closer to him, cups her hand around his face. "Polydamas and who else?" she asks.

"Lycomedes." She is not surprised. Lycomedes is usually silent, but whenever he speaks, he opposes her. He rarely even looks her in the eye.

"Where is this servant now?"

"In my room."

"Good. Let him stay there."

"Should I guard him myself?"

"Let some of your men do it. You are coming to the *megaron* with me."

When they enter the high-roofed hall, the elders are already inside, whispering in groups. At the sight of her, they fall quiet and make space. Polydamas stays apart from the others, brooding. Cadmus stands closer to the throne, wringing his hands nervously. It makes her think of an ant moving its front legs.

She climbs onto the throne and lets Orestes sit on the high chair next to it. Aegisthus wanted to take the place beside her, but she has forbidden it. No one will respect her if she lets a man sit there—they will look at him for a decision. And it is obvious what the elders will think of Aegisthus's decisions. With Orestes, though, she can show them that she is still queen. If the elders see that her son, strong and charming, always looks for her judgment and respects her decisions, then who are they to refuse to do the same?

Next to the throne, Leon stands as still as stone, his hand on his sword. He will watch and see what happens to those who betray her.

"I have called you here to discuss my affair with Aegisthus before you can gather and discuss it among yourselves, behind my back," she says calmly.

Some elders look down, awkward. Others straight at her.

"You told us you had a plan," Cadmus starts. "That you would take care of Aegisthus yourself."

"What did you think that was?" she asks. "That I would poison him at dinner?"

"Not this. We didn't expect this," Lycomedes intervenes. He

is hunched, pale and fearful, and his lips are cracked, like baked earth.

"Agamemnon, your king, is in Troy," she says.

They nod with reverence, as always when her husband is mentioned.

"I imagine he is fighting like a true hero, taking enemies down one by one during the day."

"Of course," Lycomedes says. She wishes he would do something about his lips: the sight is annoying her.

"And during the night," she continues, "fucking his little war prizes."

Lycomedes looks down and so do a few others. Polydamas, of course, keeps his chin up, his face impenetrable.

"Among all the news we discuss from Troy, we never speak of this. Though if I have heard of it, I am sure you have too. How did the plague begin? Because your king took a virgin priestess to his bed and refused to give her back to her father. And when he finally relented, he took another, the slave of the hero Achilles, causing him to abandon the army and lose battle after battle.

"Agamemnon sleeps with young girls with no regard to the consequences that his choices have on his army and his war. Still, you bear him no ill will. You don't even speak of it." She smiles at them. "I, on the other hand, take one man to my bed for reasons you don't know and shouldn't care to know, and we have to gather here to talk about how wrong my choice is."

"Aegisthus is the enemy," Cadmus says.

"So are the slave girls. Aren't they Trojan?"

Lycomedes's pale face breaks into red blotches. This must be his angry look. "Warriors take prizes when they win battles. It is their privilege to do so. Your choice of bringing the traitor Aegisthus to your room has consequences."

"What kind of consequences?"

He looks to her right, at Orestes. With a low but clear voice, he says, "Why should we follow you, a woman who sleeps with the enemy, when your son is of age to command us until your husband returns?"

"I trust my mother's choices," Orestes says. "And you should trust your queen."

A few men nod. No one replies. She looks at Leon's profile, rigid and quiet in the bright light. Then she turns to her right, where Polydamas is standing in the shadow by the frescoes of the running lions.

"Polydamas, you are quiet," she says. "Do you agree with Lycomedes?"

"If a man sleeps with a queen," he says in his screeching voice, "he will soon expect to be king. This is how alliances are formed and power is acquired. With marriages."

She raises her eyebrows. "I do not need power. I already have it."

"Aegisthus will claim the throne," he says, coming out of the shadows. "Lycomedes speaks true. Your choices do not make you the right ruler."

She stands and walks down the steps of the throne, fixing the boar skin around her shoulders. On her left, Lycomedes darts his tongue across his lips. "I wonder," she says, "what a right ruler would do with traitors?"

"Imprison them," Lycomedes says. "Kill them."

She smiles. "I am glad we agree on this."

Lycomedes opens his mouth, then closes it stupidly. But Polydamas can smell mischief.

"It depends on the type of treason," he says. "Some are for the good of the kingdom. Others are not."

You have an answer for everything, don't you? He told her she was like the plague, but he is infecting everyone around him with conspiracy.

"I would love to discuss types of treason with you, Polydamas," she says. He raises his eyebrow, just slightly. She looks him straight in the eye and adds, "But unfortunately, a crowd is gathering by the Lion Gate to watch your execution."

Lycomedes makes a sound like choking. The other elders shift. The movement is like wind among leaves, barely audible.

"I do not understand," Polydamas says calmly.

"You conspired against the throne. You and Lycomedes spread whispers that your queen wasn't fit to rule Mycenae. A fit ruler, as you say, doesn't let treason go unpunished."

Lycomedes drops to his knees. "We didn't conspire, my queen." He gulps the last two words. She looks away from his cracked lips.

Polydamas holds his ground. "I follow the orders of the king, not yours."

"That is unfortunate, because the guards do. And even if they didn't, it wouldn't matter, because I will kill you myself."

Lycomedes starts sobbing. It is a pitiful sight. Cadmus reaches out and clasps his hunched shoulder, forcing him upward.

"You don't have to do this," Polydamas says. His voice scratches the air, like nails against stone. She wishes he would beg for mercy, not Lycomedes. But that isn't Polydamas's way.

"My father always said that a ruler has to effect the punishment himself, or his people won't respect him."

"Your father was a wise man, I am sure," he says. "He would have listened to his elders, not killed them."

She scoffs. "You didn't know Tyndareus. He never listened to the elders. I have listened to you, to your insults and treachery, for nine years. I am tired of listening now."

She has them dragged to the Lion Gate under the cold sun. People are gathered in the streets, watching and whispering, mothers' hands on their children's shoulders, men's eyes on Polydamas and Lycomedes, like a herd looking at its weakest members. She sees an old woman with a chicken under her arm, two boys pushing through the crowd to get a better view. Dogs bark, men yell, women sigh.

Outside the Lion Gate, her guards make space, pushing the two prisoners to the middle of the path. People are also coming from the villages at the foot of the mountain, baskets and rags in hand, their heads cocked with curiosity.

Clytemnestra stands in front of Polydamas and Lycomedes, Leon on her right, Orestes on her left. Dust from the alleys has clung to Lycomedes's tunic and he brushes it away. She thinks of Iphigenia, who couldn't brush sand from her dress before she was murdered. She clears her throat and turns to the people around her.

"These men stand accused of treason and conspiracy." The crowd is quiet, and a hundred eyes watch her, as big as eggs.

"They walked around the citadel to spread the word that their queen wasn't the rightful ruler of this city. They called me a plague upon Mycenae and conspired to make my son king while my husband fights in Troy."

Lycomedes is mumbling, his pale forehead sweating despite the cold. The wind cuts across their cheeks like ice. Polydamas stares at her, his tunic rich and clean. His wife and daughters must be somewhere in the crowd. Still, no one pleads for him.

"I believe mercy can be shown to those who repent, but these men had many chances to do so and never took them. Their disrespect shan't go unpunished."

Polydamas's face is like stone. She can hear the silence around her and Orestes's breathing next to her as if it were her own. She is glad Electra and Chrysothemis aren't here. Her hand goes to her mother's jeweled dagger as she turns to the elders.

"Your treacherous words have caused your own death."

Lycomedes's knees tremble and he bends forward, praying to the gods. *See how the gods listen. See how they care about us.*

Polydamas looks at him, then back at her coldly. He spits on the dusty ground, a small wet smack at her feet. His voice as loud as thunder, he says, "You are no queen of mine."

Her dagger flies, and with one single movement, she cuts their soft throats.

31

Landslide

EVERY CHOICE ONE makes has consequences, like a rock that falls from the top of the mountain.

Perhaps as it rolls down, it will take only a few trees in its path.

Maybe it will cause other stones to fall and turn into a landslide.

Right now, standing by her chair in the high-roofed dining hall, Clytemnestra watches the stone she has thrown. Leon is pacing the room, madness and disbelief spreading in his eyes. He didn't move as Polydamas and Lycomedes choked and wriggled on the dusty path, but she could see the fire on his face, consuming him from the inside. "You would kill your advisers so," he says.

"They were not loyal advisers. They were traitors." Their blood is still on her hands, and she tries to wipe it away with a cloth.

"Then you would do the same to me if I opposed you?"

"You haven't opposed me so far."

His face twists. He grabs a ewer, and for a moment, she thinks he will fling it aside. But he puts it down, controlling himself, his hand shaking.

"You did this for Aegisthus? You plotted with a traitor?"

"I plotted nothing with him."

"Then why didn't you tell me of your decision? I am your guard and protector!"

"I didn't know if I could trust you anymore," she says simply. "You showed me no respect when you came to my room and insulted my relationship with Aegisthus."

"Your relationship with Aegisthus," he repeats bitterly.

She wishes she could sit and eat something. But Leon walks closer to her, his face looking as ugly as she has ever seen it. He has always been incapable of hiding his feelings: everything is written upon him and easily read.

"Aegisthus wasn't there when your daughter was murdered. He wasn't there to bring you back to Mycenae from the camp. He wasn't there when the soldiers in Aulis wanted to beat you." He is breathless, spitting each word. "I was there. I was beaten again and again to prevent them from touching you. I was there on the road back when you wanted to take your life and again in the palace when you wouldn't rule. Did you use me for pleasure? Am I nothing more than a tool thrown aside now that you have another?"

She feels as if she has been plunged into the ocean, her body weighted with stones. "You didn't protect my daughter!" she shouts.

He looks back at her, his eyes defiant. "You didn't protect her either. Her death weighs on you as much as on me."

How dare he? Her rage is so strong she can't move. She tightens her grip on her dagger.

"Go on," he says. "Are you going to kill me too? Because I wasn't *loyal?* I almost gave my life for you!"

Almost.

"It wasn't enough." The words come out before she can stop them. She sees the hurt on Leon's face. He straightens up, his fists balled.

"Then I will find some other queen to serve," he says. He speaks as if his throat is broken. He sounds as he did after the men in Aulis strangled him. "One for whom I am enough."

He starts toward the door. She grabs her dagger and throws it. It hits the wooden handle, and splinters fly. He flinches, turns back. In his eyes, there is shock, as if *she* is betraying *him*.

"You do not walk away from your queen," she says. Their eyes lock, and she wants to shout, to hurt him, to do something to stop this.

"I know you for what you are," he says. "Not this tyrant who'd kill anyone who walks away from her." He swallows and his voice thickens. "As cold and ruthless as you have become, I know you won't kill me."

He turns and leaves then. She should follow, run after him. But her feet are heavy, rooted to the ground. She hears his boots on the stone floor until the sound fades into silence.

In the *megaron*, she sits on her husband's throne. *Her* throne. The hall is empty, light thinning on the floor. There is the faint smell of the frescoes, the dying embers of the hearth. The red columns look like flames, lapping at the painted ceiling. The dogs come inside, nestling at her feet, looking up at her as if asking, *Where is he?*

"He will come back," she says to the dogs, to herself, to the empty hall. *He always does.*

And if he doesn't?

Once they were in the armory together, tidying the spears and arrows. Outside, the yard was ringing with the clatter of wooden swords and the boys' laughter. It was peaceful, more so than the *megaron*, where she had to bear the elders' distrust, or the bedroom, where she spent her nights under a slab of grief. As if hearing her thoughts, Leon had smiled at her and pressed his body against hers. She'd kept still in his arms until it was time to go back to the palace, wearing her mask of indifference once more.

He knows I can't love him. He knows how I am, he has always known, and yet he left me. Let him live with his choice.

She feels flat and calm. No grief, no anger, just emptiness. The light dies, the room turns to gray, and yet no one comes. She curls up on the throne and falls into a dreamless sleep.

Electra finds her in the morning, nestled on the throne as if she were a child. Clytemnestra hears her daughter's quick steps on the floor and opens her eyes. It is still early, and she turns to her right, expecting Leon to be there. Then Electra speaks. "You sent Leon away." Her voice is thick with accusation.

Clytemnestra sits up, her joints aching, and fixes the boar skin around her shoulders. It must have rained: the air smells of wet earth, and the morning light is soft and bright. "Leon decided to leave," she says.

Electra takes a few steps forward, her eyes shining with rage. "But you drove him away! You went with the traitor Aegisthus and he left us!"

What an interesting choice of words, Clytemnestra thinks. Didn't Electra ask her if Aegisthus was handsome and say that broken people fascinated her? When she speaks again, she seems on the edge of breaking down.

"Leon was like a father to me, to Chrysothemis, to Orestes. He cared for us because he loved you." She stops, catching her breath. "You knew he would leave if you went with Aegisthus."

"I didn't."

"Why did you have to go with him?" There is an edge to her voice. For a moment, she sounds almost like a child, whining.

Did Electra really desire Aegisthus? Clytemnestra had thought her fascination with him was nothing more than a whim, a result of his fathomless nature.

"Why did you go with him and send Leon away?" Electra repeats.

"I didn't want to push Leon away."

"Then why didn't you tell him so?"

"Queens aren't meant to beg."

"So your pride sent him away."

Clytemnestra stands. "Are you angry with me because you wanted Aegisthus?"

Electra narrows her eyes. "I did desire him, but I would never have gone with him, because I understand that some things must not be touched. Some people must not be taken." The pain in her eyes is a living thing. "You, though, have always taken what you wanted, ever since I was a baby. You have taken Father's attention, Iphigenia's love, everything."

"You think I wanted your father's attention?" Clytemnestra almost shouts, her body racked with anger. "The very monster who slaughtered the man I loved and took me for himself?"

Electra doesn't back down. "What about what I wanted? You took that too. The people's loyalty, Orestes's respect, Leon's adoration."

Everything I have I have earned. "You think this is a challenge? A fight between me and you?"

"Yes."

"You do not know a real challenge," Clytemnestra says, sharpening her words like axes. "You do not understand a real fight. When I was a child in Sparta, my mother would beat me if I lost a race. She humiliated me. My father starved me. The priestess flogged me. Those are challenges. Those are fights. The things you complain about are nothing more than childish whims, but you are no child."

"Don't you understand?" Electra replies. "Your childhood...that is something else you have won. You have won games and wrestles, you have survived beatings and floggings, you have been on hunts and killed a lynx! And what have I done? Nothing." Rage is gone from her face, and now she is back to her unsettling coolness.

Clytemnestra takes a deep breath. Speaking to her daughter is harder than fighting a match, for Electra's words are always unexpected blows.

"You do not see the things that make you special," Clytemnestra says. "You make everything a challenge and refuse to see that you are different from me, and that is good. Your aunt Helen did the same when we were younger. She once told me she was jealous because I had everyone's attention, but Helen has always been a much better person than I will ever be."

"I am not like Helen," Electra replies. She is standing fixed, like a tree that won't be bent. "Nor am I like Iphigenia."

"No, you aren't." *Iphigenia was never jealous or unkind. She was unlike anyone else in this world.*

Electra stares at her as if trying to pierce her skull, listen to the thoughts inside. Then she speaks the words that Clytemnestra has hoped she'd never hear: "Sometimes I think you wish I had died and Iphigenia had lived."

She stumbles out of the *megaron* and into the courtyard. The guards move aside to let her pass, and when she looks at their faces, they are ugly, disfigured. She moves past them, past the griffins that seem to be bleeding. Everything is breaking down around her, losing shape. The columns become blades, the servants wild animals. The jars and baskets they are holding are like corpses.

Sometimes I think you wish I had died and Iphigenia had lived.

She finds her way to Chrysothemis's room. The light is bright in this part of the palace, and contours fall back into place. She clutches her chest, feeling her heart beat wildly.

Chrysothemis is still in bed, sleeping with her hair spread around her. Aileen is sitting by the window, polishing some jewels. She stands when she sees her. "You are feeling unwell," she says.

Clytemnestra gestures her to sit and takes the place beside her. She catches her breath as Aileen cleans the gems, giving her space. Holding each to the light to make sure it is shining, she rubs it gently with a cloth whenever she finds an opaque spot. Chrysothemis's rhythmic breathing behind them is as soothing as a cradle song.

Sometimes I think you wish I had died and Iphigenia had lived.

"My daughter despises me," Clytemnestra says.

Aileen puts the tiara and cloth down, looking at her with her gentle eyes. "Surely she didn't use those words."

"She said worse."

"You know how Electra is," Aileen says, taking her hand. "She harbors sadness in her heart and makes it come out as hatred. But she loves you."

"I don't think she does."

"Electra has grown up in the shadows. Iphigenia was older, better than her at everything, and Orestes was a boy. They had all the attention. It has been difficult for her."

Clytemnestra draws away her hand. "You know what is difficult? Losing a child. I gave my life to these children. I made them strong, fought so that they could learn how to rule." *And I expect their loyalty in return.*

"Electra lost a sister." Aileen sets down the tiara and picks up a pair of earrings. "When you came back from Aulis, she would spend every night outside your room, listening to you as you cried. When she couldn't bear the sound and wanted to hurt herself, Leon would find her and stay with her until dawn." She gives her a small, sad smile. "He might not have been her father, but she loved him."

Clytemnestra feels a rot inside her body. "He left, and I did nothing to stop him."

"You had no choice. If you had stopped him, he would have stayed here and hated you. If you had followed him, you would have disgraced yourself."

Chrysothemis stirs in her sleep. The sun pours on her like a shower of golden light. Clytemnestra used to cradle her in the sunlight when she refused to sleep as a baby, and Chrysothemis would drift off in a second—she liked the warmth on her skin.

"Sometimes I fear that I am becoming the person I am pretending to be," she says quietly. "I felt nothing when Leon left."

Aileen shakes her head. "The first night you came to Mycenae, you saved me from flogging. Remember that? You may not, but I do not forget. Then a few days later, you came into the kitchen and asked if I wanted to walk around the garden with you. You said, *You remind me of my sister*. When Agamemnon wanted to sleep with me, you intervened. When I had the fever, you gave me herbs. You taught me to read so I could help you with the inventories. Would a cruel person do any of this?"

She reaches out and takes her queen's hand once more. This time, Clytemnestra doesn't draw away.

"Even when you are pretending," Aileen says, "you are still better than most people."

That night, she lies wakeful, looking at the stars that swirl outside the windows.

Electra had come to the *megaron* to give her some sliced apples while she was speaking to the warlords. A peace offering. Aileen must have spoken to her, or Chrysothemis. Clytemnestra sent the men away and ate the apples in silence with her daughter, the fire of the hearth sizzling and crackling like their thoughts.

Aegisthus cups his hand around her shoulder, moves her gently so that they are facing each other on the large bed. His eyes hold her, pulling her in. She isn't scared of the frost anymore: it quietens her, healing her pain like ice against a wound.

"Did you love him?" he asks. "Your guard."

She shakes her head. "I can't afford to love anyone."

But even as she says it, his hands warm on her body, she can feel something breaking down inside her, the walls she has built so carefully around herself cracking. Just a tiny fracture, nothing more, but spacious enough to let light through.

As if he felt it too, Aegisthus falls asleep. She watches his lips part, his eyelids fluttering. His slumber is always restless, filled with nightmares and murmurs. Every night, he twists under the sheets like a fish in a net, and every time, she cups her hands around his face and he stills. Then she can sleep too, somehow heartened by his presence despite the nightmares and the tossing. It is as if in sleep they are fighting shadows, but at least they are doing it together.

She is sweating, her cloak tossed aside, her tunic covered with sand and dust. Aegisthus walks around her, waiting for the right moment to attack again. In his eyes, the fear and alertness that haunt him every time he holds a sword. They are fighting in the practice yard in the late afternoon, the sky swollen and yellowish, like a blister.

Aegisthus's blade whirls, flashing in the fading light. She catches the blow with her own sword, sliding away from him. They have been practicing for a long time, and on Aegisthus's cheek, there is blood. When she cut him, rage had danced in his eyes, and for a moment, she was afraid. But the rage dissolved and he smiled—the smile he keeps for her every time she challenges him. She has never seen him smile like that with anyone else.

Now his foot lashes out and catches her leg. She stumbles but keeps her feet while Aegisthus brings his sword up, cutting her shoulder. She laughs and their blades kiss, then fly apart again.

"My queen," someone behind her says.

She kicks Aegisthus's hand, and he drops his sword. Breathless, she turns and stops. The man is young and swarthy, his black hair oily—one of her scouts. He is looking at Aegisthus, frowning.

"You bring news," she says.

"Yes," the scout says, his attention back to her. "From Sparta and from Troy."

She stiffens, cleans her sword on her tunic, then puts pressure on the cut on her shoulder. Blood trickles over her fingers. Aegisthus takes the place next to her. She wishes he wouldn't.

"What of Sparta?" she asks.

The man looks around, at the weapons spread on the yard and again at Aegisthus. She has ordered every scout to come to her in private rather than to meet her in the *megaron*, so he must be wondering why Aegisthus is staying now.

"Your brother Polydeuces proposes a marriage between your niece Hermione and your son Orestes. He says that Hermione has blossomed into a wise young woman and that she will have to marry soon."

"I imagine he is proposing this because no one wants to marry the daughter of the woman who left for Troy," Clytemnestra comments.

The scout frowns. "He didn't say so."

"If Orestes marries her, will he become king after Menelaus?"

"Your brother knew you would ask this, and he said that he will. Polydeuces has no interest in the throne."

"Good. Then I will speak to my son, and I will give you an answer. Is that all from Sparta?"

"Yes."

The scout comes closer, wringing his hands. She looks at Aegisthus, waiting for him to leave, but he does not move.

"I will meet you in the palace, Aegisthus," she says.

She half expects him to complain, to look hurt, but his expression betrays nothing. He picks up his weapon and walks away, fallen leaves crunching under his feet. She will have to deal with him later, she knows, but now her body is tense, her heart beating fast. Her scouts haven't brought news from Troy in a while.

When Aegisthus's figure has disappeared into the citadel, the scout speaks in a low voice. "You told me to hurry to you first in case anything new came from Troy."

"Is the war over?" she asks.

"Not yet. But it will be soon. The word is that Odysseus, son of Laertes, has devised a trick to get our soldiers into the city gates. The Greeks are building a giant wooden horse. What they will do with it, no one knows yet, but it must be part of Odysseus's plan. My informants tell me that the people in the Greek camp expect the war to be won in a matter of weeks."

A matter of weeks. How long has she been waiting for this? How many sleepless nights? How many grieving days?

"Who are your informants?" she asks.

"The bed slaves in the camp talk."

"I see. And how certain are we that the war will end in the Greeks' favor?"

"Odysseus is quite certain, according to my sources."

Then we will win. Her shoulder is still bleeding and she ties a piece of tunic around it. The scout keeps talking.

"Some generals are already deciding on which Trojan women they will take once the war is won. Priam has many daughters, most of them of age."

"And Helen?"

"Your sister is still inside the city, though Menelaus has sworn to kill her once Troy falls."

She takes a deep breath. *I am sure my brother will forgive her,* Agamemnon had said before leaving. *Your sister can be quite convincing.* She clings to the words like a limpet to its rock. "How many generals survive?" she asks.

"The Prince Achilles died, my queen. Paris killed him with an arrow."

She knew this already. Cadmus had told her in the *megaron*. She imagines Paris, handsome as a god, eager to please his father after bringing ruin on his people's heads, riding on the Trojan plain looking for the best of the Greeks. A boy who was raised as a shepherd killing the greatest soldier of his generation.

"What about the others?"

"Among those closest to the king, Menelaus and Diomedes both live."

"And Calchas?" she asks, keeping her voice as firm as she can.

"He is alive, though some say he is falling out of King Agamemnon's favor."

"Good." She leans against a tree, trying to control her excited thoughts. "You bring good news," she tells him. "You may rest in the palace tonight, but tell no one about this. Tomorrow you go back to your outpost. When the city falls, light a bonfire and order your men in the mountains to do the same so that the news might come here as soon as possible."

For a moment, she is tempted to cut his throat, because she doesn't trust anyone with such a secret. But a body to burn would be much more suspicious than a scout sleeping in the palace, so she lets him go.

Orestes is in the lower part of the citadel to have a new sword forged. Inside the blacksmith's shop, the air is as hot as a furnace. When he sees his mother, Orestes smiles and walks to her, away from the apprentice smiths he was talking to. She takes him aside, in the darkest corner of the shop.

"Your uncle Polydeuces sent us a message today. He wants you to marry your cousin Hermione."

Orestes gives her an amused look. "What do you think of his proposal?"

"Hermione is a good girl, strong and wise. She has endured the loss of her mother and has grown up under Polydeuces's wing, which means she will know the difference between the things that matter and those that don't. My brother has always been a very practical man."

Orestes nods. Earlier today, she saw a servant girl coming out of his room, giggling. When the girl noticed her, she fell silent and hurried away.

"If I marry her, will I be king in Sparta?" he asks.

She smiles at the question. "Yes. I have already made sure of that."

"But who will rule Mycenae?"

"Our family will." This is what she has always wanted for her children—to take back control of Mycenae *and* Sparta, to establish a dynasty much more powerful than the Atreidai's. With her son in Sparta, Electra and Chrysothemis soon ready for marriage, she will build a web of alliances throughout their land. *But first, Menelaus and Agamemnon must come back from the war.*

Orestes is looking at her. "Yes, but who?" When she doesn't speak, he adds, "Aegisthus is not our family."

She leans against the wall. "He isn't."

"If he rules with you, the people will judge you, condemn you."

It is her own fault, she thinks. She has trained her son too well, taught him to be distrustful. "You spend too much time worrying about the people," she says. "I've told you many times that the people do not rule. We do."

"Perhaps you spend too little time thinking about it, Mother." He doesn't mean it as an insult, simply as an observation.

She scoffs. "I am a woman with a crown. Of course I think about the others. I have to, or the crown would be on someone else's head."

He looks at the blacksmiths working the bronze, sparks flying across the room. His profile is dazzling, his skin like ripe olives and his eyes dark like charred wood. Like his father's, Clytemnestra thinks bitterly.

"I will marry Hermione," Orestes says.

When she goes to her room, Aegisthus isn't there. It is already dark, so she walks to the guests' quarters, knocking on his door before she enters. He is eating cheese and pears by the window, his daggers on the table next to him. She has been thinking about what to say to him, whether a lie or the truth. Lies have come more easily to her lately, but not with Aegisthus.

Without turning to her, he says, "Have you decided I'm not worthy of your trust any longer?"

"No one is," she says simply.

"So what now? Will you throw me into prison, like the elders suggested? Or kill me before your husband comes home?"

He is like a child sometimes, she thinks, making such a scene just because she told him to go back to the palace. "If I wanted to kill you, you'd already be dead."

He turns to her. Under the torchlight, his eyes are the color of ash. "Do you know what the people in the villages say about you?"

"Something horrible, I imagine."

"They say that you are mad with ambition and distrust. That you execute people who aren't loyal."

"I can't argue with that. What do they say of Agamemnon?"

"That he is a great leader."

"Ah, of course." She goes to him, takes one of his daggers, and presses her finger against the blade. "If you heard such stories about me, why did you come back here?"

"To kill you." He isn't looking at her. She sees the tension in his shoulders, the white knuckles around the wine cup.

At last, the truth.

"And yet here I stand," she says. She is surprised to hear the coldness in her own voice, the indifference.

"Yes," he says, so quietly it feels like a breath of wind.

"You have just told me you wanted to murder me, yet you expect me to trust you with secret information."

He puts down his cup, softness on his scarred face. "The first time I heard of you was when Agamemnon brought you here. I was living in the woods then. One night as I slept in a shepherd's barn, I heard him say that the king of Mycenae was marrying a Spartan woman. He said you had already been married, that Agamemnon killed your husband and your infant son so he could have you for himself."

It is the first time he speaks of this in front of her. Her body feels numb. "I didn't know shepherds enjoyed that sort of talk."

He shrugs. "Everyone spoke about you then. *The sister of the most beautiful woman in our lands. A Spartan princess marrying a powerful king.* I thought you must be either a beaten dog, some unlucky girl doomed to live a life of unhappiness, or a ruthless woman who shared Agamemnon's cruelty.

"Then I heard that my cousin was off to Troy to fight a war for a woman who couldn't stay in her husband's bed. I laughed then, for Menelaus was always the one women never refused, not even when we were boys. It must have been hard for him to see his beautiful wife leave him for the enemy.

"I thought this was my chance to retake the city, to make those loyal to the Atreidai pay once and for all. But then I heard that *you* were ruling Mycenae, far better and more efficiently than Agamemnon, and that you were both loved and feared by many. I thought I would come here and see for myself. If you were indeed to be loved, I would ask for mercy. If not, I would murder you and make my cousin pay."

"You were wrong about that. Agamemnon cares only about himself. I am just a tool for him to show others what a strong woman he has managed to bend."

"I was wrong about many things," he says.

She puts the dagger down. "Before I executed him, Polydamas said that if a man sleeps with a queen, he will soon expect to be king."

"You make a far better ruler than I ever would."

"What do you want then, if you don't wish to kill me?"

"I want to be where you are. To advise you and protect you."

Aileen was right then: she will never get rid of him. Does she want to? His eyes are huge and cold.

"I have fought for the respect of my people," she says. "And your position here threatens my work. They might see you as a traitor, but you are a man, and in their eyes, a man will always be better suited to rule."

"I have always wanted the throne only to take it from someone else. That doesn't make me a good king."

She takes his face in her hands, feels the scars under her fingers. He doesn't relax at her touch but gazes at her with a fervency that could make even the sky burn. This is a man ready to kill for her, she can see that.

"Troy will fall soon," she says. "And Agamemnon will come back."

"How do you know this?"

"The scout told me today."

His face is barren. "You want to send me away, then."

"No." She steps away from him, takes his cup to sip some wine. He looks at her, waiting. Inside her, the familiar anger, raw, relentless.

"I used to tell the story of Artemis and Actaeon to my daughters when they were little. Iphigenia loved it, just like my sister used to love it. They felt safer hearing it, I think. Here is a beautiful woman who isn't at the mercy of men, a woman who takes revenge. Beauty can be a curse sometimes. It blinds men, makes them do horrible things.

"When Iphigenia was a child, merchants and envoys used to call her 'goddess.' They gazed at her with lust, and I would have clawed their eyes out if I could. But she was safe next to me. No one dared to touch her.

"When she was fifteen, a boy tried to rape her. She hit his face with a rock, and when the boy's father demanded justice, I didn't give it to him. He was lucky to be left alive.

"When she was murdered…" She stops, bites her lip until she can taste blood. "When my daughter was murdered, I spent days obsessing over how she'd be remembered. Gentle, lovely, an innocent virgin sacrificed… That is how bards sing of her. She was nothing like that. She was fierce, defiant. She wanted everything from this world. She was like the sun, and my husband took her from me. And for what? He didn't kill her for vengeance, ambition, or greed. He killed her *for a puff of wind*.

"I've heard the elders talk about that wretched day as if their king had a choice to make. 'What could he do? Obey the will of the gods or desert the fleet? Pain both ways,' they said. 'An impossible choice,' they said. But that is not the truth. The truth is my daughter died *for nothing*."

She puts the cup aside and looks Aegisthus in the eye. He is still, his face dark with pain. She cradles each word carefully in her mind before speaking. "You speak of your own thirst for vengeance, but what about me? What about my revenge?"

His fingers tighten against the table.

"You say you want to be with me and protect me," she says. She feels a surge of emotion inside her, anticipation and exposure. "Then you will stay in the palace when my husband comes back from the war. You will hide as I welcome him and his soldiers. Then you will help me murder the man responsible for my daughter's death."

32

Friends and Foes

THE TREES BLOSSOM, the branches heavy with cascades of white and purple flowers. The sky grows lighter, the days longer. Yet no news of Troy arrives at the citadel.

Clytemnestra is restless. She doesn't sleep at night, and in the mornings, her eyes are swollen and her head hurts. As she hears the people's requests in the *megaron*, she often stares out the windows, trying to glimpse a fire lighting up the mountains. But each day, the horizon is the same, the valley bright and warm under a cloudless sky.

Orestes is fidgety too. At night, more and more servant girls visit his chamber, and Clytemnestra worries. She doesn't want her son to end up like Menelaus, making his wife miserable because of his stupidity. There is also Aegisthus, who seems to trouble Orestes with his presence. Sometimes, at dinner, Clytemnestra catches her son staring at her lover with a challenging, playful face. It reminds her of Castor's childish face before he made mischief.

"Isn't Hermione too young to be married?" Chrysothemis asks one evening. They are dining all together, the torches spilling light, like flowers of gold. Chrysothemis is frowning as she plays with her food. Clytemnestra understands her worry: her daughter is her niece's age, after all.

"For a Spartan, yes," Clytemnestra says. "But in other Greek cities, girls marry young, as you know."

"At least she'll have someone *experienced* beside her," Electra says, staring at her brother. Her eyes are as bright as polished silver. Orestes laughs, unbothered by his sister's teasing.

"Do you and the warlords share your spoil now?" she insists, her voice carefully expressionless. "I've seen Kyros in an alley with one of the new servant girls."

"I'd never go so low as sleeping with a woman who has been in Kyros's bed," Orestes replies with a smile.

"And yet you fight with him," Electra says. "A man who once tried to rape your sisters. Do you think he is different now, a better man?"

"Electra," Chrysothemis says quietly. Her voice fades in the silence, like the last light of the day.

Electra sips her wine, her lips the faintest shade of purple. "What do you think, Lord Aegisthus? Do people change?"

Aegisthus looks up, as if surprised to hear her talk to him. "Once greedy, always greedy," he says quietly.

Orestes smirks. "Isn't it curious that you would say so? Surely then you agree with me when I say once a traitor, always a traitor."

Aegisthus slams his knife onto the table. The servants slide back into the shadows with heavy platters of food. Orestes remains in his chair, relaxed, though his eyes are shining, like burning coal.

"If you wish to quarrel, leave me," Clytemnestra orders. "Taunt one another, tear each other apart, I do not care. I won't listen to any of it."

Her children keep seated, quiet as tombs. Aegisthus drinks his wine, his anger under control. Clytemnestra tries to focus on the food, her mind tired, her body drained. Once, it was Leon who soothed the tension with kind words, who shielded Clytemnestra from her children's moods. Now he is gone, and in his place, there is Aegisthus, who struggles with his own suffering.

She feels she has woven a web too large and complicated, and now she is caught in it too.

Aileen wakes her, shaking her arm. Clytemnestra springs up, panting. She was dreaming about her sister, captured by the Greeks and executed on the walls of Troy. The nightmare still lingers on her skin.

"What is it?" Her eyes are dry, her limbs tired as if she has spent the night fighting.

"Orestes and Aegisthus are fighting in the practice yard."

She slips into a *peplos* and hurries outside, followed by Aileen. She is running fast, and her servant is hard-pressed to keep up.

"Maybe they are just playing," Aileen says tentatively, breathless, "but I have heard some men cry out, so I thought…"

They are not playing. Aegisthus doesn't fight with anyone except her. Orestes must have challenged him, taken him by surprise. And though she knows her son is strong in close combat, Aegisthus can be dangerous.

They run down the stone steps that lead to the yard. They can hear the grunts and cries, the clashing of blade against blade. There is a small crowd around the dusty ground, young boys who were probably meant to train at this hour. They are staring at the two figures dancing in the yard, swinging their swords to strike each other down. Clytemnestra makes space between them and stops at the edge of the yard, Aileen's breath on her neck.

Orestes is fighting with his newly forged sword, his curls bouncing on his sweaty forehead. In front of him, Aegisthus is using two daggers, and there is blood running down his face. He is moving like a wolf, his blades hitting her son's sword like lashes.

"Look who's here," Orestes says, amused, seeing Clytemnestra out of the corner of his eyes. "Do you wish to join us, Mother?"

Aegisthus looks in her direction, and her son's blade cuts him again on the temple. He doesn't complain, but Clytemnestra sees the fire in his eyes, the fury. He would cut Orestes's throat if she weren't here. He leaps toward her son, slashing at his head. Orestes ducks under his blade and moves aside. When he stabs at him, Aegisthus bends and throws himself forward, dragging Orestes down with him. Their blades keep clashing on the sand, and when Aegisthus hits Orestes in the throat, he gives a choked laugh. Aegisthus moves back, his blades held forward as a warning.

Clytemnestra grabs a spear and throws it. It sinks into the ground between them, and the combatants turn to her. Orestes's smile doesn't fade, and she feels the need to slap him, to remind him that this is no game. The rage on Aegisthus's face is gone, and in its place, fear. He's afraid of her reaction.

"It is time for the boys to practice," she says and walks away. The sky above her is empty, and she is reminded of when she ran on the sand to save her sister from Cynisca. An easier time, when friends and enemies were stark and clear and she thought she always knew what was right.

Aegisthus follows her inside the palace, a guilty dog desperate to earn back her love. When she turns to him under the torches near the dining hall, he stops abruptly, his muscles tense.

"He attacked me," he says, his mouth a thin line. His eyes are wild.

She has never seen him so angry. "He would have killed me if I hadn't fought back."

How many times had he endured this while he was growing up, young men taunting him, forcing him to fight back? It must be exhausting.

"My son would never do such a thing," she says, walking inside the hall. He follows close behind. She can feel the air around them thickening with his fury.

"He is jealous of our relation," he blurts out. "He is poisoning everyone in the citadel against me!"

"You are bleeding," she says.

He touches the trickle of blood that runs down his temple and wipes it away carelessly. "You must send him away," he says. "Or it will be the end for me when Agamemnon comes."

"I won't."

"So you would choose him instead of me?"

"He is *my son*. There is no choice to be made."

His face turns cold, his eyes bitter. "But you must make a choice. What happens if Orestes stays here when your husband comes home?" *Your husband.* He must really be angry to refer to Agamemnon so. "What happens when you put a blade in his heart? A son must avenge his father. It is the law."

She knows he speaks the truth. A son's highest duty is to honor and avenge the father, no matter how cruel the father. Aegisthus is living proof of that.

A wanderer, born to kill his father's enemies, bound to bring ruin to his house—the words the elders had used all those years ago as they sent spies across the mainland to look for Aegisthus. "Aegisthus's father was a monster," Clytemnestra had said, but the elders had shaken their heads.

"You are a woman. You cannot understand loyalty to the father."

They were wrong, as always. She understands Justice, the ancient spirit that lives inside each of them, ready to burst forth for every crime. It is a web, each thread stained with the blood of mothers and fathers, daughters and sons. It grows and grows, the Furies always weaving more traps.

Yet would Orestes really side with a father who had murdered his sister like an animal bred for slaughter? Would he gather an army against his own mother? She has taught him everything he knows. She has shown him the other boys' weaknesses and told him that mercy *never* helps one win. She was there when he wielded his first sword, when he rode his first horse. She wanted him to grow into a strong *and* decent man, fierce but not savage. Maybe she has gone too far. Maybe she should have taught him to be loyal, first and foremost. *Do good men make good warlords?* Orestes asked her with a smirk.

Unease floods her, a warning. She looks up. Aegisthus is staring at her, like a wolf stalking a sheep.

"Orestes is promised to Hermione," Clytemnestra says. "He will go to Sparta before the Atreidai come back from the war. That way, he will start to build his web of alliances. He will command respect *before* the king of Sparta is at home." The expression on Aegisthus's face warms her, like the first spring morning after a long winter. "Then, after I have dealt with his father, he will come back to Mycenae. He will show me his loyalty."

She sends her son away in the last days of spring.

At dawn, they go to the Lion Gate together. The citadel is still waking up, some women walking half asleep to the stream, carrying dirty tunics. Orestes ties his dagger to his belt, his profile sweet in the orange light.

"Be kind to your cousin," she says. "Treat her as your equal, not as your inferior."

"I will," he says, giving her one of his handsome smiles.

"Don't take other girls to your bed," she adds, and he breaks into a laugh. "That is how your uncle lost Helen in the first place."

He places his hands on her arms. "You worry too much. Besides, I know what Uncle Polydeuces will do to me if I wrong his beloved niece."

She looks at his dazzling face, at every faint line and jagged angle. "Be careful. Look around, find those loyal to you. Your uncle will help you, but never underestimate your counselors. Sparta has changed. Most families are faithful to Menelaus now. They will look upon you as an intruder."

He gazes at her seriously, and in his eyes, she sees his father, the same intentness when he listened to something he knew was important.

"Everyone has friends and foes, but kings and queens even more so," she adds. "Remember it when the time comes."

The horses are ready, and his men call for him. She wants to cling to him, never let him go. But she has made a choice, and she can't turn back.

He kisses her forehead. "I will remember," he says. She thinks he will turn now and leave her, but he cups his hand around her face. "And you be wary of Aegisthus, Mother. He's not your foe, but he's not your friend either."

She goes straight to the walls to watch Orestes ride into the sunrise. Aegisthus is already there, his eyes on her son. She feels sudden uncertainty at the sight of him, as if the ground were collapsing under her feet. A tiny sun rises with a splash of color, and the last pale, resilient stars disappear. Aegisthus turns to watch her, unblinking.

"Orestes believes I shouldn't trust you," she says. "The elders thought I shouldn't trust you. Leon warned me not to trust you. Should I worry that I was wrong about your loyalty?"

Below them, Orestes is a small point moving quickly across the land. Soon he will ride beyond the hills and disappear.

"Your faithful dog Leon is gone," Aegisthus says. "Orestes is gone. The elders are gone. You yourself saw to that." He holds her gaze. "There's only me and you now."

It is strange how frightening he can be. She knows he loves her, yet sometimes he slides back into his hole of fear and distrust, a hole he has dug for himself during all those years of loneliness.

He kneels and takes her hand. His palm is cold and dry against hers. "I will always be loyal to you, *my queen*."

33

The Lion Comes Home

THE WATER IN the bath is cool and pleasant against her skin. The lights are dim inside, and outside, the hills stretch like ocean waves. She closes her eyes and lets her body sink deeper into the bath. Is this how death feels? she wonders. Is her beautiful Iphigenia floating somewhere peacefully, her golden hair dancing around her? She emerges, and her hand finds the cold blade of her dagger lying on the floor next to her. The sharpness soothes her, and she tries to distract herself from painful thoughts. There was a fight in the citadel today, and she will have to speak to the warlords about it. Two men were killed. The elders mentioned it was about some deals the merchants have made, some gold they refused to give. She is thinking she should summon the merchants directly to the *megaron* and teach them obedience once and for all…

That is when she sees the fire. Something is burning in the distance, on the mountain in front of the citadel, the flames rising in the sky like a flock of scarlet ibises. She climbs out of the bath and runs to the high window, water dripping from her body. There is another fire behind the mountain, flickering on the hills toward Athens and Delphi. And then another, the light so small in the distance it looks like the white of an eye open in the darkness.

Troy has fallen.

She stands by the window, frozen, watching the chain of beacons send burning sparks into the starless night. The fire grows larger, hungrier, and soon her eyes are alive with brightness. The sight makes her ravenous. Violence gorges on more violence—it is insatiable, always craving more blood. She closes her eyes, lets the pain flood her mind.

Iphigenia's blood on her knees as she was dragged toward the altar stone. Leon's battered face, the purple eye and the damaged throat. The redness on Clytemnestra's hands, the broken nails and finger joints torn as she tried to anchor herself to the sandy ground—anything to be close to her daughter. The memories make her choke, like the sickly smell of putrefying bodies. But there are more.

Her mother holding Clytemnestra's dead baby in her arms, her face twisted in desperation. Tantalus's empty eyes staring back at her. She couldn't touch him. Someone was holding on to her, and no matter how much she clawed and screamed, they wouldn't let her go. And then Agamemnon, staring at her across the corridor. He wasn't speaking, but she knew what he thought: *You are mine now.* But he was wrong. She is nobody's.

She walks slowly back to the bath and picks up her mother's jeweled dagger. The first time she touched the blade, she cut herself—but her skin has long been thicker. *More blood will be spilled soon, but it won't be mine.*

She throws the dagger into the wooden door of the bathhouse, where it sticks with the smallest sound. It is like the sound of a dead bird falling on the ground.

Her daughters are sleeping together in Chrysothemis's room, their chests moving up and down like the wings of a butterfly. Clytemnestra sits at the edge of the large bed and strokes Chrysothemis's cheek. Electra opens her eyes, suddenly alert.

"What is it, Mother?" she asks. Her sister stirs in her sleep. Clytemnestra moves a strand of hair away from her face.

"The war is won," she says quietly. "Your father is coming back."

Electra flinches, and her deerlike eyes gleam in the darkness. Clytemnestra knows it is because she has called Agamemnon "your father," which she hasn't for a long time. Chrysothemis opens her eyes too. Maybe she has been awake all along, because when she sits up on the bed, the first thing she says is "What will happen?"

Clytemnestra doesn't reply. Her daughters stare at her, their heads cocked to one side, their breath held. She can tell they have waited to ask this question. Unable to keep the silence, Chrysothemis speaks again, her small voice no more than a breath of wind. "Will he hurt us?"

The question cracks Clytemnestra's heart open. "He will never touch you," she says.

Electra sits up too, jaw set, body tense. "How do you know?"

"Because I won't allow it. While he was gone, much changed."

"Some things didn't," Electra replies. "You still hate him."

She is almost tempted to draw back as she looks into Electra's eyes. It is like staring into deep, dark water.

"He took my children away from me," she says. "My perfect daughter and my baby boy. Would you not *hate* someone like that?" She knows "hate" is the wrong word. But in all these years, she has never found the right one. Some feelings aren't meant to be captured.

Chrysothemis seems alarmed. She leans forward and takes her hand. "We understand, Mother. We always have."

Electra draws her knees up to her chest. "Do you think the gods are watching us? Do you think they know that you hate him?"

"Listen to me," Clytemnestra says. "Gods do not care about us. They have other concerns. That is why you should never live in the shadow of their anger. It is men you must fear. It is men who will be angry with you if you rise too high, if you are too much loved. The stronger you are, the more they will try to take you down."

Her daughters' profiles are sharper now. Soon it will be dawn, and the summer heat will become unbearable.

"Father doesn't love us, does he?" Chrysothemis asks.

Clytemnestra looks away, the words carrying her to a painful place.

A scorching heat.

A purple tent.

Iphigenia's sweet voice. Her daughter had asked the same question before she died.

"It doesn't matter what he feels," Clytemnestra says. "It doesn't matter what he thinks. *I* love you both, as I loved your sister, more than anything in the world."

Her daughters' faces brighten like shields in sunlight. She takes their hands.

When vengeance calls and the gods stop watching, what happens to those who have touched the people I love?

Aegisthus is waiting for her in her room, wide awake. She finds his body in the dawning light, takes his head in her hands. When he kisses her, she can taste his hunger for revenge. *The lion comes home and finds the wolf ready to welcome him.*

"The fire," he says, his voice flat. "He is coming back."

She nods and walks to the window, looking at the golden sky. He follows and brushes his lips against her shoulders. She feels herself growing tense, her mind sharpening like a blade. She closes her eyes and imagines killing her husband—the thought that has fed her for years, the seed that has grown into a vine. She couldn't stand if she stopped thinking about it. It is the same tightness one feels before a fight—and this is a fight for which she has been preparing for a long time.

"Agamemnon is always watchful and will be even after a ten-year war," she says. "He is clever enough not to trust anyone around him, ever."

Another man would tell her to relax, to be sure of herself, but not Aegisthus. He knows that those who relax fall easily into spiders' webs. His face is full of malice. Maybe in another life, he might have been innocent, a life where he wasn't caught in games of cruelty and power. Could a life like that even exist?

She stares at him. "Which is why we don't play the heroes. We need to strike like snakes. We crawl and kill when no one is watching."

He gives her his wolflike smile. "I was never much of a hero anyway."

The next day, she has the elders gathered in the *megaron*. They take their places around the throne, bowing to her. As soon as they are seated, her guards drag Aegisthus inside.

"As you know, the king is coming back now," she says. "He will decide what to do with his prisoners."

A murmur of assent, like a breeze, runs through the old men. How easily they are fooled. How trusting they become when she gives them exactly what they want.

Last night, as she lay on the bed sleeplessly, she told Aegisthus that he had to trust her. *I trust you*, he said, reaching for her, pressing his body against hers. She felt his warmth but it wasn't enough. She wanted him to tear through her skin, to hold her so tightly that she might break.

"Throw him into a cell," she orders, each word as bright as a knife.

"Traitor," Aegisthus says as the guards drag him away again. She keeps her face expressionless, thinking of a stone before it is carved, until his figure disappears beyond the hearth. Silence looms and the elders stare at her.

"Agamemnon will return and find his wife loyal and true," she says.

The elders are wide-eyed, watchful. They suddenly fear this is a game or that she has gone mad. *Isn't this what you wanted? For me to be no more than a watchdog, licking the mighty king's feet?*

"Give the news to the people in the citadel," she says. "Agamemnon is sailing back, and the queen readies to welcome him." Cadmus nods, and so do a few others. "Tell them also how the city was taken. Tell them that Troy was sacked, temples destroyed, priests killed."

The elders frown. There is no greater offense to the gods than to spit on their holy places.

"Remind them that Agamemnon and his men come home as true heroes." She stops for fear that her malice will show between her honeyed words.

Cadmus clears his throat. "War has its necessities, my queen."

She smiles. "Of course. But remind the people of what those necessities are."

He nods quickly and takes his leave. The others follow him closely, perhaps not wishing to be left behind.

Light comes into the hall, touching the frescoes. She walks past them, tracing the lines of every figure, every painted blade of grass. It hurts her to see that lies come easily to her now. Once, it was decency, courage, goodness. But that was another lifetime.

The next morning feels like the hottest day of the year. Electra and Chrysothemis wait patiently as Clytemnestra stands by the window, staring at the citadel while Aileen does her hair. People are running their errands, cleaning and clearing the streets for their king's arrival. Some men move carts and chests aside, while others pour water on the cobbles. As the crown is placed gently on her head, she turns to her daughters.

"You won't dine with us tonight," Clytemnestra says. "You will welcome your father and then disappear."

Electra doesn't answer. She plays with her rings, precious stones on glittering gold. Clytemnestra looks at her daughter's arm, clean and smooth, then at her own scars.

"Guards will be stationed outside your quarters. Whatever happens, do not come out."

Chrysothemis frowns. "Mother?" Her hair is adorned with little gems plaited into each strand and ribbons. Clytemnestra kisses her forehead, her lips barely brushing the skin.

"Come now. The army is here."

Her daughters share a look before they hear it: horses' hoofs beating on the dust in the distance.

They hurry to the top of the walls to watch the army coming, right by the Lion Gate. Aileen keeps adjusting Electra's dress, even though

Electra pushes her away. Chrysothemis wrings her little hands, standing on tiptoe, trying to see better.

At the foot of the mountains, a long line of warriors is marching in their direction. They look like ants, spread across the arid land. In the hands of the two soldiers at the top of the line, the banner of Mycenae. There is something different about it, and it takes Clytemnestra a moment to make out the dark-red stains on the lion. A Mycenaean victor, gorging on the blood of Trojan kings.

The air is furnace-hot, but Clytemnestra keeps still. She lets each ant pass until her eyes rest on her husband. He isn't hard to find. He rides at the front, next to a large chariot filled with war spoils. She expected to feel pain or anger at the sight, but there is nothing inside her. This is how vengeance transforms you: it makes you pale and cool, like a sea goddess.

She watches him ride, his breastplate glistening in the scorching sun, his men following, scattered and limping, like wounded dogs, among the shrubs and rocks. Closer now, their broken bodies come into focus—missing limbs and eyes, wounds still festering.

A girl sits on the chariot next to Agamemnon among the gold, rugs, and vases. Her hands are bound, her skin brown as oak bark. There is an old bruise on her face, half-covered by her loose hair. A war slave. Clytemnestra would rather die than live like that. "Even a slave has a choice," her mother once said. "Slavery or death." Is that a choice? Clytemnestra isn't sure.

She looks down and the girl looks up. For a moment, their eyes lock. Then she disappears beyond the gate.

34

The Queen's Justice

Feast

THE DINING HALL is lit and loud, servants running around with platters of food, warriors gulping wine as if they had never tasted it before. The king sits at the head of the table. Clytemnestra takes the place on his left, just as she always did. To have his greedy face close to her after all these years… It is pressing memories to her skin like a burning blade. Yet she doesn't flinch. Calchas is in front of her, on the king's right, which means she cannot escape the seer's gnarled face. But that is good—she wants to look at him for as long as she can. Ten years have left no sign on him: he still looks twisted and puffy, like a dead body left on the shore by the tide. Agamemnon's slave has also been brought to the table and ordered to take the place next to Clytemnestra. She sits with her back straight, like a queen, though her hands are trembling. For a moment, Clytemnestra fears she will take a knife and stab her.

"I haven't introduced you," Agamemnon says. "This is my war prize and *pallake*." Concubine. The word, spoken aloud in front of everyone, is meant to humiliate them both, Clytemnestra knows. But the girl doesn't look down as a slave would. She stares back at

Clytemnestra, challenge burning in her eyes, as though she is daring her to pity her. She doesn't know that Clytemnestra pities her only because she understands. *I was once sitting like you at this very table. Not a slave, but a prisoner in the king's home.*

"What is your name?" Clytemnestra asks.

"Cassandra," the girl says. She waits before adding, "Daughter of Priam." *The king of Troy.* Her Greek is slow and rusty, each word rolling like a jagged stone.

"She is difficult, this one," Agamemnon says, staring at Clytemnestra. He tilts his head in the girl's direction with an amused expression. "You should see how she fights. I thought you might like her."

"Cassandra is lucky our king chose her," Calchas intervenes. His warm, sickly voice makes Clytemnestra gasp for air. She feels as if she is plunging into boiling water and struggling to breathe for the pain.

"Lucky," she repeats.

"Princess Polyxena was sacrificed on Achilles's tomb like a heifer," Agamemnon says, biting into his meat. Cassandra's eyes are as dark as ashes. She clenches her fists so tightly under the table that Clytemnestra fears her fingers will snap—Polyxena must have been her sister.

"And many other women were taken by brutes." Agamemnon pauses, as if weighing a thought. "You do not wish to be Diomedes's bed slave, trust me."

"But the worst fate was Andromache's," Calchas says. "Do you know what happened to her?" His eyes never leave Clytemnestra's.

"I am not sure I care," she replies. She wishes she could save Cassandra from further pain. But Calchas likes pain: he would bathe in it if he could, as long as it is someone else's.

"Hector's wife was hunted down by Achilles's son, Pyrrhus. He took Andromache's baby and smashed his head open against the walls of Troy."

Clytemnestra stops herself from biting her lip. She thinks of an egg when it is dropped and its yolk spreads on the floor. Her baby, dead in Leda's arms.

But Calchas isn't done with her. "Pyrrhus then took Andromache for himself." He keeps staring at her, waiting for some sort of reaction. Clytemnestra's face betrays nothing.

"A great warrior, but too proud," Agamemnon interrupts, swigging his wine. "Sooner or later, the gods will punish him."

Clytemnestra turns to Cassandra, but the princess isn't crying. Maybe her eyes have been emptied already. That is what her husband does. He empties people.

Clytemnestra stands, lifting her golden cup. "A toast, then!" she says, and the hall grows quiet. The men turn to her, their faces raw and wrinkled. "To the gods who helped true heroes come home, and to the best victory of our times, a war that will be remembered for generations!"

Agamemnon stands too. "Everyone whispered that Troy was impregnable, that the Trojans were unbeatable. But we raped their city, broke through the walls, and took everything down." The men cheer, and Clytemnestra sits down.

"Our men's blood wets the earth of Troy, and we mourn them." More cheering, cups and fists slammed into the table. "And now we drink in honor of everyone we have lost, whose memory will never fade."

There are shouts of agreement, and the room grows loud again as cups are quickly emptied. When Agamemnon sits down, Clytemnestra chooses a piece of cheese from the platter. "You have always enjoyed lying to your men," she says. She is aware of Cassandra staring at her and of Calchas licking his lips, thinking of something wise to say. Agamemnon snorts, but she continues. "The memory of most men who died on that field will be gone soon. No one will remember them. No one will care."

"If they fought valiantly," he says, "they will have their reputation."

"They had their reputation in life maybe, but not in death. Only a few survive the passing of time." She wants to make him angry. She wants him to speak about the dead, about the men who died because of his war, and about the daughter he killed.

Calchas's neck twists, like a snake's. "Time can play strange tricks. Often the gods pluck dead men from the shadows and carry them into the light for future generations to remember. They let others shine in their lifetime, then bury them too deep to be talked about in the future."

She smiles, as guilelessly as she can. "And what do you think your fate will be, seer? Will you be forgotten, or will you be remembered as the man who sat with kings during the greatest of wars?" *And who ordered them to kill little girls for a breath of wind?*

Calchas draws back his lips, showing his teeth. "I do not know what will become of my name. All I know is that those who gave their lives for the greater purpose of our victory will be held like torches in the ages to come." He pauses, and she hopes he will close his mouth. But of course, he doesn't. "Your daughter included. Iphigenia will have more in death than you could ever give her in life."

He dares to speak her name. He dares to mention her beautiful daughter. Agamemnon and Cassandra are looking at her, and she finds her mildest voice, the one she had used to lull her babies to sleep. "That is good to hear." Her eyes set on Calchas's chapped lips. His cold, scarred skin. His snakelike face.

You are going to die tonight, she thinks. *Enjoy your feast while you can.*

Temple

Cassandra looks at the seer, thinking of ways to kill him. She has cradled the thought ever since the greedy Greeks sacrificed her sister. Eyes like precious jade, skin like olive oil, hair like polished bronze—no one was as good and beautiful as Polyxena. And yet the cruel seer ordered her death so they could sail home. Nothing good and shining is safe in the hands of the Greeks, Cassandra has learned.

Soldiers were still drinking in the hall when she and Calchas left "to pray to the gods." She has been eager to be alone with the seer since they sailed from Troy. Now they are walking in a garden toward a pale temple, and Calchas's footsteps in front of her make no sound, as if he were wan and fading. Cassandra tries not to stumble on the path. She has stolen a knife from the dining hall, and her hand around it is so damp she is afraid it might slip and drop to the ground.

They reach the temple and Calchas steps inside. Cassandra stops, sickness taking hold of her. She remembers the cold columns of another temple in her homeland, her hands clinging to them so tightly that her fingers were bruised, her screams echoing all over as the ones of a trapped bird, and the pain, so severe she feared it might break her in two.

Ajax was the name of the man who raped her. The many-minded king told her when they were distributing the women for the Greek generals.

"Come, pray with me, Cassandra," Calchas's voice calls from the temple. She steps inside and crouches at the seer's feet. He touches her head as if she were a dog and closes his eyes.

Her mother has taught her to be kind, and her god has told her to be just. But where are they now? Hecuba has lost everything, and Apollo has stopped speaking to her ever since Ajax took her. She fought and cried for help and no one came. That is what everyone does in the face of atrocity: they look away. No one is brave enough to acknowledge the truth, not even a god.

Forgive me, Mother. Forgive me, Apollo.

She has never hurt anybody. How will it feel? She is drawing the kitchen knife when she hears steps behind her. She turns just in time to see the Mycenean queen.

She catches her breath as if about to dive underwater and slides closer to the seer.

Sacrifice

Clytemnestra turns up her nose, covering her face. Inside the temple, the air smells wet and pungent. She doesn't come here often. The stillness of the place disgusts her—it's like a tomb. Under the big statue of Hera, Calchas is praying. Next to him, crouched in a sitting position and staring at her, the Trojan girl. There is a strange light in her eyes, dazzling and dangerous.

"Leave," Clytemnestra orders her. The girl springs up and walks to the door, but Calchas doesn't turn. Clytemnestra examines the back of his head, like an eggshell whose surface has been cracked.

"I knew you would come," he says.

"Did some sheep's intestines tell you so?"

He turns, and his little black eyes seize her, like a hook with a fish. "I prayed for you in these ten long years."

He prayed. She almost strangles him there and then. Men like him, who pretend to be holy while others do their dirty work, have always enraged her the most.

"How generous of you," Clytemnestra says.

His lips curve into a hideous smile. It is calculated, like everything he does. "Your father and mother are gone. Your brother was killed, your sister abducted. Yet here you are, queen of the most powerful Greek city, with an army of men at your command. I find that admirable."

She steps closer to him, her feet light on the marble floor. Why are people so eager to remind her of her family's fate? It must be because they wish to weaken her.

"You are an ambitious woman married to a ruthless king. In my experience, ambitious people fall quickly. But not you. You have a talent for survival."

She stops close enough to touch him. "So do you. Though while I fight my way till the end, you crawl and whisper in kings' ears. Not heroic, but you do what you must to survive."

He tilts his head to the side, his hollow eyes sucking her in. "We all do what we can with the gifts of the gods." She remembers that Odysseus once said something similar and feels a deep pain inside, like a splinter festering within the flesh.

"Yes. And what do you do with your *godly sight*?" She pauses, but he keeps silent and utterly still, like animals in the woods when they sniff danger. "You order an innocent girl to be butchered like a goat. A mistake, one might say, but no, because in Troy, you give the same order, this time sacrificing a Trojan princess, Polyxena. It was you who ordered the sacrifice, wasn't it? How brave of you. What a great use of your *gift*."

"I do what the gods order me to do. It is unwise to challenge their will."

She laughs. The sound echoes all over the temple. "Do you know what was unwise? To keep me alive once you slaughtered my daughter. My brother always said that when you make enemies, you must eliminate them before they eliminate you. That was the mistake you made."

"Our mistakes matter little in the eyes of the gods. We all die in the end, like your brother did."

She licks her lips. "Yes, we do."

She is about to draw her dagger, but he moves first. With a gesture far too quick for a man of his age, he takes a knife out of his sleeve and points it at her. She doesn't step back but grabs his wrist without effort and twists it. He drops the knife. She lets her own dagger trace the contours of his face, from his hollow little eyes to his thin lips. He doesn't struggle.

"You won't spill blood in here," he says. He doesn't sound scared, only a little surprised. "You are not that bold."

She is amused he would say that after drawing a knife out of his vest. "You do not know how bold I am," she says.

She sticks the dagger into his eye, the very same eyes that *saw* her daughter must be sacrificed. He drops to his knees, screaming, and she cuts his throat quickly before anyone can hear. He falls onto the floor, his body small and decrepit in the large vest. In the shadows, it looks like an empty sack.

She remains standing, catching her breath. Everything inside her is cold and hateful. She can feel it like tendrils spreading around her bones.

She turns to the door, and there is the Trojan girl. Clytemnestra approaches her with caution, putting away her jeweled dagger. Cassandra takes a step forward, her chin out, challenging. She is not afraid.

"Do it," she says when Clytemnestra is close enough. "Do it now."

She truly is a princess. Only royalty would give orders like that.

Clytemnestra reaches out and touches her arm gently. "Hide here," she says. "No one will hurt you, I promise."

The look Cassandra gives her is of utter distrust. Clytemnestra understands. If she were the girl, she wouldn't trust her either.

Dungeon

Aegisthus has promised himself that he will trust Clytemnestra, but an entire lifetime of wariness is getting the better of him. This saddens him. If he can't trust the only woman he has cared for in all his life, then maybe it is too late for him.

He is sitting in the dungeon, his hands tied to a wooden column, a guard standing by the door. They can hear the cheers coming from the dining hall, the whispers and clattering from the kitchen.

The place is bringing back bad memories. Atreus had once thrown him down here after he had lost yet another wrestling game. "So you learn what it means to lose," he had said, and Aegisthus had spent two days alone in the dark with rats creeping around him. Agamemnon had come to see him, and when Aegisthus asked him for food, Agamemnon frowned. "You wouldn't learn anything, would you?"

There is also the memory of Thyestes in a cell, how he told him that the sword Aegisthus was wielding was his and that he was his long-lost son.

Aegisthus banishes the thoughts and focuses. He had gotten out by himself all those years ago, hadn't he? He needs to do the same now. The ground stinks of piss and mud, but he sinks his fingers into it. His tied wrists ache as he searches for a stone, a shard, anything. His hands unearth a bone, a dead rat, then something that feels like a pin. He feels it between his fingers. Sharp enough.

He cuts the cord that binds him and waits. When the guard turns toward the door, he jumps on him. They tumble down and Aegisthus bangs the man's head against the wall. The guard drops, unconscious, and Aegisthus steps over him.

Upstairs, he runs through the corridors, a familiar fear tearing him apart. Clytemnestra is strong and knows her husband, but Aegisthus knows him better. He grew up with him, fought with him, has hated him since he was a child. And he knows Agamemnon always wins.

He stops running by the entrance of the *gynaeceum*, flattening himself against the wall to avoid two guards. Here the corridor divides. He could go left, toward the baths, where he knows Clytemnestra will have the king cleaned. Or he could go right, toward the temple, where the mad seer will be hiding. He can smell blood and fear coming from the garden. He follows the scent like a wolf.

♛

Garden

Cassandra has learned that the Greeks are two-tongued. She has watched, speechless, as Clytemnestra killed the seer by the statue of

Hera, blinding him first. The queen spoke of her dead sister Polyxena, and Cassandra cried in the shadows of the columns. She thought the queen would kill her too, but she left her here.

This is a strange land, and it breeds strange people. They have no respect for gods or men. They kill and rape each other in holy places and lie to their enemies with no mercy. That is how they won the war, by lying. Her mother kept saying, "We will prevail because we aren't greedy or false." But greed and cunning win wars, as Cassandra tried to tell her. Her mother didn't listen, but then, no one ever really listened to her. Her sister Polyxena was the most loved, and so was her brother Hector. They were beautiful and charming, while Cassandra always said uncomfortable things.

Then, back in the Greek camp, after Troy had fallen, the king of all the Greeks had chosen her. She couldn't understand it. "This one is tough," Agamemnon said, dragging her away among the tripods, golden weapons, and rich tapestries. "At least I won't be bored."

Now she'd rather die than go back to him. *Maybe you won't have to.* She could leave now, run to the woods. And then? She could cross the sea again and search for other survivors. She holds her kitchen knife tight. Maybe that is what the Mycenean queen wanted to say when she told her to hide.

She walks out of the temple and into the garden. The valley looks menacing from up here, dark as the deepest parts of the sea. Her shadow leaps ahead of her like a frightened spirit, and the sweet scent of flowers drifts around her. It reminds her of home, of the sounds of flutes and lyres, of her sisters dancing under the branches of the courtyard, of the stallions neighing in the stables. She should steal a horse, she considers, and then, before she can realize it, a man comes out of the shadows. She stumbles, trying not to fall, her hand clutching the knife.

"Shh," he whispers. He is tall and handsome, his face scarred, his eyes like ice. He watches her, and she watches him. She is good with people, always has been. She can sense their feelings as her own, and Polyxena always said that she should be a seer, not a priestess. But seers aren't good with people. They care only about gods.

"Who are you?" the man asks. His voice is kind, but there is something inaccessible in his eyes… Rage? Hurt?

"Cassandra," she says. "Slave and concubine to King Agamemnon."

The expression on the man's face changes. Something dangerous has slipped between them. Cassandra steps back, and the man draws a long sword.

Trial

Clytemnestra steps into the bathhouse. The air tastes of salt. It is a sharp smell that seeps into her and makes her think of Aulis. She closes the door gently behind her and takes in the scene.

Agamemnon is lying in the bath with his back to her, his large, scarred arms around the edges. There are no weapons in sight and no guards. She has made sure of that. *This is it, then*, she thinks. *No false steps, no mistakes*. She can't afford them.

"Here comes my wife at last," he says. "The mighty queen of Mycenae, as they call you now." He chuckles, amused by the idea. "I am sure you have earned the name."

She walks to him and stands by the side of the tub. The row of smoking lamps hanging on the wall makes his face shiny. "Once it was you who were called mighty," she says.

He looks at her. "Now I am the lord of men."

Clytemnestra takes the cloth Aileen uses to clean her and kneels to scrub her husband's arm. He doesn't flinch, but he doesn't relax under her touch either.

"I heard a few stories on my way back here," he says. She waits, listening to the silence that stretches between them. "Stories of you and my dear cousin Aegisthus."

Of course he would talk about Aegisthus. Any other man would ask about his children, about Orestes's departure, about Electra's growth. But Agamemnon is not like any other man. "People like to talk," she says.

He snorts. "He was always a beggar, even as a child. We would beat and humiliate him, yet he always came back, pleading for mercy and *love*." He says the word with revulsion. "He never understood how the world works."

"I think he does now."

"Didn't he come here and beg for shelter?"

"He wasn't looking for shelter. He wanted to murder me to make you pay for what you did to his father."

Agamemnon laughs bitterly. "Atreus was Aegisthus's father as much as Thyestes was. He took him in and brought him up with the rest of us. And Aegisthus killed him."

She passes the cloth over his shoulders, the scars carved on his skin. "That is why I threw him into a cell."

His back grows tighter. "But you fucked him first. Isn't that true?"

She walks around the tub and takes his feet into her hands, wipes each toe with the cloth. Ten years of dirt and blood to be scrubbed. Ten years of pain to be avenged.

"Aegisthus is a weak man," she says.

"You have always liked weak men."

She keeps her movements slow and controlled. "What about the Trojan princess? Did you take her?"

Agamemnon's eyes never leave her. "She reminds me of you. That was why I chose her. When we took the city, all the other women were crying and cowering, but not Cassandra. She kept glaring, and when one of my men struck her, she spat at him."

"It takes courage to do that."

"Or stupidity. She was proud and didn't accept that her role had changed."

"You wouldn't accept it either."

He shakes his head. Outside, the stars are coming into view, bright and clear like lamps. There is the distant sound of men stumbling to their beds, drunk, dragging their lovers with them.

"I would have slashed my own throat long before that," he says. "People like me don't make good slaves." He adds, "And you would have done the same."

Something tightens inside her. "I am not like you."

"You have always prided yourself on thinking so, but you are no good either. You take things from people, just like me. You lie when you don't trust others with the truth, just like me."

She wrings the cloth. "I am not like you," she repeats. The words sound empty in her mouth. Agamemnon must feel it too, because he smirks.

"Polydamas and Lycomedes are dead," he says. "Did you kill them?"

She knows where this is going but answers him anyway. "They didn't respect me. They plotted against me."

He waves his hand. "People always plot behind a ruler's back. They didn't do your bidding, so you got rid of them."

"Still, that doesn't make me like you."

He ignores her. "And I see that Leon is gone as well. Did he leave you after you lied to him about Aegisthus? He always had a soft spot for you."

She keeps her voice calm. "Leon was faithful to me because he saw that you are greedy and cruel, heartless and vicious."

He laughs. "Go on, keep hating me. But future generations will hate you as much—the woman who slept with the enemy, the queen who disrespected her elders, the wife who didn't submit to her husband."

The words are blades, cutting her skin. "And how will they hate the man who murdered his own daughter?" she whispers.

He shakes his head. "Your father once told me that our lives are nothing more than a fight among those who have the power, those who want it, and the people who find themselves in the middle—casualties, sacrifices, call them whatever you want."

Her eyes find his. "So my daughter was a casualty to you."

"She was my daughter too, and I mourned her."

"You murdered her!"

He rests his head back, exposing his thick neck. "Calchas played with my mind. But we sailed for Troy, and then we won." A drop of sweat trickles down his face. "Now I need to deal with Aegisthus. Then all our enemies will have been destroyed."

Her throat is raw, but she forces herself to speak. "And what about my enemies?"

He is staring at the ceiling when she throws the wet cloth at him. It sticks to his face, blinding him, and before he can grab it, she draws her dagger from her sleeve and plunges it into his arm. He makes a choking noise. She pulls it out, and blood spatters on her face. Grunting, he tosses the cloth aside. There is energy in his eyes, like rage and pleasure together. She knows that expression—it is the fervency that takes hold of him before he hurts others. Still, she isn't careful enough. When her arm strikes to stab him again, he takes the blade in his hand, stopping her. His eyes are wild. With his other hand, he punches her in the face so hard that her head smacks the wall. For a moment, she loses her balance, her sight blurred. She takes a few steps back, feeling the wall under her hand.

Agamemnon is standing in the tub, water drops falling down his naked body, his hands a bloody mess. He is smiling like a madman, looking at his wounded arm with amusement.

"Did you think I wasn't ready for this?" he says, breath rasping in his throat. "You have always been difficult, Clytemnestra. The things I have to do to make you learn your place…"

She moves forward again, each limb tense with rage. Her blade only tips at the hollow of his throat before he grabs her hair and throws her sideways. He is stronger than she remembered. She falls, sliding on the stones away from him. He steps out of the tub, and water wets the floor. The knife has fallen out of her hand and is now between them, shiny in the feeble light. She crawls toward it.

"When will you ever understand?" he says. Her hand reaches out, but he kicks it with his foot. There is the sound of bones breaking and she screams.

"You can't kill me," he says, and on his face, there is a small smile. "We're one and the same."

She can hardly breathe for the pain. Her hand is swelling, fingers twisted like tree roots. *No false steps. No mistakes.*

He bends to pick up the dagger, and she throws herself against him with all her strength. Together, they drop down, and she manages to take the knife. This time, she sticks it into his chest. The sound he makes is of utter surprise. It gives her pleasure, and she twists the blade deeper inside.

"Aegisthus might be weak and broken," she says, "but at least he can love."

He tries to grab her, but she stops his hand with her knee, pinning him to the floor.

"You do not know loyalty or affection." His eyes are wide, and for the first time since she has known him, he looks afraid. "You will die alone, as you have been all your life, killed by your own wife. You see the irony in that? You take things from people, and sometimes they take things back from you."

She stabs his chest again and again until his ragged breath stops. Even then, there is no peace. She stands, her body red with her husband's blood, and looks down at him. His eyes are open but empty, his lips parted. He doesn't look like a king, his large body slumped gracelessly on the floor. He looks like a nameless beggar.

Bathhouse

Electra takes the hood off her face and stops to think behind a painted column at the entrance to the palace. She has been following Aegisthus ever since he escaped from the dungeon, but now that he has gone into the garden, she doesn't know where to go.

She wasn't surprised to find him sneaking around. She suspected he would try to do something as soon as her father returned, and even when her mother threw him into a cell, something hadn't seemed quite right.

She crept out of her room when Aileen and Chrysothemis fell asleep. She crushed some herbs into the guards' cups of wine and looked at them as they slumped on their stools, spittle at the corners of their mouths.

Noises are coming from the dining hall, and she slips past the door to peep inside. A few men are stumbling around, sweat pouring down their arms, the house dogs eating leftovers at their feet. Two servant women are standing among them, their tunics torn, their eyes staring blankly.

Electra retreats into the shadows before anyone can see her. Agamemnon isn't here. She quietly walks toward the baths, her mind buzzing. Her father has committed a horrible crime, it is true, but as much as she wills herself to hate him, she can't. Maybe it is because she has always been his favorite, the only child he actually paid attention to. Orestes was too generous, Iphigenia too competitive, Chrysothemis too shy. And after all, they already had Clytemnestra's love. But Electra has always been too quiet, selfish, defiant. It couldn't have been easy for her mother to love her. Yet her father would always talk to her, ask her questions when her siblings weren't around. It made her feel special.

She is close to the baths when she slips. Her back hits the floor, and when she pulls herself up, her hands are red. She gasps.

Aegisthus is dead is the first thought that comes to mind, though she knows that he can't be here. She moves into the bathhouse slowly, her breath held, like a slave walking toward the altar where he must be whipped.

There is water everywhere, and the torches have burned out, shadows circling overhead like crows waiting. Electra limps to the center of the room, her ankle hurting. There is a naked body in front of her, and she brings her hand to it. It is cold and wet. She passes her fingers over the wounds on his chest, blood drying and crusting.

She remains there for a long time, her shoulders hunched, like wings. The world around her is too quiet. Finally tears come, like winter rains, flooding her heart.

"Father," she whispers. "Father, please, wake up."

Darkness

Clytemnestra runs back to the temple of Hera, eager to find the Trojan girl and take her somewhere safe. The palace is silent, each corridor flooded with darkness. She has ordered the guards to feast and rest tonight, and now they must be sleeping, half drunk next to their lovers.

She is already in the garden when she hears a shout. It is coming from the temple, and she hurries in its direction, her bare feet still wet. At the entrance, Aegisthus stops her. He is holding his sword, and there is madness in his eyes. She tries to walk past him, but he holds on to her. His hands are sticky with blood, though he doesn't look hurt.

"It is done," he says.

She feels a numbness coming over her. "Where is Cassandra?" she asks.

She can see a small shape at the foot of the columns, curled up like an infant. She pushes Aegisthus aside and runs to it, face contorted. When she bends over the body, she sees that her throat is slashed. Her skin is still warm, though life is ebbing away.

"She was trying to run away," Aegisthus says, "but I found her."

Clytemnestra screams. Cassandra's face, young and lovely in her desperation…like her daughter's before she died. "She did nothing to you! Why did you have to sacrifice her?" she shouts, spitting at him. The expression on Aegisthus's face shifts. Pain and fear—fear of her—are tearing him apart.

"I thought you wanted her dead," he says.

She sinks her head into Cassandra's robe and weeps. She weeps for the Trojan girl, but mostly for everything she has lost. Her tears belong to Castor, who was caught in a cruel man's net; to her baby son, whom she didn't name and thus will always float in the afterworld in anonymity; to her dear Tantalus, the king who loved her and died because of her; and to her beautiful daughter, whose heart against her chest she can still feel, like the feeble beating of wings.

Mother, I am at peace now.

She keeps still, barely breathing.

You avenged me, now let me rest. I will meet you in the darkness when you are ready.

Leda was right. The dead do speak. She lifts her head and reaches out, almost expecting to see her daughter. But in her arms, there is air and nothing else.

35

House in Order

THE KING'S BODY is taken to the garden, and they all gather around it—the elders, the women of the palace, Agamemnon's faithful warriors, and Clytemnestra's men.

She stands to the side with her daughters as servants arrange the wood before bringing the torches to it. The fire builds and the flesh starts to burn. *You can't kill me*, he'd said. But he is dead, his body—what is left of it—quickly turning to ashes.

Chrysothemis kneels and cries. She covers her face with her hands, wailing. The other women are wailing too, calling for the gods. Electra keeps silent, her eyes fixed on the flames as if she were burning the body herself. She was the one who found him, who shouted for help and awakened the palace.

Clytemnestra takes her broken hand in the other. She tries to move the fingers, pain shooting through her. *I have killed the lord of men, Agamemnon. My debt is paid.*

Somewhere down by the walls, Calchas's body is burned too, away from his king. He talked about being remembered in the times to come, but all that people will know of him is this: an ugly, freakish man who ordered little girls to be sacrificed.

Calchas will wither away, while Agamemnon's name will live on. But Clytemnestra doesn't care: she knows that kings tend to become

heroes to future generations. Heracles, Perseus, Jason, Theseus…
songs about them are sung, and their cruel deeds are turned into
sunlight.

As for queens, they are either hated or forgotten. She already
knows which option suits her better. Let her be hated forever.

In the dining hall, she stands at the head of the table while Cadmus
and a few other elders take their seats on one side and, on the other,
Aegisthus, Electra, and Chrysothemis. Some of Agamemnon's faithful warriors stand opposite her, surrounded by her most loyal men.
The light that comes from the windows is reddish, streaked with fire.
Clytemnestra catches sight of Aileen in the shadows by the door, the
other servants crowding around her.

It is Cadmus who speaks first, his face grave. "My queen, we ask
you to execute the man who committed this hideous crime."

A murmur of assent. She almost smiles. As she predicted, everyone
thinks Aegisthus killed Agamemnon. It must also be Electra's doing.
When they took their place around the pyre, Electra whispered in her
ear, "Your lover killed my father." Now she sits next to Aegisthus, the
hatred in her eyes like a burning whip.

"Act for act," a large man intervenes—one of Agamemnon's com-
manders in Troy. "Justice demands it."

Aegisthus shifts in his seat. He trusts her, yet he can't help fearing
an angry crowd.

"Vengeance is our way of life," Clytemnestra says. The men nod,
their faces gray in the light of the torches. "But what about Aulis?
What about Princess Iphigenia, who was sacrificed like a beast, her
blood still wetting the altar stone?"

No one speaks.

"Did anyone avenge her? Her father murdered her, yet you didn't demand that he was banished. You didn't hunt him down, as you are ready to do with Aegisthus."

Everyone stares at her, confused. Her eyes meet Electra's, and she sees realization dawn on her daughter's face. She is the only one who understands.

"The princess gave her life willingly," a warrior says, "for the war."

Are these the lies you have been telling yourselves all these years?

"You were there," Clytemnestra says coolly. "You saw how she screamed and cried. My daughter came to Aulis for a marriage, and she never left."

"We mourned the princess, my queen," Cadmus says calmly. "But now our king is dead."

"Was his life more important than Iphigenia's?" she asks.

Cadmus hesitates. She wants him to say it—she dares anyone to say it.

"He was our leader," the large man says. "A king and lord of men." He steps forward, his finger pointed at Aegisthus. "And this man murdered him!"

Clytemnestra takes a deep breath. She thinks of her father when he talked in the *megaron*—how deep his voice was, how his men revered him. She will never have that kind of devotion, no woman can, but she will have respect.

"You are wrong in accusing Lord Aegisthus," she says quietly. She doesn't look at her daughters as she speaks, for she is afraid her heart might break. "The work is all mine. I killed your *lord of men*, and I did it to avenge my daughter."

The silence is as deafening as when a predator passes through the forest. Then, very slowly, Cadmus says, "You exult over a fallen king."

"He was no king of mine," she says.

Agamemnon's men step forward as one, their swords drawn. In a second, Clytemnestra's guards are around them. Blades meet blades.

"You are a murderer and a traitor!" the large warrior spits in her direction.

She meets his gaze. "Yes, I murdered him, but I will not stand here and let you call me traitor—you who watched a king sacrifice a little girl and did nothing."

"We understand your grief, my queen," Cadmus says, "but what you did cannot be forgiven."

Who decides what can be forgiven? Her heart is beating too loudly, and she is afraid they will hear it.

"I was raised to be a warrior and a queen," she says. "Most of you don't know this, but I was married when your king took me for himself. Tantalus was his name, and he was king of Maeonia, one of the richest lands our world has ever seen." The name in her mouth tastes like tears. "I loved him and he loved me, and together we had a baby boy."

Aegisthus's face is in the shadows, and she wonders what he is thinking.

"Then Agamemnon came and murdered him. He took the baby from my husband's arms and smashed him onto the floor. He did something *that cannot be forgiven.*

"All my life, people have wronged me. I was whipped and shipped like a cow. My own father betrayed me. I was raped and humiliated, marred and beaten. But I am still here. All the things I have done, I did to protect the ones I loved. Wouldn't you have done the same?"

For a long time, no one speaks. The wait is painful, and she feels as if she is plummeting through the sky, with no wings to raise her. Finally, something in the air shifts. Cadmus steps forward and kneels.

His thin white hair looks like feathers on his head. "My queen," he says, "you have made this city thrive with richness beyond imagining, and you lead us with strength and valor. What is done is done. All I can do now is choose to follow you for the rest of my days. You are the true keeper of the House of Mycenae."

He looks up and she looks down. When she nods, he rises to his feet again.

Agamemnon's warrior sheathes his sword. "For a woman, you are brave and worthy. But what you did cannot be forgotten."

"I don't ask you to forget. I ask you to make a choice. Follow a queen who has proven her worth, who rewards loyalty and justice, or leave your city to the vultures."

The men hesitate. They would ask Orestes to rule if he were here, but her son is away to be king of another city—Aegisthus has made sure of that.

"Our queen, keeper of our house," the large leader says, "we will serve you."

The others follow his lead and repeat the words—they echo in the hall, slowly fading to silence.

"Gather every man, woman, and child," she orders. "Give the news to the citadel."

Their shadows leap high on the walls as they leave, the light falling behind the mountains into the shadows.

"Mother," Chrysothemis says. Her daughters are standing together, their faces bathed in the light of the torches. Everyone else is gone—elders, warriors, Aegisthus. Clytemnestra knows he will be stalking Agamemnon's men, listening to their every word, checking their every move.

She extends her hand, and Chrysothemis falls into her arms. Clytemnestra feels her daughter's heart beating against her own.

When they separate, Chrysothemis turns to Electra and gestures her to do the same. But Electra's eyes are sharp. Clytemnestra feels her daughter slip away quickly, like ashes in the wind.

"You may have their love and loyalty," Electra says quietly, "but you took a father from me." Anger shines on her face and something else—spite. "You speak of justice, but what you did isn't just. You are no better than him." She turns and walks away, leaving nothing but emptiness behind her.

Chrysothemis touches her mother's hand. "Give her time," she says, her voice faint, as if she were afraid of speaking louder. "She will forgive you."

Clytemnestra closes her eyes. She would give anything to believe that, but she knows Electra. Her daughter doesn't forgive.

When Clytemnestra walks into the garden, the pyre is burned out and all that remains are ashes. Electra is sitting on a fallen tree, the moon creeping overhead. She has tortured her fingers so much that her hands are like an old woman's.

"Go away," she says when she sees her mother approaching.

Clytemnestra walks closer but remains standing. She can feel her daughter's anger on her own skin, not warm and burning, like a flame, but ice cold, like snowflakes.

"I don't want to speak to you." Electra's voice is thick with grief, though she tries to control it.

"I do not care."

Electra scoffs. Her face is pale, like the wild crocuses under her feet. Clytemnestra wants to reach out and cup her hands around it.

"You don't understand why I did what I did," she says, "but you have to live with that, and so do I."

Electra lifts her chin, defiant. "Why do I have to pay the consequences for something I didn't do?"

"Life is like that."

"Life isn't as simple as you want us to believe. And there is a difference between what is and what should be."

On that, Clytemnestra agrees. But it is the spite in Electra's voice that aches, like a rotten tooth.

"You can't forgive me for killing a father who would have hurt you? A man who slaughtered your sister? I have loved you since the moment you were born. I have fed you at my breast, cried for you, laughed with you, understood you when no one else would." She stops because her eyes are wet with tears. She recomposes herself. "But if you loved him so much, then kill me. It won't bring him back."

The air between them feels spoiled with smoke. Electra doesn't flinch. "Do you think Orestes will forgive you? Do you think you'll rule our land together, take it away from the Atreidai?" She shakes her head, a cruel smile on her face. "He won't. He will come back with a sword in hand. And he will avenge his father."

She stands in the garden for a long time. She keeps still among the trees, under the thinning light of the moon. The blades of grass seem to crawl over her feet. She bends and rips them out by the root, one by one. *I will never forgive you*, Electra said. She knows that, in moments of pain, some words are spoken with a harshness that is not truly meant. But even so, words can grow roots inside one's heart. You can bury them, hoping they will wither and die, but roots keep finding something to latch on to.

A bird darts through the shadows, flying away from the trees and up toward the mountain peaks. She takes a crocus and presses it against her heart, then walks inside.

Aileen is lighting the torches in her bedroom when Clytemnestra comes in. "Your fingers are still broken," she says gently. "I need to tend them."

Clytemnestra sits on the stool and puts her hand into her servant's. Aileen takes it with care, as if she were handling a newborn baby.

"You are not surprised I killed him," Clytemnestra says.

Aileen takes a piece of linen and wraps it around the fingers as tightly as she can. "He was a cruel man," she says.

"And yet Electra hates me for it."

"You can't have justice and everyone's approval," Aileen says, touching her queen's thumb carefully, trying to move it.

I don't want everyone's approval, just my daughter's.

"Electra knows what her father was," Aileen continues, "but I think she would have wanted you to show him mercy."

"Would *you* have shown him mercy?"

Aileen makes a knot to keep the linen tight around her hand. "I have never been in your position. I wouldn't make a good queen."

Under the torches, her hair is so bronze it seems to catch fire. There is nothing for a while, only the sound of their breaths in the warm air.

"An envoy came for you today," Aileen says finally. "You were busy with the elders so he gave me the news."

"From Sparta?"

"Yes, but not from Orestes. From your sister."

Clytemnestra stares at her, frozen.

"She is alive and well," Aileen says. "Menelaus has forgiven her."

Menelaus has forgiven her.

She walks to the window, her hand clutched to her chest. The relief is so strong it is taking her breath away. Her sister, "burning men to death with her beauty." She has heard the warriors who walked on the Trojan fields speak of Helen: the "bringer of agony," "the scourge of Greece."

What is left of the girl who was afraid to speak in front of her father? Who followed Clytemnestra everywhere? Who couldn't lie, not even when her sister asked her to? She has survived a war that destroyed a city—a war that *she* started—and now is at home, safe in the arms of her brother. Clytemnestra holds on to the image, refusing to let it slip away.

And Menelaus?

She can hear Helen's voice, as she used to when they were little. *Do not worry about him, Sister. I can take care of myself.*

Clytemnestra almost laughs. Lately kings and heroes have dropped like flies, but just as her grandmother predicted so long ago, queens outlive them all.

Dawn in the *megaron*. The light is feeble, like the first rays of sun on the water in the summer mornings. The frescoes rest, trapped in their still eternity. She walks by the throne. She once asked herself, what does it mean to be queen? Now she knows. It is daring to do what others won't.

She has dared much in life and paid the consequences each time. She has been called "proud," "savage," "single-minded," "mad with ambition," "a murderess." She has been called many things, but none of those matter. "It is the will of the gods," the priestess had told her all those years ago. "You will be despised by many, hated by others, and punished. But in the end, you will be free." She doesn't know if the gods had anything to do with it, but the prophecy was true. For more than half her life, she has worn vengeance like a second skin. Now it is time to shed it. Who will she be without her anger, her pain? What will her freedom taste like?

Human lives are based on pain. But to have a few moments of happiness, lightnings tearing the darkness of the sky, that is worth it.

Inside her, the image of a Spartan girl waiting on the terrace for a foreign king, thinking about her future. *When I ask your sister about you, she says you always know what you want.* What does she want?

She has fought her war and won. Now she can rule.

Aegisthus comes. He is silent as air, but she has learned to feel him in different ways. Rooms always grow colder when he steps into them, as if his thoughts and feelings float around him, bringing waves of darkness with them.

"The warlords are patrolling the streets," he says. "The people rejoiced at the news."

"Did the elders say how the king was killed?" she asks.

"They didn't."

Good.

His face is blurred in the rose light. His hair has been cut, and the scars on his face are faded. The wolf has been domesticated.

He reaches for her, and their hands touch. "For a moment, I thought you were going to betray me," he says. "But you didn't."

"Don't you know? I don't betray those who are loyal to me."

The frost in his eyes is cracking and, behind it, the green of the first buds of spring. "When I was young," he says, "I was afraid of everything. Atreus's hounds, Agamemnon's games, mutilated bodies, angry slaves. Wherever I looked, I feared.

"I learned to overcome those fears. I had to, or I would have died. But something stayed inside me, a feeling of rootlessness, of floating through life trying not to drown."

She listens, though she doesn't know that sensation. Every step she has taken since she was a child had a direction. And it brought her here.

He stares at her. "But now I know that I belong with you."

She closes her eyes and savors the feel of his hand against her own. He doesn't know this, but he gave her a chance too, which no one else did. He told her: Look, I am as damaged as you, but here I am.

She thinks of those white flowers blooming against the rocks of the Ceadas. For years, she wondered how they survived down there, among the corpses and darkness.

But maybe this is how broken people keep living. They find someone as broken, fit him into the empty spaces of their hearts, and together grow something different.

Outside, the light is golden. It shines on them as if they were gods.

There will come a time when songs are sung about her, about the people she loved and the ones she hated.

> *They will sing of her mother, the queen seduced by a god,*

of her brothers, boxers and horse-breakers,
of her sister, a woman so vain who couldn't stay in her
     husband's bed,
of Agamemnon, the proud lion of Mycenae,
of the wise, many-minded Odysseus,
of the treacherous, cursed Aegisthus,
of Clytemnestra, cruel queen and unfaithful wife.

But it doesn't matter. She was there. She knows songs never tell the truth.

An Ancient Greek Glossary

Aristos Achaion—"best of the Greeks," a title that, in *The Iliad*, belongs to Achilles.

Atreidai—patronymic of Agamemnon and Menelaus, literally "sons of Atreus."

Aulos—double-reed wind instrument. According to the myth, the satyr Marsyas found the *aulos* that Athena had thrown away and challenged Apollo to a musical contest. The god defeated him, tied him to a tree, and flayed him.

Barbaros (plural: *barbaroi*)—term used by the Greeks to define all the non-Greeks. Literally "foreigners," "barbarians," "uncivilized people."

Basileia—word for "queen" in the Greek Heroic Age.

Boreas—purple-winged god, bringer of the wind.

Ceadas—ravine on Mount Taygetus where Spartans threw criminals and ill-born babies. This notion comes from Plutarch, though archaeological evidence suggests that the bodies thrown down the cliff were traitors and prisoners, not children.

Chiton—a short tunic that fastens at the shoulder, made by a single piece of wool or linen.

Furies—ancient goddesses of torment and vengeance. They

represent the law of "blood will have blood" and are also
the spirits of avenging dead that can bring regeneration.
Daughters of Gaia (Earth), they sprang to life from the
blood of Ouranos's genitals when Kronos flung them into
the sea.

Gymnasium—training facility. The word comes from *gymnos*,
meaning "naked," as the men (and women, in the case of
Sparta) practiced naked.

Gynaeceum—women's quarters in the palace.

Harpazéin—"to marry" but also "to take with force."

Homoioi—literally "those who are alike," it refers to the elite of
Spartan citizens.

Hubris—the arrogance and pride of men that is always punished by the gods.

Megaron—the great hall in early Mycenaean and ancient Greek
palaces. It was a rectangular hall that contained the throne
of the king, an open hearth that usually vented through an
oculus in the roof, frescoed walls, and a columned portico.

Moira—the fate from which mortals can't escape. The Moirai
were deities who ensured that every being lived out their
destiny as it was assigned to them.

Mousike—music, dance, and the performance of poetry.
Mousike was an integral part of life in the world of ancient
Greece.

Myrmidons—Achilles's devoted soldiers. The word comes from
the Greek *myrmex*, "ant," as according to the myth, the
Myrmidons were once ants from the island of Aegina,
which Zeus then transformed into men.

Oionopolos—bird-savant, seer, diviner. Literally "someone who
observes the flight of birds."

Orthia—epithet of the goddess Artemis in Sparta and Arcadia.

Pallake—concubine.

Pelides—Achilles's patronymic, literally "son of Peleus."

Peplos—a body length garment for women, belted at the waist.

Polutropos—the man "of twists and turns," "ingenious," "cunning" beyond measure. Odysseus's epithet.

Spartiates—members of the ruling class of ancient Laconia.
Elite citizens of Sparta, usually male, though we can
assume that in Mycenaean times, women belonged to the
group too, since Spartan women were free citizens.

Teras—word to describe both a portent and a freak.

Tholos—tomb where the royal ashes are placed.

Xenia—the law of hospitality, one of the most crucial concepts
in ancient Greece, where protection and generosity toward
guests were a moral obligation.

Xiphos—short sword with a curved blade.

Reading Group Guide

1. At the start of the novel, Clytemnestra intervenes in a fight involving her sister, Helen. When told that she must let people win their own battles, she thinks to herself, "What if the loser is your loved one?" How does this mentality guide Clytemnestra throughout her life?

2. Clytemnestra and the rest of the girls in Sparta are trained to fight as children. How does this warrior mentality guide her throughout the novel? How does this set her apart from other heroines you have read before?

3. The murder of Clytemnestra's first husband, Tantalus, and her baby is not told from the perspective of Clytemnestra herself. How did you read this change in perspective? What did it add to the narrative?

4. Clytemnestra and Helen's relationship is tested many times, yet there is always love between them. How might you describe the evolution of their relationship? How does the theme of forgiveness play a role between the two?

5. Describe Clytemnestra's relationship with her father. How did his betrayal make you feel, and how does it shape Clytemnestra?

6. The story of Clytemnestra and her family is foreshadowed by an inescapable prophecy. Did the priestess's vision play out the way you though it would? What roles did prophecies and religion have in this world?

7. This story does not have obvious good characters and bad characters; all of them make decisions that are morally questionable. Were there specific moments that made you think differently about any of the characters? Were there some you found unforgiveable?

8. Why do you think Odysseus allowed for Clytemnestra's daughter to be sacrificed?

9. How did you feel about Clytemnestra's final act against Agamemnon? In the end, were her actions warranted? Who do you believe is ultimately to blame?

10. Vengeance is a common theme that courses throughout the story. How does vengeance play a role in all the characters' lives, especially Clytemnestra's?

11. Clytemnestra has been portrayed by history as an evil queen. How does the author question that role? Do you think Clytemnestra is truly evil?

12. Are you familiar with any of the myths that are presented in this novel? Were they told differently than you remember?

A Conversation with the Author

Of all the women in Greek mythology, why Clytemnestra? What drew you to her story?

I fell in love with this extraordinary character more than ten years ago. In the ancient texts, she is fierce, clever, powerful, and unbending, unlike any other heroine I'd read before. The most fascinating thing about her in the ancient sources is that she is feared and respected for the power she holds in Mycenae. I thought, here is a woman who commands a city as her husband is away, who makes him pay for all the wrong he has done to her, and who doesn't let the men around her belittle her. I felt the need to explore her story.

Her backstory was also incredibly fascinating with all the myths surrounding her. Clytemnestra grows up in Sparta, where women, compared to other Greek cities of the time, were much freer, so she is taught to hunt and fight just like the men around her. And then she is connected to some of the most fascinating characters from the myth: she is sister to Helen, cousin of Penelope, wife of Agamemnon, lover to Aegisthus, daughter of Leda. She might have been called an "adulteress," "bad wife," and "murderess" for centuries, but I believe that once people get to know her whole story, they can't help falling in love with her.

How much research did you have to do to weave these myths together? What was the writing process like?

I was already familiar with the myths, having read and studied *The Iliad*, *The Odyssey*, and the *Oresteia* when I was younger, as well as many other plays such as Euripides's *Electra* and *Iphigenia in Aulis*, for instance. Before writing the novel, I went back and studied them again, especially Aeschylus's *Agamemnon*, where Clytemnestra is the main character, despite the title. The fascinating thing about these myths is that there are so many different versions of them: for example, Clytemnestra's brothers, Castor and Polydeuces, in *The Odyssey* are both sons of Tyndareus, but in Hesiod's *Catalogue of Women*, they are sons of Zeus. So before writing the story, I had to choose how to deal with these different versions and also how to weave them together in a way that felt both true to the sources but also fresh and surprising.

I also did a lot of research that focused on details of everyday life: How did the characters wash? What did they eat? How was the *gynaeceum* structured? And the gymnasium? However, the most important part of my research was what I call "cultural," namely the way in which ancient people (in this case, Greeks in the age of heroes) thought and behaved. How did they experience grief? Were vengeance and justice the same thing for them? I then wove those elements into the narrative as seamlessly as I could, in a way that would be also understandable for a contemporary reader.

Clytemnestra is an immensely complicated character. What was it like to write about her? What did you feel was most important when portraying her?

I've always felt a great empathy for her. To me, she wasn't so complicated to write because she is guided by values that are strong and clear—loyalty, courage, vengeance, and the need to do the thing that is right. In her motivations, she is straightforward as a character. Then, she is obviously a complex woman and a character who is constantly evolving as the events in the narrative shape her and make her more ruthless and vengeful. To me, the most important thing when portraying her was writing a heroine who took part in the action, who dominated every exchange and dynamic. A woman who, despite doing plenty of right and wrong, readers can root for right until the very end.

There are many hard topics in this novel, specifically violence against women and the need for revenge. How difficult was it to write about these themes? What about having to write characters that were morally corrupt?

Clytemnestra's tale is extremely brutal—a child sacrificed to the gods, a husband and baby murdered—so I needed to write scenes that reflected that brutality. I believe that if you include violent scenes in a book, it needs to be for a reason, and those scenes were purposeful for the narrative: the tragedies that happen to Clytemnestra make her the queen she eventually becomes.

This is also a world that lauded violence: fights and wars are how heroes are made, so I couldn't shy away from it. It was essential for me that these scenes were raw and brutal but also showed a perspective that we don't see often: fights from a woman's eyes.

As for writing characters that are morally corrupt, I love novels that bring to the fore people who are capable of both generous, heroic acts but also horrible things. Every character has its wounds and secrets, its motivations for doing the things they do, and I love exploring that. That is the beauty of the myth too: it offers heroines who are morally ambiguous—see Phaedra or Medea, for example—but still unforgettable.

You retell a famous Greek character through a feminist perspective. Why do you believe this new lens is important?

Having a woman at the center of the narrative and at the center of the action—a woman who has been hated and vilified for centuries—is incredibly important because it proves that women's stories can be as epic as the ones of the men.

In the ancient texts, from epic poems like *The Iliad* and *The Odyssey* to plays like *Agamemnon*, there are incredibly intriguing heroines, but most of the time, they are not given the space and love they deserve. They are either relegated to the margins, see Circe in *The Odyssey* or Helen in *The Iliad*, or seen as misogynist archetypes: ruthless schemers, scandalous adulteresses, vengeful murderesses. Retelling their stories through this new lens allows us to go back to these myths with a fresh perspective and show that women can be as powerful, as complex, as layered as the men.

Ancient myths are often resonant to every society throughout history. Did you find any connections between the Greek myths you were rewriting and our current world now?

Absolutely. Clytemnestra to me has always been a very modern character, a woman who refuses to know her place and, because of that, is hated and vilified by the men around her.

Clytemnestra, like Helen and other women from my novel, has always been the embodiment of men's fears around female power and sexuality. In *The Odyssey*, Clytemnestra is called "treacherous," "deadly," and "bestial," and Helen in *Agamemnon* is an "angel of war, angel of agony, lighting men to death." As I was writing the book, I wanted to show these characters in a more multifaceted way, peeling away all the sexist stereotypes that have been attributed to them.

I was also aware that I was tackling some themes we're not

completely comfortable with as a society, such as female ambition and female rage. But I believe that exploring these topics in a book set in the past raises important questions: on our perception of women's pain, our distrust in women's ambition and power, our judgment on women's sexuality.

What do you hope readers get from this story?

I hope that readers will fall in love with these timeless myths and stories (if they don't love them already) and, most of all, with these extraordinary female characters. *Clytemnestra* can be a challenging book for all the reasons we mentioned—violence, vengeance, betrayal—but I believe that challenging reads are thought-provoking and, in that sense, can have a positive impact on us, pushing us to reflect and empathize more.

What are you reading these days?

I love reading across different genres. Books that I've loved and recommended recently are Jenny Tinghui Zhang's *Four Treasures of the Sky*, Miranda Cowley Heller's *The Paper Palace*, and Kamila Shamsie's *Home Fire*.

Acknowledgments

Thank you:

To Victoria Hobbs, my dream agent, who gave me a chance and changed my life. I still pinch myself that I am lucky enough to be represented by you.

To Jillian Taylor, simply the best editor a writer could ask for. You understood the book and the characters and helped me make them shine. Thank you for being next to me every step of the way.

To everyone at Michael Joseph: Ciara Berry, Sriya Varadharajan, Stephanie Biddle, Courtney Barclay, Beatrix McIntyre, Emily van Blanken, Lee Motley, Becci Livingstone.

To the brilliant rights team: Chantal Noel, Jane Kirby, Lucy Beresford-Knox, Rachael Sharples, Beth Wood, Inês Cortesão, Maddie Stephenson, Lucie Deacon, Agnes Watters.

To my U.S. editor, MJ Johnston, for your passion and exemplary work, and to everyone at Sourcebooks, especially the wonderful Cristina Arreola.

To my early supporters, who gave me strength and love as I was submitting this novel, especially Erica Bertinotti, Anna Colivicchi, and Annie Garthwaite.

Thank you also to Hazel Orme, Jessica Lee, Andrew Davis, and the wonderful teachers at the University of Warwick, where I started writing Clytemnestra's story.

Finally to my family, my whole heart:

To my father, who fills my life with books and happiness. There is nothing I love more than the moment we talk about a new chapter I sent you.

To my mother, who read me stories when I was little and taught me I could be anything I wanted. You are the fiercest, most special person on this planet. Thank you, for everything.

About the Author

© Arianna Genghini

Costanza Casati was born in Texas in 1995, grew up in a village in northern Italy, and lived in the UK for five years. Before moving to London, she attended a classical Liceo in Italy, where she studied ancient Greek and ancient Greek literature for five years. Costanza is a graduate of the prestigious Warwick Writing MA program where she earned a distinction, and she currently works as a freelance journalist and screenwriter. *Clytemnestra* is her debut novel.